Miles To Go

A Sweet Western Romance & Small Town Saga Novel

Cowboys of Three Rivers
Book 10

Liz Isaacson

ISBN-13: 978-1-63876-485-4

Reader Note

Hello Fabulous Christian Cowboy Readers!

I love a good cowboy romance, don't you? And give me a grumpy, injured, feels-unworthy cowboy? Mm, yes, I'm hooked.

I hope you'll love reading about Ty's journey to himself, to God, and ultimately to Winnie as much as I loved writing it. I want us each to cling to the hope that no matter how injured or damaged or hurt we feel, that we can still find a place to belong.

Ty's journey is really about finding that place for him — inside his family, his friend group, his small town, and with Winnie.

And YOU, my friend, belong right here in Three Rivers, with Finn, Henry, Alex, Link, Dawson, JJ, Conrad, Paul, Mitch, Wilder, Brandon, Ty, Colt, Trap, Jake, Smiles, Gun, Rock, Libby, Angel, and all the Glovers, Walkers, and everyone at Three Rivers Ranch.

Welcome to town. We're glad you're here!

xoxo

~Liz

The Small Town of Three Rivers

Welcome to Three Rivers! There have been three complete series here already - Three Rivers Ranch, Seven Sons Ranch (Walker Brothers), and Shiloh Ridge Ranch (Glover Family).

That's 37 books. Loads of characters. I'm going to list them here, but you don't need to know them all comprehensively for this book. I just know some of you like seeing these amazing small towns and who lives here!

SHILOH RIDGE RANCH:

Lois & Stone (deceased) Glover, 7 children, in age-order: (Lois is now married to Donald Parker)

　　1. Bear — Sammy, wife

- Lincoln (34), adopted son, married to Misty / Dallas (nickname: Diesel, son 8), Scout (son, 5), Meadow (daughter, 1)
- Stetson (Smiles, 28), son

- Russell (Rock, 26), son, married to Clover Broadbent
- Heather (23), daughter
- Sunnie (19), daughter

2. Cactus — Allison, ex-wife / Bryce, son (deceased) // — Willa, wife

- Mitch (36), adopted son, married to Lacy Hayes (**Signs for Success Deaf Academy**)
- Cameron (30), adopted son
- Kyle (28), adopted son
- Charlie (Chaz, 26), son
- Lynn (23), adopted daughter
- Melissa (21), daughter

3. Judge — June, wife

- Lucy Mae (40), step-daughter
- Birch (21), son
- Willow (19), daughter
- Linden (16), son

4. Preacher — Charlie, wife

- Betty (24), daughter
- Hank (22), son
- Daisy (18), daughter

5. Arizona — Duke Rhinehart, husband, living at the Rhinehart Ranch, just south of Shiloh Ridge

- Shiloh (25), daughter
- April (21), daughter
- Dwayne (19), son

- Dallas (15), son

6. Mister — Libby, wife

- Bell (20), son
- Marley (18), daughter
- Hazel (15), daughter
- Brantley (12), son

7. Bishop — Montana, wife

- Aurora (41), step-daughter and married to Oliver Walker
- Robbie (26), son
- Georgia (21), daughter

Aurora and Oliver have 5 children, who are Bishop and Montana's grandchildren:

- Jewel (14), daughter
- Laramie (Lara, 11), daughter
- Mason (9), son
- Lennon (7), son
- Nicole (18 months), daughter

DAWNA & Bull (deceased) Glover, 5 children, in age-order:

1. Ranger — Oakley, wife

- Wilder (26), son
- Fawn (24), daughter

2. Ward — Dot, wife

- Glory Rose (25), daughter, married to Conrad Walker
- Silver (23), son
- Flint (21), son

3. Ace — Holly Ann, wife

- Gunnison (26), son, married to Camila Walker
- Pearl Jo (24), daughter
- Ashton (20), son

4. Etta — August Winters, husband

- Hailey (33), adopted daughter
- Joey (23), son
- Nash and Nellie (twins - 19), son and daughter

5. Ida — Brady Burton, husband

- Johnny and Judy (twins - 25), son and daughter
- Riggs (21), son
- Sonora (18), daughter

BULL AND STONE GLOVER were brothers, so their children are cousins. Ranger and Bear, for example, are cousins, and each the oldest sibling in their families.

SEVEN SONS RANCH:

Momma & Daddy: Penny and Gideon Walker

1. RHETT & EVELYN WALKER

Son: Conrad - 31, married to Glory Rose Glover, Sarina (Sari, daughter, 6)

Triplets: Austin, Elaine, and Easton - 27

2. JEREMIAH & WHITNEY WALKER

Son: Jonah Jeremiah (JJ) - 28, married to Ruby Reynolds, Jade (daughter, newborn)

Daughter: Clara Jean - 25, married to Tate Reynolds (they run the farmland that feeds **Wilde & Organic**, the grocery store Clara Jean also manages)

Son: Jason - 24

Daughter: Emily - 21

Daughter: Hattie - 20

3. LIAM & CALLIE WALKER

Daughter: Denise - 35

Daughter: Ginger - 31

4. TRIPP & IVORY WALKER

Son: Oliver - 41, married to Aurora Glover

Son: Isaac - 31

. . .

5. Wyatt & Marcy Walker
    Son: Warren - 28
    Son: Cole - 26
    Son: Harrison - 25
    Daughter: Rachel - 21

6. Skyler & Mallery Walker
    Daughter: Camila - 28, married to Gunnison Glover
    Son: Sawyer - 26
    Son: Gideon - 23

7. Micah & Simone Walker
    Son: Travis (Trap) - 28
    Daughter: Daisy - 25
    Son: Jensen - 21
    Daughter: Laurel - 19

Coyote Pass:
    Alex Baxter, wife Nikki (twin boys - Shane and Hank, age 8)

Three Rivers Ranch:
    Frank and Heidi Ackerman - patriarch and matriarch. Frank died 20 years ago; Heidi is remarried to Malcolm Rust.

Squire and Kelly Ackerman
    Son: Finn - 39, wife Edith, Theo (son, 9), Bubba (son, 6), Dustin (son, 2)
    Daughter: Libby - 33, husband Rusty Jackson, Nora (daughter, 2)
    Son: Michael - 30

Son: Samuel - 28

P**ETE AND** **C****HELSEA** **M****ARSHALL** **(Chelsea is Squire's sister, and they own Courage Reins, which is housed at Three Rivers Ranch)**

4 sons:

Paul - 35, married to Brielle, Spur (son, 8 months)

Henry - 33, wife Angel, Wrangler, (son, 2.5), Starr (daughter, 3 months) (**Lone Star Ranch**)

John - 30, married to Virginia Switz

Rich - 28

R**EESE AND** **C****ARLY** **S****ANDERS:** They're the admins for Courage Reins, Pete and Chelsea's equine therapy unit at Three Rivers Ranch. They have no children.

G**ARTH AND** **J****ULIETTE** **A****HLSTROM** **(former foreman; vet technician)**

Son: Jake - 33

Son: Carson - 30

C**AL AND** **T****RINA** **H****ODGKINS** **(he's the full-time vet at Three Rivers Ranch)**

Daughter: Sabrina - 42

Daughter: Abby - 34

Daughter: Olive - 30

E**THAN AND** **B****RYNN** **G****REENE** **(they own Bowman's Breeds, which is housed at Three Rivers Ranch)**

Daughter: Carolina - 33
Son: Tyson - 31
Son: Bryan - 29

Beau Peterson (foreman at Three Rivers Ranch) and Charlotte Wisenhouer
Son: Walter - 17
Daughter: Michelle - 13

Bennett and Ellie Peterson (he's a cowboy, she works on the finances on the ranch with Kelly)
Daughter: Joy - 18
Son: Jaxon - 15

Tad and Sandy Jorgensen (he's a cowboy, she owns the pancake house in town)
Son: Nathaniel (Nate) - 32
Daughter: Helen - 39

Kenny and Taryn Stockton (he's a cowboy, she works for a local online newspaper in town)
Daughter: Joelle (Jo) - 30

Jon and Grace Carver (he's a cowboy, she helps Heidi run the bakery in town)

Andy and Lawrence Collins (he's a cowboy, she owns a clothing boutique in town)

. . .

SUMMER AND TANNER WOLFE (he's a cowboy, she's a nurse at the hospital in town)

GAVIN AND NAVY REDD - they own their own single-family ranch on the northeast side of Three Rivers

BOONE AND NICOLE Carver (Squire's cousin) - they own and operate the full time veterinary clinic in town

CAMILA AND DYLAN WALKER (he's a cowboy and an electrician, she owns a plumbing shop in town)

RHINEHART RANCH:
1. Dawson (39), wife, Caroline / Colt (son, 6), Joy (almost 3), Bronco (son, almost 1)
2. Brandon (37), married to Lenore Sawyer (they live on a homestead northeast of town)

1

Tyson Greene slipped into the apartment he shared with his roommate and quietly closed the door behind him. He twisted the deadbolt, glad Jacob had left the light on above the sink.

Ty didn't normally stay out past nine PM, let alone midnight, as he worked at Lone Star stables three days a week and had recently started to run a crew at the apple orchards for one of his best friends, Colt. He reminded himself of that as he limped along the back of the couch, using it to steady himself.

But today was technically New Year's Day, and he didn't have to work at all. He'd need the rest after the big barn party-dance out at Three Rivers Ranch, which was like a second home to him.

Ty moved into the kitchen, every move causing a new pain to shoot through his body. He really couldn't let himself get like this, and he stood at the kitchen sink and ran the water cold while a flash of gratitude moved through him that he'd made it home safely.

His physical body often gave out before his mind, and he'd been progressing nicely in his physical therapy, and felt nearly fully recovered from his injury, that he sometimes thought he could do more than he actually could. His body would literally shut down at that point, and it didn't matter if Ty was behind the wheel, had access to a chair, or managed to make it to a bed.

He looked out the window and into the darkness beyond. During the day, he could see the playground across the sidewalk from the apartment where he and Jacob lived. Right now, he only saw his own reflection—and wow, he looked exhausted.

He reached to the slim cabinet beside the sink, and he pulled down a bottle of painkillers. In his back pocket, his phone buzzed, but Ty kept his focus on swallowing the pills he'd need to make it through the night.

He'd have to look at his phone, because ten to one, the text he'd just gotten had come from his mother. She'd want to make sure he'd gotten home okay. He couldn't blame her for asking, though at almost thirty-two years old, Ty was tired of being checked up on.

No, it's not that, he thought. He'd run the rodeo circuit for years without his parents checking on him all the time. It had just been in the last couple of years, since his catastrophic and career-ending injury, that his momma and daddy felt the need to drop by just to "see how he was doing," or text to see if it was "a good day or not," and then call if he didn't respond.

He couldn't blame them. He'd had a series of surgeries, and at one point, the doctors had told him he might not be able to walk again.

He'd completely lost his hearing in his left ear and, right now, a massive headache throbbed behind his eyes, in his temples, and along the back of his skull. The entire left side of his body felt like someone had weighed it down with a fifty-pound sandbag, and no matter how many times he drew his left shoulder back to try to make his body square, it drooped forward again.

He threw back two acetaminophen, four ibuprofen, and one *Simply Sleep*, then chugged several more swallows of ice-cold water to chase the pills all the way down.

He tried not to take painkillers if he could avoid it at all, knowing that it didn't do great things for his kidneys. But after a New Year's Eve dinner with a live band and dancing, games, and after-dark horseback riding, every cell in Ty's body felt like someone had hammered on it with an electric jackhammer.

He reached to flip off the light and turned to face the house, leaning into the corner of the kitchen cabinets to give his eyes a chance to adjust. As shapes became lighter and darker shades of gray, Tyson pushed away from the corner and, leaning on the fridge and then the walls for support, he went down the hall to his bedroom.

He closed the door behind him and picked his way over to the bed, discarding everything except his boxer shorts. When his boots came off, pure relief sang through Ty's soul.

His back spasmed as he sat on the bed, and while it didn't truly hurt, the involuntary motion definitely felt weird and triggered in his nerves as pain.

He positioned his pillows up against the wall, then lay down on his right side and scooted back into them so that the towers of foam could support his body for him.

He sighed when he remembered his phone, and he reached for the grabber he had positioned in the slim space between his bed and nightstand. It was about four feet long, and he could pull a trigger that would make two prongs come together, so he could grab things without having to bend over or get out of bed. He had to lean forward enough to reach his jeans, and it took his last ounce of energy to pull the denim close enough that he could grab the pants and extract the phone from his back pocket.

He'd kept his phone on silent all night, because he hadn't wanted to justify himself to his parents about how much he could handle at the New Year's Eve party. Falling down at the summer dance, though it had been six months ago, had renewed their concern over him. It didn't help that he'd never been back to another dance until this one.

Yes, he'd stayed out of the spotlight and near chairs. He'd danced with a few friends, and even his cowboy friends' wives.

Ty had not been on a date in six months either, and that had prompted the second reason why he'd kept his phone on silent. His older sister Carolina had gotten engaged over Christmas, and the family group text that kept Ty so connected to his two siblings and his parents now felt like a war zone of emotions that he had to navigate on an hourly basis.

Of course, he was happy for Carolina, especially since she'd been trying to find a husband for a lot longer than he'd even considered dating. His younger brother Bryan had a pretty serious girlfriend too, and not having anyone simply solidified Ty's role in his family as the black sheep.

His two siblings had stayed around Three Rivers, and he'd left the moment he could. They'd gone to college or trade schools and worked in agriculture or business.

He'd joined the rodeo, and the only classes he'd ever taken were American Sign Language classes, and only in the last year.

If he hadn't been thrown from that two-ton bull a couple of years ago, he'd still be on the rodeo circuit. Heck, he might even be married to Jenn.

A scoff fell out of his mouth, because in the stages of grief over losing that relationship, he'd definitely entered the angry one. Some days, he thought he'd moved on from her completely, but after a disastrous date with someone he'd had no romantic feelings for, he certainly didn't want to try a relationship with someone he did want to impress.

After all, what was impressive about him?

A calm, quiet feeling came over him, and his mind cleared, save for the thought of Trevor White. He too had been injured in an awful accident almost a decade ago, and the man had just gotten married in October.

Ty's anger faded, and while he hadn't quite made his pilgrimage back to organized religion and attending church meetings, he could acknowledge God's hand and love in his life. In quiet moments like these, he knew his life had been spared for a reason he didn't know yet.

In the past two years, he'd been reminded of what an amazing family he had, and how much he loved small towns like Three Rivers, and what having good friendships felt like. He hadn't had any of those things on the rodeo circuit, and that had gone right down to the woman he'd dated and thought he'd been in love with.

He swiped on his phone and found that he had several messages. Yes, his mother had texted, and he quickly responded to her: *I made it home, and I'm in bed. My head is killing me, and you're right, I probably overdid it.*

That would validate her and worry her, and Ty hoped she'd already gone to bed, though her message had only come in a few minutes ago.

He'd gotten a couple messages from Colt about doing the New Year's Day brunch at the restaurant his friend had built into the apple orchards this past fall. He'd thrown himself into that when his attempts at blind dating had gone terribly. Ty said he could be there at eleven to help out for a couple of hours, and he navigated to Wilder Glover's text next.

Hey, I meant to grab you at the dance tonight, he said. *But something came up with Savannah's daughter, and we left early. I'm just wondering if you're bringing a date to Judy and Trooper's wedding.*

Ty sighed and looked away from the brightness of his phone, though he'd put it on dark mode.

"The wedding," he grumbled to himself.

He tapped back over to Colt's message and saw that his friend had said, *Thanks, brother.*

Hey, are you taking anyone to Judy and Trooper's wedding? Ty sent off quickly.

Colt started to respond, and Ty held his breath. Maybe he and Colt could be each other's plus-one, the way they'd been before.

While he waited, a pretty brunette paraded into his mind. She wore scrubs, and bright purple shoes, and her dark hair up into a high ponytail.

"You're not asking Winona," he muttered to himself.

The very idea was laughable, though she seemed to show up everywhere Ty did in Three Rivers. He had to see her a couple of times per month for their therapy appointments, and since she challenged him to do exercises he didn't like and use his body in ways he didn't think he could, he was never very happy to see her—and always glad when she walked away.

He could admit she was beautiful, but only to himself, and only in quiet, exhaustive moments like this. She'd integrated herself into their small-town community far quicker and easier than Ty ever could or would.

In every way she was his opposite, so why she'd come into his mind when thinking about a date for a wedding, he had no idea.

Yeah, Colt said. *I went the safe route and asked Wilder's sister, because I know she thinks I'm too old for her and she's not interested. She'll have to be there anyway, and this way neither one of us have to be alone.*

"That's a pretty good idea," Ty said, grinning at his phone. *Are there any other Glovers that don't have dates?*

Colt sent a couple of laughing emojis. *I don't know, man. Ask Wilder.*

He's asking me about a date, Ty said.

Maybe he's got someone in mind, Colt said back.

Ty tapped back over to Wilder's string and said, *I don't have anyone. Do I need someone? Does one of your cousins need a date?*

Wilder didn't respond, and Ty scrolled up to see that he'd texted a couple of hours ago. They'd left early, and Savannah had little girls, so Wilder was probably already home and in bed.

A new text from his momma came in, and Ty's heart jumped up into his throat.

I'll bring you some soup tomorrow, she said. *Did you take medicine tonight?*

Yes, he said. *I have to work at the orchards tomorrow from eleven to one. I can stop by your house after for lunch.*

Let's do that, Momma said. *I can't believe you have to work on New Year's Day.*

Colt just asked last minute, he said. *I don't mind.*

All right. Love you, buddy.

Love you too, Momma. Ty sighed as he put his phone down on his chest. He did love his mother, and he loved his freedom and living with Jacob here in this apartment.

Yes, he'd been attending the small ranch owners' meetings for over a year now, and he loved all of his friends there, their wives, and their kids. So when Ty closed his eyes and started thinking about what he lacked in his life, it was definitely a wife and children.

His phone buzzed against his sternum, and he picked it up.

Yeah, I've got someone in mind for you, Wilder said. *Not one of my cousins. But Savannah and I were talking to her at the dance, and she seemed, I don't know, lonely.*

"Great," Ty muttered, his thumbs hovering above the screen as he tried to figure out how to respond. The last thing he wanted was a blind-date-set-up with some lonely spinster. He could find someone like that himself, thank you very much.

You're not answering, Wilder said after a moment. *Does this mean no?*

I don't even know who it is, Ty said.

You already know her, Wilder said. *And I don't know—she seemed to be watching you during the dance.*

Yeah? Ty swallowed, his pulse ratcheting through his body for a different reason now. *Who was watching me during the dance?*

Winona Landry.

Ty dropped his phone, a corner of it landing hard against his breastbone as Winnie's first and last name burned into his retinas.

Of course she was watching him. Winnie was always critiquing his movement, his core support, and his strength. It didn't mean anything, did it?

He picked up his phone as it buzzed again.

I told her I'd give her your number, but she said she already had it. That's when Savannah's mom called and we had to leave.

Ty started to type something, but Wilder came in with another message. *I don't know. Maybe it's a bad idea. I think she's your physical therapist.*

Ty erased what he'd started to type. *Yeah,* he said. *She is.*

So maybe she'd be safe? Wilder said. *I know you tried that one time over the summer, and it didn't go super well.*

"Yeah, because of Winnie," Ty muttered to himself. He could just see her pressing through the crowd at the summer dance and bossing his friends around for how to help him stand up.

At the same time, Winnie never judged him. She never looked at him like he couldn't do what everyone else could do, and she always positioned herself on his right side so he could hear her. She was gorgeous and thoughtful and a great physical therapist.

I'll think about it, Ty said.

Okay, Wilder said. *Let me know, because I know Trap doesn't have a date either, and I thought maybe he could ask her too.*

The idea of Trap Walker going out with Winnie made Ty's blood run like molten lava through his veins. "Absolutely not," he muttered, and his movements almost became stabs instead of taps as he started a new text, put Winnie's name in it, and sent her a message.

His eyelids grew heavy, and he couldn't fight off the effects of the pain in his body and the *Simply Sleep* medication he'd swallowed a half-hour ago. He managed to plug in his phone and set it on his nightstand before succumbing to the blissful wash of unconsciousness, where he dreamed of a beautiful brunette brushing his hair off his forehead to gently wake him in the morning...and she looked gloriously like Winona Landry.

2

"Three Rivers Ranch is *really* far out here," Winona Landry said, peering through the dark night ahead of her. It hadn't seemed that far when she'd driven out for the New Year's Eve dance, and she told herself that was because she hadn't been alone on the way out.

She huffed, her fingers tightening on the wheel. It was just like Taylor to bail on her for a handsome face and a sexy cowboy hat. "Honestly, did you think your sister had changed *that* much?"

Yes, yes, she had. Winnie thought the best of people, and she was still learning that not everyone could be trusted, that not everyone told the truth, and that not everyone was nice. Her own sister included.

She glanced at her infotainment screen as a text popped up. The sound came a moment later, covering up the low warble of the radio she had on to keep her company on the long drive back to town.

Tyson Greene flashed on the screen, and a blue button sat there that said *READ ALOUD*.

Winnie reached out and tapped it, her pulse picking up the pace as her mind fired questions at her. Was Tyson all right? Why would he be texting her? He'd never done that before, despite her giving him her number and telling him to text about anything that came up between their therapy sessions.

The cowboy remained as elusive as ever, even if he'd improved by leaps and bounds since Winnie had started working with him six months ago. He never smiled. He barely said hello, and at least eighty percent of the time, he didn't say good-bye at all. Still, he kept coming back, and his work outside of their sessions showed, because he'd only gotten straighter, stronger, and more square since she'd taken over his treatment.

Winnie pushed against the pride flowing through her. It wasn't her doing the work, but him, and she did try to praise him at any opportunity. "The problem is," she said aloud. "That only seems to irritate him further."

The text didn't play, and Winnie checked the road in front of her again, found no one, and reached to tap the button again. Her finger landed right this time, and the car said, "Message from Tyson Greene. What are you doing a week from Saturday? My friend is getting married and I need a date."

Without thinking, Winnie lifted her foot from the gas pedal and pressed on the brake. The car began to slow, obviously taking its cue from her mind. Before she knew it, she'd come to a stop right there in the middle of the highway leading south to Three Rivers.

She'd become friends with Libby Jackson, who owned and operated Three Rivers Ranch, after the woman had hurt herself during the harvest season. She'd been coming to Winnie to regain the full range of motion in her right shoulder, and she'd extended the invite to the New Year's Eve party Winnie and Taylor had attended tonight.

Winnie had been in town for a little over six months now, and about four months ago, she'd made a personal pact with herself to say yes to anything she got invited to. The Town Council needed volunteers at the first aid station at the summer dances?

Winnie said yes.

Her co-worker wanted to trade shifts?

Winnie said yes.

Her mentor at the clinic wanted her to go out for appetizers and drinks with him and his wife?

Winnie said yes.

So when Libby had asked if she'd like to attend the party, Winnie had, once again, said yes.

She picked up her phone from its riding spot in the cup holder. She should've known Ty would be at the party tonight; he was friends with every cowboy in town, having grown up here. "Practically at Three Rivers Ranch itself," she muttered.

She'd seen his mother's training facility, right there on the left-hand side of the road at the ranch. Of course, the handsome-hot cowboy who could barely tolerate her would be at tonight's ringing in of the New Year.

He hadn't looked happy to be there, and she'd actually wondered if he'd made a personal pact the way she had, and said yes to things simply to feel like he was part of a community, part of something bigger than himself, not forgotten in the billions of people in the world.

The words her car had read to her shone on the screen. *What are you doing a week from Saturday? My friend is getting married and I need a date.*

The text honestly represented Ty to a T. Blunt, straight to the point, no wasted words.

Winnie looked up as a pair of headlights approached her. To her great horror, the car began to slow, and the truck came to a stop with the two driver's windows lined up. The man across from her flipped on his interior light, and she rolled her window down halfway.

"Are you okay?" he asked. His wife rode in the passenger seat, and they both wore concern in their eyes.

"Yes." She held up her phone. "I got a strange text is all."

The man blinked at her like she'd lost her mind.

Humiliation painted its way through all of her internal organs.

"I'm fine," she said. "Thanks for stopping to check." She rolled up her window and lifted her foot from the brake.

The car inched forward, and Winnie got herself going again. She drove home with the music on low and her mind running on high. A half-hour later, she pulled into her garage, tapped the button to close it behind her, and waited for the door to shut all the way before she got out of her sedan.

She entered her house to a brightly lit kitchen, because she always left those lights on if she'd be gone after dark. Rocky, her gray and white cat, said, "Mrow," and then, "Mrow," and then, *"Mrrrrrow."*

The cat wove through her legs, begging for a pat, and Winnie bent down to stroke him absently. "Where's Salmon, huh?"

She wasn't surprised her black cat hadn't come to greet her; he never did. She'd find him in his cat palace, or asleep on her bed, or judging her from atop her grandmother's china cabinet.

She noted Taylor had not returned to the house, and she wondered if her sister would come stumbling in at three o'clock in the morning or not at all.

"She's going home on Friday," she told Rocky. And it couldn't come fast enough.

She straightened and looked at her phone as if it were a foreign object that had fallen to earth from outer space. Winnie already knew she wasn't doing anything a week from Saturday, but she tapped to get to her calendar, just to check.

She'd spoken to Wilder Glover about Tyson tonight, and she rolled her neck, her stomach mimicking the side-to-side movement. "Idiot," she muttered to herself. Wilder had said he was "good friends" with Ty, but *he* was the one who'd suggested Ty take her to the wedding.

Winnie hadn't even known there was a wedding next weekend.

Can you call me? Winnie typed out the words and sent them to Ty. It had been a while since he'd texted, and she wasn't surprised her message sat there, unread and unanswered.

Winnie went into her bedroom, Rocky hot on her heels, and she methodically pulled the pins out of her hair, washed her face, and brushed her teeth. She shed her party clothes and slipped into a soft pair of pajamas that testified of her love of reading, the color purple, and hot tea.

She sighed, a round of tears pressing into her eyes for a reason she couldn't name. Perhaps the fact that her own sister had abandoned her at the dance. Maybe because she didn't want Ty to think she'd been fishing for a date when she'd talked to Wilder about him. Maybe because he'd asked her out, and she didn't know if she could—or should—keep her personal pact and say yes.

Sinking to her knees at her bedside, Winnie bowed her head and let herself cry for several long moments. She didn't vocalize anything, but she believed God could hear the prayers in her heart, and tonight, that would have to be good enough.

———

THE FOLLOWING MORNING, Winnie's phone rang just as she stepped through her sliding back door and onto the deck. She carried a plate with a rewarmed chocolate croissant in one hand and her morning cup of pomegranate tea in the other, and she couldn't fish her phone out of her pocket immediately.

She did manage to get the croissant on the table and her hand in her pocket by the second ring.

"Tyson Greene," she breathed out. Then she cleared her throat, lifted her head, and swiped on the call. "Hello?"

"Hey," he said, and oh, that word could've just as easily been categorized as a bark.

Winnie waited, because he had initiated this conversation with that two-line text last night. Along the edge of her backyard, the river bubbled, filling the air with the cheery sound of running water that had won her over the first time she'd looked at this house.

"You wanted me to call?" he asked.

"You want to go to your friend's wedding with me?"

"Well, I can't go alone."

Winnie sat down and lifted her tea to her lips. She blew gently on it as she watched the squirrels in her backyard run up the oak tree. "Why not?" she finally asked. "Lots of people go to weddings alone."

Nothing came through the line at all, but Winnie imagined him growling, because it would fit his personality perfectly.

"All my friends have dates," he finally said, his voice one flat monotone. "And I don't want to go alone. If you have plans—"

"I don't have plans." Winnie's heartbeat zoomed through her body, making her head spin.

"So you just don't want to go with me."

"I'm a little surprised *you* want to go with *me*," she said.

"Why—I mean, why's that? Why wouldn't I want to go with you?"

Winnie tried to hear the ingenuine quality in his tone, but she couldn't. He seemed honestly confused, and that only added to *her* confusion. She cocked her head and took a sip of her tea as a blue bird landed on her bird feeder.

A smile spread across her face. "Do you like bird-watching?"

"Bird-watching?" Ty repeated. "No. Who likes bird-watching?"

Winnie's smile faltered. "I do."

"I mean, yeah, of course. Bird-watching." He cleared his throat. "It's fine. Well, I have to get to work—"

"Why did you ask me?" she asked.

He coughed this time, and Winnie couldn't believe it, but all the physical signs she could hear told her he was...nervous. To be talking to her?

Impossible.

Preposterous.

Ridiculous.

"Do you want me to be honest?"

She set down her teacup, the liquid still too hot to sip, and she wasn't exactly sure where this conversation was going. "I generally advocate for honesty, yes."

"I heard that my friend might set you up with another friend of mine, and it irritated me. Okay? I didn't want him to ask you, and I didn't want to see you there with him. Yeah. That's why. That's why I asked you."

Pure disbelief tore through Winnie, and she was so glad she'd put down her tea. Otherwise, she might have spilled boiling liquid all over herself when the muscles in her arm failed her.

"You didn't want him...." She pressed her eyes closed. "I'm confused."

"Welcome to the club," Ty muttered. "It's okay. You just don't like me."

Her eyes flew open. "Hey, I like you fine. *You're* the one who acts like *I'm* the black cloud ruining your otherwise sunny day."

"You make me do things I don't want to do," he shot back.

"It's my *job*." Winnie blew out her breath.

"I don't want to go out with my physical therapist," Ty said without missing a beat. "So if you can't just go as Winnie, a really beautiful woman, with a cowboy, who yes, happens to have a limp, then I rescind the invitation."

"You rescind it? *Rescind* it?" Winnie had never even heard a regular person use that word in normal conversation before. "You can't just *rescind* a wedding date invitation. It's out there. It's scinded."

A pause filled the line while Winnie's pulse stamped through her body. Then a low sound entered her ears. It took her a few seconds to even recognize it as laughter.

Ty was *laughing* at her.

"Scinded is not a word," he said, still chuckling.

Winnie held her head high, though he couldn't see her. *A really beautiful woman.*

Had she really heard that? Or had her tired brain simply made it up?

He quieted, and Winnie made her decision. "I can go as myself," she said. "Not a physical therapist."

"Okay," Ty said.

"Is there a color scheme I need to adhere to?"

"A color scheme? It's a wedding in Three Rivers."

"Yes, and I've heard that some brides, even in small towns, want things a particular way," she said dryly. The moment she said the word "brides," Winnie's chest collapsed. How could she have forgotten that *she* should've been a bride only eleven months ago?

How could she possibly go to a *wedding* without thinking of the one she'd planned for and never got?

"I can find out," Tyson said. "But I highly doubt it. Any dress you have will be gorgeous."

"What if I don't own any dresses?" she asked.

He scoffed. "You don't own any dresses?"

She thought of the many she'd left behind in Redwood, Oklahoma. Carver had told her once that he preferred her in a dress, and she'd worn one on every single date they'd gone on since then.

"I own a great many of them," she said matter-of-factly. "But I left them all in Oklahoma." She *rescinded* the part where she'd burned a couple of them. Better to save that crazy tidbit for when she knew Ty well enough that he'd understand.

"Well, what would you wear if you couldn't go get a dress?"

"I'm absolutely *not* going to go get a dress."

"Ohhhh-kaaay," he said, drawing the word out. "Am I picking you up and you're going to the wedding in scrubs? What are we talkin' here?"

Winnie smiled at the very idea. "I own an amazing black jump-suit," she said.

"I'm not even sure what that is," Ty said. "And I'm also not sure black is appropriate for a wedding."

"I'd be willing to buy a jumpsuit in a different color," Winnie said. "Will we be dancing?"

"I don't want you there as my nurse," he said.

"I thought I already agreed to that," she said. "I was asking to know if I should wear heels or not."

"I have no idea what the itinerary is," he said. "It's a *wedding*, Winnie. For the love of eight seconds."

Winnie burst out laughing, though she didn't think Ty had meant to be funny. Nope. He didn't join her, but she couldn't help the giggles streaming from her mouth.

She sobered and asked, "What time do I need to be ready?"

"I don't know."

Winnie grinned out into the peacefulness of her backyard. Yes, Taylor would be up soon, and Winnie would have to pretend to care about her new boyfriend, but for now, she could enjoy the mid-morning sunshine, the squirrels, and teasing Ty. She could hardly believe that last one, but well, she was just trying to live in the moment.

"I've got to be honest, too, Ty—"

"When are you ever not?"

"It sure seems like maybe you pocket-texted me," she went on. "I didn't see you drinking last night, and I'm pretty sure you drove away in your truck, but...you text me at almost one in the morning, and it was practically a demand to go to a wedding with you in ten days. But you don't know what I need to wear, or if there will be dancing, or what time I need to be ready?"

"I—I don't drink."

"That's a relief." Winnie pictured his dark eyes and all that hair, which he'd admitted he kept long to annoy his mother. "Shoot straight with me, cowboy, because I've had enough of men who lie right to my face."

She took a deep breath and hoped she wouldn't regret the next words out of her mouth. "Did you ask me to the wedding because you were jealous?"

Silence.

Two seconds, then five, then seven, passed.

"Yes," he barked. "Okay? Yes. I don't want to watch you go out with someone who isn't me, okay? Yes, I was jealous of this other guy who might ask you out." His breath heaved on the other end of the line, and then he quieted again.

Winnie ducked her head, her soul practically singing. She wasn't sure if her heart was ready to take on a man—another cowboy—like Tyson Greene, but oh, she wanted to find out.

"Okay, then yes," she said, using a lot of the same words he had. "I'll go to the wedding with you next weekend if you can get me some additional details very soon."

"I can," Ty whispered.

"Great," she whispered back. "Well...Happy New Year, Ty."

"Yeah," he said. "Happy New Year to you too, Winnie."

The call ended, and Winnie sighed into the silent morning air. "I don't know what this will be, Lord," she murmured. "But can You please make it something good? I don't know if I can take any more sad, bad, or lonely."

She ate her croissant and sipped her tea, and when her phone chimed, she found a text from Ty.

The ceremony is at five o'clock on Saturday, up at Shiloh Ridge Ranch. There's a dinner, reception, and dance party right after. Judy says there's no color requirements, so wear whatever makes you smile —heels or no heels. I think I need to pick you up at four for us to be there on time.

Winnie smiled and watched a pair of squirrels chase each other along the back fence. "It might be nice if Ty and I could get along," she added to her prayer. "Okay? Just for a couple of hours." She nodded and tucked her phone back onto the side table with her now-empty teacup.

Yeah, it sure would be nice if she and Ty could learn how to get along...maybe for longer than it took to attend a wedding together. But Winnie didn't want to ask too much of God too soon, so she simply said, "Amen," and left it at that.

3

Tyson finished unloading the dishes he'd just brought in from the veranda and retied his apron around his waist to make it tighter.

The kitchen at Colt's new restaurant at the apple orchard bustled with cooks whipping up French toast stuffed with apples, frying bacon, or poaching eggs. Tyson didn't love restaurant work, and he normally ran a crew in the southwest part of the orchard.

They cleaned up slash, pruned trees, and checked irrigation systems, and while he'd only been involved in one harvest, he'd managed that part of the orchard to make sure all the fruit came down, got checked, and delivered where it needed to go.

Thankfully, his section of the orchard wasn't open to the public, who could come pick their own bushels. In fact, Ty had had no idea that people actually did that, but he'd learned last fall that they came and picked apples to make sauce, juice, and dried snacks for their kids.

Colt had opened a farm store a couple of years ago, and he'd added a food-kitchen operation to the orchard, and they made applesauce, apple juice, apple butter, apple cider syrup, and other appley products. They sold canning supplies and pie spices and caramel apple kits, and his latest addition to the orchards since taking over for his mother was this restaurant and café.

Ty had eaten here several times, and the food was delicious, as Colt had brought in talented chefs and cooks.

"Table eleven needs to be bussed," Julie said.

Ty nodded at her. "I got it." He grabbed onto his cart and headed back out onto the veranda.

Table eleven sat out on the edge, one of their couples' tables that overlooked the orchards. In the evening, Colt lit up the trees with fairy lights, creating a romantic atmosphere. Word had quickly gotten out around town, and most evenings had to be reserved a couple of weeks in advance.

Ty knew most folks here at brunch, and around town. He deliberately kept his focus on his goal, concentrating on taking the strongest, most even steps he could. He remembered all the things Winnie had taught him in physical therapy and employed them, so no one would have a reason to have his name in their mouth.

Winnie sneaked into his thoughts again the way she had been for a while now. He'd woken up with the woman in his mind, and he'd spoken to her only two hours ago on his drive to the orchards, in fact. That conversation had left him feeling a little chaotic inside, but the texts afterward had soothed him, and hey, he had a date to Judy and Trooper's wedding now, and Trap would *not* be taking Winnie.

He arrived at the table, still not quite sure why the prospect of one of his best friends going out with Winnie bothered him, only knowing that it did. He started stacking plates and putting them in his plastic bin. When he had to reach toward the middle of the table, he grabbed onto the back of a chair for support. His balance wasn't great when leaning forward or backward—something he definitely needed to work on.

As long as he had some support, he was fine, and he had a little pole with a hook on the end that he could use to pull glasses or salt-shakers closer to him.

Laughter at the table next to him rang out, but Ty didn't look up from his chore. Now that he'd heard them, though, his ears seemed in tune with what they were saying, and he heard a woman ask, "Don't you know him, Winnie?"

He flinched, his head coming up. He looked out into the orchard, using every ounce of willpower he possessed not to look over at table ten. But how many people named Winnie could there be in Three Rivers?

His physical therapist—and his wedding date—was the only one he knew of.

Ty's heart pounded as he finished wiping the table and setting the condiments, salt and pepper shakers, and sugar substitute packets where they belonged. He deliberately turned his back on table ten and swung his cart around the other way, scanning that half of the veranda for more tables that needed to be bussed. If he could just go that way, he could—

"Hey, Tyson."

It wasn't Winnie's voice that interrupted his thoughts, but he definitely heard the feminine tone, because she stood on his right side. In fact, she came around his right side and appeared precisely in front of him.

"Taylor, he's working," Winnie said from somewhere behind him, her words barely registering in his ears, but Tyson simply took in the woman in front of him. She had dark hair, similar to Winnie's, but with plenty of blonde streaks through it, suggesting she saw a stylist often. Her dark eyes crinkled when she smiled, and something familiar about her tickled in Tyson's memory.

Winnie arrived and linked her arm through the woman's standing in front of him. "Taylor, come sit down," Winnie practically hissed at her. She flashed a smile at Ty that only lasted a breath. He took in the two of them, and they were definitely related.

"You didn't introduce me to him last night," Taylor said. "But I know I saw him at the party."

Tyson wished he had a boss that would come storming across the veranda and demand he get back to work. Instead, he stood there and stared at the two women in front of him.

"Come on, ladies," a cowboy drawled, and Ty turned his attention to table ten, his heartbeat now kicking against his ribs. He found Burt Hallahan and Cross Gables sitting at table ten.

Of course.

Great. Just great, Ty thought.

They wore their New Year's Day brunch finest, which for cowboys was a clean pair of jeans and a button-down shirt.

Burt and Cross lived together in a cabin at Lone Star, and they were elite farriers in the exclusive program there. They apparently did everything together and had dressed as twins that day, with matching long-sleeved black shirts and dark cowboy hats. Burt also wore a stormy look, and Winnie tugged on Taylor's arm to get her to go back to the table.

"I just wanted to meet the man you're going to that wedding with," Taylor said, a definite pout in her tone.

"Yes, well, he's working," Winnie said. "And besides, you met him last night."

Tyson had *not* met Taylor last night, at least not with a formal introduction from Winnie with words like, *Hey, this is my sister,* or maybe, *This is my cousin from Alabama.*

Taylor wore a pink dress that swished around her knees as she walked the few steps back to the table, with a pair of impossibly high heels and the teeniest tiniest pinpoint heel. Ty had no idea how they didn't go down through the slats in the veranda, but she managed to stay upright and make it back to table ten.

Winnie wore a loose pair of wide-leg pants that mimicked a skirt but weren't a skirt, and Tyson remembered their conversation about how she didn't own any dresses. Her pants shone like navy water, and she wore a silver shirt underneath a matching jacket.

Ty narrowed his eyes as Cross stood and pulled out her chair for her, as if they were on a date. Was she seriously on a date with that guy a couple of hours after agreeing to go to the wedding with him? Ty felt frozen, his feet stuck to the veranda and both hands gripping his dish cart.

"Hey, man," Burt said. "We've got some stuff you can clear away here."

"Burt," Winnie said, clearly chastising him. "We're not even done eating yet."

"I'm done with mine," he said in a loud voice.

Ty fixed a mask on his face as he walked over to the table. "Yeah, sure," he said, his voice a monotone. "Let me clear this stuff away for you guys." He picked up Burt's empty plate and put it in his bin. "You guys off today at Lone Star?"

"Just until this afternoon," Cross said, and he was definitely the nicer of the two of them.

Ty worked with them a couple of times a week, but he wasn't a farrier. He moved horses from one stall to another, or hooked up equines to a walking circle, or brushed them down after their workout.

He loved nothing more than his time alone with a horse, making it feel good, getting it clean, and securing it somewhere safe, warm, and dry. The sense of accomplishment that came with taking care of an animal appealed to Ty's protective nature, and he loved training the dogs at Mitch's academy and taking care of the horses for Henry and Angel.

Sometimes, he got paperwork for the farriers and helped them clean their tools, and he definitely knew his role at Lone Star was subservient to both Cross and Burt, though Henry and Angel made sure every person there understood their role was critical, no matter how small it was.

He picked up a couple more plates and surveyed the table. Taylor hadn't even eaten a third of her breakfast yet, and Winnie had a few bites of eggs left, a little pile of hash browns, and all of her bacon. He could barely meet her eyes but managed to do it.

"Anything else?" he asked.

"No," she said quickly. "Thank you, Ty."

He nodded and shuffled his feet to turn around and get the heck out of there.

Thankfully, Julie caught his eye and held up three fingers, and he headed toward the other side of the veranda, feeling the weight of the world on his back, as if everyone at table ten was still watching him.

He made it to table three, where a sense of relief moved through him as he reached for the first plate. He tossed a napkin on top and picked up a bowl that had once held hollandaise sauce when someone arrived at the table beside him.

"I'm really sorry about that," Winnie said, and she picked up two glasses and put them in his plastic bin.

He straightened and stared at her. "What are you doing?"

Winnie pulled her hands back as if just now realizing she'd started to bus the table but didn't actually work at the restaurant. Her hands twined around themselves, and she finally dropped them to her sides, as if they'd suddenly had bricks tied to them.

"I don't know," she said. "I just—Burt was really rude to you, and I'm really sorry about that."

"I can handle Burt Hallahan," he said. "I work with him. It's fine."

He picked up one of the glasses she'd put in his bin and emptied the few swallows of liquid into the other one, then stacked them. He looked at Winnie and pulled in a breath, her beauty making it catch in his throat. He didn't want to fight with this woman. Quite the opposite, in fact.

"How long are you working here?" she asked.

"Brunch just goes until one," he said. "It's usually about an hour cleanup after."

Colt had fed them the stuffed French toast that morning for

breakfast, and he had his momma's soup to look forward to that afternoon.

"What about you?" he asked. "Enjoying your date with Burt?"

"I'm not on a date," Winnie said quickly. "Taylor—" She blew out her breath and looked over to table ten. "I'm just trying to keep my sister from getting herself into too much trouble."

"Ah, so she's your sister," Ty said. "You know we didn't actually meet last night."

Winnie's gaze flew back to him. "No, I know."

"You don't like your sister?" he asked.

"She's flighty," Winnie said, her voice crisp and coming out in bursts. "And I never know what she's going to say or do and, yeah, that makes me a little nervous."

He grinned at her. "I bet it does. Where does she live?"

"Oklahoma," Winnie said. "She's still in the small town where we grew up."

"Is that where you moved from?" Ty asked.

Winnie nodded and swallowed. "Yeah. She goes home tomorrow." She looked back at Ty, her shoulders deflating. "And I can't wait."

Ty wanted to draw her into his chest and help her feel safe and comfortable the way he did horses.

"Well, today's already half over," he said. "How much trouble can she get into?"

"You'd be shocked," Winnie said dryly.

Ty was pretty sure he'd met and known women like Taylor on the rodeo circuit, and doubly sure that Winnie would be shocked if she knew all the wild and crazy things that happened in that life. Ty realized in that moment that he didn't miss it at all anymore, and that God had led him exactly where he needed to be—back here in Three Rivers.

He blinked at the beautiful brunette in front of him, wondering if God had put her in his life too. He cleared his throat, his mind suddenly buzzing with all kinds of questions and words and fragments of sentences that wouldn't come together in complete thoughts.

"Anyway," Winnie said, "I just wanted you to know—" She waved her hand and didn't finish the sentence. She turned back to table ten again, and this time, Ty reached out and grabbed her hand as she started to leave. She gasped, but Ty held on as the electricity flowed from her fingers, through his, and up to his shoulder. Every cell in his body buzzed and—holy-eight-second-ride, he was attracted to this woman.

He cleared his throat. "Maybe you'll just want a relaxing weekend after your sister's been here." He ducked his head and tilted it away from table ten, lowering the brim so he wouldn't be able to look that way and see anyone watching him.

Winnie's eyes stayed on his face, though he wasn't directly meeting her gaze.

"I work with Mitch on Saturday mornings. We train the hearing dogs, and afterward, I always treat myself to lunch. Maybe I could stop by and pick you up and we could go together."

He had no idea what he'd do if she said no to a casual Saturday lunch date a week before the wedding they were already set to attend together. A moment went by and then another, and Ty raised his eyes to hers. He found Winnie smiling, and her fingers in his tightened.

"Is this like a dry run for the wedding?" she asked. "To see if we can get along?"

He grinned at her. "If you want to call it that, that's fine with me."

"Well, if that's not what it is, what is it?"

"I'd call it a date, ma'am."

Winnie swallowed too, an edge of fear creeping into her expression now. "Ty, there's something I should tell—"

"We're ready, Winnie," Taylor said as she arrived.

Winnie dropped Ty's hand instantly and put another foot of space between them. She held his gaze, and he found pleading in it this time, and he understood her to be begging him to please understand and that she would explain later.

Ty nodded and went back to bussing table three as Taylor and the two cowboys collected Winnie and they all left.

"As long as there's a later," he muttered to himself, catching sight of Winnie's shiny, earthy hair as she ducked out the door, wondering how long he'd have to wait for her to call or text him and let him know if she would—or wouldn't—go out with him on Saturday.

4

Winnie sat curled into the beanbag in the corner of her living room, her favorite spot in the whole world. Behind her, the New Year's Day sun shone over her shoulder, and she had two purrers on her lap. Salmon had finally given up pawing her to pet him, and she'd been texting with her best friend back in Oklahoma about Ty for the past twenty minutes.

Just text him and tell him you'll go to lunch with him, Amelia had said. *He's probably going crazy by now, and I'm not going to answer you again until you've told me you've texted him.*

Amelia could be hard-nosed if she needed to be, and right now, Winnie really appreciated that. She'd been staring at Tyson's name on her phone for the past several minutes, and she sighed as she looked up to the movie she'd put on.

When Taylor had gone down the hall to get ready for her evening date, Winnie frowned because she didn't understand why her sister had turned her visit into a *date-as-many-cowboys-as-possible* fest.

To be fair, Taylor was going out with Burt again tonight, and Redwood only sat two hours from where Burt lived and worked near Amarillo. Still, Winnie wouldn't want to do a long-distance dating thing, and the reason she hadn't texted Ty yet was because she wasn't sure she wanted to do "a dating thing" at all.

"It's been ten months," she whispered to herself.

Ten months since Carver had shown up on her doorstep, his cowboy hat in his hand, his bags packed, and his truck still running in her driveway. Ten months since he'd left town the moment he'd finished telling her he didn't want to marry her. Ten months since he'd left Winnie to pick up the pieces of her life and the life she thought she'd have, as well as the shards of her heart.

Ten months of being alone again, after so long of being part of a couple.

She'd stayed in Redwood for a couple of months before starting to look for another job, and she had moved to Three Rivers almost seven months ago now.

She looked up again and watched the characters on the TV trying on dresses. She kept the volume low and the captions on, but she didn't hear them or see them. Instead, Winnie took a few moments to really evaluate how she felt. Right now, right here, in this moment.

"Guide my hands, my feet, and my life," she prayed. "Please, God."

She didn't need big, grandiose shows of God's love for her. She'd always known He was there and always believed that He would take care of her. She didn't need to test Him, and as a peaceful feeling came over her and settled in her heart, Winnie took a breath and blew it out.

With it went all the negativity of the last ten months, all the ways she felt inadequate to be a girlfriend or a wife, how her hair wasn't the right color, and how she carried too much weight, and how she pushed people too far, and that she spoke too loud, and she volunteered too much, and she inserted herself in conversations where she wasn't wanted.

Winnie had been through it all and blamed herself for everything that had gone wrong—between her and Taylor, between her and Carver, between her and everyone.

After all, she was the common denominator, so didn't that make the problem exist within her?

As she opened her eyes, she saw her house with new vision. No, she wasn't perfect, but neither was anyone else. She'd rather not be married than married to a man who didn't love her and didn't want to be with her.

She wanted to be around people who appreciated her for her opinions, and her knowledge, and her ability to refuse to text them back until they texted the cowboy who'd asked them out.

She looked down at her phone, turned it back on, and tapped to start typing a message to Tyson.

I'm not sure I ever said it, but I'd love to go to lunch with you on Saturday.

She stared at the words, knowing she hadn't told him yes or no while at brunch earlier. They'd gone into one of their back-and-forth banters, and the man had outright used the word *date*. Winnie liked that she didn't have to guess at his intentions.

And honestly, she'd rather know now if she was walking into a disaster next weekend. There'd probably be hundreds of people at the Glover wedding, many of whom Winnie had started getting to know in the past few months. She wanted to belong to this small town, and if she couldn't even go to a lunch date with Tyson, they certainly shouldn't be attending a wedding together.

"It'll probably save us both," she whispered, and then she dropped her thumb onto the arrow to send the text.

A circle appeared and went around once, and then the text said *Delivered*.

If you let me know what time I need to be ready, that would be great. Here's my address. She typed that in, because Ty would certainly have no way of knowing it, and he'd need it for the wedding anyway.

Great, Ty said back. *Mitch and I usually work with the dogs until about eleven-thirty, so I bet I could be to your place by about twelve. If that works.*

That's the perfect time for lunch, Winnie said. 😀 🍗

Is that emoji an indication of where you want to go? I'm taking requests.

Winnie grinned at her phone, feeling flirtatious and fun—something she hadn't felt for a long time.

I'm new to town, cowboy, and I like to eat. So I'm sure anywhere we go, I'll be able to find something I like.

Okay, that's easy, Tyson said.

Since she'd been working with him in a professional capacity, Winnie knew he wasn't particularly verbose. He didn't volunteer information, and he never said more than he needed to.

A flash of loneliness struck her, and she looked back at her phone, hoping a question wouldn't annoy him too much. She stopped and gave herself a mental shake.

"If a question annoys the man, you don't want to date him." Winnie didn't want to live her life on eggshells, which was why she'd had to leave Redwood in the first place, and why she couldn't wait for Taylor to hit the road tomorrow morning.

What soup did your momma make?

You'll die, Ty said. 😋 *It's called Cabbage Patch Stew, and believe it or not, it's actually really good.*

Vegetables? 🥬🥬🥬 Winnie's smile felt bigger than it'd been since she'd moved to town.

It's mostly vegetables, yeah. Cabbage, crushed tomatoes, black beans, and ground beef. She puts a lot of chili powder in it, and it makes my nose run in the best way possible.

A picture started to come through, but it didn't load before his next text popped up.

Of course, the real prize is the cornbread with lots of honey butter.

The buttery, glistening cornbread made Winnie's mouth water.

Wow, that looks amazing.

What are you having for dinner? he asked. *Wait—if I only get one question, I don't want it to be that.*

Her smile started to fade. *Who said you only get one question?*

I don't know, he said. *I guess if you're willing to answer more than one, you can tell me what you're having for dinner.*

Well, now I want to know the other question.

I was going to ask if you're really not going out with Cross.

Warmth moved through Winnie's chest, and her smile came roaring back. *No, I'm not going out with Cross. Apparently, they had tickets to the brunch at the orchards today, and the woman he was going to take backed out at the last minute, and Taylor made me tag along.*

She sent that text, her thumbs already flying across her screen for another message.

And I was probably going to order Chinese for tonight. Taylor's going out with Burt again, so it's just me and the cats.

Two more questions, Ty said. *And you can stop answering anytime. What Chinese restaurant and what kind and how many cats are we talking?*

Do you not like cats?

I'm more of a dog person myself.

I've got two cats. Rocky and Salmon.

And I'm probably going to get the chicken rice teriyaki bowl from Wok This Way. It was the first restaurant I ate at after I moved to Three Rivers, and I loved it.

Winnie wasn't sure if it was the food she loved or the freedom of being in a new town and picking whatever she wanted to eat, where no one knew her name and no one looked at her with an edge in their eyes that said they knew she must be hurting inside.

After all, wasn't everyone?

Winnie intimately knew that a person could look okay on the outside—happy even—show up to work every day, pay all their bills, and still be shattered and bleeding on the inside. Some people, like Tyson, had to wear those wounds outwardly, but she knew they carried an inner hurt as well.

I've never been to Wok This Way, Tyson said. *It's your favorite place?*

It was good, Winnie said. *I've had the noodle bowl and the fried rice bowl, and I like them both.*

I'm not sure the last time I ate Chinese food.

No? Are you more of a steak, burgers, sandwiches kind of guy? And soup, obviously.

Obviously, he said back. *Honestly, I could eat eggs for every meal. They're fast and easy and full of protein.*

Winnie shook her head, a flirty buzz sliding down her spine. *This is going to be bad news, but I don't like eggs.*

How can you not like eggs? he asked. *Every person on the planet likes eggs.*

Obviously not, she sent back.

You had eggs on your plate at brunch today.

Yeah—when I was finished eating.

What's your favorite food?

Winnie started looking for an emoji she could send, but she didn't think one existed for chocolate lava cakes or biscoff cheesecake.

Now that I know your favorite food is eggs, tell me your favorite animal, she said when she came up empty.

Horses, he sent back. 🐎🐎🐎

🐈🐈🐈

Winnie giggled like a little girl getting tickled by her daddy when Ty sent, *I can send random emojis too -* 🌙🌙🌙

Winnie finally found a food she liked and sent it. 🥚

Her love for guacamole arrived front and center, and she was already scrolling through the emojis for something else to send Ty.

I don't like: 🍄🍄🍄🍄🍄🍄

She sent a row of emojis just as Taylor asked, "Who are you texting?" and Winnie instantly slid her phone under her leg, her left hand moving to stroke Rocky's back.

"Just someone from work," she said, and while it wasn't exactly true, it also wasn't exactly a lie. "When is Burt going to be here?"

Taylor didn't answer verbally, but stuck her hip out as her manipulative, cutesy smile appeared.

"Taylor." Winnie sighed and reached to rub her fingers across her forehead, because a look like that meant only one thing: Burt wasn't coming here to pick her up for their date, and Taylor needed a favor.

"I'm just meeting him at this barn dance," she said. "I promise I'll be back before midnight. I have to be on the road by nine tomorrow morning."

Winnie looked at her sister, her weariness making her sink further into the beanbag. "What do you need?"

"Just fifty dollars for gas." Taylor pressed her palms together as if praying. "I promise I'll pay you back."

Winnie sighed and gestured to the credenza holding up the TV. "Bring me my purse. You can have whatever cash is in it."

Taylor squealed and danced over to her purse, practically throwing it at Winnie. She'd deliberately made sure she didn't have much cash, and she pulled out a single twenty dollar bill, along with a ten. "This is all I have."

"Thank you," Taylor gushed. "I'm sure Mom and Daddy will help me with the gas to get home."

Winnie simply watched her tuck the bills into her bra and turn to leave the house. She wanted to tell her sister that if she didn't go gallivanting all over town, she wouldn't have to beg for gas money.

Oh, and if she'd get a job, she could afford to buy the things she needed.

The front door clicked closed behind Taylor, and Salmon jumped down from Winnie's lap as she pulled her phone out to see if Ty had responded.

He hadn't; he'd gone silent after her row of mushroom emojis, and Winnie sighed, deflated and a hint of dejection running through her that the flirtatious moment between them had fled.

"Mrow," Rocky said pathetically, and Winnie grinned at him.

"Yeah, let's get you guys some dinner." She heaved herself out of the beanbag, then quickly sent a text to Amelia.

I did it. I have a date with him on Saturday.

Yes! Amelia said instantly. *Way to go, Winnie. I want outfit pics and a full run-down afterward.*

Winnie tucked her phone in her back pocket and headed into the kitchen, first to feed her cats, and second, to bake something delicious for dinner.

"Maybe brownies," she mused, because while Winnie didn't love to cook, she did enjoy baking, and she had full freedom to eat only dessert for dinner if she wanted to. After all, she had a date with a handsome cowboy, and it felt like something to celebrate.

5

Ty gave his phone a glare as it blared out his mother's ringtone. He'd already interrupted his conversation with Winnie to talk on the phone with his brother, Bryan. Maybe he hadn't exactly been enthusiastic to help his younger brother propose to his girlfriend.

"On Saturday afternoon, the *one time* I have a date," he grumbled as he wiped his hands on a dish towel and reached for his phone as it started to shriek for the third time. His momma was not an easy woman to put off, though Ty had tried many times in the past. He swiped on the call, tapped the speaker button, and moved the phone closer to the stove.

"I'm cooking dinner, Momma," he said.

A beat of silence came through the line, and then she said, "Dinner? You just got soup from me a couple of hours ago."

"Yeah, and I ate it. Then Jacob brought home some steaks that Mitch got from his daddy up at Shiloh Ridge."

"Oh, well, you can't beat steak from Shiloh Ridge."

Ty smiled at the obvious happiness in his mother's voice. "You sure can't." He glanced over to his roommate, who looked up as if sensing Tyson's gaze. Jacob raised his eyebrows, and Ty simply shook his head. He didn't say anything else, because his momma had called him, and Ty already knew why.

"Bryan said you were…short about coming out to Three Rivers on Saturday."

"Yeah, Momma, it's a long drive," he said.

"Your brother is proposing to his girlfriend," his mother said, as if no more important thing in the world could be done on Saturday.

"Yeah, I heard," Ty said. "I don't know why I have to be there."

"He needs you, Ty, to get the table all set up out in the fields."

Ty could have made any excuse about how he wouldn't be able to make the drive from *Signs for Success* in time, and Bryan had already told him he would time it according to Tyson's schedule. "I don't know why you and Daddy can't do that."

"Because we have to act like it's a regular workday," she said. "And I've got two clients coming on Saturday."

"Well, maybe Saturday's not a real great day to do it," Ty barked out. "Did he ever think of that?" He held the tongs in his hand and watched as the steaks sizzled in the pan, his grumpy attitude about his younger brother getting engaged flowing through him and infecting every cell in his body.

"What's really going on?" Momma asked.

Ty sighed and let the irritation he had allowed in seep away. "It's nothing," Ty said. "I'll reschedule."

"What do you have to reschedule?" Momma asked.

"I just said it was nothing," he said, because he wasn't ready to tell anyone that he'd actually asked Winnie out to lunch.

I'd call it a date, ma'am.

The words rang through his head, and he liked that she hadn't been upset with him for calling her ma'am, and she hadn't balked at their lunch on Saturday being called a date, either.

Ty's face heated. He put his hand on the towel over the handle of the cast iron skillet and gave it a little shake. The steak didn't move, which meant it wasn't ready to turn. He could be patient, and he glanced at the clock, knowing he had less than sixty seconds to flip this thing and keep it at a medium temperature.

"Is this why you're calling?" he asked. "To make sure I have a good attitude on Saturday?"

"It would be nice," Momma said. "It's not like your brother's going to get engaged every weekend or anything."

Ty rolled his neck and wanted to blast her with a grumpy sigh. He repressed it and said, "You know, I'm allowed to be upset if I have to change my plans to accommodate him with less than forty-eight hours' notice."

"He acknowledged that," Momma said. "Did he not, Ty?"

"Yeah, he did," Ty admitted. "He said he could do it anytime that worked for me."

"So if you have plans, you just need to say," Momma said.

"I already told him it was nothing that can't change," Ty said. "But I don't get done at Signs for Success until eleven-thirty and I gotta have time to eat."

"I just got off the phone with him," Momma said. "And he's hoping to get there around two o'clock. As long as you're there about fifteen minutes before him, you'll have plenty of time. Libby is going to help too."

"I'm aware, Momma." Ty reached to turn over the steak. It came up easily, and he flipped it, the satisfying sizzling meeting his good ear and making his mouth water. "I already talked to Bryan about all of this. Why are you micromanaging this?"

"I just want to make sure everyone's happy," she said.

"We're all just fine," Ty said. "We're grown adults."

"He doesn't want to cause a problem," Momma said. "And I know this is already going to be hard for you, and I just want you to be okay."

Talking to death wasn't going to make it okay. Ty wanted to tell her that, but that would only spark more conversation. Instead, Ty stepped back from the hot skillet and then reached to turn the flame off underneath it. The steaks could finish in the pan in the next couple of minutes. Then they'd eat, and with his belly full of really good beef, he could text Winnie and ask for a rain check.

"Momma, I'm okay," Tyson said.

"Bryan's worried that you're going to be upset about the engagement."

"Well, I don't know how to fix that," Ty said. "Am I super jazzed both of my siblings are going to get married this year, and I don't even have a girlfriend? Of course not. Would *you* be?"

"No one thinks anything of it," Momma said.

"*I* think something of it, Momma."

"Well, maybe you don't need to," she fired back at him, and it was no wonder Ty had a grumpy, fiery streak. His daddy had one too, which meant Ty had been doomed from birth.

"Besides, I heard you had a date to the Glover wedding next weekend," she said, her voice moving into that fake *this-doesn't-matter-to-me-but-so-does* tone.

Ty dang near dropped his tongs. "How in the world did you hear that?"

"Janice Mulberry was at the New Year's Day brunch today," she said. "And I guess she overheard something. She didn't know who it was with, but as I was taking the last of the leaves out to the green-works bin, she caught me and said something about it."

Ty pulled the cast iron skillet off the stove and turned to the peninsula behind him. "I've forgotten where I live," he said. "Dear Lord, is there any way to escape the rumor mill in this town?"

Momma laughed, and Ty turned to get down two plates and picked up the phone from beside the stove. "I heard that," she said. "But you definitely moved away from the phone."

"That's because our dinner's done," he said. "Do you have more lecturing you need to do, or can I go?"

"I didn't call to lecture," she said.

"I know," he said. "I didn't mean that. I'm sorry. I'm going to be fine on Saturday. I will be there. I will be in my best clothes. I will smile, I will be happy, I will cheer the loudest."

"Oh, you're not going to make it a show," Momma said. "Bryan won't like that either."

"Momma," Ty said. "I will act so normal you won't even know what hit you."

"I don't even know what your normal is anymore, Ty," Momma said with a huff. "All right, go enjoy your steak. If you're not going to tell me who you're taking to the wedding...."

Ty thought about it for a moment. As he removed the steaks from the pan and set them on a plate to rest away from the heat, he said, "You know what? No, I don't want to tell you right now."

"Well, it's not that far away," Momma said. "I'm going to find out."

"Yeah, everyone's gonna find out," Ty said. "And maybe it's not that big of a deal."

"Well, if it's not that big of a deal, why don't you tell me who it is right now?"

"Because you really seem to want to know," he said. "And it might just be a friend date or a safe date, so that I don't have to be by myself, with my sister and her fiancé, *and* now my brother and his fiancée, and everyone else in the world who has someone else to be with."

His chest hurt, and he took a deep breath. "My steak's done, Momma. I'm fine. Everything's gonna go amazing on Saturday. Bryan and Ellie are going to be engaged and blissfully in love. We'll have another wedding on the calendar this year. What could possibly go wrong?"

"I can think of a lot of things," she said. "And they all start with T-Y-S-O-N."

"Okay, Momma." He rolled his eyes and turned to the fridge to get out the condiments. "I already talked to Bryan about this, and he was fine." He signaled to Jacob and signed that their food was ready. "Love you, Momma. See you on Saturday." He ended the call and tried to remember how to sign *medium* for Jacob, who got up and pulled a pan of potatoes out of the oven.

They moved around their apartment in silence, though Jacob could speak; he simply rarely did. Ty was still learning sign language, but he could communicate well enough to say dinner was ready.

They sat back down at the bar, and Jacob doused his potatoes in ketchup and his steak in A-1 sauce, and then Ty did the same.

Jacob put his first bite in his mouth and moaned, his eyes rolling back in his head. *So good*, he signed, and then he pulled his phone closer and tapped a message for Ty.

What are you taking to the Signs for Success party tomorrow night?

Ty blinked at the phone, having completely forgotten about the *Signs for Success* party tomorrow night. He'd be back at work at Lone Star, and he looked up at Jacob. He seemed to be able to read his expression, no signs or words needed. He started to laugh and then said, *You forgot.*

Ty grinned at him and nodded. "I forgot," he confirmed, saying the words as he signed them. "I don't even remember what I signed up for," he said next, and that took him to his own phone, where he went to his calendar, sure he'd made himself a note.

He had, and he saw that he'd signed up to bring rolls for the *Signs for Success* company potluck dinner tomorrow night. The new semester didn't start until Wednesday, and a lot of students had gone home for the Christmas and New Year's holiday.

A few stayed, and of course, Mitch and Lacy lived on site, and they'd wanted to do a faculty and staff party before life returned to normal again. Ty only worked with Mitch training the hearing dogs, and the rest of his experience with *Signs for Success* was actually as a student.

Do you know what they're having for the main dish? Ty typed into Jacob's phone, as Mitch and Lacy had said they would provide the meat.

Smoked turkey, Jacob wrote. *And steak bites. I'm supposed to take cheesy potatoes to go with.*

"Sounds like we'll eat well tomorrow, at least," Ty said as he typed the words into the phone. He grinned at Jacob, and he did enjoy his steak—every scrumptious bite.

He cleaned up the kitchen, wiping down the stove of all the steak splatters and wiping out the cast iron skillet with a paper towel before he took his phone and headed outside. Darkness had started to fall, and Ty walked the sidewalk between two pads of grass—the playground on the right that he could see out the window over their kitchen sink—to a bench on the left side in the corner, about one hundred yards from his front door.

Winnie hadn't strayed far from his mind, as she had been the one to tell him to make this walk every day, focusing on his steps and his stride, where his shoulder was, and how he could pull it into position and find the natural gait that he'd once had.

He'd done it too. Even on his busiest days, he made the one-hundred-yard walk to the bench, thinking of her the whole time before making his way back.

Tonight, he sighed mightily as he sank onto the bench and looked at his phone. Winnie hadn't texted again, but she hadn't seemed to mind his questions, and surprisingly, he hadn't minded hers either.

He'd learned that her favorite food was avocados and her least favorite foods were mushrooms or eggs. She had two cats, and that was her favorite animal. And he'd told her that he loved horses and the full moon and the scent of dust and dirt in the air, and the way the earth felt so clean after rain. She loved a good rainstorm too, and Ty thought it might be the first and only thing they'd agreed on yet. She loved the color purple, and he already knew she was a people person. He wasn't, but he figured lots of people found happiness with someone who wasn't exactly like them.

Why couldn't he?

I'm going to need a rain check, he typed out. *My brother called this afternoon, which is why I kind of disappeared. Then Jacob came home with steak and well, now you know where you rank against fresh steak from Shiloh Ridge.*

She seemed to like the emojis, and he sent a couple of laughing ones.

Then my momma called and, wouldn't you know it? My brother's getting engaged on Saturday, and apparently he needs my help to do it, so I can't take you to lunch.

He sent that message and sighed as he looked up.

Maybe we can find another time before next weekend to make sure that we don't embarrass ourselves in front of the whole town. Since, you know, my momma already knew I had a date to the wedding.

His phone buzzed only a few seconds later, and he looked down at it.

Your momma knew you had a date? Winnie asked.

Out of all the things he'd said, that was what she'd latched onto?

I guess someone picked up on something at the brunch today, he said. *Maybe you and Taylor were talking about it.*

Yeah, we were, Winnie said. *Maybe someone at the table next to us overheard.*

Welcome to Three Rivers, Ty said. *This place is notorious for its rumor mill, especially with someone like me.*

Someone like you? Winnie asked. *What does that mean?*

And someone like you, he said. *You're new to town, so of course people are curious about you. And I'm not new to town, so everyone knows everything about me from the time I was born, and they feel— like, I don't know—protective of me. At least that's how my momma explains it. I just find it annoying.*

Cry me a river, cowboy, Winnie said. *I left my small Oklahoma town because everyone there knew every single thing about me, and I couldn't stand the way they looked at me.*

Ty sensed a story there, and his memory flashed back to earlier that day, when she'd said she had something to tell him, and then her sister had interrupted her. He wanted to press her, but at the same time he didn't. Instead, he said, *I'd love to hear about it when we finally get to go to lunch together.*

Then, fearing she might never go to lunch with him if she

thought she had to tell him something she didn't want to talk about, he added, *Or whenever you want to tell me. It doesn't have to be the first time we go out.*

Okay, she said. *We'll see how it goes.*

Does the reason you left Oklahoma have anything to do with why you won't wear dresses? he asked. That little tidbit had intrigued him more than anything else she'd said.

Yes, they're related, Winnie said. *And maybe if we can figure out how to get along, I'll tell you about it.*

I think we've been getting along pretty great over text.

Well, let's see how we do in person, cowboy. Now my cats are demanding dinner. And I have to make the dessert for the party tomorrow night, and then I'll be back if you want to text some more.

Ty's smile widened by the second. He'd forgotten that Winnie was going to start as a sign language instructor at *Signs for Success.* She was supposed to begin in the fall semester, but her workload at the physical therapy clinic had been too much, and she'd asked Mitch and Lacy if she could postpone her assignment. They'd made things work with Lacy taking on the beginner classes that Winnie was supposed to teach.

Ty had been really grateful, because he wasn't sure if he could see Winnie at the physical therapy office and in his beginning sign language classes. He'd graduated out of that one now, though, to the Intermediate ASL class, so she wouldn't have to be his therapist *and* his teacher.

"And hopefully your girlfriend," he whispered to himself as he turned his attention back to his phone.

I'll be around later if you want to chat. At least tell me what you're making for dessert, because that's the best part of any meal.

She didn't answer right away, and Ty got up to do his walking exercises, because while he'd been on a vacation schedule at the orchards and the boarding stable, his healing never took a day off, and he suddenly wanted to become as whole and as strong as possible...for Winnie.

6

Winnie pulled up to the beautiful red-brick Academy, a twinge of nervousness singing through her. She hadn't even started at *Signs for Success* yet, and it felt a little strange to be coming to a faculty party and potluck.

She got out and moved to the back of her sedan, where she popped the trunk. The brownies she'd spent last night making sat there, and she smiled down at them. She'd made a huge sheet pan of them, doing a different flavor in each quadrant.

She'd put big chocolate chunks in the mint brownies, which she then frosted with icing she'd tinted a lovely light green.

She'd done a vanilla cake batter and swirled it with the brownies and topped that with apple-pie spices and a drizzle of white chocolate.

She'd put Rolo chunks in a third corner, and they definitely looked the messiest. Winnie frowned at them, wondering what she could do to make them look more appetizing for future events. The caramel usually oozed out of the candy and kind of left little craters through the brownie surfaces, which were delicious but not that pretty.

In the fourth corner, she had gone for a German-chocolate variety, and the coconut-walnut frosting made her forget about the little Rolo disaster she had going on next to it.

Lacy had texted her to say they were expecting up to two dozen people, which included custodians, groundskeepers, her and Mitch, of course, and the few other professors that they had there. She said they were inviting any students and Resident Assistants to come eat as well, and that brought the total up.

Each quadrant held sixteen brownies, and Winnie wasn't worried that someone wouldn't get what they wanted. She wasn't sure what she was worried about at all, only that she couldn't seem to reach down and pick up the brownies and turn toward the building.

In the end, the fact that she'd done many things here in Three Rivers that were new for her gave her the courage to tuck her car keys in her pocket, check for her phone, and then reach for the brownies. She got them out and managed to close the trunk, and then she walked across the parking lot and through the front door of the main building, which had been propped open.

A sign in the foyer pointed her straight back, which she did, and she exited out the back doors after she went past the big lecture hall where Lacy said she'd be teaching beginning sign language on Tuesday and Thursday evenings.

She found the group under several tent shades in the courtyard, the fountain bubbling merrily behind them.

Her eyes roamed the group even as she moved closer, and she found Ty standing off to her left, positioned with Jacob and another man Winnie hadn't met yet. Her nerves doubled, and once again, she didn't know why. She'd known he was going to be here.

Maybe not looking so cowboy-country-boy-dreamy in those dark denim jeans and a short-sleeved shirt the color of pale pink cotton candy. Her mouth watered, and she quickly looked toward the main group, the image of Ty's white cowboy hat and oh-so-sexy beard burned into her mind's eye.

Lacy Glover turned her way and dropped the hand that she'd

been resting protectively on her pregnant belly. Winnie's mind blanked and she couldn't remember when Lacy was due, though it had to be in the next three or four months.

"Oh, wow, these look incredible," Lacy said, her eyes on the huge tray in Winnie's hands. "When you said you had a knack for baking, you weren't kidding."

"I didn't say I had a knack for baking," Winnie said with a light laugh. "I said I enjoyed it. I just hope these won't poison anyone."

Lacy gestured her forward. "Bring them down here. Let's make sure they stay in the shade."

Winnie went with Lacy, because she knew the woman would then take her around and introduce her to everyone. She slid the tray onto the end of the table in the shade, and not two seconds later, Mitch himself arrived and wrapped one arm around her shoulders and squeezed her. He signed something with his free hand that Winnie didn't quite catch because she was looking up at his face instead of at his hands. He wore a smile as wide as the sky, and he'd grown his beard longer in the last few months since she'd seen him.

"I'm sorry, say again?" she said, signing as she spoke.

I'm only gonna eat brownies for dinner, Mitch said. He laughed, and Lacy and Winnie joined in.

"We're just waiting for a couple more people," Lacy said. "And then we'll do our welcome and we'll eat." She nodded toward a couple of others standing over near the fire pit, which roared with flames and made everything feel charming and homey.

"This is our office manager," Lacy said. "Geraldine Maude. She goes by Dina."

"Hello," Winnie said, remembering to sign as she did. Besides Lacy, she was the only hearing instructor here at *Signs for Success*, and she knew she needed to do sign language for everyone else.

She met Fletcher Palmer, who taught specialty sign language classes, specifically in agriculture and finance.

Lacy did the intermediate and advanced sign language classes, and she kept getting introduced as, "Winnie is going to be taking over the beginning classes for me on Tuesdays and Thursdays."

She shook hands and swept her lips across a couple of cheeks. She met their full-time custodian and the nighttime part-time custodian, and then Lacy's brother, Jacob, who did all the groundskeeping.

"And I think you probably know Tyson already," Lacy said.

Winnie had been glancing at him from the moment she'd stepped outside. She wanted to maintain her cool, professional demeanor, but she couldn't stop the smile that spread across her whole face. "Yeah, I know Ty."

"Winnie's my physical therapist," he said.

She tilted her head a couple of inches, trying to get a better read on him.

"She basically tortures me a couple times a week," he said, his smile kicking up further on the right than it did on the left.

Winnie giggled and shook her head. "That's not true." She glanced over to Lacy. "He only comes in a couple of times a *month* now."

Lacy grinned at them and then turned when Mitch put his hand on her arm. Mitch signed something, but he spoke so fast and Winnie only caught a couple of words—*begin* and *starving*.

She nodded and said, "All right, you guys, we're going to go ahead and get started." She moved through the crowd, and Mitch helped her stand up on the edge of the fountain. She raised both hands above her head and waved her arms while she called, "All right, everyone."

It took a moment for the message to be conveyed through the crowd, because Deaf people couldn't hear her calling, and they had to see her to know she wanted to talk to them. She signed much slower than Mitch, and she spoke aloud everything she said as well, bridging the gap between hearing and Deaf perfectly.

"Welcome to the Signs for Success potluck party." She grinned and started to clap. Winnie joined in with the others.

"Mitch and I love a good party, and we want to foster a sense of family here at the academy. If it's not obvious, I'm going to have a baby at the end of March, and I'll miss the end of this winter semester, and we will not be running classes in the summer.

"Mitch wants to continue the community classes, so some of you will be staying with us, but our students and Resident Assistants will likely be leaving for a couple of months. We'll make sure we know who's coming back for the fall before this little rascal is born."

She put both hands on her belly and gazed down at it with such love that Winnie's heart sighed. She wanted children too, and she glanced over to Tyson. He stood a few feet from her, not too close as to be too personal, and not so far as to be cold. He wore an unreadable expression, of course, though Winnie was normally pretty good at telling what others were thinking or feeling anyway.

"Mitch has steak from Shiloh Ridge, and we've done steak kebabs and beef tips with gravy. Jacob made his famous scalloped potatoes, and we have smoked turkey breast that Mitch helped his uncle Ward do up at Shiloh Ridge as well. Thank you to everyone who brought something to go with the food, and we'll go ahead and start with a prayer."

She scanned the crowd and then looked at Mitch. He got up on the fountain wall too and swept off his cowboy hat.

"Mitch is going to say it," Lacy said, and more movement went through the crowd—including at Winnie's side, as Ty reached up and pulled his cowboy hat as well.

Mitch pressed his to his chest with his forearm, pressed his eyes closed, and bowed his head before he started to sign. Lacy dictated it, and Winnie simply let the feelings of speaking with the Lord flow through her. She didn't need to know so much what was said, but how she felt about it, and when the crowd murmured "Amen," she quickly added her voice to the sentiment.

At a normal party, chatter would break out immediately after the "Amen," but at a party where the large majority of people there were Deaf, silence prevailed.

Winnie turned toward Ty and signed. *I think me and you are the only people who speak here.*

He blinked at her and said, "I've taken a few months of beginning sign language. I'm not really sure what you said."

Winnie grinned at him and moved a little bit closer. "I think we're the only hearing people here—me, you, and Lacy," she said.

Ty glanced around. "Yeah, I think you're right." He shifted his feet and adjusted his cowboy hat on his head again. "You're doing beginning sign language on Tuesdays and Thursdays?"

"Yeah," she said. "Seven to eight-thirty."

He nodded and pressed his lips into a tight line. "Yeah, that's when it was last semester too. I'm thinking I better retake it."

"Did Lacy pass you up to Intermediate?" Winnie asked.

"Yeah," Ty said, and he watched as Jacob said something to one of the RAs. "But I only caught about half of what he just said."

"He said he's been looking forward to the smoked turkey all week," Winnie said. "Come on, I want some of the steak from Shiloh Ridge after you bragged about having it last night." She threw him the flirtiest look she could muster and went to join the food line.

"Did Taylor go home today?" he asked, clearly right behind her.

Every muscle in Winnie's body tightened at the mention of her sister's name, and then it released just as quickly. "Yes," she said. "Thank goodness. Although I think she and Burt are really going to try to stay in touch."

Ty chuckled. "Well, that'll be something."

Winnie glanced over her shoulder to him. "Is he not a nice guy?"

"It depends on what you mean by *nice guy*," Ty said. "He's a good worker and a good farrier. He just...goes with a lot of women."

Winnie's heartbeat skipped. "I've heard the same thing about rodeo cowboys."

Ty didn't exactly gasp, but his intake of breath made a sharp, if low, sound. She looked at him and their eyes locked.

"I'm from Oklahoma," she said with a shrug. "Plenty of rodeos there."

"Well, blanket statements are rarely true," he practically growled. "I didn't say all farriers dated a lot. I said Burt Hallahan did."

"Well, my sister does too," Winnie said. "Maybe they'll be perfect for each other."

"Maybe," Tyson said.

"Are you saying you never dated anyone while you rode the rodeo circuit?" Winnie reached the end of the table and picked up a plate.

"I dated plenty," he said. "I mean, enough." He coughed a couple of times. "I've had a few girlfriends."

"Anyone serious?" Winnie reached for the tongs and put a healthy pile of green salad on her plate.

"Yeah, my last girlfriend was pretty serious," he said. "I figured I'd probably marry her, but she cut me as soon as I couldn't ride anymore."

Winnie swung her attention back to him, though the whole-wheat rolls in the basket next to the salad made her mouth water. "She broke up with you when you got injured?"

"Yep." Ty did not reach for the salad tongs. "I haven't been out with anyone since I've been back home."

"Well...." Winnie trailed off, not quite sure what to say. She exhaled in a tight burst. "Had you asked her to marry you yet?"

"No," Ty said. "But Jenn and I were together about two years, and we'd definitely talked about getting married." His dark eyes glared holes in her. "You're holding up the line, sweetheart."

Embarrassment flooded Winnie's cheeks, and she quickly grabbed a roll and moved down to the potatoes.

"What about you?" Ty asked, and Winnie inwardly cringed, though she'd opened this door. "Have you ever had a real serious relationship? Tell someone you love them?"

"Yes," Winnie whispered.

Ty leaned closer. "I didn't hear you, sweetheart."

"Yes," she said louder, lightning striking through her body as all of her memories of Carver stormed back to life. "I've been engaged—just once. It didn't work out."

"Engaged?" The level of surprise in Ty's voice pitched it up.

"Wow." He chuckled. "I don't know what I was expecting, but it wasn't that."

"You don't think someone would like me enough to want to marry me?" She threw him a smile that pinched against her cheeks.

"No, of course not," he said. "It's not that—I just...."

Winnie took a couple of beef kebabs, and then moved down and added two slices of smoked turkey to her plate, all while Ty tried to figure out what to say.

When she reached the end of the table, where she ladled some gravy over her turkey and then turned to face Ty, she said, "This isn't good party conversation. We don't have to talk about it right now."

"Is he why you left Oklahoma?" he asked.

Winnie's eyes widened, and Ty seemed to get the message without her having to say anything. He frowned. "I'm really sorry, Winnie."

"Like I said, it's not good party conversation." She turned away, scanning the tables for somewhere to sit. She'd literally just met everyone here, and she could admit she was looking for a table with two seats.

"There," Ty said. "Next to Jacob." And he led the way to a table in the corner, where Jacob sat with a male RA named Redd and the nighttime custodian, an older man named Mark.

Ty sat next to Jacob and asked, "Can we sit here?"

Jacob nodded and grinned first at Ty and then at Winnie.

Ty signed and said, "I live with Jacob. Did you know that?" He moved with a graceful, fluid motion, but his signs did seem a little hesitant.

"Yes," Winnie said, and she smiled over to Jacob. "Now tell me— is he a clean roommate, or is he messy?"

Jacob laughed and said, *Ty's a neat freak.*

Winnie looked at Ty. "Ah-ha. Good information."

"I am *not* a neat freak," Ty said. "I just think things have their place, and that's where they should go."

Jacob laughed again, and Winnie couldn't stop smiling. "Sounds like a neat freak to me," she said.

"I better watch my job," Mark said, and he signed and spoke too. Winnie looked at him, because she hadn't realized that he could also hear. "Sometimes I don't think I'm as neat as I should be."

Oh, you're fine, Jacob said, and they settled in to eat their dinner. There wasn't tons of conversation in a Deaf meal while people used utensils to eat instead of their hands to talk, but Winnie really enjoyed the camaraderie that came with simply being with another person.

She really wanted her date with Ty, and after she finished her dinner, she leaned over to him and said, "I'm going to go get the brownies. Do you want me to get you some?"

"I want one of everything, sweetheart." He ducked his head toward hers, and their eyes met again. The whole world fell away from Winnie in that moment. If she just tilted her head a little bit more, and Ty moved another eight inches, she could kiss him.

Panic flooded through her, because when Carver had left, she'd never thought she'd be whole again. She thought she'd never feel anything for a man again, and yet, there she sat at a nine-foot round table with a cream-colored tablecloth on it, imagining kissing Tyson Greene.

"What are you doing tomorrow night after your brother gets engaged?" she asked.

Ty blinked at her. "I don't rightly know."

"Do you have a family obligation? Surely he'll want to go out with his fiancée alone."

"Yeah, I think they're planning on doing something by themselves," Ty said.

So Winnie tiptoed her fingers across the table and down Ty's arm. She tapped his wrist a couple of times. "Maybe you're not free for lunch, but maybe you're free for dinner."

Ty slid his hand back and curled his fingers around hers. Everything tight inside Winnie sighed away at the warmth and comfort of holding hands with him.

"Are we ready for a Saturday night date?" he asked. "Lunch is more casual, and I didn't want there to be a lot of pressure."

"I think we could at least try," Winnie said.

Ty nodded. "All right. Let me talk to my brother, so I don't have to cancel again, and I'll let you know what time."

She nodded, and then gently slipped her hand out of his and stood. "I'm going to get brownies for the table," she said, and she left to do that. A new measure of happiness threaded through her, something that Winnie could barely believe.

She picked up a plate and loaded four of each type of brownie onto it before returning to the table. She set it down in the middle, and then returned to get the little dessert plates, one for each of them. She passed those out, and as she retook her seat, Ty nudged her phone a little bit closer to her.

"You got a message," he said.

Her heart did a cartwheel—perhaps it was Taylor saying something about how Burt had already broken up with her, or maybe she'd met a cowboy at a gas station on the way home and had a date with him that night.

But she saw the message was from Ty, and it said, *Bryan said I'll be done by 3:30, and that puts me back in town around five. How about dinner at six?*

She looked up and found him watching her with the same intensity on his face that he always wore while doing his physical therapy, even while at a New Year's Eve party with his friends or at a summer dance on a blind date.

A smile crossed her face. "Six is great for me." Then she reached out and picked up the mint brownie, declaring, "Let's do a taste test, and you guys can tell me which one you like the most."

7

"Like this?" Ty set an enormous vase of red roses in the middle of the table he and Libby had just finished setting up. While he'd limped back to the truck, she'd spread a tablecloth over it and set out two plates.

"Yes," she said. "That looks great." She set down a couple of candles, then picked one back up to switch it on. Ty really didn't see the point of all of this. It was broad daylight, for crying out loud, and he couldn't even see the fake flickering of candlelight.

No wonder he'd never proposed to Jenn. He didn't want to go through the whole show of this. No, when he asked a woman to marry him, he simply wanted to show up on her doorstep, tell her he loved her, and beg her to be his for the rest of this life.

Maybe that was why he'd never gotten close to engaged.

He thought of Winnie, because the woman had embedded herself in his mind. She'd been there for a while, and he just hadn't realized it until someone else had pointed her out.

"Do women like this stuff?" he asked as he peered into the box Libby had carried from the truck. He found a bright teal stuffed dinosaur, and he lifted it out. "Like...."

He met his friend's eyes, and she beamed a smile at him. "Yes, Ty." She took the dinosaur from him and positioned it on one of the plates. "Women like this stuff." She stepped back and looked at the table, set for a romantic meal for two in the shade.

"It's not about the roses or the candles or the trinkets." She turned and picked up the box, holding it toward him.

Ty plucked out the only remaining item: a scrapbook, by the looks of it.

"Open that so they can both see it, behind the roses," Libby said.

He did what she said. "If it's not about the stuff, what's it about?"

Libby smiled at the table display. "The roses might be the most generic thing here. But Ellie works at the museum." She reached out and tapped the dinosaur. "She leads school groups through the dinosaur exhibit. Bryan knows that, and he knows she loves her job."

Libby looked over to Ty. "Let's go get the food out." She stepped that way, and Ty took one more look at the table before he went with her. She never made him feel like he wasn't good enough now that he was permanently injured, walked with a limp, and had to walk on her left side to hear her.

"The book is filled with pictures of them," he said. "Bryan made that."

Libby smiled at him. "Yep. It'll be full of all their intimate moments together. All of the little things they've done, all of their experiences that have made them into them. Ellie will love it, and she'll fall even more in love with Bryan when she sees stuff like that, because it tells her that he listens. He pays attention. He knows what's important to *her*, and he's going to spend his life making sure she's happy."

Ty watched the ground, though they hadn't gone too far out into the field. "What if a man has a bad memory?" He tossed the now-empty box into the back of his truck, and together, he and Libby reached for the cooler.

Libby met his eyes. "Most men have phones," she said coolly.

"They can send themselves emails or take notes on the things they want to remember."

Ty blinked, and they started the trip back to the table. "I can't believe we're the two people out here doin' this," he grumbled. "I can't walk, and you hurt your shoulder during the harvest."

"Bryan trusts us," Libby said simply. "Besides, I'm pretty much better. Winnie's helped so much."

Winnie again.

"Yeah," Ty said as they reached the table and set down the cooler. He let out a long sigh. "Okay, I think Bryan said he just wanted the Rice Krispy treats out." He bent with a groan, already tired after a long morning of dog training, and took out the treats his brother had made and packed.

"When do you think they'll get married?" Libby asked while Ty arranged the treats between the two plates.

"Ellie wants pumpkins and corn stalks," Ty said as he stepped back and surveyed the table. "And my momma said Bryan couldn't have his wedding within three months of Carolina and Hugh, so...." He grinned over to Libby. "It's September or later, and I don't really know when the exact date will be."

"Carolina is getting married the first week of June?" Libby asked. "I'm pretty sure that's what I have on my calendar."

"Yeah," Ty said, though he didn't have the exact date memorized. Perhaps he really did need to write down more information.

"I think it's only a week before I'm due." Libby sighed and wiped her hair back, then put her cowgirl hat back on her head.

Ty gaped at her. "You're pregnant?"

Libby gave him a smile that suddenly seemed very tired. "Yeah. I haven't made it to the ranch owner's meetings to tell people, so I figure the more people I tell, it'll spread through town without me having to say anything."

Ty blinked at her. "And you're telling me?" He chuckled and shook his head. "I'm not part of the rumor mill, Libs."

"No, but your mother is," she said.

"So is yours," he said without missing a beat.

"Yeah, and that's how I know you have a date with a mystery woman to Judy and Trooper's wedding next weekend." Libby bumped him with her hip and nodded to the cooler. "Push that further under the table, and let's get out of the sun. I'm tired, and the bright light hurts my head."

She shaded her eyes while Ty did what she said. They returned to his truck, and Ty drove them back to the epicenter of Three Rivers Ranch. Libby lived in the big ranch house with her husband and little girl—and apparently a new baby come summer—and Ty waited until she'd gone up the stairs and into the house before he turned his attention to the horse training facility his momma owned.

Bowman's Breeds.

Ty sighed at the sign, at the trucks parked out front, at the fact that in about another thirty minutes, he'd be the only un-engaged member of his family. His mother had said she had clients today, and that she'd sent Bryan and Ellie out on horseback to "get rid of them," so she could get through her day.

His phone buzzed, and Ty pulled it out of the cupholder to check it. Momma had said, *They just left. You guys have about ten minutes to be out of there. Status?*

I just dropped Libby off at the farmhouse, Ty told her. *Everything is set and ready for them.*

Great! Thanks, baby.

I'm headed home, he told her.

Dinner with everyone tomorrow? she asked. *After church? I'm making that chicken cheese bread you love.*

Ty didn't want to commit to dinner at his parents' house, with Carolina and Hugh and Bryan and Ellie and all their diamond-shiny-happiness. And that only made him feel worse about himself. Guilt drove through him, because his siblings had spent their lives cheering him on, and he couldn't even be happy for them?

"I am happy for them," he told himself. "And I drove over an hour from my morning job to put out some Rice Krispy treats for my brother's proposal."

He now had to drive forty-five minutes back to his apartment, shower, and get ready to go out on a weekend evening date with Winnie.

"Definitely too much pressure," he said to himself, which was what a Sabbath Day meal with his family would be too. He'd wanted things with Winnie to be more casual from the beginning, because he needed time to figure out how he felt about her before they got too serious.

"She was engaged," he whispered to himself as his phone vibrated again. That told Ty that Winnie knew how to be in a serious relationship.

His phone buzzed, and then it rang. His mother, again.

Ty exhaled slowly and tapped to answer the call. "Hey, Momma."

"I can see you sittin' in your truck."

Ty looked out his side window and found his mother standing against the post at the end of the fence. He waved, sighed, and got out of the truck.

"You don't have to act like seeing your momma is the worst thing that could happen to you," she said. Then she shook her head, rolled her eyes, and hung up the call.

"I didn't," Ty called. "I was just leavin' is all, but I can't just drive away without giving you a hug." He smiled at her, glad when his mother softened. She opened her arms to him as he neared, and Ty sank into his mother's embrace.

"Mm, a boy is never too tough or too old to hug his mother."

"All right, Momma." Ty squeezed her extra tight and then stepped back. "The table looked beautiful, and as long as Bryan can get the question out, I think they'll come back engaged."

Momma grinned at him. "Daddy and I are going to hide out in the upstairs office and watch for them to come back."

"Sounds like a fun time," Ty said in a deadpan. "I'm headed home."

"You've had a busy day," Momma said. "I noticed you were limping a little bit more than I've seen you do lately."

"I'm fine, Momma," he said. "I'll text you when I get home."

"Who are you taking to the wedding?" Momma asked, reaching to adjust her sunglasses against the winter sunshine. "And did you see it's supposed to snow in the ten-day forecast?"

Ty blinked at his mother. "Really? We're going from dating to the weather within a breath?" He chuckled and shook his head. "I have a date with her tonight, actually, and if it goes well, I'll tell you who it is, okay?"

His mother's hopes shone on her face. "You have a date tonight?"

"Yes, Momma, so can I go now?" He wiped the grin from his face and cocked his eyebrows at her.

"Did you reschedule it from lunch to dinner?"

"Yes," he said, though technically, Winnie had done that. "And no, I don't check the ten-day forecast, so I didn't know it was going to snow."

"We're hoping to have the roof done over the end of that stable rebuild by then." Momma looked over her shoulder and toward her facilities. "And Daddy's going to make sure we have fuel for the generator and extra potable water."

A slip of worry moved through Ty. "Really, Momma? It's going to be that bad?"

"Up here in the Panhandle, it can get that bad," she said. "You've been gone for a while, and we've had some wicked winter storms before."

"I live in an apartment," Ty said. "How do I get extra potable water?" He wasn't even sure he knew what that was.

Momma grinned at him. "You just come stay with us," she said.

Ty leaned against the fence, because he had been walking and working a lot today already, and his body ached. "Momma, I'm almost thirty-two years old. What am I doing with my life?"

She sighed and joined him, the two of them looking out over the horse-dotted fields.

"I don't have a house," he said. "I don't check the ten-day forecast so I can be prepared. I don't have any education, and the woman I'm going out with tonight barely seems to like me." He sighed. "I'm working someone else's farms, and I'm lame, deaf in one ear, and completely surly all the time."

Momma linked her arm through his. "Someone will love you for all of those things, Tyson."

"How do you know, Momma?" he whispered.

"Because, my amazing son, someone fell in love with me, and I'm just as salty as you are, and I started this place in debt, and while I don't have a physical disability, I don't believe those limit people."

They did, but Ty didn't argue with her.

"You do just fine at Lone Star, right?" Momma asked.

"Yeah," Ty said.

"And Colt loves you at the orchard."

"Yeah."

"And I'm sure whoever you're going out with tonight likes you more than you think."

Ty thought of how Winnie had tapped her fingers down his arm at last night's potluck party. Bursts of fire erupted on his skin at the mere memory of her touch. He'd held her hand for only a few moments, and it had been the highlight of the last twelve months. Heck, the highlight of his life since he'd returned to Three Rivers.

"I just feel like everyone else has gone so far," he said. "And I'm way back at the beginning, and I have miles to go."

"Until what?" Momma asked.

"I don't know," Ty said. "That's the hardest part. I don't even know." He faced her, and he caught the caring, kind look in her eyes. "Do you think I could ever work my own farm? Like, maybe what Finn has. Like, hobby-sized. Or just somewhere I can keep Jupiter, so I don't have to drive out here to see him, and I don't have to worry about my roommate calling me a neat-freak, and I could just—I have plenty of money."

Momma smiled at him and quickly reached up and wiped her eye. Ty hated making her cry, but honestly, everything he'd asked had come from his heart.

"Of course you could work your own farm, Ty." She smiled at him with everything maternal in her. "And it's okay to be a neat-freak."

"It just makes me feel in control of something," Ty said. "Anyway, I have to go. I told Winnie I'd pick her up at six."

Momma's face lit up. "Winnie? Winona Landry?"

Ty rolled his eyes and aimed his gaze heavenward. "Dear Lord, I've made a mistake. Please bless my mother not to make a big deal out of this, and bless her to not repeat anything she's learned today to anyone else in town."

He lowered his eyes and hooked them into his mother's. "Please, Momma."

"You're taking her to the Glover wedding,' Momma said. "Everyone in town is going to see you there."

"Yeah, well, Colt is taking Fawn," Ty said. "It could be a throw-away date. There's nothing to gossip about." He took a couple of steps away and glanced over his shoulder. "Besides, Bryan is getting married, so won't that keep the ladies buzzing for a while without them talking about me?"

"No one can predict what the ladies will find interesting," Momma said.

Ty chuckled and headed out, the drive back to his shared apartment taking no time at all as he thought about everything he'd told his mother, about his date with Winnie that night, and about the upcoming wedding.

He showered, shaved his beard up nice and trim, and stepped into clean clothes. He pulled on a pair of cowboy boots with insoles that helped with his limp, and tucked his wallet in his back pocket before shrugging into his leather jacket.

Jacob wasn't home, and Ty quickly texted him. *I'm going out with Winnie tonight. I should be home by midnight, but I'll keep you updated if anything changes.*

I'm at Mitch and Lacy's, Jacob said. *I think I'm going to stay the night here. Let me know if you need anything.*

Will do.

Tyson headed out again, glad he had someone besides his siblings or parents to check-in with. He could've done the same thing with Colt or Trap, or even Conrad or Wilder or JJ. He'd learned on the circuit to make sure someone knew where he was and who he was with, just in case anything went wrong.

It was something his daddy had taught him from his days of riding in the rodeo, and Ty had kept the habit alive even now.

He'd already looked up Winnie's address, and she lived in a cute little part of town called Old Town. It sat just north of the main river that ran through town, and he checked her address one more time before heading out.

He arrived in front of a perfect white-sided house only twelve minutes later. His headlights shone against the closed door of the one-car garage, and he swept his gaze across the lit windows and kept yard.

He glanced at the clock and found he'd arrived a couple of minutes early. His pulse bounced against the back of his throat as he warred with himself about what to do. In the end, he found it less creepy to just go ring the doorbell, rather than park in her driveway, truck idling, until precisely six o'clock.

So Ty dropped to the ground, slammed his door nice and loud, and made his way up Winnie's front sidewalk, his cowboy boots ringing like gunshots through the quiet neighborhood.

Let the ladies start talking, he thought as he climbed the steps and rang the doorbell.

8

Winnie flinched with the *ping-ding-dong* of the doorbell. Every time that happened, she got thrown back in time to when Carver had rung her bell, waited on the front steps of a house very much like this one, and told her terrible, awful, no-good things.

"It's not Carver," she told herself, though her pulse had already driven her adrenaline toward the roof. "You're not in that house anymore. You don't even live in Oklahoma."

She looked into her own eyes in the mirror in her bathroom, ran her fingers through her loose curls one more time, and marched herself out of the bedroom and on down the hall.

Still, once something as scarring and life-changing as what Carver had done to her happened to a person, something as simple as a doorbell could cause all kinds of fight or flight reflexes.

Things like that changed a person, and Winnie had never felt so out of control as she did in that moment, going to answer the door and expecting to see another cowboy standing there. After all, she'd been expecting Carver too. They were supposed to be going to pick up his tux from the tailor the day he'd ended things with her.

Winnie made it into the living room and paused as she faced the still-closed front door. Her breath shook in her lungs as she inhaled, and she dang near choked on it. *I am not that woman,* she recited to herself. *This is not Carver.*

A couple of knocks landed on the wood. "Winnie, sweetheart, it's me. I know I'm early, but I figured it would be okay."

The sound of Ty's voice, even muted through the door, got her feet moving again. She practically ran to the door, her skin-tight jeans pulling along her calves as she did. Winnie yanked open the door, and she had no idea what Ty would see when he looked at her.

A panicking mess of a female? Most likely.

Someone he couldn't get along with no matter how hard he tried?

Oh, come on, she thought through the chaos in her head. *You guys got along fine at last night's potluck.*

Even though Ty had voted for the German chocolate brownies, which so weren't as good as the mint ones, Winnie still liked him.

"Hey," Ty said. "Are you okay?"

Winnie realized she wasn't breathing, and she sucked at the air. "I don't know," she gasped out, one hand reaching for the doorframe to anchor her.

Ty stepped up and into the house. "All right, well, hold onto me, because you look like you're about to fall over." He encircled her in his arms, bringing her flush against his chest and holding her there.

Winnie's arms did the natural thing—they went around him and clutched him tightly too.

"Shh-shh-shh," he went, making soft noises with his mouth. "You're okay, Winnie-girl. I got you." He backed her up a slow step at a time until he could get the front door closed, and that broke the spiral Winnie had fallen into.

After all, Carver had not entered the house on that fateful date in February.

Winnie stepped back, pure foolishness now filling her. "S—Sorry," she said. Her hands flitted about, touching her cheek—that felt too hot—and then sliding through her hair. She'd probably ruined the curls by now, and she had no idea how to explain what had just happened to Ty.

He said nothing, and several seconds clicked by while Winnie continued to calm down. She finally managed to take a breath and get her thoughts to quiet, and she looked up and met his gaze.

He gave her the most perfect thing in the whole world—a smile. "There you are."

"I...I guess I did get lost there for a second."

"Nervous about going out with me?" he asked, his voice low in both volume and pitch, almost like he was trying not to scare her.

"A little," she admitted. She spun on her heel and picked up her purse from the end of the credenza. As she faced him again, she decided to rely on her mouthiness—something she'd blamed herself for in the past.

"When my fiancé came to break up with me," she said. "It was only six days before our wedding date." She gestured to the door behind him. "He rang the doorbell, and I knew there was something wrong the moment I opened the door."

Ty's smile faded into that trademark frown that drew his eyebrows down and in.

"He was already packed. Truck idling. He said he didn't love me and couldn't marry me. And then he just left." She snapped her fingers and told herself she wasn't the problem. After another breath, she calmed even more, found her center, and this time, casually brushed her hair back off her face.

"When something like that happens, every time the doorbell rings, my heart stops for a moment."

Ty took a step toward her and reached out one hand. His fingers brushed hers in a non-verbal way of saying *I'm sorry, Winnie.*

"I made it to the door, but I don't know. I was in full panic-mode by then," she said.

"Have you ever not made it to the door?" he asked.

"Yes," she admitted. "I've ignored the doorbell many times in the past ten months."

His eyes came up from where he'd been watching her hand, the tips of his fingers just barely playing with hers. "This only happened ten months ago?"

"Almost eleven," she said. Her chest finally loosened, and she felt like sagging to the floor. "I'm sorry. I've started this date out all wrong." She turned away from him and redeposited her purse on the TV cabinet. "We don't have to go to dinner."

"Why wouldn't we go?" Ty pressed in close behind her, his right hand sliding down her bicep, over her elbow, and along her forearm to her fingers. He took them fully into his now, his left hand coming to rest on her hip. "Unless you don't want to, that is. I get panic attacks and how they can wear you out."

"You do?" she whispered.

"For the first six months after my injury, every time I woke up, I'd panic," he whispered back. "It's exhausting and demoralizing all at the same time. So...yeah."

Her stomach growled, and Winnie didn't want to send Ty away and call for Chinese food. Not when she'd gone shopping for a new jumpsuit for next weekend's wedding, and not when she'd picked up these cute flowered pants she now wore.

Bright, vibrant pinks, purples, and white petals danced across a black background, and she'd paired it with a black blouse on top. The jeans disappeared into the tops of her ankle boots, and Winnie wished she could rewind time and open the door as the confident, beautiful woman she wanted to be.

"You look real nice," Ty said, still in that same low voice. "And if I'm right about where you live, you should have the river running along your backyard. So I can order dinner here, and we can eat it outside if you want."

She turned, glad when he simply let his left hand slide along her back. She ran her hands up his chest and yes, leaned into him again. "Do I strike you as the kind of woman who likes to eat outside?"

"Yes." He grinned at her. "Because you told me last night that you take your pomegranate tea on the back deck every morning."

She smiled back at him. "That's cheating."

He chuckled. "Cheating? I'm *cheating* now if I remember what you've told me? That doesn't seem fair."

"I don't want to eat on the back deck."

"Okay," he said. "I don't care about the panic attack, Winnie. I just won't ring that doorbell ever again." He wore fierceness in his expression, and his tone turned a touch harsher than he'd used so far that evening.

"Where are we going to dinner?" she asked.

"I got us a garden table at Squared Away. It's a nice little bistro on the square downtown." His eyebrows went up even as his gaze dropped to her mouth. "If you still want to go."

Winnie watched his mouth as he spoke too. "I do," she whispered. "I like this shirt. It's very soft." She played with the buttons up near his throat that he'd left undone. "I promise I won't freak out every time you come get me."

Ty nodded, then simply turned, dropped his hand to hers again, and led her out of her own house. She hadn't grabbed her purse, and part of her felt naked without it. She had her phone in her pocket, though, and she figured she could call a ride, pay for things, and pretty much survive with just that for tonight.

"How did the engagement go?" she asked, once they both sat in his truck.

Ty glanced over to her. "Great. She said yes."

Winnie smiled out the windshield. "That's great."

Ty backed out of her driveway and started down the lane. "You have a very cheerful attitude about marriage for someone who's been through what you have."

She looked over to him, and with the sun already down tonight, with only tones of gold and violet in the sky, she couldn't see him as clearly as she'd like to. "I still want to get married someday," she said. "I'm just...well." She blew out her breath, searching for the right words.

"I guess I just need to be more selective about who I spend my time with."

"Seems to me you've been spendin' time all over town," he said.

Winnie watched him come to a stop at the end of her street, the orange lamp there painting his features in harsh light. "What do you mean?"

"You're everywhere, Winnie," he said, that lopsided smile making an appearance. "You volunteer at the summer dance, you're teaching at the Deaf academy, you work with all my friends."

"*One* friend," she shot back. "And that's just luck. I don't *pick* my patients. They get assigned to us at the clinic."

"Hey, it's not a bad thing." Once he'd turned, Ty reached over and took her hand in his again. "I like holding your hand. Is this okay?"

"Yeah," she said with a sigh. "It's nice—I haven't...." She trailed off, something inside her turning her tongue shy.

"You haven't what?" he asked.

"I don't want to air all my insecurities on the first date," she said.

"Hey, it puts us on even ground," he said.

"What do you mean?"

He glared at her for a moment, then focused on driving again. "I mean, you've seen me at my worst. Angry, hurting, falling down. It's nice to know that even the sunniest pictures can still have real problems."

Winnie wasn't sure if she should be hurt or not. "No one's perfect," she finally said.

"No," he murmured. "No one is."

"I've missed this." Winnie squeezed his hand. "I left my family in Oklahoma. I left all my friends, and I miss this...this human touch. No one ever hugs me. The closest I get to this is petting my cat."

"I'm better than the cat is what you're saying." He kicked her that flirty grin again, and this time, Winnie returned it.

"So far," she said.

Ty tipped his head back and laughed, and oh, Winnie had never heard such a glorious sound. She let it drip through her ears and paint her soul with the golden light it possessed. She even giggled for a few seconds near the end, and when he quieted, Ty looked over to her again.

He seemed completely transformed from the angry, hurting cowboy who she'd first met at the physical therapy clinic. He hadn't barked at her once tonight the way he had when he'd called on New Year's Day. None of the frustration over having to reschedule this date had accompanied him on it, and Winnie let herself sink further into the seat of his truck, a sense of comfort sweeping through her she hadn't anticipated she'd feel on tonight's first real date with Ty.

"Do you dance, ma'am?"

Winnie barely caught the movement of his throat as he swallowed. "I can," she said cautiously. "Why?"

"Squared Away is a bistro," he said. "With a dance hall attached, and I thought you might like that."

"You thought *I* might like dancing," she said. "So you're taking me to a place where we dine and dance, when it's the thing *you* dislike most."

He shifted in his seat. "We don't have to do it."

"Ty," she said, and she heard her physical therapist voice come into play. "I would like you to look at me."

"I'm driving," he said, and oh, the stubborn cowboy actually looked out his side window instead of over to her.

"I want this date to be fun for both of us," she said. "So no, I don't want to dance with you tonight."

"Well—that's rude."

She heard the teasing undercurrent in his tone, and she turned her head away from him as a soft smile came to her face too. "I've had a busy day," she said. "And I just endured a panic attack when I didn't know I got those. I want something delicious to eat, and I want to linger over coffee and dessert, and I want you to tell me something hard you've been through, so I don't feel so alone."

"You already know all the hard things I've been through," he said.

"Although, there was this one time on the circuit when I lost by a half of a point to this cowboy named Wuth, and boy, I was *so* angry."

"Wuth?" Winnie repeated. "That is not a name."

"You'll find a lot of not-names on the rodeo circuit," Ty said. "And Wuth was a real tool, and losing to him put me in a lower bracket for Nationals. I was so mad, I punched a wall in the arena, and that was a huge mistake too."

He flexed his hand on the steering wheel. "That was not a good year for me. My manager ended up calling it a *rebuilding* year." He glanced over to her then. "I hate that word, by the way. No one wants to be *rebuilding*, and yet, here I am rebuilding my entire life from the ground up. So I'm not having a picnic or anything."

"I like picnics," Winnie said with a smile. "Maybe our next date can be a lunchtime picnic, with a basket and a red-checkered blanket and everything."

"Maybe tomorrow," Ty said. "It would save me from having to eat Sabbath Day dinner with my family." He pulled into a side parking lot at the end of Main Street, swung into a parking space with precision Winnie did not possess, and put the truck in park. "Do you go to church, ma'am?"

"Yes, sir," she said. "Do you?"

His eyes held hers for a few long moments, each one filling the truck with a delicious tightness that bound Winnie to Ty again, and then again, and then again. "Sometimes," he said. "If I could sit by you and hold your hand, I'd go more often."

She grinned at him and pulled her hand away. "You'll behave at church."

"Yes, ma'am," he murmured just before he unbuckled his seatbelt and opened his door. "Stay there, sweetheart. I'll come get your door."

His door closed, and Winnie breathed out, feeling flushed and semi-whiplashed about. She'd always felt like that after being with Ty, and she actually liked it. He opened her door and crowded into her, his chest about the same height as hers now.

He reached up and tucked her curls behind her ear, and wow, Winnie hadn't been touched that intimately in a long, long time. A yawning need for it opened in her heart and soul, and all of the flirtatiousness between her and Ty evaporated.

This was *real*, and this was *good*, and Winnie didn't want to sugarcoat it. "Ty." She fiddled with that top button again. "I don't care if you go to church or not, but you should go because you want to, not because you'll get to hold my hand."

She met his eyes and found a storm in his before he blinked it into submission.

"You're right," he said as he backed up, took her hand in his, and gave her space to use the runner to get out of the truck. "I could check the weather for tomorrow, though, and we could definitely have a picnic after the sermon."

He led her down the street, which had a great small-town vibe, with Saturday evening shoppers, couples heading to their restaurant of choice, and that bubbling fountain in the middle of the roundabout.

"I don't know if I can get a basket and a red-checkered blanket in less than twenty-four hours, but I'm pretty sure my momma said the weather would hold for another week or so."

"I believe you can do anything you set your mind to." She grinned over to him, but he scoffed.

"Well, you'd be wrong about that," he said. "Because I can set my mind to hear again out of my left ear, but that ain't gonna happen." He nodded toward a door, and Winnie stepped that way.

He reached past her to open it, and she entered Squared Away first, her pulse stampeding through her veins. She quickly turned into Ty in the tight space, as others had arrived ahead of them and currently milled about in the front waiting area. "I didn't mean anything by it," she said. "I just meant I think you're amazing, and if I wanted a basket and a red-checkered blanket in less than twenty-four hours, I know you'd get it for me. That's all."

He wore a tightness in his jaw that relaxed as he nodded. He opened his mouth to say something, but a deafening country music song began to play, and Winnie blinked as she turned to see what in the world was happening here.

Ty's hand in hers tightened, and the next thing she knew, he'd pulled her back out onto the sidewalk. "I don't want to eat here," he said. "It's too loud."

Flustered, Winnie looked down the block. "Where are we going to go, then?" She certainly didn't know all the options, and it was a Saturday night at peak dinnertime. In that moment, her stomach growled, just to remind her she hadn't fed it in hours.

"Come on." He dropped her hand and started back down the street toward where they'd parked, drawing his phone out of his back pocket as he moved. "I know the perfect place, and I just have to make a phone call real quick...."

Winnie scampered after him, because he was her ride and she needed to eat. Oh, and wherever Ty was, she wanted to be too.

9

"Yeah, I know where Goose Creek Lane is," Ty said. "Thanks so much, Link."

"I'll call right now," he said. "They should be able to get you a table that will be exactly what you're looking for."

"Thanks," Ty said again, and he ended the call as he took a deep breath. He really did need to calm down a little bit. He, once again, felt the pressure of a Saturday night date having to be absolutely perfect for him and Winnie. Maybe because it was their first one, maybe because she looked so pretty with her hair curled and her lips all shiny, or maybe because it had started with her face as pale as the moon and her eyes as wide as that, and her body shaking against his as he held her.

No matter what, he didn't want to go back to Squared Away, where the music played too loud, Winnie wouldn't dance with him, and they wouldn't even be able to hear each other talk.

He turned toward her, and his left leg sent a twinge of pain up to his hip. "It's only a five-minute drive from here," he said, new hesitation inside him that hadn't been there a few moments ago.

Thankfully, Winnie linked her arm through his and took the first step toward the truck. "Okay, cowboy. I'm willing to go five more minutes."

Ty smiled at her. "Link says he's gonna call ahead, and he has enough clout to pull some strings." Link's status around town, as well as his money, did that, even though he didn't use them.

Ty got Winnie settled back in the truck, and he made the quick five-minute drive over to Goose Creek Lane, which was far quieter than Main Street had been. Festive Christmas lights decorated the house which bore the label of *Home* that Ty parked across the street from.

"Home," Winnie said the word out loud and then turned to look at him.

"Yeah, it's supposed to be really good," Ty said. "Down-home, good Southern cooking. Quiet tables, and Link says the Americano is to die for." He chuckled as he unbuckled his seat belt. "Of course, I've never met anyone who loves an Americano more than Link."

He once again collected Winnie from the truck, and they crossed the street to the house, which still had Christmas decorations in the windows and a couple of birdhouses out front, with Santa Claus gnomes and rocks with painted handprints on them.

"This is really cute," Winnie said. "I like it already."

He had to climb nine steps to get to the porch, which spanned the entire front of the house and had a table for two on each end of it. They went inside, and no bells rang as they did, and his boots landed on carpet as he approached the hostess stand.

"You must be Tyson," the woman there said, and her smile shone as brightly as the northern star.

"Yes, ma'am," he said.

"Give me two seconds to check with Davy," she said. "To see if your table is ready." She picked up two menus and moved away from the station. She had only taken a few steps before she turned back and gestured for Ty to come with her. "I see he's ready. You can come with me."

She led him into the living room where four or five tables had been populated with people. They went into what had to have been the house's formal dining room at some point, and right there, looking out a big bay window, stood a man wearing black from head to toe and an apron very much like the one Ty wore when he worked the restaurant at the apple orchards.

"This is Davy," the woman said. "This is Ty and Winnie. He's going to be your waiter tonight, and I'll let him take you two from here."

Ty pulled out Winnie's chair for her, and she sat down. He did the same, feeling sparkly all over as Davy handed him a menu.

"Have you guys been with *Home* before?" he asked.

"No," Ty said. "But my friend has told me how amazing it is."

"Oh, that's great to hear," Davy said. "We offer what's called a split menu. You pick either Track One or Track Two, and you eat off that menu. Tonight, we've done a Southern fried chicken meal for Track One, and it comes with buttermilk mashed potatoes, lemon-pepper asparagus spears, homestyle gravy with plenty of black pepper, and a dark chocolate pistachio cheesecake that is to—die—for." He grinned over to Winnie. "Yeah, I think you're the dark-chocolate lover."

Winnie beamed right on back at him. "I have been known to consume quite a bit of dark chocolate in the past."

Ty made a mental note of that, hoping he wouldn't forget it before he could write it down.

"On Track Two," Davy said. "We've gone seafood, with a beautiful blackened salmon that comes with a sweet pea risotto and heirloom multi-colored carrots. All of our meals come with crusty homemade bread, apple butter from the orchards right here in town, and a signature salted butter that I'll bring out and talk to you more about. Can I get either of you anything to drink?"

"I'd love a ginger ale," Ty said. "With lots of lime wedges, if you've got them."

"I do," Davy said. "And for you, ma'am?"

"Can I have this orange-cranberry spritzer?" she said, peering at the menu. "It says you have a nonalcoholic version. Can I get that virgin?"

"Absolutely," Davy said. "I'll be back with the bread and the drinks in just a couple of minutes. Oh—we have a common appetizer for both Tracks One and Two, and tonight it's a cheesy sausage and polenta with a house-made marinara. Would you guys like that?"

"Absolutely," Ty said.

Davy grinned, knocked a couple times on the table, and walked away.

Ty picked up his silverware packet and unwrapped the utensils so he could drape the napkin in his lap.

"This is really nice," Winnie said, glancing around the restaurant. She met his eyes, a hint of trepidation in hers. "But there are no prices on this menu."

"It doesn't matter," he said.

Winnie's lips pursed for a moment, and then she nodded and looked down at her menu. "I think I'm going to get the chicken. I've never been much of a salmon fan."

"Me either," he said, and she looked up. An electric zing moved through him, and he cataloged that they had another thing in common. It might be ridiculous, but it made him smile.

In the background, low, lilting music played, and the people at the other tables kept their voices quiet and their conversations private, making the atmosphere here exactly what Ty wanted it to be.

"So tell me," he said. "Do you have any other siblings besides Taylor?"

"Yes," Winnie said. "We've got an older brother—Brad. He's seven years older than me, and he's been married for a few years and has a little girl named Windy, like the weather."

"That's cute," Ty said. "So you're a middle child too."

"I don't think I ever said Taylor was younger than me," she said.

"Yeah, but she is," Ty said, raising his eyebrows.

"Yeah, she is." She unwrapped her silverware too. "You've got an older sister and a younger brother, is that right?"

"That's right," Ty said.

Davy returned with their drinks and a gloriously huge basket of bread that contained a dark bread with oatmeal on top, a couple of Asiago cheese rolls, and a soft honey whole wheat bun that Ty couldn't wait to taste.

"And we've got two salted butters," Davy said. "This one is plain sea salt from the Dead Sea. And this is our smoked pink Himalayan sea salt."

"Wow," Winnie said, leaning closer to examine the pink-salted butter. "It's so beautiful. I don't even want to eat it."

"I totally want to eat it," Ty said, and his own stomach rumbled at him to give it something good.

Davy chuckled. "Have you two decided what you're going to have?"

"Yes," Ty said, reaching for Winnie's menu. "We both want the chicken dinner."

"Excellent," Davy said, and he took the menus from Ty. "Your sausage and polenta is almost done, and I'll bring it right out."

"Thank you," Winnie and Ty said together.

Once Davy left, Ty once again found himself at a loss for what to say to Winnie. She hadn't seemed to want to expound on her familial relationships, especially Taylor, and Ty scrambled to find something else to ask her. He didn't want tonight's date to be a repeat of some of his previous ones lately, where he'd sat there like a fool—mute, unable to come up with anything to start a conversation.

"Tell me how you learned sign language," he said, because that seemed safe enough. "Is someone in your family deaf?"

"No," Winnie said. "I just started taking it in junior high, and I loved it." She reached for a straw and unwrapped it to put in her virgin cocktail. "I've always known I'd work in a service industry, and for a while, I thought I might be an interpreter."

Ty reached for one of the honey whole wheat rolls and the regular salted butter. "Colt will be thrilled that his apple butter is here," he said. "I'm going to take a picture of it for him." He did that, and then he held up his phone and added, "Let me get a picture of you with your drink."

She lifted it up to her face and wore the widest smile Ty had ever seen. He snapped a photo, something that felt so much like joy painting him from the inside out. He hadn't felt this way in such a long time, he hardly knew what to do with it.

"Here's the sausage polenta," Davy said. "I can get a picture of the two of you, if you'd like."

Ty's heartbeat stuttered, and he wasn't sure when he'd last taken a picture with a woman. But Winnie said, "Yeah, sure. You can use my phone." She handed it to Davy, and then she folded her arms on the table in front of her and leaned forward.

Ty followed her lead, the scent of marinara meeting his nose. He hitched a smile to his face, hoping he didn't look absolutely ridiculous.

"Right there," Davy said, and then he lowered the phone. He handed it back to Winnie, who beamed her sunshine down at the screen. While she sighed over the photo, Ty scooped out some polenta and a few pieces of sliced sausage, put them on a plate, and pushed it in front of her.

"There you go, sweetheart," he said.

"Look at us, Ty." She ignored the food and got up. She came around the table and sank into a crouch at his knee. She held up her phone, but Ty could only look at her.

She exuded such joy, and Ty loved the light she put off. She looked up at him, and he quickly cleared his throat and looked at the photo on her phone. The sunset shone through the window behind them, and Ty looked happy enough while Winnie bore pure radiance.

"Send that to me, would you?" he asked.

"Of course." Winnie did it right there, crouching at his side, and then she straightened and went back to her seat. "This looks amazing." She got herself situated while Ty served himself some sausage and polenta, and he'd just speared some meat when she said, "Let's taste it together on three, two, one."

Ty put his bite in his mouth at the same time Winnie did, and the spice, tomatoes, and fatty salt hit him all at the same time. "Oh, yeah," he said around the creamy polenta, with plenty of that sharp cheddar flavor in there.

"Mm, this is spicy," Winnie said, and she chewed quickly, swallowed, and reached for her spritzer. She took two big gulps and then coughed. "Wow. How are you not coughing?"

In response, Ty forked up another bite of the spicy sausage, the creamy polenta, and swiped it through the marinara sauce. "It's *good*." He popped the bite of food into his mouth as Winnie's cheeks pinked up.

Winnie ran the tines of her fork through the polenta and ate a little bit of that, but she didn't take another bite of the sausage. She picked up a chunk of brown bread and spread the polenta on that as if it were butter. "Let's do the yes-no game."

"The what now?"

She smiled at him. "I ask you something, and you can only say yes or no. Then you can ask me something."

Ty hated games, but he didn't have any amazing conversation topics. He supposed he could've asked more about her formal sign language training, but that ship seemed to have sailed. "All right," he said, taking another bite of spicy sausage.

"Did you go to college?"

"No," he said. When he didn't immediately voice another question, Winnie waved her fork at him.

Ty got the message. "Uh, when did you get your cats?"

"That's not a yes-no question," she said.

Ty huffed at her and wanted to roll his eyes. He refrained, but he seriously couldn't come up with a yes-no question he cared to know. "Can you drive a bus?"

"Can I *drive a bus*?" Winnie blinked at him and then burst out laughing. Pure humiliation ran through Ty, but soon enough, he joined his laughter to hers.

"Can't we just talk?" he asked. "I'm no good at games."

"The only thing I'm good at is games," Winnie said.

"See? Now I know that about you," he said. "What kind of games do you like?"

"Word games." Winnie looked up as Davy arrived with their chicken dinners. A woman had come with him, and both he and Winnie were served at the same time.

"Anything else I can get you two?" Davy asked.

"This smells amazing," Winnie said, and she grinned up at Davy, as if he'd prepared their food.

"I think we're good," Ty said, and the waiters left. He tucked into his food, noting that Winnie didn't find anything with the black pepper too spicy. In fact, she exclaimed multiple times about how much she enjoyed the food, and Davy checked on them several times, finally boxing up their leftovers and offering coffee with their dark chocolate cheesecakes.

By the time the meal wrapped, Ty realized that the restaurant had quieted even more, and he and Winnie were a few of the last to leave. He'd managed to eat and chat, no games required, and he laced his fingers through Winnie's as they stepped back out into the January night.

"Mm, it got cold," he said.

"I hate to break it to you," she said. "But it's been cold for weeks now."

Ty ducked his head and chuckled. "I don't mind the winter. I mean, it's not summer, but it has its own type of beauty."

"Yeah." Winnie sighed, and while Ty wanted to prolong their evening together, he led her back to the truck and got the heater blowing.

"So," he said. "Do you want a tour of my childhood?"

She leaned her head back against the rest of the passenger seat, her smile barely there and oh-so-beautiful. "Yeah, that sounds amazing."

"We'll be seated and warm," Ty said. "And if you're lucky, I'll find us a hot chocolate stand that's open, and you can have a second cocoa fix."

Winnie giggled, and Ty reached over and took her hand in his. "I really like holding your hand," he said, his chest suddenly storming. "I don't have a lot of human contact either, and it's nice."

"Yeah, it is."

"I'm...." Ty mentally cursed himself, but he just wanted tonight to be perfect, and if he tried kissing her.... "I'm not sure I'm ready to do more."

"More?" Winnie spoke with the cutest uncertainty.

"It seems like everything I do lately," he said. "Has to go slowly, and I think that's going to include me and you." He glanced over to her. "Is that okay? I mean, I want to kiss you, but I'm not sure I'm ready."

You're definitely not ready.

Winnie blinked at him and then released the cutest, lightest laugh. "Yeah, Ty, it's the first date. I don't even *want* you to kiss me."

Ty dang near drove up onto the curb as he stared at Winnie. Then he realized she was teasing him. "Well." He huffed. "That was rude."

She laughed again, and then they settled into comfortable silence. Ty made a turn and nodded out Winnie's window. "There's the elementary school. There's only one in town, and we all went there."

And for some odd reason, Ty's embarrassment about taking this trip down memory lane to prolong his time with Winnie didn't feel so ridiculous after all.

10

Winnie closed her eyes and let the Sabbath Day sunshine coming in through the tall windows behind the dais pour through her soul. She took a deep breath and exhaled away all the busyness of the holidays, all the stress of having her sister in town, all the newness of going out with Ty.

They had not made plans to attend church together, though dinner last night had turned into one of the best meals she'd ever experienced. She opened her eyes and looked down at her phone, which rested in her lap.

She swiped it on and navigated to the picture of the two of them. They both leaned into the center of the table, and she smiled at the slightly asymmetrical shape of his smile, and then took in the joy on her own face.

Yes, that had been the best date of her life, the doorbell panic attack notwithstanding.

The services started, and Pastor Glover got up to deliver her sermon. Winnie sank further into the upholstered pew, as she'd come to enjoy the woman's lectures.

"Today, I would like to start with a couple of scriptures. I love diving into the Bible, because each verse can hold so much personal meaning to the one reading it."

She gripped the sides of the pulpit where she stood, and she had a way of sweeping her eyes across the crowd while seeing every single person individually. At least Winnie felt seen by her, and she tapped away from the picture of her and Ty and over to her digital app for the scriptures.

"Jeremiah, chapter twenty-nine, verse eleven," Pastor Glover said. "For I know the plans I have for you." She looked up and lifted her glasses up on top of her head. "Stop for a moment and consider this simple verse. Do you believe it? Do you believe that God has a plan for you? An individual plan, and that He knows it?"

She shook her head, reseated her glasses, and murmured. "I love thinking about the Lord like this—that He knows me personally, and getting that affirmation right here in the Bible." She drew a breath. "Now, let's couple that with Hebrews, chapter ten, verse twenty-three."

Winnie couldn't tap fast enough to get over to the new book of scripture. So she simply looked up and took in Pastor Glover's energy as she read it.

"Let us hold unswervingly to the hope we profess, for He who promised is faithful." She looked up and removed her glasses again. "Unswervingly, my brothers and sisters. What have you ever done in your life with absolute *unswerving* energy?"

She put one hand down on her Bible, which rested on the pulpit in front of her. "God is asking us to hold to the hope we have in his plan unswervingly. And He will deliver. He alone is positively unswerving, and He alone keeps every promise He has made, and He will absolutely be faithful to those promises."

A smile bloomed on her face. "Isn't this amazing? Don't these two verses just make you want to raise your hands toward heaven and say, 'Thank You, Jesus.'?" She beamed her faith and happiness out to the congregation. "That's how I feel. God knows me, and He knows you, and He knows each and every one of His children. Not only that, but He has a plan for each of us—me, you, and everyone—and He is unswervingly faithful to us each in guiding us toward and along that path."

She nodded then, and Winnie's heartstrings sang with truth. Pastor Glover continued to speak, telling a story about a time in her life when she'd lost her way, when the path and plan God had for her had been obstructed by darkness, but Winnie once again simply let her feelings take shape inside her mind and heart and soul without needing the words.

No, she might not know exactly why God had brought her to Three Rivers, but Winnie did know without a doubt that He had.

Hold unswervingly to my hope, she thought, and Winnie's thoughts started moving through all the hopes and dreams she had for herself.

Marriage. Motherhood. Maybe a small-town farm with her cats, as well as a donkey or a couple of pygmy goats. Something simple and small that would feel big to her, the way the sky existed right around her but also extended across the whole world.

Definitely a donkey, she thought, and her smile touched her mouth and emanated through her whole body.

Before she knew it, Pastor Glover had finished her sermon, and the choir sang their closing number. Winnie stood after the benediction, and she smiled to the couple across from her, an elderly man and his wife, and let them enter the aisle first.

She followed them out of the chapel and into the foyer, where Pastor Glover stood with her husband and brother. Winnie joined the line of people to shake her hand, and when she got to them, she actually leaned in and hugged the pastor.

"I loved that sermon," she said brightly. "You're so good at public speaking."

"Thank you, dear," she said.

"How was the party at Signs for Success?" Cactus asked, and Winnie suddenly remembered that these two were Mitch's parents.

"Amazing," she said. "The steak was delicious—almost as good as the brownies I brought."

"Oh, Mitch told us *all* about the brownies," Willa said. She grinned over to her husband. "I bet Cactus would trade you beef for brownies, because I'm terrible at baking."

"Cactus would," he said, and they laughed together.

Winnie moved out of the way, tightening her jacket across her chest as she exited the church and the January wind tried to steal her sleeves right off her body. She leaned into the weather and hurried toward her car.

"Whew." She pushed her hair back and pulled out her pantleg that had gotten stuck under her body for how quickly she'd dove into the car. She looked up and out the windshield to see Tyson with one hand pressed to the top of his head, holding his cowboy hat in place, and driving forward against the wind too.

So he'd come to church today. She wondered if he'd seen her, and her pulse ricocheted through her body with what to do. By then, he'd passed her row, and she couldn't see him anymore. Winnie fished in her purse for her phone, and she turned the volume back up so she'd hear notifications of texts and calls.

They hadn't made definite plans for a picnic today, and the grayness in the sky told Winnie she didn't really want to spend any significant time outside. She also felt like she'd been quite forward with him already, and part of her wanted to be wooed. Chased. Asked out.

"He *did* ask you out," she whispered to herself. But *she* was the one who'd turned their canceled lunch date into a Saturday night dinner date.

Her phone chimed, and Winnie nearly jumped out of her skin. "That's way too loud." She pressed on the button on the side of her phone to lower the volume, and she caught Ty's name as the text got sucked back up into the top of the screen.

She tapped over to his text, her giddiness returning. *Hey, I just saw you at church, and I was wondering if you still wanted to do that picnic.*

A picture came in, also from Ty, and a moment later, a picnic basket with a red-checkered cloth spilling out the top brightened her screen. It appeared to be riding shotgun in Ty's truck, and Winnie wanted to be there too.

It's looking gray today, cowboy, she said.

I know a great place, he said. *Very quiet, and we can sit in the back of my truck. I brought a couple of blankets, and if I open the little window, the heat blows right down the back of your neck.*

Sounds nice, Winnie said. *I saw you walk through the parking lot. Did you want to meet me at my house?*

Yeah, I've already left.

Okay, see you there. Winnie set her phone back in her purse, and she too left the church parking lot. She made the drive, a few rain-drops splattering her windshield, and when she turned onto her lane, she found Ty's big, dark brown truck parked in front of her house.

Winnie smiled and smiled and couldn't stop smiling as she pulled into her driveway, then her garage. She closed the door while she still sat in her car, something she always did, and then quickly ran into the house.

I just need to feed the cats. She sent the text to Ty, rushed through giving Rocky and Salmon their midday meal, and then she paused in front of the full-length mirror on the inside of the coat closet door only a few feet from the front windows.

"It was good enough for church," she said, taking in her black slacks and sage-green blouse. She wore a pumpkin-colored jacket with cream trim, and she reached for her purse at the same time Ty knocked on the front door.

She took the couple of steps to it, pulled it open, and grinned at him. "Sorry. Was I taking too long?"

"Not at all," he said easily. "I thought I'd put Valerie Thompson's worries at ease, since she's been glaring at me from her front porch since I pulled up." He kicked her that adorable grin, and Winnie reached for his hand.

"I don't even know who Valerie Thompson is."

"She lives next door to you," Ty said. He glared to the house located just north of hers. "Right there." He lifted his free hand to a woman standing there with a watering can, doing absolutely nothing.

Winnie smiled and waved at her too. "I haven't met her yet."

"I'm stunned by that," Ty said as he led her down the steps. "You've lived here for what? Seven months?"

"Yeah," Winnie said. "But she was out of town visiting her daughter when I moved in, and I work a lot. So."

Ty reached his truck and opened her door for her. "Who feeds the cats their lunch while you're at the clinic?"

"What?" Winnie blinked at him and then got in the passenger seat.

"The cats." He slammed the door between them and went around the back of the truck to get behind the wheel.

"No one feeds the cats while I'm at work," she said. "I just like to keep them guessing on the weekend, and I only gave them my left-over chicken for breakfast."

"Wow." He chuckled. "That's one expensive feline breakfast." He grinned at her. "And double wow—it's so great to see you."

Winnie lifted her chin and kept smiling. "Thanks. It's great to be seen by you." She peered over the seats and into the back of the truck. "Where's that picnic basket?"

"Right behind you, sweetheart." Ty eased away from the curb, waved once again at her neighbor, and headed out of the neighborhood. He went back toward the little white church on the south side of town, and then took the highway that led away from Three Rivers.

"How far to this 'quiet place'?" she asked.

"Fifteen or twenty minutes."

"Perfect," she said. "Let's do the one-minute game."

"The what?" He looked over to her with a blank look on his face.

Winnie settled into her seat and looked at all the buttons on the dashboard. "Where's the one to turn on my seat heater?"

"I got you," he said, and he reached over and pressed a button for her.

"The one-minute game is something my parents made us do on road trips," Winnie said. "They'd give us a topic, and we'd have to talk about it for sixty seconds. Our thoughts, our feelings, whatever we wanted to say." She watched his reaction. "No judgment, of course."

"No judgment," he said. "So who's going to set the topic?"

"I'll give you yours, and you can give me mine." Winnie swallowed, not quite sure where this would go. "You can go first if you want."

"Sixty seconds is a long time," Ty said.

"We can make it the thirty-second game," Winnie said.

"Does it have to be the truth?" he asked.

"Oh, my word." Winnie rolled her eyes. "Or—what do you say? For the love of eight seconds?" She gave him a glare. "For the love of eight seconds, Ty. Just say whatever you want."

"I just want to know the rules of the game," he said, his voice a touch darker now. "So I can play it right."

"It's not a game, Ty. It's just talking."

"Well, that can be hard for some people." He drove in silence for a couple of beats, then released his tight grip on the wheel and exhaled. "But I want to...talk to you."

Winnie lifted her chin for a new reason now. "I've been told I talk too much. I don't mean to be so *extra*."

"You're not extra," he said. "Or if you are, I don't mind it."

"Okay." Winnie took a deep breath and tried to give the oxygen a moment to settle into each brain cell. "Well, I'd kind of like to start with what the pastor talked about today. Hopes. Dreams. What are your hopes and dreams?"

Ty sighed, rolled his right shoulder, and looked out his side window. "Going straight in, I see."

"Surely you have some hopes and dreams," she said.

"You said you'd go first."

"But it should be a question from you," she said.

"Fine." He shot her another dark look. "Do you like Three Rivers?"

"Yeah," she said, ignoring his attitude. "First, I really like the clinic here. My boss is great, and my co-workers are easy to trade shifts with, that kind of thing. They're fun." She smiled and noted that Ty slowed the truck and made a right turn off the highway.

They now drove down a gravel road that turned to dirt, and Ty's truck handled it like a champ.

"I think Three Rivers is beautiful in the summer and fall, and it's not been too bad in the winter either—we get way more snow in Oklahoma for sure—and I have a cute little house. The cats like it here, and it's a good buffer for me to Redwood."

"And that's where you're from?"

"Mm hm," she said, though he wasn't supposed to get to ask follow-up questions. "There are a lot of good restaurants in town too, and I don't know. When I take my evening walk, I just feel good here, you know?"

"Yeah," Ty said. "Three Rivers has some magic to it."

She waited, and when he didn't ask her something else, she grinned at him. "When you're done, you have to tell me."

"More rules I didn't know," he shot back at her. "I'm done."

"Okay." She sat up a little straighter. "Your hopes and dreams."

He looked at her out of the corner of his eye, barely moving his head as he did. "Fine. I have some money saved from my time in the rodeo, but I can't just do nothing all day. So I like working at Lone Star and the orchards, but I think I'd like my own place."

"Like a ranch?"

"I can't run a ranch, no." Ty shook his head. "Nothing like a whole ranch. I was thinking more along the lines of a hobby farm. I have a few friends who have their own farms. They feed their animals, and grow big gardens, and sell their excess alfalfa. I think— well, I think I could do that. Maybe."

"Why wouldn't you be able to?"

"Because running a farm is a lot of physical labor," he said. "And sometimes, after a really busy day of *walking*, I need to ice my hip and take a lot of painkillers." He looked over to her fully, lightning and thunder in his expression.

"Sure, but you could hire in help."

Ty sighed. "Yeah." The truck slowed again, and Winnie switched her attention out the windshield instead of scrutinizing Ty. "I just know I can't live in that apartment forever. Heck, I'd like to be out by summertime."

"Really? That soon?"

Ty came to a stop and nodded. "Eagle Bear Lake. I'm going to turn around and back in." He started doing that while Winnie gazed at the rippling water in front of her. "The name is kind of interesting, because there was a pair of eagles who used to nest here, like, forty years ago. So it used to be called just Eagle Lake. Then, someone saw a bear, and now it's Eagle Bear Lake."

Winnie smiled at him. "It's simple. I like it." She exhaled, wondering if they could just picnic from the front seats of the truck. "It's really windy, cowboy."

"I have a couple of blankets." He stopped talking as he got the truck where he wanted it, got out and collected the picnic basket, and then opened her door. "Ready?"

"Yes, sir." She dropped to the ground beside him, and she stayed out of the way as he lowered the tailgate, slid their lunch inside, and then unfolded a single-step step-stool. He gripped the side of the truck as he put his right foot on it, and he half-pulled, half-pushed himself up the step.

He grunted as he did it, but Winnie stayed silent and still. Ty made it into the bed of the truck, and he knelt down to help her up. Nerves ran through her body, because while Winnie took her evening walks, they were more like strolls.

She managed it, and then found that Ty had created a nest in the back of his truck. A nest of blankets and pillows, and she sank onto a perfectly purple one with a wide smile. "This is great."

He toed the basket over to her and sat down beside her. "Okay, let's see what we've got in this thing." He took the red-checkered cloth off and spread it over her legs.

She grinned harder.

"Chicken croissant," he said, handing her a golden crescent croissant in a zipper bag. "Red grapes. Sliced caramel apples."

He handed her each item as he pulled it out of the basket, and when he gave her an oatmeal chocolate chip cookie as big as her face, she asked, "Where did you get all of this?"

"I made it," he said simply.

Winnie stared at him as he settled next to her and opened his chicken croissant sandwich. "You made it?" She looked down at the cookie. "All of it?"

"I mean, I bought the grapes," he said. "And the apple—but I cut that up myself."

"When?" she asked. "I mean, we were out until forever last night."

Ty grinned at her. "Forever? I kept you out until *forever*?" He shook his head and lifted his sandwich. "And you don't sound happy about it." He took a bite of his croissant, his grin making him so stinking handsome.

"I'm happy about it," Winnie said, looking down at her lap covered with that red-checkered cloth. She picked up her baggie of sliced caramel apples. "I had a great time last night."

"Good," Ty said. "Because so did I. Good enough to make chicken salad and cookies this morning, stop by the grocery store for a picnic basket, and *still* make it to church on time."

Winnie lifted her gaze to meet his, and Ty leaned toward her. She pulled in a breath and let her eyes drift closed. Ty's soft beard brushed her cheek as he pressed his to hers.

"You sure are pretty, Winnie," he whispered. "Sorry I made the game so hard, but thanks for coming on this picnic with me."

He retreated then, leaving Winnie's body buzzing with want. He sighed and popped a grape into his mouth. "I love this lake," he said.

"It's out of the way, and there's no services, so not many people use it."

Winnie bit her apple slice in half and looked out at the lake too. "It can't be very deep."

"Nope," Ty said. "And it sometimes dries up in the summer. It's a great thinking spot."

She leaned her head against his shoulder, glad when he lifted his arm and brought her closer to his side, tucking her next to him before he took another bite of his croissant.

Winnie felt like something as simple as a picnic had made her whole world brighter. Ty had rescued her from so many things... including herself, and she hoped their relationship would continue to develop into something beautiful and lasting and real.

Please let it be real this time, she prayed. *Because I don't know how I'll survive if it's not.*

11

Tyson pulled open the door to the physical therapy clinic, his anticipation for today's appointment already off the charts. He hadn't seen Winnie in a professional capacity since before Christmas, and he hadn't seen her in a personal capacity since their Sunday picnic at Eagle Bear Lake.

They'd been texting a lot, but with the holidays over and the vacation schedules at the ranches and orchard where he worked done, Ty had returned to Lone Star on Monday, and was working with his crew at the orchard on Tuesday.

Classes had resumed at *Signs for Success* yesterday, though Winnie's first beginning sign language class actually started tonight. Ty had gone ahead and signed up for that one as well, knowing he needed to do a lot more work to be proficient in ASL.

A new receptionist waited at the desk when Ty arrived, and he said, "I'm Tyson Greene. I have an appointment with Winnie Landry at eleven-fifteen."

The girl, who seemed to be about fifteen, looked up at him with wide blue eyes. "Did you not get our message, Mister Greene?"

"No," he said, pausing though he'd already picked up the pen to sign in. "What message?"

"Miss Landry is out today," she said. "I called a couple of hours ago and wondered if we might reschedule you with Melissa Ryher? If that doesn't work, we'll have to reschedule you with Winnie next week."

"Winnie's out today?"

"Yes, sir," the woman said. "Yesterday, too. She's not feeling well."

Ty immediately wanted to leave the clinic, find her favorite Chinese food, and go see what she needed. He'd texted with her last night, and she had not mentioned that she'd stayed home from work, nor had she told him that she would not be at their appointment today.

He signed his name and pulled out his phone to text Winnie. *You're sick? Can I bring you lunch?*

"So are you okay with Melissa?" the receptionist asked, and Ty nodded absently, watching his phone and willing Winnie to respond. She didn't.

"Yeah, sure," he said, already calculating how long it would be before he could get to Winnie's house to see how she was doing.

Melissa spent half of his appointment reviewing his notes and making him show her things that he'd been doing for months. Then she told him to continue to do those things, and said he should come see Winnie next week.

"Glad I paid for that," he grumbled as he stepped onto the elevator and left the clinic.

It had started to rain while he'd been inside, and he hurried to his truck and got it started so the heater would begin to blow. Then he pulled out his phone and checked his notes, because he couldn't remember the name of the Chinese restaurant Winnie had given him exactly a week ago now.

"Wok This Way," he said. "That's right. Chicken teriyaki rice bowl."

He texted Winnie again: *I'm getting lunch and stopping by. Tell me now if it's a bad time.*

She still didn't answer, and Ty didn't want to wait for her permission anyway. She was sick, and he wanted to make her life easier if he could.

So he looked up the restaurant and navigated to what old-time Three Rivers residents called New Downtown, which was a series of high-rise buildings filled with various companies, offices, and yes, restaurants. In fact, one of the buildings housed several restaurants on the top floor or the roof, providing amazing views of Three Rivers and the surrounding Texas Panhandle.

Wok This Way stood at street level, but Ty had to park down the block and make the walk to get there. He found a lunchtime crowd waiting in line and a complicated menu board that he thankfully had time to figure out before it was his turn to order.

He thought about all the things he would like in a teriyaki chicken bowl, and then ordered the opposite of that for Winnie.

He got a noodle bowl with steak and wok sauce, water chestnuts, and sugar snap peas—something he would take a picture of and send to his mother, just to prove to her that he ate vegetables from time to time. With everything finally in his possession, he limped back to his truck and aimed himself toward Winnie's house.

She always pulled all the way into her garage and closed the door before she got out of the car, something Tyson had witnessed her doing after church a few days ago. When he'd asked her about it, she told him it simply made her feel safe, and she couldn't imagine getting out of her car with the door still open.

He couldn't tell if she was home or not, but her quaint little cottage made him smile. He collected their lunch and texted her for a third time.

Okay, I've got lunch and I'm at your house. You haven't answered, and I'm a little bit worried that you might be asleep.

He waited a couple of minutes and still didn't get a response.

He looked at the rice bowl, the empty-for-now front porch next door, and then Winnie's front door and made a decision. He once again hurried through the rain and up Winnie's front steps, his hip twinging with pain and reminding him that Thursday was supposed to be his day off.

He didn't work at Lone Star or the orchards, and he only had to go to *Signs for Success* for a couple of hours to work with Mitch and the hearing dogs. The rest of the day was his, and Ty could admit that he often took a nap on Thursday afternoons and sometimes meal-prepped for the coming weeks if he was feeling strong enough.

He bypassed the doorbell and instead knocked on the front door, leaning close to where it sat shut against the frame. "Winnie," he called. "It's Tyson."

He heard nothing, not the sound of footsteps or anyone saying they were coming. He didn't hear a cat meowing and, in fact, the Panhandle wind rushed across his face, stealing any sound he may have heard. He didn't think for a moment Winnie would leave her front door unlocked, but his fingers twined around the knob and he twisted. To his great surprise, it opened.

"Winnie," he called again, his heart suddenly pounding in the back of his throat. "It's Ty. I heard you were sick, and I brought lunch."

Still nothing.

He tilted his head toward the house, and he heard the soft padding of tiny feet on the carpet. In the next moment, a gray-and-white cat appeared at the mouth of the hallway about fifteen feet into the house. Ty had been inside before, of course, and his eyes swept the couch to his left, the TV on the credenza in front of that where Winnie usually kept her purse, and the little bit of the kitchen he could see. He didn't find Winnie or her second cat, but he did see her bag sitting next to the TV and the whole house in silence.

"Is she home?" he asked the cat, as if it would answer.

He would have to consult his notes if this was Rocky or Salmon, though he suspected Rocky, because Winnie had said Salmon liked to hide out by himself even when she was home.

"Meow," Rocky said, and Ty made another decision.

He stepped into the house and gently closed the door behind him. Her furnace blew, and there was no reason to make it work overtime.

Something beyond the scent of the Chinese food met his nose, growing stronger as he moved into the kitchen and set the plastic bag of food on Winnie's kitchen counter.

Her trash overflowed, and he took a couple more steps and found her sink full of dishes.

The neat freak inside of him frowned, but mostly because this was evidence that Winnie had been sick for a while. Why hadn't she told him?

He turned and faced the cat who'd followed him into the kitchen. "Have you guys had breakfast?" he asked, though the second feline had not made an appearance.

Ty looked around and found the cat bowls against the wall behind the small dining room table. They did not look like they had been refreshed that morning, and, by balancing himself with one hand on the back of a kitchen chair, he managed to bend over and pick them up. He washed them out and refilled one with fresh water.

Winnie wasn't exactly messy, and he only had to open two cupboards to find the cat food. The dry kibble actually sat in a plastic container labeled with masking tape, and he sprinkled some of that into the bowl, then opened one of the wet cat food containers and mixed it all together.

That must have been a siren's call for the felines, because when he turned around, he not only had her gray-and-white cat staring at him, but her black cat too.

"Oh, hello," he said. "You must be Salmon."

"Meow," Rocky said, and Ty moved to put down the bowl of food. Both cats moved over to it and started to eat.

Ty didn't know how many bedrooms this house had, though from the outside he was guessing at least three. Not many people had basements in Three Rivers, and Winnie's house only stood one story tall.

He flipped on her hot water and opened her dishwasher, finding it half-full of dirty dishes. He filled it with the dishes from the sink, washing any that didn't fit and setting them to dry on a dish towel. He started the appliance and wiped down all the counters.

By then, the cats had finished their lunch, and he found them curled into the beanbag in the corner of the living room.

"Is she asleep?" he asked them. When neither feline answered yet again, he returned to the kitchen and emptied the trash, taking it out the side door and into the garage. He didn't find the big outdoor can there, and he opened the garage door and found it on the side of the house.

Back inside with all the doors securely closed, he paused at the sliding back door and looked out over her deck, half-expecting to see Winnie sitting there, sipping her tea, the way she'd told him she did on weekend mornings.

He didn't, and he reached into his back pocket to text her that he'd brought lunch and he'd leave it for her on the counter.

"What are you doing here?"

Ty spun at the sound of Winnie's voice. She stood there in an oversized T-shirt with a pair of cartoon dogs on the front. If she wore shorts, he couldn't see them, and the T-shirt skimmed the top of her knees.

"Hey," he said. "I brought lunch, because the girl at the clinic said you were sick." He took a couple of steps and stopped on the other side of the peninsula from her. "Why didn't you text me and tell me you were sick?"

"I don't know," she said, and she did sound a little bit stuffed up. "It just started yesterday, and I didn't think it would be too bad." She moved over to the plastic bags containing their food. "You went to Wok This Way."

She looked at him, and a smile tugged up the corners of her mouth. "Thank you." She glanced over to the kitchen sink, and then along the counters. "You've cleaned my house." Her eyes came back to his. "How long have you been here?"

"Maybe twenty minutes," he said. "The front door was unlocked, and no cops have arrived, so I don't think your neighbor called nine-one-one."

Winnie giggled, which quickly turned into a cough. "I don't feel good," she said miserably, and she was so stinking cute Ty couldn't help his smile.

"Let's get you back to bed," he said. "I'll bring you something to drink and some medicine. I fed the cats, so they're happy."

Winnie looked down at her feet and along the seam where the kitchen met the living room. "Oh, where are they?"

"They're snoozing in the beanbag," he said.

"That's where I want to be," she said.

"All right." He moved around the end of the counter and took her hand. "Come lay in the beanbag then, sweetheart."

She looked pretty pathetic as she went with him, and she collapsed next to the cats, both of whom meowed their displeasure about being displaced to the couch while Ty tucked her in with a fluffy blue blanket. Then they returned to her lap, and he returned to the kitchen to get her lunch.

He poured the teriyaki rice bowl into a big bowl he found in the cupboard, opened a couple of drawers to find a fork, and then took everything out to her.

"I had some Gatorade delivered last night," she said. "There should be a green one in the fridge."

"Green Gatorade," he said. "And where's your apothecary?"

She blinked at him. "My what?"

He grinned at her. "My momma used to have a cupboard full of pills," he said. "Band-Aids, medical wraps, vitamins, you know. Stuff like that. She called it the apothecary."

Winnie blinked at him. "I have a couple boxes of cold medicine next to the toaster."

He grinned at her and returned to the kitchen to get her meds and a drink.

Her hair flowed loose and wild around her face, and Ty realized for maybe the first time just how much of it she had. He took a moment to admire her as he crossed the living room, and he recognized the fondness he felt for this woman as it flowed through him.

He handed her the box of cold medication and the bottle of Gatorade, then sat on the end of the couch beside the beanbag.

"Thank you so much, Ty," she said, and she looked and sounded truly grateful.

"What else do you need from me?" He turned more toward her, since she was sitting on his left. She reached over, and Ty fumbled for a moment but managed to slide his fingers between hers.

She squeezed, and smiled, and said, "Just you, cowboy."

The words echoed in his head. *Just you, cowboy.*

"What do you have going on today?"

"Nothing until tonight," he said, trying to get her words to not sound so sweet inside his head. "It's your first class...or did you call out sick?"

Just you, cowboy rang through his ears and filled his head and slithered straight into his heart. While he wished it didn't mean so much to him, it did. Yeah, it really did.

"No, I'm going to go," she said. "If I take some meds now, I can take some more right before class and make it through."

Ty nodded. "I can drive you."

"So you'll stay with me this afternoon?" She wore an expression of pure hope on her face, and Ty nodded.

"Yeah, I can stay."

"Perfect," she said. When she released his hand so that she could continue eating, Ty went to get his noodle bowl. As he rejoined Winnie and her cats in the living room, he felt like his life finally held some purpose, because he'd been able to help Winnie in a world where she didn't have anyone but him.

And he wanted to be that man for her more than anything, and gratitude filled his heart that he had the time and means to be sitting with Winnie, in her house, in the middle of the day, eating her favorite Chinese food.

12

Winnie slept on and off all afternoon, her belly full of delicious Chinese food and her heart filled with happiness that Ty had shown up in her hour of need. At one point when she'd awakened, she'd found him stretched out on her couch, fast asleep.

He'd breathed in and out, soft and steady, and he hadn't moved at all though she'd gotten up, gone down the hall to the bathroom, and returned.

She lay cradled in the beanbag now, her kitties warm along her side, and the sound of Ty humming in the kitchen. Everything about it felt domestic and homey and absolutely wonderful.

When they'd both been awake earlier, he'd opened up the front window and the back screen door and let the Panhandle wind air the house out. He'd done her dishes and taken out her trash and fed her cats—which he was actually doing for the second time that day right now.

"Come on, guys," he called, and Winnie opened her eyes. The scraping of the cats' feeding bowl on the linoleum in the other room filled the house, and both cats catapulted off the beanbag and ran toward the kitchen. She heard his low voice murmuring to them, and it caused a smile to fill her face.

He came around the corner, wiping his hand on one of her dish towels. "Do you need to eat?" he asked.

Winnie shook her head. "I want to get something after class, like you suggested."

"All right," he said.

"Just something fast on the way home," she said. "And then you can tuck me in bed and go home."

"I'm fine for whatever you need me for, sweetheart."

"Yeah, but you have to go to work tomorrow, right?"

"Yeah," he said. "Out at Lone Star. I can come back in the afternoon."

"I've called out again for tomorrow," she said. "I have a doctor's appointment in the morning, so if I have a virus, hopefully I can get some antibiotics."

"What about the wedding?" he asked.

"Don't worry," she said. "I'm not going to miss the wedding."

A frown settled over his expression, drawing down his mouth and making that tight V appear between his eyes. "I don't want to go to the wedding anyway. This would be a great excuse to miss it."

"Because I'm sick?" Winnie asked.

"Yeah. Why not?" Ty threw her a look and went back into the kitchen. She heard the water run in the sink, and then he called, "Can I have one of these bottles of water?"

"Of course," she called back.

"Do you want anything?"

"No, I'm good." Her throat felt scratchy and dry, but the cold medicine she'd taken a few hours ago had definitely done its job. She didn't feel nearly as stuffed up, and if she could stay hydrated and rested, she knew she'd make a full recovery.

Ty came back into the living room, and it did seem a little bit strange to see him walking around her house in his socked feet. He'd taken off his cowboy boots at some point and left them by the front door.

"Is there room for me on that?" he asked, nodding to her left side.

Winnie scooted over, pure anticipation dancing through her at the thought of cuddling with Ty on the squishy beanbag. It was like swinging in a hammock with a person, and she wouldn't be able to hold her body up away from his. He sank onto the other half of it, and he turned toward her, wrapping her easily in his arms.

As he drew her into his chest, she pulled the blanket up and over his shoulder and sighed as she sank into his warmth. She breathed in the scent of his shirt and his skin, getting notes of cedar and sunshine and something spicy that was probably labeled *waterfall* in his cologne.

"You're probably going to get sick," she whispered. "You should've kept your distance."

"I can't," he said. "You're just so pretty."

Winnie smiled to herself. "I got a new jumpsuit for the wedding," she said. "It came last night, and I tried it on, and it fits pretty good."

"And I didn't get a fashion show picture?" he asked.

"A fashion show picture?"

"Whenever my sister gets new clothes, she sends us all fashion show pictures."

"I didn't know I needed to do that," Winnie said.

"It's kind of like the games you play in your family," he said. "Remember how I failed at all of those?"

She laughed against his chest. "You haven't failed at anything, Ty."

"What color is the jumpsuit?" he asked.

"Red," she said. "And it's got white animal print all over it. It's pretty cute."

"Red and white animal print." Ty chuckled. "I actually can't wait to see that, so I guess we'll have to go to the wedding."

"I guess?" She almost scoffed but held it back at the last moment. "I don't know why you're so grumpy about going to this wedding."

"I don't know why you're so jazzed to go," he shot back. "It's not like you know Judy or Trooper."

"No, but they're *your friends*, and I like meeting new people."

"Another thing I don't understand," he griped.

She pulled away and looked up at him. His eyelids fluttered open, and Winnie wondered if she should hold her tongue, but she wanted to be able to speak her mind with the people she spent her time with. If Tyson didn't value that, then she didn't want to be with him.

"Oh, you've got that look in your eye," he said.

"What look?"

"It's the same look my momma gets when she has something she wants to say, and she knows I'm not going to like it."

Winnie pressed her lips together and looked over to the entrance to the living room. As Rocky entered, he meowed several times before joining them on the beanbag. She stroked her hand down his side, trying to find the right words.

"Are you going to be super surly at the wedding?" she asked.

"I'll probably just be myself," Ty said.

"Well, if that's the super surly version of yourself, then I'm not sure I want to go with you." She looked up at him. "I think true love is amazing, Ty. And even if we're a little bit jealous, or we wish it was for us, or we don't know the person, it's something that can touch our hearts and we can appreciate it. If you can't even *try* to do that, then I'll just wear my jumpsuit to church on Sunday."

He searched her face too, his eyes sharp but everything else about him soft. "I just can't believe you want to go to a wedding for people you don't even know," he said. "Just to meet a few of my friends."

"Well, your friends are important to you, aren't they?"

"Yes," he clipped out. "But how are you not angry and bitter about the wedding that you didn't get to have?"

"Who says I'm not?" she asked.

"I do," he said. "You acted a little sad about it, for like, four minutes. And then your response was literally, *I just need to find the right person.*"

"Well, that's true," she said.

"I don't understand how you can be so, so, so...*cheerful* about the bad things that have happened to you."

"I'm not *cheerful* about them." She put her palm against his chest and pushed him a few inches further away. "But there's no point in wallowing in it. What's done is done. Carver walked out. He didn't love me. Why would I want to be in a marriage with a man who doesn't love me? Everything would be worse if we'd gotten married."

Her chest stormed and Winnie felt her emotions running away from her. She tried to grab onto them, because when that happened, she said too much and almost always the wrong things.

"Are you implying that I've been wallowing in my injury?"

"Haven't you been—?"

"You don't know me *at all*," Ty said.

"I know you a little bit," Winnie said. "And no, I don't think that you've been wallowing."

He pressed his lips together, clearly fighting what he really wanted to say. "What *do* you think?" he finally asked.

Winnie studied his face, the pure unhappiness in his eyes and the sharp daggers he threw her way.

"I think you've been a very fortunate man," she said. "Who has a big bank account, so when he got hurt, he was able to take all the time he needed away from the responsibilities of life.

"I think you have amazing parents and siblings and friends and a small-town community who welcomed you home with open arms, and it took you a while to realize that you appreciate that, too."

He dropped his eyes, some of his fight deflating and easing the tension in the air between them.

"I think you fought really hard to be where you are," she said next. "Probably harder than I, or anyone else, even knows, because

I've read your chart, Mister Greene, and you had doctors telling you you would never walk again."

She took a breath and reached for Salmon as he joined them on the beanbag. She drew comfort and strength from her grumpy cat, realizing that Tyson reminded her a lot of Salmon. And all she'd ever had to do was take care of him, and the cat loved her for it.

"I think you've been coming around to yourself more and more in the past several months," she said. "I don't really know how long before I met you, but *since* I met you, you seem like you want to build your life here in Three Rivers, and you want your own place, and you want to be able to walk out your back door and go ride your horse."

"Yeah," he whispered.

"And I think you haven't had a lot of luck with women, and for a while, you figured, *Why should I try at all?*" She slid her hand up his arm and along his jaw, gently lifting his chin so he would look at her.

"And we may see things differently, because I never think, *Why try? I think, Why shouldn't I?* I might fail, but it's at least worth a shot, and maybe I'll learn something along the way."

"Yeah, I don't think like that," Ty said.

"But you *have* taken a shot," she said, her eyebrows coming up and a small smile first crinkling her eyes and then extending to her mouth. "I see you, Tyson Greene, and I know that it took a lot for you to ask me out."

He didn't argue with her, which meant she was right—or he simply didn't want to argue anymore.

"Was it very hard to bring me lunch today?"

"No," he whispered. "The hardest part was remembering the name of the Chinese restaurant, but I'd written it down." A tiny smile played with his lips too, and Winnie focused her attention there.

"I think I naturally see things in a more positive light," she said. "And I think it takes work for you to do the same, but you eventually get there."

"Yeah. Maybe." He dipped his head and ran the tip of his nose across her cheekbone. She couldn't help pressing into his touch, because he was so strong, and so warm, and Winnie liked him so much.

With his lips practically catching against her earlobe, he whispered, "I promise I'll try to have a good attitude at the wedding."

"Mm-hm," Winnie hummed, because she couldn't get her mouth to form words, not with him so close and his breath tickling her neck.

"Okay?" he whispered.

"Yes, okay," she said.

His arms around her tightened, and Winnie relaxed into his chest.

"I'm thinking pizza for dinner," he said, his voice soft and sexy. "I can order it from the app when your class is almost over, and it will be here when we get back."

Winnie pulled back and smiled at him. "Let me guess: you're an I-don't-eat-fruit-on-my-pizza cowboy."

He grinned at her. "Wrong. I love a good ham and pineapple pie, but it has to have Alfredo sauce, not the red sauce. Otherwise, everything's too sweet."

Winnie shook her head. "I've never met anyone who changes their order and does so many substitutions as you."

"Are you kidding?" he said. "We've been out once, and I ordered the chicken dinner as-is, same as you."

"Yeah, but you're always telling me how you like this—*but*—and you like that—*but*."

"Well, there are some modifications worth making."

Winnie cradled his face in her hand, and the moment between them softened and also strengthened. "I really appreciate you coming to take care of me today, Ty."

"It might sound crazy," he whispered back. "But I really like taking care of things. Mostly, I've only had the opportunity to do that for horses, but doing it for you is twice as good as helping out a horse."

Winnie grinned and giggled. "Wow, that's so romantic."

Ty laughed, the sound free and full of joy. "Don't make fun of me," he said. "That *was* romantic for me." He sobered, and their eyes met. "You know everyone is going to pepper you with questions at the wedding."

He sighed and let his eyes drift closed again. "You're going to have to meet my parents, my siblings, all of my friends. Every single one of them is going to wonder what we are."

Winnie's pulse stormed through her body. "Part of having Carver leave a week before our wedding taught me that people can think whatever they want. As long as I know what's true, then it doesn't matter."

"I like that." Ty opened his eyes and looked at her. Really looked at her. "And what's true for us?"

He leaned closer, his lips barely skimming the soft skin along her cheek. "Am I your boyfriend?" He touched his lips in a full kiss right below her ear. "Are you my girlfriend?"

"Yes," she gasped. "I'm not seeing anyone else, and we've been out a few times now."

"So the wedding *isn't* just a couple of casual hours, so I don't have to go alone."

"If that's what you want it to be, you better say so right now," she said. "Because I think we've come a long way in a week, and I can have casual friendships with my coworkers."

Ty pulled back just slightly, his eyes oh-so-serious as he gazed at her. "Good, because there's nothing casual about this for me."

He laid his head back down on the beanbag, and Winnie tucked herself back into his arms, a sense of safety and comfort filling her that could only come from having another person care about her and take care of her.

"But for real," he said. "What do you want on your pizza tonight?"

"Anything but mushrooms," she said. "Remember, Ty, I like to eat, and I can find almost anything that I like."

"All right," he said. "There's an amazing barbecue chicken pizza from The Bullpen. How does that sound?"

"Sounds like an amazing third date," Winnie said, and while

attending the wedding with him did send a stream of nerves through her—mostly because of how many people would be watching her and wondering how she and Ty had met and how serious they were and how long they'd been together—Winnie was still sure that her time on Saturday would be her fourth incredible date with the handsome, if a little surly, Tyson Greene.

13

Wilder Glover adjusted his tie for the third time as he stood at the back of the ballroom, watching snowflakes drift past the tall windows. He prayed the weather would hold long enough for him to get Savannah and the girls back home, as the drive into town had been a bit sketchy. The wind had been relentless lately, and it currently sent the snow into a blur, making everything white in all directions.

January in the Texas Panhandle could be unpredictable, and this morning's storm had been on the calendar for the past ten days. Aunt Ida had started making contingency plans immediately, and while Judy and Trooper hadn't wanted to have their wedding at the ranch, in the family barn where so many others had tied the knot, they'd chosen a beautiful old church in town that had been converted into a wedding venue.

The Perennial had indoor and outdoor space, and Ida had rented the whole building, so they'd simply had to reconfigure some of the seating for the reception, and Aunt Etta had stepped in to help her twin call around and find a tent rental company that could handle the snow.

In the end, the wind had canceled some things, and Wilder reached up and wiped a thin sheen of sweat from underneath the brim of his cowboy hat.

"It's hot in here, isn't it?" Savannah appeared at his elbow, wearing a smile that made his heart skip one, two, three beats.

"There's too many people here," he said.

She reached up and straightened his burgundy tie, her engagement ring catching the light from the blinding snow-light overhead. "You look perfect."

He swept one arm around her waist, as she was the one broadcasting perfection. "I'll take handsome and distinguished."

She laughed, that musical sound he'd fallen in love with the first time he'd heard it. "How about *devastatingly gorgeous cowboy who cleans up real nice?*"

"Mm, yes. A cowboy with his queen." He leaned down and touched his lips to hers, marveling at how natural it felt to have her beside him. Seven months ago, he'd stood at a wedding very much like this one, feeling sorry for himself and completely convinced he'd never find what his cousins had.

Now, with his own wedding only three months away and Savannah wearing his diamond, he could barely remember what all that misery had been about.

"Where are the girls?" he asked, scanning the crowd of family milling about the ballroom.

"Your mother has them," Savannah said, nodding toward the front where Momma sat on the right side with Gallery and Sequoia flanking her like tiny bodyguards. Both girls wore matching silver dresses which Judy had sewn specifically for them, their hair braided with ribbons that coordinated with Wilder's tie.

His chest tightened with affection as he watched Sequoia turn toward his mother, who nodded, smiled, and smoothed her fingertips along the little girl's hair. The twins would be turning six years old in a couple of months, and his momma had already started planning the party.

As Wilder watched, Daddy arrived, and he handed one juice box to Gal and reached past Momma to give the second one to Sequoia. He ducked his head as he smiled, because his parents' hearts had been melted by the twins once Wilder had made it very clear that he and Savannah were serious.

"They're doing great," he said. "I don't know what you were worried about."

"Really?" Savannah scoffed. "You don't know what I'm worried about? Gal asked me this morning if she could catch the bouquet, and when I told her it was for unmarried *women*, she announced she was going to marry Harry Parker—who is this rascally boy in her kindergarten class." She rolled her eyes, but Wilder threw back his head and laughed.

"She's the best," he said, because Gal definitely had a larger-than-life personality.

"She certainly thinks so." Savannah smoothed an invisible wrinkle from her forest green dress—one that Aurora had made. Judy had wanted everyone in specific clothing, and to do that, she'd made everyone come in for a fitting, and she and Aurora, Aunt Etta and Aunt Ida, and a seamstress out of Amarillo had been sewing for months.

Savannah's dress fit her like a glove, the straps wide and flowing over her shoulders. Judy had a silver shawl that looked like chain mail for each woman, and Savannah adjusted hers as she surveyed the crowd that just continued to swell, and swell, and swell as more aunts, uncles, and cousins arrived.

"Is this where we're hiding out?"

Wilder grinned at Link and drew him into a hug. "I'm not hiding. We're just staying out of the way for the moment." He released the co-foreman at the ranch and hugged Misty too. "Where are the kids?"

"Sitting with Janey and Trevor," Misty said.

Wilder nodded, though he couldn't locate them, or see Link's kids anywhere. Misty carried their little girl on her hip, and she passed her to Savannah when she reached for her.

"The weather's not looking good for the next couple of weeks," Link said with a sigh.

"Tell me about it," Wilder said, a dark note entering his voice. "Shadow called and said he's not sending his crew out until it clears up."

"It'll be fine," Savannah said, a hint of warning in her tone. "The house will be done in plenty of time." She turned her back on him to greet Clover, who'd just arrived with Rock.

"Howdy, brother." Wilder took Rock's hand and pulled his cousin into his chest. They bumped there, then separated. "Where's Smiles?"

"Oh, he met some woman," Rock practically growled. "I swear, the man knows everyone."

Link chuckled. "Yeah, leave it to Smiles to come to a family wedding alone and end up leaving with a date."

Wilder grinned too, though he couldn't find the shiniest star in the Glover family either. "Did Gun make it off the ranch?"

They'd been out since dawn, moving animals into barns and stables, and Wilder had had to leave before anyone else to get all the way to Llama Mamas and back to the wedding on time.

"Yeah, he and Camila are here." Link pointed toward the far side of the room where Gunnison stood with his wife, both of them laughing at something Ashton was saying.

"Okay, good," he said. "Brandon and Lenore said they're not going to make it."

"That's because she's pregnant," Clover said.

Wilder whipped his attention to her. "She is? How do you know?"

"She texted us." Clover gestured to Savannah, herself, and Misty. "We wives have our own thread, remember?"

Wilder blinked at his fiancée. "You're on the wives thread?"

She grinned at him. "Oh, did I forget to tell you that?"

Rock laughed right out loud, and he linked his arm through Clover's. "Come on, you. We've stirred up enough trouble for one day."

"Yeah, *we're* the ones causing trouble," Clover said dryly, and that made Wilder grin all the wider.

"I didn't know Lenore was pregnant," Link said.

"Me either," Wilder said.

"I did," Finn said, sidling up to them and taking Rock's spot. "Edith told me last night." He lifted a can of Diet Coke to his lips, took a sip, and then grimaced. "Ew, that's warm."

"You had to bring in your soda pop?" Wilder teased. "They're going to serve dinner in less than an hour, buddy."

Finn grinned at him, shook his head, and turned. He found a garbage can a few steps away, and tossed the can into it. "Hey, when you have children, you'll learn you'll do anything to get them in the car so you can get somewhere on time."

Link laughed and said, "Yeah, you sure will."

"What are you lot doin' over here?" Dawson Rhinehart came their way, first stepping into Link and hugging him hard. "Thank you so much for coming to help with that mudslide. My word. I don't know what we'd have done without your excavator."

"Yeah, no problem," Link said, and Wilder basked in the camaraderie and brotherhood that seemed to beam off Dawson and Link. They'd been friends for a long time, and they'd been through a lot together as they both worked neighboring ranches.

"Did y'all see who Ty Greene just walked in with?" Finn asked. He nodded toward the door, where Ty, wearing black from head to toe—boots, belt, cowboy hat included—stood with a gorgeous brunette wearing a bright red pantsuit with white zebra print zigzagging everywhere.

"Well, they're not trying to hide, are they?" Link murmured.

"He is," Wilder said, his smile only growing.

"Anyone know who she is?" Dawson asked.

"That's Winona Landry." Wilder nodded at Conrad Walker as he joined them. "Ty's out with Winnie."

"Yeah, we walked in with them," Conrad said. "But Sari had to go to the bathroom, though we made her go before we left." He sighed. "She is not adjusting to the new baby as well as I'd hoped."

"It gets better," Link said.

"She asked if we could take him to Grandma's and leave him there." Conrad shook his head, and he did look tired. "I mean, I get it. He cries a lot, and I swear he throws up everything he eats."

"Does he?" Savannah asked, and Wilder flinched. He'd forgotten she stood nearby, as more and more cowboys had been crowding around him. "Has Glory Rose taken him to the doctor?"

"Yeah, he's got some reflux thing," Conrad said. "We've switched his formula now, and he's doing a little better." He smiled at Savannah. "Also, those llamas you sent me? You're going to be so mad you didn't get them."

"They're amazing, aren't they?" Savannah didn't happy about it, though.

"Incredible."

"Dang it." She shot Wilder a look. "I knew I should've snatched them up."

"It'll be good for the guardian llama report," he said. "And when our place is done, you can get as many llamas as you want."

"Oh-ho-boy," Finn said as he laughed. "That's a big promise, cowboy."

"What are we promising?" JJ arrived, and he carried his darling baby girl in his arms. Jade was as dark as midnight, just like her daddy, and she had big, soulful eyes like her momma.

"He said I can get as many llamas as I want," Savannah said with a smile.

"Good man," JJ said, also grinning. "I mean, I buy all the longhorns and horses I want, so I can't really tell Ruby no about anything."

"Her dress is *incredible*," Savannah said, and she took a few steps away from the men to gush over Ruby's dress.

"She realizes she's wearing the same dress, right?" Link whispered, and that caused everyone in the group to laugh.

"Incoming," Conrad said, and Wilder found him watching as his cousin, Trap, approached with a pretty blonde.

"Howdy, fellas," Trap said, and he wore an air of nervousness about him. "This here is Fiona Colwood." He indicated the woman at his side. "She's a barista at The Coffee Cart."

"Howdy, Fiona," Conrad practically bellowed, and Wilder looked at him with wide eyes. "Wow, your dress is stunning."

"I didn't get the wedding color memo." She shot a look at Trap.

"It's only for family anyway," Wilder said. "I'm Wilder Glover." He stepped forward and shook the woman's hand. "See? Look—Ty's date isn't wearing silver or green either."

Tyson arrived at the edge of the group, and he'd found Colt and Fawn—who was wearing a dark green dress with the silver chainmail shawl. Wilder grinned at them too, noting that Fawn held hands with Colt's son, Jonas.

Colt was about five years older than Wilder, and Fawn was younger than him and had no romantic interest in the apple orchard owner. But she was great with kids, and she'd wanted a date to the wedding. Wilder had been the one to suggest Colt ask Fawn to go with him, and that had worked out nicely.

He'd also suggested Winnie to Ty, and he looked through the crowd to find the usually quiet, reserved, grumpy cowboy leaning in close to Winnie, whispering.

Oh, ho, and they were holding hands in a very more-than-friends gesture everyone in town could see.

Brave, Wilder thought as a chime sounded through the ballroom.

"You know what that means, guys," he said.

"What does it mean?" Trap asked.

"We got an extensive text with instructions," Link said. "And that chime means you have five minutes to find your seat."

"We'll be closing the doors in five minutes," a cool female voice said. "Please take your seats, remembering that the first five rows on either side are reserved for family of the bride and groom."

"My family needs about fifty rows," Wilder said, and he happily went to collect Savannah and lead her over to the end of the row where his parents sat with the twins.

Light, twinkling music filled the room, and the chatter died down. When the music stopped, Wilder looked over his shoulder and quickly got to his feet, for no less than two dozen police officers had just entered the room.

Uncle Brady had been named the Chief of Police about a year ago now, and he stood at the front of the formation, dressed to the nines in his full uniform, with every button, pin, and flag in precisely the right spot.

He wore snowy white gloves as he lifted one hand to his mouth, and the shrill, shocking peal of a whistle filled the air. All conversation cut off then, and every eye riveted on the brigade about to march down the aisle.

"Is there a Trooper Wellington here?" Uncle Brady yelled in his most authoritative tone. As a child, Wilder had been a little bit afraid of his uncle, but the older he'd gotten, the more he realized Uncle Brady was only tough when he had to be.

"Yes, sir," a man called.

Wilder swung his attention up a couple of rows and across the aisle, where Trooper's father stood. The rest of Trooper's family had stayed seated, which only made the older man more obvious.

"Right here, Chief." He pointed to his son, who got to his feet in a seemingly reluctant, sheepish way.

"I didn't do anything wrong," Trooper called, his shoulders coming up and turning boxy.

All eyes flew back to Wilder's uncle, including his. Uncle Brady stood there unyielding, every officer behind him wearing a mighty frown.

"Being totally in love with your daughter isn't a crime," Trooper yelled next, and Wilder relaxed, realizing what this was. "I asked you for her hand in marriage and everything."

One of Uncle Brady's deputies stepped forward, put his own

white-gloved hand on Brady's shoulder, and leaned in to say something. Uncle Brady's frown only deepened.

"I don't know—" he yelled.

"I'm going to love her with everything I have until the day I die," Trooper said, moving out into the aisle. He took a microphone from someone, and his voice reverberated through the ballroom as he continued with, "I'm going to take good care of her, sir. In hard times, and easy times, and all the time. I will protect her, and I will support her, and I will do everything I can to be the man she deserves."

He stood tall and proud at the end of the aisle, his gaze unwavering as he met his soon-to-be father-in-law's gaze.

"What is the hold-up here?" Aunt Ida came bustling through the line of officers. "Brady, what are you doing?" She reached her husband and mock-glared up at him. "We have a whole line of people waiting."

She leaned in closer, but she was clearly miked, because Wilder could hear every word she said loud and clear, though she whispered, "Did you forget the first step? Remember, you lead with your right—"

"I didn't forget the step," he hissed back at her.

"This young man loves our daughter," she said. "And we have hungry people here. I don't think you know what you'll be dealing with if you make Bear wait a moment past six to eat."

Laughter filled the hall, and Wilder sought out his uncle Bear. He grinned and grinned, and even started to clap.

Then, the loudest music Wilder had ever heard filled the hall, and he actually ducked as if the roof might be coming down. He grabbed onto Savannah and moved toward Sequoia too.

Then the beat dropped, and reality caught up to his reflexes. His gaze flew to the doors where the officers had gathered, and to his great astonishment, Uncle Brady took the first step with his right foot.

He did a double-bounce there, then took another step forward. On his next step, the two officers flanking him moved forward with him. By the fourth measure, they'd added hand and arm motions, and the crowd whooped and cheered as every man in the Three Rivers Police Department danced their way down the aisle.

They all hugged Trooper, and when he finally stood at the altar alone, he wore a badge someone had pinned to his tuxedo.

"Him is a policeman now too, Mister Wilder."

Wilder scooped Sequoia into his arms. "Yeah, sweetie, he's going to the Police Academy right now. He'll be done in a few months."

And then Trooper really would be a police officer, just like Uncle Brady.

The ladies came down the aisle next, the music calming to something less nightclub and more frilly, and Judy had wanted every one of her female cousins in the wedding party. They came alone, so Judy hadn't had to pair them up with an escort, and Wilder took Savannah's hand in his free one while he watched the people he loved best walk down the aisle.

When they reached Trooper, they each gave him a flower, and when they all finally finished, he held an assembled bouquet that Aunt Etta quickly swept a ribbon around to hold it in place.

The wedding march started then, with an extra beat or two thrown in to jazz it up. Judy and her twin brother Johnny appeared in the double-wide doorway, and he looked at her, and she beamed up at him.

As long as Wilder had known her, Judy had loved girly things. Big ballgowns, and makeup, and false eyelashes. She loved getting her hair and nails done, and she loved taking vintage clothes and making them into new pieces.

He should've expected her dress to fit her personality, because it did. She wore a stunning gown with a fitted bodice gleaming with gems, and a skirt that ballooned out at her hips and had to be at least six feet across.

"Wow," Savannah breathed.

"She is so pretty," Gal said right out loud. "Momma, I want a dress like that."

"Shh, baby," Momma whispered, and she bent to pick up Gal. "Look, you can see better now, but just whisper."

The dress shimmered the way gasoline did in sunlight, and when Johnny offered his sister his arm, she tucked her hand in the crook of his elbow, and they finally stepped into the room.

The song changed again, the march becoming even more like a rock song. Judy and Johnny took a few more steps, definitely adding more bounce to their feet—and their shoulders.

Then Judy came to a complete stop. She waved both hands above her head, and yelled, "Stop the music."

It came to a grinding halt, that awful record-scratching noise screeching through the ballroom.

"I think I'm a little over-dressed for this party." She grinned around at everyone, and while Wilder had known his cousin to be theatrical, this wedding sure wasn't what he'd expected.

She reached down and grabbed her burgeoning ballgown skirt on both sides—and pulled.

A gasp flew from Wilder's throat, along with everyone else's. Fine, some people actually yelped as Judy's dress ripped—right—in—half.

She flung the skirt aside and cocked one hip as Johnny kicked the rest of the now-mangled dress out of the way. "Better?"

Judy now wore a slinky skirt made of pure silver, the kind that shone in the sunlight and changed colors on a fish's scales. "I mean, this is more of the party vibe I wanted this wedding to be."

Johnny reached up and took off his tie, flinging it away too. "So can I unbutton a couple of these? Because holy horses and figs, it's hot in here."

They grinned at one another, and then Johnny—with a couple of his shirt buttons undone—and Judy in her new, sleek wedding-slash-party-dress linked arms and walked the rest of the way to Trooper.

He laughed with every step she took, and Johnny took something from his father before passing Judy to her almost-husband.

Wilder basked in the glow that reached all the way back to the second row, even over on the side, that emanated from Judy gazing up at Trooper.

Then Johnny jumped at least four feet straight up into the air, shrieked, and landed in a crouch. He straightened, put on a pair of sunglasses, and yelled, "It's time to say I-do!"

The crowd responded to the energy that the police officers had first brought, then from the bride and her brother jiving down the aisle. Wilder laughed right out loud, and he loved the way Savannah snuggled into his side, both of her hands wrapped around his forearm.

"This is the best wedding I've ever been to," she said.

"We're fun sometimes," he said as the congregation started to settle down and sit.

"Yeah, but I don't want a wedding like this," she said.

Wilder swung his attention to his fiancée, his smile fading. "No, I know. We're doing simple, farm-themed, with ducks as ring-bearers."

"And you're okay with that?" She actually wore worry in her expression, which only made Wilder want to burst out laughing again.

"Savvy, I would go anywhere and do anything to have you say 'I do.' Whatever you want is fine with me." He ducked his head as his uncle Judge started to speak.

"Okay?" he whispered.

"Yeah, okay," she whispered back, and then Wilder tuned into his uncle, because he always heard good things when a Glover got married.

14

Ty had had a taste of celebrity in his life. He'd accepted awards in the past and sat at signing tables to scrawl his own name over his scowling picture for fans. He had three championship belt buckles—two in bull riding and one in team roping—and yet he'd never felt like as big of a celebrity as he did with Winnie on his arm.

She'd curled her hair, and she wore more makeup than Ty had ever seen her wear before. She'd painted her lips bright red to match her jumpsuit, and she wore shiny, sleek white heels and great big enamel-coated hoops in her ears. Every person who looked at her smiled, and that meant their positive energy hit Ty as well.

"Well," she said, still clapping as Judy and Trooper ran down the aisle, hand in hand. "That was incredible."

"The Glovers know how to throw a party," Ty yelled, and he put his fingers in his mouth and whistled. Several moments later, the cheering and clapping subsided, and the same cool female voice who had told them to take their seats came over the public address system in the building.

"Due to the weather, we will be unable to mingle in the gardens while we change over the facilities for dinner. If you'll please exit the ballroom, we have set up a few seats and bar tables with snacks and drinks in our Regency Room, located directly across the foyer."

Ty took Winnie's hand and led her down the row, stepping just in front of JJ. When they reached the end of the aisle and the space opened up, he said, "Hey, Ty, introduce me to your girl."

Ty slowed and stepped out of the way. "Yeah, sure," he said, though his heartbeat thrummed like tiny bird wings in his neck. "This is Winnie Landry. We just started seeing each other last week."

"Oh, so it's *really* new," JJ said, wearing a smile that could light the city.

"Yeah." Ty said, "Winnie, this is JJ Walker. He runs Seven Sons Ranch just about fifteen or twenty minutes south of town. You've probably passed it on your way out to Signs for Success."

"If you take the south highway, at least," JJ said with a genuine smile. "You turn left at the junction right past Seven Sons."

"Yeah," Winnie said, recognition brightening her face. "Yes, I have seen the signs. You guys have a lot of stars on your fences."

"Yeah—seven of them," JJ said with a laugh. "My daddy has six brothers, so there are seven sons."

"Ah, got it," Winnie said. She reached out and tickled baby Jade in JJ's arms. "What's your baby's name?"

"Jade," JJ said, smiling down at the little girl. "This is my wife, Ruby." He drew her closer to his side, and the three of them shone with what Ty could only describe as joy. J-O-Y all day long, everywhere.

"Oh, like the gems," Winnie said. "She is just the most beautiful baby I've ever seen."

JJ and Ruby did have a gorgeous baby, as they both came with dark features, though Ruby's were a little bit lighter in her hazel eyes and her auburn hair.

"What do you do, Winnie?" Ruby asked.

Winnie's smile filled the hall. "I'm a physical therapist," she said. "I work at the Premier Family Clinic in what Ty has informed me is

New Downtown. I've only been in town for about seven months." She beamed over to him and linked her arm through his.

Ty saw the moment that JJ and Ruby realized what was going on. But thankfully, neither of them raised their eyebrows and said, *So you started dating your physical therapist?* as if he'd done something wrong.

"You should've seen JJ and Ruby's wedding," Ty said, half his mouth lifting up on the side. "I wasn't here for it, but it's still talked about around town."

"Oh, it is not," Ruby said with an added eyeroll, as if her wedding hadn't been the premier event of the year a couple of summers ago.

JJ looked at her and then over to Ty. "Is it really?"

"It was featured in *Texas Country Living,*" Ty said to them, then he turned his attention to his lovely Winnie. "She wore a *red* wedding dress, sweetheart. You'd have loved it."

"I clearly like red," Winnie said with a laugh and swish of her wide pantlegs. "That sounds amazing."

"I'll find the article for you," Ty said, just as Finn Ackerman joined them.

"Hey, fellas," he said, "I just wanted to say hi. Edith took the boys out to get a little snack, and I saw you standing here."

"This is Finn," Ty said. "He runs our small ranch owners' group at the IFA." He nodded to Winnie. "This is Winnie Landry, Finny. We just started dating."

"Winnie Landry," Finn said, cocking his head slightly. "Yes, I think my wife said she knows you?"

"Oh? Who's your wife?" she asked.

"Edith Baxter," Ty and Finn said together.

"*Ohhh,* she's the author," Winnie said, and she bounced on the balls of her feet slightly. "When I moved here and I found out she lived here, I sent her an email."

"Yep, that's it," Finn said.

"You read Edith's books?" Ty asked. "Aren't they for kids?"

"They're *middle grade* novels," Winnie said with a hint of haughtiness in her voice, though it was hard to hear with the mass of wedding guests flowing past them.

"Link, Misty." Finn waved at the couple moving by. "Come meet Winnie."

"Really, Finn?" Ty asked.

His friend turned and looked at him. "What? They'll want to meet her."

"Yeah, *everyone* wants to meet her," Ty said.

Winnie's hand in the crook of his elbow tightened and he met her eye. The silent conversation they then had started with Winnie saying, *It's fine. I want to meet your friends. Remember?*

Ty ducked his head in acquiescence and then lifted it when Link said, "Howdy. I'm Lincoln Glover."

"Yep, he's Lincoln Glover," Ty said. "He's co-foreman with Wilder—who's around here somewhere—and they run Shiloh Ridge together, with a couple other Glovers too."

"Yeah, Gun, and Rock, and Smiles—when he comes home," Link said. "We have a couple of uncles still doing a few things."

"Shiloh Ridge is just a little bit further south than my place," JJ said.

"Mm, everyone knows Shiloh Ridge," Winnie said. "My brother wanted to get a job there about a decade ago."

"Oh, did he come?" Link asked, his eyes bright with hope.

"No. He ended up getting somewhere up in Oklahoma, where we're from," she said. "But trust me, *everyone* knows Shiloh Ridge."

Link chuckled. "I don't know if that's a good thing or a bad thing."

"Oh, it's a good thing and you know it," Ty said. "They're like a billion-dollar ranch or something."

"It's not quite a billion with a B," Link said, and Misty scoffed.

Ty gestured to her and said, "See? She knows. This is Link's wife, Misty. They've got three kids—a couple of boys—and that's their youngest, Meadow."

"Wow, you guys make the cutest babies ever," Winnie said. She looked from Jade to the baby in Misty's arms. "Is there something in the water here in Three Rivers?"

Everyone smiled, and Finn shook his head. "Mine are monsters most of the time, but we love 'em."

"Finn's got three boys," Ty said. "And—oh, what do you know? Here's Finn's cousin, Henry." Ty grinned and leaned closer to Winnie. "They're my bosses at Lone Star, so try to act like I'm really amazing."

"You *are* really amazing," Angel said.

He smiled at her. "This is Angel Marshall and her husband, Henry," Ty said. "They own and operate Lone Star—that big boarding stable I work at out near Amarillo."

"Sure, sure," Winnie said. "Ty loves his job there. I think he talks more to horses than he does people." She giggled, and everyone in their little huddle joined her.

A hint of heat climbed into Ty's face. "Hey, horses don't talk back," he said. "And I don't have to worry about offending them."

"They are good listeners," Henry said, stepping in to shake Winnie's hand. "It sure is great to meet you, ma'am."

"How do you get your hair to hold that curl?" Angel asked. "Mine refuses to do it no matter what."

"My hair is a little bit naturally curly," Winnie said. "But I have this really great dry spray that I put in before I curl it. I'll show you."

"That would be great," Angel said. She carried their daughter on her hip, and the little girl fussed. She passed her to Henry and took Wrangler's hand in hers. "Well, we promised the kids snacks, and they know how to organize a coup if we don't follow through. It was lovely to meet you, Winnie. Good to see you, Ty."

Henry bumped his fist, and the two of them left with their kids.

"I'm going to take the kids to get treats too," Misty said, and she herded their boys toward the exit.

Ty stood there with Link, JJ and Ruby, and Finn, not surprised at all when Dawson Rhinehart joined them.

"This is Dawson," he said dutifully. "Dawson, this is my new girl-friend, Winnie."

"Oh-ho, you're calling her a girlfriend?" Dawson grinned. "I was not expecting that."

"She's handling questions a lot better than I am," Ty said.

"Well, you answered the only one I had." Dawson reached out and shook Winnie's hand. "It's great to meet you. I think you work at the physical therapy clinic?"

"Yeah," Winnie said.

"Yeah, Libby was talking about you in one of our meetings," Dawson said.

"Oh, sure," Winnie said. "Libby's great. She doesn't come anymore, because I'm pretty amazing at my job." That caused a few people to chuckle as well, and Ty marveled at how well she met new people, how easily she could flow with conversations and names, how she didn't get riled up by anything.

"And," Dawson said, glancing around at everyone. "I'm going to send a reminder out, but Caroline wanted me to let you all know about Bronco's birthday next Saturday."

"I've got it on the calendar," Finn said.

"It's just at our place," Dawson said. "We're praying that it won't be snowing, but the ten-day forecast looks pretty good."

"Yeah, it's supposed to clear up again," Winnie said. She met Ty's eyes. "Is this a big birthday party?"

While the other cowboys continued to talk, he leaned in close. "His youngest is turning one," he said. "Dawson and his older brother, Duke, run the Rhinehart Ranch, which borders Shiloh Ridge on the south. It's quite the drive, but I was planning on going."

"And I don't work weekends."

He grinned at her. "Well, then I guess *we're* planning on going."

In a pause in the conversation, he said, "I'm gonna go get a soda pop. I heard there were specialty drinks designed by Trooper and Judy. All this talking has me parched."

Finn laughed again. "Yeah, all right. Let's go get drinks."

Ty had only taken one step when he heard, "Tyson Joseph," in his mother's voice.

"Oh, boy," JJ said. "That's your mother. I'll go get you a drink." He herded away the other cowboys while Ty turned toward his mother, taking Winnie with him. If he ever got out of this ballroom, it would be a miracle.

She usually wore jeans and a tank top, cowgirl boots and a hat, and her hair in a ponytail. But every week when they went to church, and any time she and Daddy went out on date nights, she let her hair down and it hung straight, just like Angel said hers did.

She'd brushed a little bit of makeup on her face, but not much, and she wore a floral print dress on a cream-colored background with a bright blue belt cinched around her waist. Daddy wore navy-blue slacks, a white shirt, and a brown leather jacket, as he knew how to dress up and be a picture-perfect cowboy, just like Ty.

They'd both ridden in the rodeo, and a flash of love and gratitude filled Ty in the couple of seconds that he took in his parents and Daddy settled at Momma's side.

"That was a great wedding, wasn't it?" Momma flicked her gaze over to Winnie and opened her mouth as if she'd say something more.

"Momma," Ty blurted out quickly. "This is Winona Landry." He omitted the part about her being his girlfriend, but Winnie stepped forward and slid her lips across his momma's cheek.

"It's so great to meet you, ma'am," she said. "Ty talks about you *constantly*."

"Does he now?" She gave Winnie's shoulders a quick squeeze, and they both stepped apart.

"And my daddy," Ty said. "Ethan. My momma's name is Brynn. They run the barrel racing training facility out at Three Rivers Ranch."

"Is that the one where we're going to go horseback riding?" Winnie asked.

"No, that's Courage Reins," he said.

They had talked about his childhood and how much time he'd

spent out at Three Rivers working, cleaning stalls—not only for the ranch but for his momma and Pete Marshall, who owned Courage Reins. He told her he saw a therapist there, in conjunction with the work he did with the horses as part of their equine therapy unit.

Winnie had told him that she thought everyone should see a therapist, and Ty really liked that she never judged him in anything he did. He'd fallen flat on his face a couple of times in front of her, and she never made a big deal out of walking on his right side.

He'd enrolled in the beginning sign language classes, because he would love to be able to talk with Winnie silently, and he knew he wasn't going to regain his hearing in his lifetime. For all the flaws Ty felt he had, Winnie didn't seem to see any of them.

"It's great to meet you," Daddy said, and he reached forward. "Is this more of a casual thing?"

"Oh, no, sir," Winnie said. "Ty's been telling everyone I'm his girlfriend." She beamed at him and then looked back at his parents. "And he's right. He's not really the type to do casual. Ty doesn't like to play games."

"I have never said those words out loud," he said.

Winnie blinked at him. "You're the one who said it wasn't casual."

"Well," he said. "*You're* the one always bringing up family games like I know all the rules."

Winnie put one hand on her hip and pushed it out in a way that made Ty's pulse bump in strange ways. "Didn't I send you a fashion show picture this morning?"

"Oh, this is fun," Daddy said, and he genuinely sounded like he was enjoying himself.

"Just be careful what pictures you're sending to each other," Momma said, and Ty's eyes flew to hers.

"You have got to be kidding me," he said.

"Just because you're a grown man doesn't mean you can't get yourself into trouble." She smiled at Winnie. "You are lovely, and I'll stop embarrassing my son now."

"You're not embarrassing me," Ty said. He dropped his hand to Winnie's and captured hers in his. "Winnie has a pretty good idea of how I am."

She nodded emphatically, her smile wide, her teeth so white against her bright red lipstick.

"Here's your drink," JJ said, and he handed Ty a fizzy, bright orange drink with a maraschino cherry floating on top. "Winnie, I went ahead and got you the other one. This one's Judy's. It's a Shirley Temple, with a citrus twist."

"It's nonalcoholic, right?" Winnie said. "I don't drink."

"It's nonalcoholic," JJ said. "The Glovers have too many kids to be serving alcohol."

"Okay, great," Winnie said, and she took the pink drink and lifted the straw to her lips. "Ooh, this is good," she said after she'd taken a sip. "You'll like it." She extended the drink toward Ty. "You love ginger ale."

"I do." He fumbled, but managed to get his lips around her straw and take a drink. He felt like a complete fool with his momma and daddy watching, as this felt like an intimate moment that only he and Winnie should be sharing.

He expected the cherry to come with his ginger ale, as that made a Shirley Temple, but he also got a hint of something sour at the end. "That's good," he said. "What is that?"

"I think it's grapefruit." Winnie took another drink. "What's yours?"

JJ had already left, and Ty tried to remember what Trooper's drink had been. "I think it's blood orange and mango," he said. "With orange juice and Sprite."

"It's a lot of citrus," Momma said.

Ty took a sip and his mouth puckered. "Yeah, this is sour—just what I like."

He offered the drink to Winnie, and she took a sip too. "Yes, I can see why you would like that."

Ty looked back to his parents, and Daddy now wore slightly

narrowed eyes. Momma's were as big as moons, and they kept moving between him and Winnie, him and Winnie, him and Winnie.

"How long you two been going out?" Daddy asked.

"Our first date was just one week ago, sir," Winnie said.

"But she's your physical therapist, right?" Daddy asked.

"Dad," Tyson said, his tone laced with warning.

Momma laced her arm through his. "It's clear that they've known each other for a while. Come on, Ethan-baby, let's go get ourselves a drink too—since no one seems to be sharing with *us*." She gave Ty a raised-eyebrow-brilliant-smile look, and reached out and grabbed onto Winnie's forearm as she passed. "It really is great to meet you, Winnie. I hope Ty will bring you around to some of our family dinners."

"I'm sure he will, ma'am," Winnie said, and she turned her head and watched as Momma and Daddy made their exit.

The breath whooshed out of Ty's lungs, and he raised his drink and took another long sip, the sourness notwithstanding. "Well, there you have it," he said. "You've met a bunch of my friends, and my parents."

Winnie swallowed another sip of her drink. "And neither one of us died."

"Yet," Ty muttered, which only made Winnie scoff and shake her head as she giggled.

The crew who would be setting up the tables and chairs for the dinner started entering the ballroom, and Ty took that as their cue to leave. As he walked with Winnie through the double doors and out into the foyer, he tilted his head toward her.

"So will you dance with me at this wedding?" he asked. "Or is all dancing off-limits, all the time?"

Winnie cozied up next to him, pressing in tight to his right side and sending fire through every cell in his body when she said in a flirty tone that told him he would have to constantly remind himself that they were not alone while holding Winnie in his arms on the dance floor, "I'll dance with you tonight, cowboy."

15

Dawson Rhinehart stood on his back porch, surveying the yard with a critical eye. The January sun beat down with surprising warmth, a welcome reprieve after weeks of bitter cold and biting wind that had kept everyone hunkered down and watching the sky for a break. The temperature had climbed into the mid-sixties, and while Dawson knew better than to trust Panhandle weather, he was grateful for the break.

"The tables look good, baby. Thank you." Caroline stepped beside him with Bronco—the star of today's show—balanced on her hip. Their youngest, who turned one today, wore a ridiculous cowboy hat that kept sliding down over his eyes, and he kept pushing it back up with chubby fingers, giggling every time.

"Do you think we have enough seating?" Dawson asked, counting the mismatched collection of folding tables and chairs they'd borrowed from his parents, Zona and Duke, or Shiloh Ridge.

"We never do." Caroline grinned at him and took the cowboy hat from Bronco. "But we'll be fine. The house will be open too."

"Like a revolving door," Dawson muttered, though he loved having his friends and family over to his house. He took the cowboy hat from his wife and placed it just-so on his son's head. "There you go, buddy."

"Da-da-dad," Bronco babbled, then lunged forward and grabbed a fistful of Dawson's shirt.

With adrenaline pumping through him, he quickly grabbed onto his son. With Bronco settled securely in his arms, Dawson kissed the top of his son's head, breathing in that sweet baby smell mixed with the outdoor air.

"Well, I'm going to start getting out the sandwich stuff," Caroline said. "April just texted me that she's on the way." She nudged Dawson with her hip. "And she's bringing her boyfriend, and she wants you to be nice."

Dawson scoffed. "I'm always nice. Did you tell her that?"

"I tried," Caroline said with a grin as she backed up. "She really wants you to like Louis."

"I'm not going to like anyone who goes out with her," he said. "She's still ten years old in my mind and shouldn't even have a boyfriend."

Caroline giggled as she went back into the house, and Bronco wiggled to get down. Dawson set him on his feet and secured his hand in his boy's, then turned to follow his wife, albeit at a much slower pace.

The truth was, April had turned twenty-one a few months ago, and she could date anyone she wanted. Heck, Dawson knew girls who'd gotten married before age twenty-one, and his heart did a backward somersault.

She and Shiloh lived in the old cabin he and Brandon had once shared, and Duke and Zona had started talking about building another cabin for their boys. None of their kids wanted to leave the Rhinehart Ranch, and right now, their oldest son, Dwayne, lived with Dawson's parents.

His daddy had gotten really advanced in his age, and he barely left the house anymore.

Dawson helped Bronco over the lip and into the house, where the little boy collapsed back to his hands and knees and crawled rapidly toward the kitchen.

"I'm going to go pick up my momma and daddy," he said.

"Okay," Caroline said, and Dawson pressed his lips to his wife's cheek before he left the house and got behind the wheel of his truck.

"Thank You, Lord, for sparing my father as long as You have." His chest turned tight, like someone had wrapped a thick rubber band around him and kept twisting and twisting.

"But it'll be okay—we'll all be okay—if You take him home." He pulled up to his parents' house and found Dwayne steadying his grandfather as they left the house.

Dawson swung out of the truck, calling, "Hey, you two."

"Hey, Uncle Daws." Dwayne grinned at him, but he didn't let go of his grandpa's arm.

Dawson jogged down the sidewalk and shored up his father on his other side. "I was comin', Daddy."

"I know," he said, his voice low and cracked like an old cement driveway. "It just takes me a minute to get moving, and I didn't want you to be waitin'."

Dawson kept a steady hand on his father's forearm. "Is Momma coming?"

"My mom is coming to get her," Dwayne said. "She has a few laundry baskets of chips."

Dawson's eyebrows went up, but he didn't say anything. He'd learned long ago to let his sister-in-law, his mother, and his wife plan the parties however they wanted to. He knew they wouldn't run out of food, and he appreciated all the work they did to celebrate him, his children, this ranch, and everyone he loved.

"Let me get the steps, Daddy."

"I can do it," his father said.

But he couldn't, and Dawson met Dwayne's eye, then released his father and hurried ahead of them to get the single step out of the back of the truck. It made getting up and into the pickup truck easier by lowering the step by half.

He opened the passenger door and positioned the step just as his daddy's boots met the gravel he'd parked on.

"There you go, Grandpa," Dwayne said. "He's already got it ready for you, and you won't have to trip the way I always do."

Daddy said nothing, but he did get a good hold on the door handle with one hand and the frame of the truck with the other before lifting his leg. He only had to lift it about six inches, which he did just fine. Another step to the runner, then another into the truck, and his daddy groaned as he finally collapsed into the seat.

"There you go," Dawson said, and he pulled the step back and let Dwayne close the door.

"I tried to tell 'im you were almost here," Dwayne said.

He gave his nephew a smile. "Well, my daddy is the most stubborn man you'll ever meet."

Dwayne grinned at him. "Must be where my daddy gets it from."

Dawson laughed, because Duke was surlier than him, and yes, extremely stubborn. He rounded the truck while Dwayne climbed in the backseat, and together, the three of them made the trip back to Dawson's house, only about seven minutes down the road and still on the family ranch.

A few more trucks had arrived, but they'd left his driveway open for him. Thankfully. Dawson didn't even want to think about what his father would say if they hadn't. He pulled up behind Caroline's minivan, and he felt like a superhero who could move faster than the speed of sound, because he managed to retrieve the step and put it in place before his father was ready to get out.

"We're just in the backyard, Daddy," Dawson said. "Or Caroline will have a place for you inside."

"Ah, the sun is out today," he said. "I want to sit outside."

Dawson nodded to Dwayne, who detoured up the front sidewalk, took the steps to the porch two at a time, and disappeared into the house through the front door. Dawson stayed with his father, moving even slower than he did with his one-year-old who'd just taken his first step last week.

But they finally made it through the garage and out the back door, which led straight out to the yard. If Daddy wanted to go up on the deck, he'd have to navigate stairs, but by the time Dawson got him over the cobblestone path and past the deck to the yard, he found Dwayne waiting by the zero-gravity chair next to Daddy's favorite flowerbed.

"Right there, Daddy," Dawson said, the sound of laughter ringing out from the house. He should be inside to greet his friends, but he kept the snail's pace with his father, balancing him as he stepped over the bar at the bottom of the chair and sank into it.

He groaned all over again, and Dwayne bent to help him get his chair reclined. "I'll go get you something to eat, Grandpa."

"Thank you, Dwayne." Daddy patted his hand. "You're a good boy."

Dwayne led the way up the steps and across the deck to the back sliding door, and Dawson simply followed him. Inside, he found April had arrived with her boyfriend, and they stood in the kitchen helping Caroline lay out all the sandwich fixings.

The other truck that had been outside belonged to Link Glover, and Dawson smiled at his best friend—at least the one who he didn't share any DNA with.

"Howdy, Lincoln." Dawson pulled the taller man into a quick one-armed hug. "No wife and kids?"

"They're here," Link said. "Caroline said you guys had some snakes out by the back fence, and my boys think snakes are pets." He rolled his eyes good-naturedly. "I put Meadow down for her nap on your bed."

"Howdy-ho," someone called. "We're walkin' in."

The clamoring of little-girl voices filled the air, and Dawson didn't have to look to know Wilder, Savannah, and her twins had just arrived.

"Here we go," April said dryly. "Once the Glovers start arriving, it's like opening the floodgates." She flashed a smile at Dawson.

"Uncle Dawson, do you remember Louis? He came to our family New Year's Eve-Eve party."

"Of course I do." Dawson put a smile on his face. "It's good to see you again, Louis."

"Thank you, sir," he said, and he focused on laying out the baby carrots just-so on the veggie tray before looking up. He smiled back at Dawson, who could admit he liked the young man. Louis Fairchild had a good family from here in Three Rivers—his daddy ran a pharmacy on Main Street downtown and his mother showed huskies in dog tournaments around the state.

She also worked with the pet adoption agency in town, and Dawson had known his family for years. Louis seemed to be the sunshiney part of him and April, who still got hot around the collar pretty quickly, though she'd learned how to channel her spirit and energy in the right direction.

And how to hold her tongue.

"So, what's goin' on with you two?" he asked, reaching for a length of celery. "Babes, can you get me the peanut butter?"

"Nope," Caroline said. "If I get out the peanut butter, then everyone wants it, and it's a veggie tray, Daws." She gave him a smile, because they'd had this conversation before.

"It's my house," he said.

"And my party." His wife passed a dripping container of strawberries to April, who looked at her and then Dawson, her eyes wide.

He looked down at the celery. "Well, I don't want this if I can't have peanut butter."

"Give it here," April said, and she practically snatched the vegetable stick from him. "I don't get why cowboys can't eat green things."

"I was going to eat it," he said, glancing at Louis in time to see him grinning. "Yeah, this is really funny, right?"

Louis burst out laughing then, and April gave him such a fond smile that Dawson really wanted his question answered.

"Are you two getting pretty serious then?" he asked. April's smile dried right up, but Louis simply grinned for both of them.

"Yes, sir," he said, giving April back the fondness she'd bestowed upon him. "I really like Miss Rhinehart here, and if she'd just stop putting me off, I'd probably have a diamond on her finger already."

"Louis," she said, her voice dark. "Don't tell him that."

"Why not? It's the truth."

"Because then he'll tell my daddy, and the whole world will be flipped inside out." April threw Dawson a look that pleaded with him not to say anything.

"You've asked her to marry you?" Dawson asked.

"And you said no?" Caroline chimed in perfectly, as if they'd rehearsed it though they hadn't.

"Yes," both April and Louis said together. April arranged the last of the berries around the fruit dip, which was one of Dawson's favorite things. Cream cheese with pineapple chunks and juice, a touch of sugar, and mandarin orange juice. Oh, and Caroline threw in a packet of Truly Lime too, and Dawson could drink the stuff, no fruit needed.

"We've only been dating for six months, and I told him I wasn't going to get engaged for at least a year."

Dawson gaped at his niece. "Sometimes you just fall in love faster," he said.

"And sometimes, you want to make sure that the other person knows what they're getting into." She shot him a look with slightly narrowed eyes.

"April, you're my favorite person on the planet," he said, his voice low but powerful.

"Yeah, I know, Uncle Daws. But that's because you're a black cat who's been rained on all day too."

Caroline burst out laughing while Dawson stood there blinking. Louis snickered with her, and Dawson marveled at everything in life in that moment.

"Well, I think you're a delight," Louis said. He swept a kiss along April's hairline. "Now, where does this veggie tray go?"

"Out on the deck, please," Caroline said, still laughing a little bit.

Once Louis had left, Dawson leaned over the peninsula a little bit. "But you really like him too, right, bug?"

She nodded, and oh, a sniffle followed.

"Let's do breakfast this week," Dawson said. April nodded again, kept her head down, and picked up the fruit tray.

"I'll take this outside too, Aunt Caroline."

"Okay, sweets." She watched April go, as did Dawson, and then he looked at his wife. "You made her cry."

"*I* made her cry?" Dawson shook his head. "That girl makes herself cry." He scoffed and watched as April stepped out onto the deck. "She's in love with him and terrified about it."

"Who's in love with whom?"

Dawson whipped his attention to the other side of the kitchen, where none other than April's mother now stood. "No one," he said to Zona. "Wilder and Savannah."

Zona scoffed and continued into the house with the laundry basket of rolls she'd brought, Momma right behind her with one overflowing with bags of chips. "Here's the bread, Caroline."

"Thank you so much, Zona."

"All right, all right, all right!"

Dawson grinned as his younger brother's voice filled the house.

"Your favorite brother-slash-uncle-slash-cowboy is here!" He appeared in the mouth of the hallway that led from the front of the house, his wife's hand in his.

"Brandon," Momma said. "You're yelling indoors."

He grinned at her and wrapped her in a one-armed hug. "It's a party, Momma, and we made it off the homestead, and Lenore isn't sick today." He beamed around at everyone in the house. "So I'm celebrating a lot more than my one-year-old nephew."

Dawson went around the counter and hugged his brother and

sister-in-law. "Congratulations," he said. "Caroline said you're due in July?"

"The very last day," Lenore said, and she did wear some extra lines around her eyes. Dawson stopped everything right then and there and said a quick prayer that she'd get the rest she needed, so she could continue to be healthy and could carry her baby to term.

"Dawson, we need a couple of towels out here," Louis called, and Dawson found himself getting whiplashed back toward the sliding glass door.

"Towels?"

"Here." Caroline threw him some, but Dawson fumbled them and sent them to the floor. He bent to pick them up as someone else came in the front door, and the very distinct sound of claws on his hardwood met his ears. That meant Mitch and his hearing dogs had arrived.

Dawson left Caroline and the others to greet him and Lacy, and he went out onto the back deck. More cowboys and their families had arrived while he'd been inside, as he found Finn and his youngest son standing with Colt and his little boy. They chatted while Edith walked across the backyard to where Misty had a whole crowd of children around her.

Gal, Sequoia, her own sons Diesel and Dallas, all of Ollie's kids except his youngest, Sari, and even Wrangler. Angel and Savannah were out there too, and Dawson supposed he should be glad for a nest of snakes if it would keep people entertained.

"We just had a ranch dressing mishap," Louis said, and he took the towels from Dawson. "I got it."

"Thanks," he said, catching sight of another arrival over the railing of the deck. Ty and Winnie had just arrived, and he paused at the end of the cobblestones, a frown between his eyes.

"You can come in the house too," Dawson said, heading over to the railing to talk to them. "There are tables and chairs out here, but the house is open, and Caroline's almost ready with the sandwich bar."

Ty looked up and tipped his cowboy hat to Dawson. "Thanks," he said. Then he nodded for Winnie to go back the way they'd come, and Dawson simply watched as Ty limped over the uneven surface.

The moment Ty and Winnie went back into the garage, Conrad and Glory Rose came out. She carried their baby, who was only five weeks old now, in a big, puffy blanket.

Dawson left the deck so he could mingle with those who'd come while he'd been begging for peanut butter in his own house. "Hey, you guys." He hugged Conrad and swept a kiss along Glory's cheek. "How's Chance doing?"

"So much better with his new formula," Glory Rose said, beaming down at her baby. "Caroline said she'd have a playpen for me?"

"Sure, inside," Dawson said. "But good luck putting him in there."

"What do you mean?" Glory Rose looked at him blankly.

"I mean, my momma is in there, and so is Arizona. They're not going to let a newborn baby languish in a playpen." He chuckled. "My momma would love to hold him."

Glory Rose's concern dissolved into a smile. "Sounds good to me." She looked at Conrad and added, "I'm going to run him inside. It's still a little windy."

"Yep." Conrad kept scanning the backyard as his wife left. "Have you seen Sari? She came with JJ and Ruby."

"Yeah, she's out with the snakes," Dawson said, indicating the large pod of women and children against his back fence.

"The snakes?" Conrad looked at Dawson with concern.

"I guess I've got some out there," he said. "Misty's boys love snakes."

"Yeah, I remember loving them too." He grinned and then yawned. "Tell me I'm going to get more than four hours of sleep at some point." He started across the grass and then up the steps, and Dawson went with him.

"Yeah, you will," Dawson said. "They make up for it by being adorable."

Conrad nodded, his eyes crinkling with happiness. "He is pretty adorable."

Ty came out onto the deck, a look of relief in his eyes. "Yeah, we can sit out here," he said. "Look; Dawson's got a heater."

"Yeah," he said. "And it's on the lowest setting, so if it gets colder, you can turn it up." He grinned at Ty, and then Winnie. "Thanks for coming, you guys. I know it's kind of ridiculous, but Bronco is our last and he'll only turn one once."

At least that was what Caroline had told him when she'd proposed this idea of having a huge shindig for Bronco's first birthday. If everyone did this for their children, they'd be going to parties every other day.

"I love a good party," Winnie said.

"Yeah, she does," Ty deadpanned, and Dawson saw two more opposites standing in front of him. Hey, he and Caroline had made it work so far, and so did plenty of other people.

Winnie wore bright purple pants with a black plaid woven through them, and a white sweater. She carried a wrapped present that had construction trucks all over it. "Caroline said the present table was out here." She glanced around. "But I don't see it."

"It's at the bottom of the steps," Dawson said, reaching for it. "I can take it. You didn't have to bring anything."

"Coming through," Duke called, and the three of them made way for him. He carried an overflowing laundry basket of gifts, all of which had been bagged or wrapped in blue paper of some kind.

"What is happening?" Dawson asked.

"My wife and our mother," Duke grumped at him. "I have another basket like this in my truck."

"You're kidding."

"I can assure you, I'm not."

Ty chuckled, and Dawson swung his attention to him. "Aren't families great?"

Dawson's disbelief and slight irritation melted away. "Yeah," he said, listening to a round of laughter from inside, and turning toward the excited calls of the children out by the fence.

Everywhere he looked, he found someone he loved—and someone who loved him.

"Yeah," he said. "Families are the best."

And things only got better when Caroline announced, "We're having cake first, everyone! Cake! First!" She moved by him and waved her arm to everyone out in the yard. "Come on up here and let's sing for Bronco, and then we'll eat."

16

Finley Ackerman adjusted the thermostat in the conference room at the IFA, grateful the heater would kick on before anyone arrived. Outside, the January wind howled against the windows, but at least the first major snowstorm of the season had finally passed through. He'd spent the better part of the last week checking on cattle at his family's much larger ranch, reinforcing his own fallen fences, and making sure every animal on his small hobby farm had shelter, food, and water.

Now, as he arranged chairs around the long table, the familiar anticipation that came with these monthly meetings ran rampant through him. The third Thursday had become sacred to him, this time when the small ranch owners around town gathered to share their struggles, celebrate their victories, and support one another through the unpredictability of working the land, raising a family, and dealing with aging parents, Mother Nature, and each other.

The door opened, and Alex pressed it all the way against the wall, toeing the doorstop into place with one boot. "Morning," he said. "I don't think people will have a problem getting in."

"No?" Finn set the last chair in place. "The plows have been out?"

"Yep. Salt and sand everywhere." Alex didn't sound too happy about that, but they both drove four-wheel-drive trucks, as they had to dig themselves off their farms when the snow came.

"We still might have a smaller crowd today." Finn gestured toward the coffee station. "But there's always coffee, and Link did text that he was still planning on bringing lunch."

He just wanted Jake Ahlstrom to come, and if the roads were bad, he might not make the drive from Three Rivers Ranch. Finn had grown up out there, and it was forty-five minutes to town on the brightest, sunniest day.

On a day that had snow blowing across the road? One might choose to stay home instead of coming to the ranch owners' meeting.

Jake had already been hesitant about it, because he didn't own a ranch. But working as the new head veterinarian on a massive cattle ranch qualified him to come, as they often talked about livestock and other animal care needs.

Finn had told him all of that, but he hadn't seemed convinced until Libby had said she'd love to see Jake at the meetings. "I have a hard time managing everything," Libby said. "I'm going to ask our general controller to come too, and if you were there, we'd have all three corners of our operation in-the-know."

Jake still hadn't committed to attending, but Finn had included him on the reminder text he'd sent to everyone for this morning's meeting.

"Oh, good, the door is open," someone said, and Finn looked up as Wilder started backing through the doorway. "We've got breakfast burritos for lunch."

He carried a heavy-duty tin foil tray with gloved hands, and Link came stutter-stepping in after him, holding the other end of the tray. From what Finn could see, individually wrapped burritos had been stacked inside, each of them in shiny aluminum foil.

"What is happening here?" Alex asked. "Who made these on a Thursday morning?"

"My momma, Aunt Sammy, and my aunt Holly Ann," Wilder said, sliding the end of the tray onto the conference room table. He grinned at them and then clapped his gloved hands together. "It's Clover's birthday, and we had a big thing at Shiloh Ridge."

"Thus, we have a lot of leftovers from Shiloh Ridge." Link grinned and picked up one of the burritos. "But these are amazing. The ones with an H on the outside are ham, and the B-ones are bacon. Otherwise, it's just egg and cheese."

"And those potato tots." Wilder picked up a burrito too. "Shoot. I left the condiments in the truck. I'll go grab them." He tossed his burrito back into the tray and headed out again.

"Hey, where you goin'?" Henry asked as Wilder nearly mowed him down in the doorway.

"Hot sauce," Wilder said by way of explanation, and Finn grinned at the answer. Then at his cousin's face as Henry entered the room.

"Hot sauce?"

"For the breakfast burritos." Finn indicated them with a gentle wave of his coffee cup.

"You Glovers always know how to feed people," Henry said. "Angel isn't coming today, but Trev's out in the store, getting some tubing for his sprinkling system."

"Great," Finn said with a grin. "I'm so glad he comes, Henry."

"Me too." Henry moved toward the coffee station. "You should see him and Janey together. They're the cutest."

JJ entered the room, and he carried an infant carrier with him. "I have Jade today," he said. "But she's asleep right now, so I'm just going to put her under the table." He moved the chair closest to the door, right near the end of the table, and set his daughter down, then pushed her further under with his foot.

He sighed and looked around the room, then at the tray of food. "What do we have here?"

"Breakfast burritos," Link said.

"Why do you have Jade?"

"Ruby's doing a consult today," JJ said, reaching for a foil-wrapped bundle. "Trap's not coming either. They're out at the Hensen place today. I guess someone is thinking of buying it, but it needs a lot of work."

"That it does," Ty said, and Finn switched his gaze to the dark-haired cowboy as he limped into the room. "I went and looked at it last week too."

"You did?" The surprise in Alex's voice matched that flowing through Finn. He'd even raised his eyebrows, same as Finn.

"Yeah." Ty sighed as he sank into the chair opposite of where JJ had just stowed Jade. "Man, I'm tired." He yawned and knocked his cowboy hat loose as he ran his hands through his hair.

"Yeah?" Henry teased. "Is your new girlfriend keeping you out too late?"

"I think it's actually this guy at the boarding stable where I work," Ty deadpanned. "Keeping me past my time to go home, because I'm so good with owners."

Henry belted out a laugh, and Finn raised a hand of hello to Paul —another cousin—and Libby—his sister—as they entered the room.

Mitch and Lacy arrived, as did Brandon and Lenore, and the room got louder as multiple conversations broke out. Trevor slipped in, and he took the seat next to JJ. Finn noted they all left that seat on the very end, at the head of the table, for him.

He heard Colt tell Brandon that he had branches down everywhere at the orchard, and Brandon and Lenore say they'd had some damage to their windbreak. Finn usually chose a topic before the meeting and texted it out, but he hadn't done that this time. Sometimes, he just needed to let the people here talk, and sometimes he didn't know what they needed to discuss until they were all in the room together.

Tate said they hadn't had any problems at the produce farm he and his wife ran for Wilde & Organic, and Finn was reminded that though they all lived in a small town, conditions weren't always the same from north to south, east to west.

He ended his chat with Alex and Wilder, who had returned with hot sauce, ketchup, and salsa, and started to move down to the head of the table.

"You just go on in," Conrad said, and Finn looked toward the door to find Jake Ahlstrom hovering there.

"Hey, hey," he said, maybe a little louder than he needed to. "You made it."

Jake nodded, looking slightly uncomfortable as he entered the room ahead of Conrad. "Yeah, I figured I'd give it a try." He looked around, his eyes finally coming back to Finn. "I know a lot of these people."

Finn chuckled and clapped Jake on the shoulder. "I knew you would. We'll do intros too." He took a couple more steps and whistled through his teeth. "Get your coffee and breakfast burritos, fellas. We're going to start in three minutes."

"Three minutes?" Dawson asked. "I swear I'm not that late."

Finn grinned at him. "Not late at all. You have three minutes." He did like to stick to a schedule, because they all had plenty to do, and no one liked meetings, even if they were with friends.

He looked around, doing a quick catalog of who'd come. Their crowd was not smaller today by any means, though he didn't see Gun or Rock Glover, and of course, Trap Walker was gone too.

"Your cousins aren't coming?" he asked Wilder as he sat down only a few paces away.

"They're on the way," he said. "You haven't checked your texts."

Finn automatically reached for his phone. Getting texts on the ranchers group string was his favorite thing. "No," he said. "Not for a while."

"We've got a mud problem at Shiloh Ridge," Wilder said. "They left about twenty minutes ago."

Finn nodded and left his phone in his pocket. "Okay, well, let's get started then."

Paul, Henry, Trevor, Libby, Jake, Alex, Brandon and Lenore, and himself made up the farmers and ranchers from the northern part of Three Rivers.

He mentally drove down the eastern highway, and he hit the apple orchards, the eastern edges of Seven Sons, and then *Signs for Success*. That put Colt, Mitch and Lacy, and JJ in that category, and Finn included Ty there too, because he lived in an apartment on that side of town and didn't have his own place. Yet.

Coming across the southern border, he could turn north and hit Conrad's hobby farm as well as the produce farm, or go south and end up at Shiloh Ridge or the Rhinehart Ranch. That put Link, Wilder, Gun, Rock, Dawson, and Tate in the southern cowboy group.

"We're waitin' on you," Alex said, and Finn realized the room had gone quiet.

"Right." He cleared his throat. "Let's do intros quickly, since we have someone new joining us today. If you have announcements or prayer requests, include them in that."

Finn touched his chest. "I'm Finley Ackerman. I run a small ranch-slash-farm that borders Three Rivers Ranch on the south with my wife, Edith, and our three boys." He grinned around at his friends, his brothers. "Edee has started talking like she might want another baby, and I'd love it if you could get the Lord to sway her differently."

He chuckled and nodded to JJ. They went around the table, each of them saying who they were, what ranch or farm they ran, and anything else they wanted the group to know.

When it landed on Dawson, he cleared his throat, threw his brother a look, and kept his head low so Finn couldn't see his eyes. "I'm Dawson Rhinehart. I run my family ranch with my older half-brother, Duke. We'd like to ask for prayers for my daddy."

He cleared his throat, his voice already deathly quiet. "He's not doing well. The doctors say it's just a matter of time now." He swallowed hard. "We've talked a lot about it, and I think we're past the point of healing. Daddy's eighty-eight years old."

He looked over to Brandon, who nodded.

"We're asking for prayers of peace for our Momma," Brandon said. "And for him to pass quickly and peacefully, and that he won't be in much pain." He too swallowed and cleared his throat. "She's much younger than him, and we're going to have to figure out what she needs once he's gone."

Dawson nodded, and both he and Brandon looked at Finn. The room stayed silent, the weight of Dawson's words settling over Finn and reminding him of how good these men and women were, of how good God was.

"Of course," Finn whispered. "We'll keep them in our prayers, Dawson; Brandon. Thank you for sharing that with us."

Several others murmured their agreement, and Finn watched as Henry slung his arm around Dawson's shoulders, and Link patted Brandon's hand.

"Ty, you're up," Finn said after another moment or two.

He first nodded down to Dawson. "I'll pray for your momma and daddy." He drew a deep breath. "I've been thinking." His voice changed on the last word, that familiar gruff edge reappearing.

"I finally moved out of my parents' house, and I'm doing great. I think the next step is for me to get my own place—like a hobby farm, or even just a piece of land where I can have horses and a big garden."

He shifted in his seat and looked around the room without letting his eyes land on any one thing or person. "Nothing huge, obviously. I can barely walk. Just like...somewhere I can keep my horse and maybe have some space to work with animals. I've got money saved from my rodeo days, but I don't really know where to start looking."

Finn looked around the room. "Light 'im up, boys. What do we know that's out there on the market?" He had a great real estate agent, and he could text the information to Ty later.

"You said you looked at the Hensen place?" JJ asked.

"Yeah, and it's a joke," Ty said. "Winnie and I just drove by."

"Well, it used to be a petting zoo," Conrad said. "I can't imagine it's in good condition."

"Ruby and Trap are there today anyway," JJ said. "I think someone may have bought it."

"Good luck to them," Ty said darkly.

"There's a property out west," Link said. "It kind of butts up against the northern edge of Shiloh Ridge." He leaned forward. "Wild? Who owns that?"

"The Knightlys," Wilder said without missing a beat. "Though, I'll be honest, there are massive drainage problems in that area." He pointed to himself. "Ask me how I know."

"How do you know?" Paul asked, kicking a grin toward Wilder.

"Because I'm building my house in the same area, and it's a swampety-swamp-swamp." Wilder did not look pleased, but Finn couldn't help the laugh that came flying out of his mouth.

"Swamp is a swear word," Link said, grinning at Wilder. "In case you're wondering."

"We're talking about swamps?" Rock asked, and Finn looked over to the doorway, where he and Gun stood. "Oh, sweet. We didn't miss the burritos."

They both entered, took a couple of burritos each, and squeezed in at the table around Link and Mitch.

"What about talking to a realtor?" Tate suggested. "Someone who specializes in small properties?"

"Yeah, I can do that," Ty said.

"I know a guy," Finn said. "I'll text you his name and number."

"There's the Lucky-H Lodge," Alex said.

Ty looked over to him. "I haven't heard of that."

"It's out on the western side too," Alex said. "His brother knows Nikki's brother...or something like that. I heard he was looking to sell."

Finn had never heard of it, but he didn't know every operation in the Panhandle.

"It's maybe ten acres," Libby said, peering at her phone. "Ty, I'll forward you this listing."

Ty's expression brightened slightly. "Yeah, thanks, Libs."

When the conversation seemed to end there, Finn looked at Jake. "You're next, my friend," he said with what he hoped was a warm smile.

The veterinarian cleared his throat. "I'm Jake Ahlstrom," he said, his voice steady despite the attention of upwards of twenty people now riveted on him. "I'm the new vet at Three Rivers Ranch. My daddy, Garth, was the foreman there for years before he retired. I graduated and worked at Buffalo Ranch for the past few years, down in the Hill Country, but I'm back in Three Rivers now."

"Jake's been a huge asset to us," Libby said from her seat. "We're lucky to have him."

"His parents are getting older too," Finn said with a nod. "And we grew up together."

"You're way older than me," Jake said with a grin. "But I loved to follow you around like we were friends."

"I'm only six or seven years older than you," Finn said. "Plus, everyone at Three Rivers was like family to me." He looked around at everyone crammed around this table, that familiar, wonderful warmth spreading through his chest.

This sense of community, of brotherhood, of shared experience, was exactly why he'd started these meetings.

"We might need to find a bigger place to meet," he said.

"Well, if you'd stop inviting everyone you know," JJ teased.

"I want Smiles here when he comes back too," Finn said without missing a beat. "And we're missing Trap and Angel today." He surveyed the group again. "This has been a great place, but I'll look into somewhere that can handle our size."

"We could even move it around," Tate said. "We have big rooms above the grocery floor at Wilde and Organic."

"Let's talk afterward," Finn said, ready to get down to business. "Okay, so I thought we'd talk about what's on everyone's mind as we move deeper into winter. We made it through this first big storm, but the forecast isn't looking great for the next few weeks. What are you all doing to prepare?"

"We're rotating animals into barns," Link said, raising his hand halfway at the same time. "Making sure everyone has shelter and that our water systems don't freeze."

"Same here," Henry said. "We've been wrapping pipes and checking heaters in every building, rotating horses, and cleaning more regularly. Wet hay is bad business for horse's hooves."

"What about feed?" Finn asked. "Everyone stocked up?"

"I'm good through March for my few horses," Colt said. "But I'm worried about the orchards. If we get another hard freeze, it could damage the trees."

"Have you been covering them?" Alex asked.

"As much as we can," Colt said. "But there's only so much you can do when you've got hundreds of acres."

"Maybe you need more seasonal help if the weather stays nasty," Tate said. "We've brought on a few extra people at the produce farm."

Colt nodded and typed something into his phone.

"Birthing season's in full swing too," Dawson said. "We're expecting about fifty calves between now and April. I'm already losing sleep over it."

"If you need help, call me," Conrad said. "I've got experience with difficult births, and my neighbor used to work on a sheep farm in Montana. He knows how to get babies through bad weather."

"Anyone can call me anytime," Link said. "We have cowhands at Shiloh Ridge I can dispatch."

"Yeah, and we have hundreds of calves being born too," Gun said. "But Wilder has been great with scheduling, and he's been teaching me, so if you need help managing that, I know we'd sit down with you and go over it."

"I'm good with horse care," Rock said. "And happy to help anyone if something comes up."

"I can help with any veterinary questions," Jake said. "Sometimes a quick video call is all it takes."

Finn beamed at him, thrilled he'd volunteered himself as a resource. The conversation continued to flow, with some of their more vocal members—Henry and Conrad and Link—speaking the most. But plenty of others piped in when necessary, and he saw more than one person taking notes.

This was what he loved most—the willingness to show up for one another, no matter what. He closed his eyes and let the words dull into a distant roar in his ears as he prayed.

Lord, thank You for bringing us together today. I ask for Your protection over our ranches, our families, and our animals as we face the challenges of this season. I pray for Dawson's daddy and his momma, that You'd grant them peace and comfort. I ask for safety as we work, wisdom as we make decisions, and strength to keep going when things get hard. And I thank You for this community—for friends who show up, who help, and who remind us we're never alone.

Finn opened his eyes, the reality of the men and women around the conference room table rushing back at him. Lacy's hands moved like lightning, and when Mitch wanted to say something, she called out, asked his questions or said his piece, and the conversation continued.

Finn's heart had never felt so full. He caught Ty's eye, who gave him a lopsided smile, and then looked at Jake. He wore bright hope in his expression, and Finn knew that despite Ty's protests about being here, or Jake's reluctance to come, they belonged.

They all did.

Pure gratitude filled him for the third Thursday of the month, for this band of brothers and sisters, and for the small town goodness that made Three Rivers feel like a little slice of heaven on Earth.

17

Elaine Walker pulled up to the gray brick historic building at the far end of Three Rivers's Main Street. She lifted her coffee cup from the console, reached across to the passenger seat for her bag, and got out of her car.

She wasn't sure why the short walk from the small parking lot into the quaint office space she'd rented filled her with such a zing of pride, but it did.

It's because you're doing something with your life now, she thought as she entered the co-op office space and climbed the stairs to the second floor.

She rented the entire floor, which had once been three bedrooms and still had its own bathroom. The big living area held an eight-foot desk for herself. A kitchenette had been built into the far wall, and Elaine set her bag on the counter there and started another pot of coffee.

After a few years of trying to figure out what she wanted to do, while she worked jobs here and there just to see what might tickle her interest, she'd decided to start a foundation that would help women in small Texas towns support themselves.

She worked with single moms, widows, married women, and singles of all ages: helping them find better educational opportunities, apply for scholarships and business funding, get the health insurance they needed, research schools for their kids, anything at all that might improve their quality of life.

She'd initially funded the foundation with her own money, which had come from her parents. All of the Walkers a generation older than her were billionaires, and she wasn't sure what her aunts and uncles had done for their kids, but her parents had set up trusts for their children when they were born.

When they turned twenty-five, they got access to the trust and no longer had to consult Momma or Daddy about what to do. Not only that, but Elaine's older brother Conrad was a financial wizard, and he had been managing the family's money for years, hers included.

So Elaine's one hundred million had become two-hundred-fifty by the time she figured out what she wanted to do with her life. She already owned a home in Three Rivers, and yes, she drove a car nicer than she needed, but she liked heated seats, the soundproofing that made her ride so quiet, and the moonroof.

Elaine definitely liked being comfortable, that was for sure. Therefore, she kicked off her heels, settled at her desk, and flipped open her laptop.

She reviewed the next day's appointments before she went home every day, and because she set her own hours, she never had to be anywhere too early or stay too late—unless a client needed it. Elaine loved the flexibility that running The Walker Foundation for Women gave her, and she'd learned so much about the educational programs and government assistance the State of Texas offered.

She'd also learned a lot about herself; namely, that it was important for her to feel significant and to know what she was doing really mattered to someone. She knew all of God's children mattered to Him, but she still wanted to do something that felt important to *her*.

With the room filling with the scent of coffee, and another storm on the way beyond the window, Elaine opened Hailey's file.

Hailey was a Glover, but only by marriage. Her daddy had married Etta about twenty-five years ago, and Hailey had grown up at Shiloh Ridge Ranch. She'd enjoyed all the privileges that came with that name, much like Elaine. But she'd never finished college, and until recently, she'd been the manager of an upscale restaurant in town.

Then, the owner accused her of stealing, fired her, and pressed charges. The poor woman had been arrested before the truth came out: that the owner's nephew had been the one with his hand in the cookie jar.

Hailey had still lost her job, though the case against her was dropped. She'd moved back to Shiloh Ridge, if only to escape the gossip that seemed so prevalent in town whenever so much as someone sneezed too close to their neighbor.

She was six or seven years older than Elaine, and Elaine had learned about her situation through Glory Rose, her sister-in-law. Elaine's mind wandered for a moment, because Glory and Conrad had a new baby boy that Elaine had fallen in love with upon first sight. She babysat for her brother every weekend, because her love life had become so pathetic that she'd put it on hold.

Starting the foundation had given her something else to focus on besides the dozen men she'd gone out with and failed to click with.

She wanted someone older, with an established career, someone who could make her laugh, and someone who knew how to cook. She didn't think her list was too demanding. She'd had a few boyfriends in recent years, but no one who made her heart sing and every cell in her body buzz. Elaine absolutely wouldn't settle for anything less than fairy tale true love.

"And now Easton has a girlfriend," she grumbled to herself.

Until now, none of the triplets had had a significant other, and Elaine had sort of assumed Austin would be the first to bring someone into their trio. He'd always been the one to break ranks, and he'd been wildly popular in high school. He'd gone to the Police

Academy, and Easton had stuck around town, and Elaine had drifted. But through it all, they'd always had each other.

Elaine had worked briefly as a secretary for HealNow, and while she didn't loathe the high-rise buildings in town like some others did, she much preferred this quaint country home that had been converted into co-op office space.

Austin worked on the Amarillo Police Department, currently assigned to their Special Victims Unit. Easton worked for the city of Three Rivers, moving his way through the ranks until he'd landed at the top of their physical facilities and operations.

He'd met his girlfriend through that job, because even though he didn't have to interact with a lot of people, plenty of scheduling went through him, and secretaries, receptionists, and department heads emailed him all the time. An expert at getting her inbox to zero, Elaine had given him some systems and filtering options that he claimed helped.

He'd been dating Marta for about five months now and had started bringing her to family events and parties, which told Elaine the relationship was getting serious.

Finally able to focus, she answered a couple of emails and set an appointment for a single mom to come in later that week before footsteps sounded on the stairs.

Her space had a glass door, and she'd been given permission to put on a vinyl sticker that read *The Walker Foundation for Women*. She watched Hailey read the words and reach for the handle.

"Come on in," she said as Hailey opened the door.

Hailey wore a cute pair of black skinny jeans and a blouse the color of dark purple plum skins with lighter violet ribbing.

"Wow, I love that shirt," Elaine said.

"I got it at the Boot Barn, if you can believe it. Clearance rack." Hailey pinched the fabric out from her body and let it fall back.

This wasn't Elaine's first meeting with Hailey, and she really liked the woman. "Coffee?" she asked, heading for the kitchenette.

"Yeah, I'd love some," Hailey said, lifting a box. "I brought those pecan buns I was telling you about."

"You're kidding." Elaine grinned. "I can't wait to try them."

"Well, I hope you're ready for your life to change on this Monday morning."

Elaine laughed. "Everyone needs their life changed on Monday morning, don't they?" She poured Hailey a cup of coffee, picked up a tray with cream and sugar, and carried it to the desk. "How are you today?"

"Good," Hailey said.

"Yeah. I'm totally convinced." Elaine grinned at her and picked up her own to-go cup of coffee.

"I'm hoping you'll have something for me," Hailey said with a sigh. "I spent the last several days searching online, trying to think of what I might like to do. And the truth is, I've never really known what to do with my life."

Elaine could relate, and a flash of sympathy moved through her. "Some people just take a little longer to figure things out," she said. "I mean, look at me. I'm almost twenty-eight, and I just started this foundation six months ago."

"Yeah, true." Hailey stirred in a sugar cube and finally looked up from her mug. "So what have you got?"

Elaine beamed and tapped the pink folder she'd labeled with *Hailey* about six weeks ago. They'd discussed a few professions—nursing, teaching, and something outdoorsy like a wildlife conservation officer or tour guide. Hailey had a people-person personality and got along with all kinds of folks. That was why she'd been so good as a restaurant manager.

She was highly detailed, organized, and smart, though she hadn't done much schooling beyond high school. She'd taken about a year of college classes before quitting, telling her parents there was no point in paying for a degree when she didn't even know what she wanted to do.

"Open it," Elaine said.

Hailey wore a dubious look, but she reached for the folder and flipped it open. Elaine watched, wanting to see her full reaction. Hailey's eyes widened; she pulled in a sharp breath. "A vet tech."

"I mean," Elaine said, trying to make her voice casual and only succeeding in pitching it up. "Veterinarian school is, like, eight years —and I know you said you didn't want to do anything like that, though I think you'd be an amazing nurse."

"Right," Hailey said, still scanning the top page in the folder.

"But because vet techs aren't doctors," Elaine said. "You can get certified and be working at a real clinic with DVMs in only two years."

Hailey dove back into the paperwork. "Is that right?"

"And there's a program right here in Three Rivers you can do mostly online," Elaine said. "You have to go to Amarillo once a month, for a week of in-person classes, and at the end you'll do an internship. They partner with several farms and ranches locally, too, and then you just have to pass a test."

Hailey turned the page, where Elaine had outlined the difference between a veterinary *technician* and a veterinary *technologist*. "Now, if you wanted to go longer," Elaine added. "Or if you find you really love it, you could continue on and do Veterinary Technology. That's a full Bachelor's degree, and you usually get supervisory roles, or do lab work, or work in research. And of course there are specializations —surgery, anesthesia, emergency and critical care—but only *if* you want to pursue one."

Elaine told herself to stop talking; everything she'd said was outlined in bullet points on the first sheet, with supplementary documentation after that. Hailey seemed to be reading every word, so Elaine lifted her coffee cup to her lips to give her friend time to absorb it.

They'd discussed a lot of service professions over the past few weeks, but when "veterinary technician" came up in Elaine's search, the idea had felt like the exact right fit.

Hailey looked up, her blue eyes still wide and filled with wonder.

"It's a service profession," Elaine said. "It's just serving animals and not people."

"I like animals more than people anyway," Hailey said.

Elaine giggled. Hailey relaxed and seemed to come back to herself. She looked at the paperwork again, flipping to the first page. "I gotta say, Elaine, this seems like something I'd enjoy."

"Doesn't it?" Elaine asked. "I mean, it *feels* good, right?"

"Yeah." Hailey glanced up. "And only two years? Are you sure that's right?"

"Yeah. It's a two-year associate's degree," Elaine said. "And like I said, you can stay right here in Three Rivers. Amarillo State has a distance-education program—as long as you can get there for a week every month."

"Well, I can move to Amarillo, too," Hailey said.

"Yeah, you can."

"I'd love to get off the ranch," she murmured.

"One of their partner branches is Three Rivers," Elaine said.

"Really?"

"Yep. They just got a new veterinarian out there, but Conrad knows everyone in town, and I've got an in with Libby, so I'm sure we can get you placed there when you're ready for your internship. But I can't make that a promise. Remember, there are no guarantees. Only connections we pray will come through for us."

"I know," Hailey said.

"I'm sure you'll look through this more," Elaine said. "But I included a packet for scholarship programs. I looked up several you qualify for based on age, gender, and previous education."

"No one's going to give me any money," Hailey said.

"Your parents' income is *not* your income," Elaine reminded her. "And if you feel like this is the right fit, then The Walker Foundation for Women has funds to cover tuition."

Hailey's gaze snapped back to Elaine. "I am not going to let you pay for my degree."

"I won't be paying for your degree," Elaine said smoothly. "The Walker Foundation is the business. I am Elaine Walker, a mere woman."

"You're a superhero," Hailey said with a laugh. She looked down again. "A veterinary technician. Yes, I think this is a good fit for me."

"I think so too," Elaine said. "You can specialize in large animals, small-animal pets, ranch animals, farm animals—even zoo animals."

Hailey giggled. "Zoo animals?"

"Oh, yeah. I watched a video about a guy doing his internship with camels and elephants."

"Wow."

"Now, he was a DVM student," Elaine said. "But they need technicians, too. It's a wide-open job field, especially here in the Panhandle. If you want to stay close to your parents, friends, and siblings, there are lots of opportunities."

"Let me guess...You know who owns both veterinary clinics in town."

"Yes, I do." Elaine leaned back in her chair and folded her arms. "And I'm not ashamed of it."

Hailey laughed, then closed the folder. "Thank you, Elaine. I'm going to look at this more and see what I need to do to apply."

"Their online programs start in either the summer or the fall," Elaine said. "That gives you plenty of time to find an apartment and move to Amarillo if you'd like—which I can help with. I know the student housing options, and a little bit about the assistance programs. You probably won't qualify since you're single without kids, but I can still talk to Belinda in Amarillo."

Hailey nodded, and her eyes looked brighter when she glanced up again. "Thank you so much for this, really," she said. "I've been so lost."

"Oh, I know you have, sweetie. But you're not the only one. We're all wandering a little bit."

Hailey sniffled and nodded. "You're right. You just seem so good at what you're doing—like you've been doing it forever."

"Finally, my obsession with the internet is paying off," Elaine said, smiling. "And making a phone call doesn't scare me, which puts me ahead of about ninety percent of people."

She really felt like she was making a difference, and Elaine needed that so badly. "It helps that I'm asking for people I genuinely care about, and not myself. That helps me fight for women like you."

"I really, really appreciate it," Hailey said. "I'm going to look at all this and see what it takes to apply."

"I put some of the financial packets and options in the back," Elaine said. "For the foundation's funding, outside scholarships, and Amarillo State, too. You might talk to your momma and daddy and see what they say. They might be happy to help."

"Yes, I'm sure they would," Hailey said. "Though, my daddy loves having me home." She smiled with a wry twist. "It'll kill him for me to be an hour away, because from Shiloh Ridge, it's really two hours."

"I heard y'all had a back road to get you to Amarillo faster," Elaine said.

"Oh, if that's common knowledge, my uncles are *not* going to be happy." Hailey laughed again, and it did Elaine's heart good to hear it. Only six weeks ago, she'd come in downtrodden and miserable, and Elaine loved watching women change their lives. She loved the tiny role she could play to help them do it.

Hailey stood. "All right, I've got to get over to the store. I'm on stationery today."

Elaine's whole soul lit up. "If you see any new notebooks, pull one out for me."

"You got it."

Elaine rounded the desk and hugged Hailey. "Let's do lunch again soon. I had so much fun last time."

"Me too," Hailey said. "Is it okay if I invite Nellie?"

"Absolutely. She's awesome, and she always makes me laugh."

"She has a certain zest for life, doesn't she?" Hailey collected her purse and tucked the pink folder under her arm. "Thanks again, Elaine. I'll be in touch soon."

"Yeah. Text me when you apply, because I can email the academic advisor at Amarillo State and let her know."

"Okay." Hailey waved and walked out, taking some of the good energy with her.

Elaine sighed, but her heart refused to be anything but happy. Her phone pinged over on the desk—the tone she'd assigned to her brothers. All three shared the sound, so she knew it was one of them, but she didn't know who until she looked.

Right now, it was Easton. *Marta wants to go on a road trip to San Antonio. Do you think that's weird and too soon, or is this normal?*

Elaine was used to answering dating questions for her brothers—she'd been doing it for over a decade—but she paused to consider his question. *Are you going alone? You and her?*

Yeah, he said. *Unless you and Austin want to come.*

Oh, honey, you can't invite me and Austin without talking to Marta first.

It's for a Beanie and Bros concert.

Elaine scoffed. She'd never willingly attend that concert, though it was Easton's favorite band—and apparently Marta's too.

I mean, I'm sure we can go if you need a chaperone, she said. *But I don't think it's weird for couples—serious couples, East—to take a road trip together. You might learn a lot about her—like if you can stand being in the car with her for more than a couple of hours.* She grinned and sent the text.

Okay, he said back.

And that was classic Easton. She'd send paragraphs, and he'd respond with, *okay.* Conrad and Austin did it too, and Elaine once again reminded herself that men and women were not the same, and that his *okay* was his validation of the things she'd told him.

For a brief moment, she considered getting back on Two Cents and navigating to the dating arm of the recommendation app. Then she flipped over her phone.

"Nope," she told herself aloud. "You need to figure out a job opportunity for Naomi, and you only have a few days to do it."

With that, she turned back to her computer, determined to stay boyfriend-free for a little while longer.

18

Ty looked up the road, the sound of the wind catching his attention and sending adrenaline straight through him.

Every flight reflex in him told him to *move*, and Ty tugged harder on the horse's rope. "Come on, girl," he said, his voice crisp and urgent. "Let's go."

He got Wonder back into her stall at the same time his phone made a series of noises. One came from the Lone Star stable-wide alert system, but it was quickly drowned out by a blaring emergency alarm. Ty fumbled to get his phone out of his pocket as he heard other cowboys' phones go off around him.

He scanned the messages quickly, trying to make sense of them. The National Weather Service had just issued a dust storm warning for a huge swath of the Panhandle, including Amarillo and Three Rivers. Ty's first thought was *Winnie*, and then that she wasn't at the clinic in Three Rivers that day.

The physical therapists had been taking turns going to the hospital for medical training in Amarillo, and today was Winnie's day.

Ty's brain moved through so many things so fast. He'd already eaten lunch, and he noted that the time was one forty-seven. So where would Winnie be right now?

Angel had said, *We need all horses inside in the next ten minutes. Anyone doing anything different needs to stop and help bring horses in.*

The sound around him felt muted, and of course, it was because he could only hear out of one ear. But voices called and boots ran.

Ty ducked around a corner and quickly tapped out a message to Winnie. *Where are you? There's a dust storm coming straight at Amarillo.*

He reminded himself that she was from Oklahoma, and certainly they'd had dust storms there in the past. Ty hadn't been in one for years. In fact, the last major dust storm Ty could remember was from when he was a little boy, probably eight or nine. He recalled the terror at seeing the sky go green, and then everything just being obliterated from sight.

His parents had sheltered them in their master bathroom, which only had one tiny window up near his father's head. Dust storms could cause a lot of damage, and though they weren't quite as destructive as tornadoes, they came with high winds and abrasive particles blasting against surfaces, whether that be a house or someone's face.

Ty pulled in a breath and held it, willing Winnie to answer him. She didn't, and he turned his phone all the way up in both volume and vibration and tucked it into the waistband of his jeans so he would feel it when it did go off. Then he pushed away from the wall and went to do his job.

He worked with a man named Caldwell, and they put away one, two, three horses before a distant siren filled the air.

"What is that?" Caldwell asked, eyes narrowed and his gaze toward Amarillo in the distance.

Ty looked west-southwest toward the city too. Lone Star sat about ten miles away, but that sound made his blood turn cold. "That's a tornado siren."

"Dear God in heaven," Caldwell whispered.

Another message blasted across their phones, and it was Angel again, giving three locations for sheltering.

We want everyone there as fast as possible. Leave whatever you're doing. The news says the dust storm is mere minutes from Amarillo, which means it will be here right after that. We've assigned your teams to specific locations. Get there and check in. Team leads, we want a report in five minutes.

Ty looked at Caldwell, and they weren't on the same team. Ty had to cross the ranch to the administration building where his team was supposed to meet, and he turned to do that.

Caldwell grabbed his arm. "Ty, you'll never make it."

"But I'm supposed to—"

"The admin building is a sure ten-minute walk on a good day," he said, his voice firm and his expression fierce. "For a man with two good legs. You're coming with me."

He released Ty's arm and started to march down the aisle at a pace that Ty could not keep up with. "My team is meeting in the North Stable," he said. "And that's like, two minutes away."

Ty moved as quickly as he could, his body protesting, as today was Wednesday and tomorrow would be his day off. He worked, or went to classes, or spent time with Winnie from sunup until long after dark, and boy did he feel it by Wednesday.

His girlfriend's beautiful face ran through his mind again, and he told himself that as soon as he reached the shelter checkpoint, he'd text her again. His phone buzzed and chimed over and over, but he ignored it, pouring every ounce of concentration he had into stepping correctly, so he didn't fall down. That was the last thing he needed right now.

He rounded a corner and found Caldwell down at the end of another aisle, gesturing for him to keep coming. "You got it, buddy," he said, and normally, Ty would hate the patronizing words, but right now he took them for what they were—encouragement.

He could do this. He just had to keep going.

He'd parked on this side of the North Stable too, and while he was sure Lone Star would have emergency supplies, he had a blanket and rations and a first-aid kit in his truck.

He had gotten there early that morning, and he'd parked right next to the door, so he felt confident he'd be able to get to his car even through the dust storm. But right now, he hurried into a tiny tack room that was usually so much bigger when it wasn't holding eleven grown men, all of whom wore grim expressions. Most of them had their phones out and their thumbs flying, and Ty went with Caldwell to check in with his team lead, a man named Flint.

"I've got Ty Greene with me," Caldwell said. "His check-in point was too far away for him to get to safely."

Flint looked at Ty. "You're on Terrance's team, right, Ty?"

"Yes, sir," Ty said.

"I'll text him." He did that, and Ty retreated to the corner of the room where he was able to lean against the wall and provide some relief to his hip. He also texted Terrance that he was in the North Stable, safe and accounted for, and then he turned his attention to Winnie.

Instead of texting, he tapped to call her, begging God that she would pick up.

"Hey," Winnie said, and she sounded breathless. "I just got in my car."

"You're in your car?" Ty's heart fell all the way to his boots and then rebounded strongly to the back of his throat. "Winnie, that's not a good place."

"They released us," she said, her voice filled with panic. "They told us to go home."

"Yeah, but you don't live in Amarillo," he said. "The dust storm's sure to be there any second."

"What should I do?" she asked. "Do you think I can outrun it?"

Ty scoffed. "No, sweetheart, you don't outrun a dust storm."

"Well, I don't know what to do," she said.

"Is there any way you can get back in the building?"

"I—" She yelped, and static shouted over the line. "I can't, Ty. It's here. I can't see anything."

"Just stay there," he said. "Winnie, do you hear me? Don't pull out. Don't drive. You won't be able to see."

Her labored breathing came through the line, and she said, "No, I can't see anything."

"During a dust storm, they tell everyone to pull over and stay put," he said. "You just have to stay right there in the parking lot," and pray that the wind didn't break a window.

Ty pressed his eyes closed to say that mental prayer, all while listening to the fear in his girlfriend's breath.

He knew where the hospital was in Amarillo, as he'd been there many times in the past couple of years. From Lone Star, it was probably a twenty-minute drive on a clear, sunny day, and he couldn't believe he was contemplating leaving the shelter of the tack room and trying to make the drive *into* the dust storm to get to Winnie.

Every part of him wanted to do that, though, and he glanced around at all the other cowboys in the room with him. Surely they all had loved ones somewhere too who they wanted to get to, and help, and protect. It would do no good to get himself killed while he went to help Winnie.

A sense of deep resignation started in his gut and moved up through his chest. "Listen, I'm going to get there as soon as I can," he said.

"Where are you?" Winnie asked, and it sounded like she had calmed down a little bit.

"I'm still at Lone Star, sweetheart," he said. "They assigned us shelter stations. I'm in the North Stable, right where I park. I'm okay."

"I'm okay too," she said, though her voice broke on the last word.

It shattered Ty's heart, and he realized in that moment just how deeply he felt about Winnie.

"Will you stay on the line with me?" she asked.

"Of course," he said.

"Tell me something."

Ty realized that she needed a distraction. He wasn't exactly loquacious and known for his storytelling capabilities, but he would do anything he could to ease Winnie's worries.

"I don't think I've told you about Marigold," he said. "She's my favorite horse at Courage Reins, and the one I always try to work with if I can. Now, we're going riding there tomorrow, and I don't want you tryin' to steal her from me."

Winnie half sobbed and half giggled, and a tiny smile touched Ty's face. He had no idea if he and Winnie would actually be able to ride at Courage Reigns tomorrow—not if the dust storm caused a lot of damage—but he launched into the story about the first time he'd worked with Marigold after his third surgery, doing everything he could to keep his voice steady and even.

It calmed him at the same time it did Winnie, and he'd just finished the story when the walls of the stable started to rumble. Cries of surprise filled the room, and Ty looked around at his coworkers, then up to the ceiling, as if it might cave in on them.

"Let's say a prayer," Flint said.

Ty relayed the message to Winnie. "I'm going to put you on speaker," he said. "So you can hear the prayer too."

"Okay," she said. "Thank you, Ty."

He moved into the circle and kept his phone in his hand as he joined the men he worked with. Flint stood in the center, and he spoke in a powerful voice as he said, "We're going to be okay, men. We've got each other and good sense. Now, if we can get the Lord on our side, nothing can harm us."

Murmurs of assent moved through the crowd, and Ty found himself nodding.

"I know you've got loved ones you're worried about," Flint said. "And for now, we still have service, so we should be grateful for that." He reached up and pulled his cowboy hat off his head. Ty did the same, barely getting his down before Flint said, "Dear Lord, we come before Thee as Thy sons, knowing that we still have much to learn in our lives, and maybe something from this dust storm itself. But we pray for safety—for ourselves, our friends and family, all of our horses here, all of their owners, and all of our facilities. We know Thy hand is strong and constantly outstretched toward us, and we pray for this blessing in Thy name, amen."

"Amen," Ty said.

No one moved and no one spoke, and Ty had never felt such a powerful spirit in his life. He stood there, marveling in it, feeling the protective hand of God come over him, and a keen sense that, yes, God was aware of him, and always had been.

And yes, he was a son of God, whether he could walk well or had a limp, whether he could hear with both ears or just one.

Someone shifted, and the mood did as well. Ty backed up to lean against the wall again, and he glanced at his phone. It had gone dark.

He tapped quickly and said, "Winnie?" lifting it to his mouth.

But the call had disconnected.

19

Winnie had never been in the situation she currently found herself in. She stared at her phone as it turned dark, her call with Ty dropped. With her pulse pounding at her, she quickly tapped to dial him again.

His phone simply rang and rang, and when his voicemail picked up, Winnie ended the call.

She didn't seem to have a problem with her service or internet, and so she sent him a quick series of messages.

I lost you, but I heard most of the prayer, and it was beautiful.

I can't wait to meet more of your friends at Lone Star.

I'm sending you my location pin so that you'll know where I am.

It's eerie here in the car—it feels like a cage—and a little bit cold. I turned off the engine because I don't know how long I'm going to be here, and I'm really glad I wore my puffy sweater today.

I'm going to lay my seat down and just try to relax.

I can't see anything outside the windows anyway, and I've never seen a sky this color before. I took some pictures because it's just so weird.

She sighed as she looked up, the dust storm raging beyond her windows.

Winnie had never been in anything like this before, and she could've looked up some information about what to do, how to shelter if caught outside, but she trusted Ty.

He'd said not to drive, and Winnie was going to wait out the storm and then figure out what to do.

Everything existed in a weird khaki-olive-green state, with thousands of particles flying by her windows, and she slid her chair back so she could recline it down. If she could just close her eyes, she could make it through this.

The car suddenly lurched forward, causing her to yelp. Just as quickly as it had started to slide, the vehicle came to a violent halt as the front passenger side hit the cement pillar she'd parked beside in the parking lot. She'd seen a few people bypass the spot that morning, because they drove bigger cars than her, but her sedan fit just fine, even though the pillar took up part of the parking space in the corner.

The back end of her car fishtailed, and Winnie cried out again, looking in the rearview mirror and trying to make sense of why her car was moving. She couldn't see another vehicle that had hit her.

In the next moment, she realized the *wind* was moving her car.

With the front corner now jammed against the cement pillar, it couldn't really go anywhere, and the back end got pushed into the truck next to her, also on the passenger side.

Everything stilled after that, and Winnie's chest felt so tight, telling her she had not been breathing. She took a quick breath and then another, almost expecting the sky to fall and crack right through her windshield.

When it didn't, she reclined her seat and started to do some deep-breathing exercises she'd learned in a stress therapy class she'd taken after Carver had called off the wedding. That only warded off the worry for a couple of minutes, because deep breathing couldn't truly erase the severity of the situation.

She lifted her phone and texted Ty again.

The wind blew my sedan into the cement light post in front of me. I'm now wedged between it and a truck.

The good news is I don't think the car will move again, so I should be able to ride out the storm. The bad news is, I'm not sure if my car is going to be driveable or not.

She sent the texts, though she wasn't sure if Ty was even getting them. She decided it didn't matter. She needed someone to talk to, and he was all she had.

Yes, she could have called her friends back in Redwood, or even her mother, but what could they do? Winnie didn't want her mom to worry anyway, and she sighed as she rested her phone on her chest and closed her eyes once more.

She wasn't sure how much time had passed before her phone rang, startling her back to full consciousness and the reality of her situation.

She lifted the phone, saw Ty's name there, and quickly tapped to connect the call. "Hey." She heard the relief and breathlessness in her own voice.

"I got your pin, sweetheart," he said. "As soon as I can, I'll get out of here and I'll come look at your car."

"Okay," she said.

"You're really all right?"

"Yes," she said.

"The storm's still raging there?"

"Yep. I feel like I'm in some sort of weird capsule," she said. "It's so strange to know the world is beyond the window and not be able to see it."

"Yeah," Ty said. "We don't have any windows in here. It's pretty dark."

She heard something come through the line. She tilted her head, trying to make it out. "Are you guys singing?"

"Yeah," he said. "You want me to put you on speaker? I might be able to whisper a few more stories, but...."

"You can put me on speaker," Winnie said, and a moment later, the singing on Ty's end of the line increased in volume.

Then sings my soul,
My Savior God, to Thee;
How great Thou art,
How great Thou art!

Winnie loved that these cowboys were relying on their faith in this hard time, and she knew she needed to do the same. She closed her eyes again and hummed along with the tune, not quite able to get her voice to sing.

Ty didn't sing either, and when the song ended, another one started.

Silent Night, Holy Night
All is calm,
All is bright.

Winnie smiled, though Christmas hymns wouldn't be sung for at least ten more months.

"We're just singing whatever we all seem to know," Ty said.

"It's oddly calming," Winnie said.

"I agree." Ty added his voice to the second verse of *Silent Night*, and Winnie joined him on the chorus.

She couldn't believe she felt as calm as she did during this ultra-stressful time, but somehow the singing of hymns had brought nothing but peace.

She was still catching up on her sleep from being sick last week, and she'd had to get up extra early for her training in Amarillo this morning. She hadn't finished it, and she let her mind wander and wonder if she'd have to come back another time.

A little while later—Winnie wasn't sure how long—the wind buffeting the car seemed to wane slightly. She lifted her phone and saw that she'd been on the call with Ty for thirty-one minutes.

"Ty?" she asked.

"Yeah, I'm still here, sweetheart," he said.

"I think the storm is stopping."

"Well, that's good news."

Winnie raised her seat, but she still couldn't see much through the windshield or any of the glass. Because she was so close to the truck next to her on the passenger side and it was black, she could see it, but only briefly in between gusts of wind and all that beige and brown dirt.

"Sweetheart, I'm getting messages from my bosses I need to pay attention to," he said. "I'm going to let you go, okay? But I promise I'm going to be there really soon."

"When?" she asked, and she hated the pathetic quality of her voice.

"Probably thirty minutes," he said. "I'm going to send you my pin right now, too, all right?"

"Okay, be safe, Ty."

"You too, sweetheart. Just stay right where you are. You don't need to try to do anything with the car. I'll take care of all of it when I get there."

"Okay," she said.

The call ended, and Winnie was once again left alone in the silence. She wasn't sure what she would do in this situation if she didn't have someone like Ty.

She supposed she could call a tow truck and then pray that they had some sort of rideshare or cab service that would take her the fifty miles from Amarillo to Three Rivers.

She thought of all the people who were alone in the world who had to figure out solutions to problems like this when they happened, and a brand-new sense of gratitude filled her that she wasn't alone right now, that she had Ty. And not only that, but she probably could've called any of his cowboy friends, and they would have come to help her.

Winnie's head hurt and her stomach lurched with anxiety, so she laid her seat down again and closed her eyes.

There was something calming and soothing about the white noise of the rushing air, and the next thing she knew, someone had knocked on her window and pulled open her door.

Her eyes flew open and she yelped.

"Whoa, whoa, it's me. It's me."

A sob tore through Winnie's throat when she recognized Ty, and she sat straight up and flew into his arms.

He caught her and held her tight. "You're all right," he said. "You're all right. The storm's over, and I'm here."

Winnie stepped back. "You scared me."

"I called and texted, sweetheart." He gave her a smile. "I can't believe you fell asleep during this."

Winnie could hardly believe it either, and she looked around at the world. Cars had been moved all over the parking lot, and the sky sat clearer than Winnie had ever seen it before. It was as if the storm had taken everything hanging in the air and blown it out.

"Wow. The world looks brand new," she said.

"Sure does." Ty took her hand and led her around the open door and then the hood. "Yeah, she pushed you pretty good into this."

Winnie looked at the front bumper of her car, which seemed to be one with the cement pillar.

"And you're right up against the truck too," he said.

Their eyes met. "Should I try to move it?" she asked.

"Maybe just away from the truck and back into the right space," he said. "And then I'll drive you home."

"Really? You don't think I can take my car?"

"No, baby." He swept his lips along her temple. "I think the tow companies will be really busy for a while."

Winnie huffed out her frustration and then moved to get behind the wheel again. The car started, and she put it in reverse and started to ease it away from the pillar and the truck. She could easily drive this home, because—

She sucked in a breath at the loud groaning of metal—really a horrible, terrible, all-encompassing roar of metal—and immediately slammed on the brake.

Ty called, "Keep going," and waved at her to continue backing up.

Since she trusted him, she did, and she felt the moment her bumper released from the truck next to her and broke free. The car almost lurched away from her, and Winnie once again applied the brake. When it didn't fall apart around her, she pulled the sedan back into the space straight, stopping when Ty held up his hand for her to do so.

She got out again and went around the front, and he nodded to her bumper. "It's dragging on the ground, sweetheart."

Yes, she could see that. "We could take it off, and maybe I could drive back to Three Rivers."

"We don't know what damage has been done to the engine," he said.

Winnie didn't want to argue with him, but having her car an hour away—unable to be driven—didn't seem like a barrel of fun either.

"I can get you to work and back," he said. "I don't even have to work tomorrow."

Winnie nodded, pressed her lips together, and went to get her bag. She collected that, her water bottle, and her purse, and she let Ty help her into the passenger seat of his truck.

"Was there a lot of damage at Lone Star?" she asked once he'd gotten behind the wheel and started to leave the hospital parking lot.

"Yeah, a bit," Ty said. "But Henry and Angel sent everyone home. They said we all have loved ones that we wanted to check on, and they wanted us to be home safe before dark. They said they'll start working on an assessment today, and we'll all get texts tomorrow."

"But you don't work there tomorrow, right?"

"I can if they need me to," he said. "And they know that."

Winnie nodded, though she really did just want Ty to be able to rest. He'd told her that Thursdays were his recovery days and that he also used Thursday to run a lot of his errands, get groceries, and fill his freezer with food for the next couple of weeks.

She liked that he knew how to cook, and he'd said he would make dinner for her one night.

As Ty left Amarillo, Winnie realized there was hardly anyone on the road. "Is it safe for us to be out?"

"It would be better if we weren't," Ty said. "After stuff like this, they call for everyone to stay off the streets if they can, to make it easier for emergency crews and rescue personnel to get where they need to go."

"Oh," Winnie said.

They started down the highway that led between Three Rivers and Amarillo, and Winnie counted fourteen cars that had been abandoned on that highway before she and Ty passed the sign that said, *Welcome to Three Rivers*.

Neither of them had said much at all, and Winnie felt like a washrag that had been wrung out. When Ty should have turned right to go to her house, he continued straight.

"Where are we going?" she asked.

"We're going to go back to my place and get something to eat," he said. "I'll cook it up at your house."

"Okay." She nodded once again, unable to get her voice to do much more.

Several minutes later, he pulled into the parking lot at an apartment complex and put the truck in park. "You want to come in with me? Are you okay here?"

Ty watched her with nothing but concern in his expression, and Winnie could admit she felt a little bit numb. Minutes seemed to be flowing by like water, and she had no memories of how Ty had navigated them here.

"I can wait here," she said.

Ty nodded, got out of the truck—but left it running—and headed around the back of his apartment building. Until this moment,

Winnie had not realized where he lived, and she now acknowledged that he'd been coming to her all this time.

They spent evenings at her house, if they weren't eating at a restaurant, and they'd been busy the last couple of weekends with weddings and birthday parties.

Ty came back out with a taller plastic container stacked on top of a smaller one. He opened the door and handed it to her, and Winnie took the frozen food into her lap, seeing a couple of big gallon-sized Ziploc bags, and then some fillets of halibut wrapped in paper.

"Wow," she said. "What is this?"

"Parmesan risotto," he said. "Halibut fillets. I can put them in the oven. They're pretty fast and easy."

She nodded, starting to feel more like herself by the time Ty pulled into her driveway. Winnie now wanted nothing more than to tell him everything that had happened while she'd been in the car alone.

At the same time, not much had happened at all. She'd sat there worried and afraid, listening to cowboys sing and the wind howl.

In the house, she fed the cats while Ty put dinner together, and then they both ended up in the bean bag. Winnie curled into Ty's chest, exactly where she wanted to be.

"Were you scared?" she asked him.

"Yes," he said. "I was supposed to meet my team lead in the administration building, and the guy I was with wouldn't let me go. He said it was too far and that I wouldn't make it."

Winnie pursed her lips, irritated that someone didn't think Ty could do anything he wanted to do.

"Do you think you could have made it?" she asked.

"I honestly don't know," Ty said. "My station was clear across the ranch, so I just went with Caldwell and checked in with his team lead."

"I'm glad," she said. "You wouldn't have wanted to be in such a hurry that you fell."

"Exactly." He stroked his hand down her hair. "I was mostly just really worried about you, and I was really glad I got in touch with you before you started driving."

Winnie thought of those abandoned cars on the side of the highway. She wondered where the people had gone, and a shiver ran down her arms.

"I shared my pin with you too," Ty said. "But I don't think you accepted it."

"Oh, right." She reached for her phone in her pocket and then realized she didn't have it. "I don't really know where my phone is right now."

"It's probably still in your bag," he said. "You want me to go get it?"

His body shifted, and Winnie tensed and held on to him. "No, stay," she whispered. She pulled away from him slightly and looked up at him.

"I don't know what I would have done today without you," she said. "I've been thinking about it a lot, and it made me realize I'm all alone here, except for you."

"I mean, kind of," he said. "You've got coworkers and neighbors, and you know people in town."

"Yeah," she said. "Maybe I just want you to be the one to take care of me."

His eyes dropped to her mouth, as they'd done on many occasions before. "And I want to take care of you."

Ty had not kissed her yet, and they had not talked about when he might be ready to do so.

Winnie reached up and cradled his face in her hand, about to ask him what he thought, when he leaned down and touched his lips to hers.

Winnie's whole world turned sideways all over again, but for a completely different and much better reason than before.

She kissed him back almost hungrily, and he matched her stroke for stroke, until it seemed the storm between them blew out and his touch became sweeter and softer.

Winnie liked all sides of Ty: the grumpy ones, the intense ones, the romantic side, and the sweet side that said things like, *I want to take care of you.*

So she didn't much care how he kissed her, as long as he didn't stop.

20

Ty had no less than forty-eight messages waiting for him on his phone. He'd silenced it in the barn at Lone Star after letting his parents and his friends know that he was fine, safe, and sheltered. His mother also had his pin, and all she had to do was look at her map app and see that he lay on Winnie's bean bag, kissing her.

Of course, she couldn't really see *that*, and Ty wasn't even sure how often his mother checked on him. But with a dust storm having just blown through town and him ignoring his phone for the past hour and a half, he figured she might be looking.

He couldn't bring himself to care in that moment, because kissing Winnie was unlike anything he'd ever done before. Ty had ridden two-ton bulls successfully. He'd bungee-jumped off bridges and flown all over the world, but absolutely nothing compared to holding Winnie in his arms and kissing her, and kissing her, and kissing her.

He couldn't quite get himself to stop, and he wondered what he'd been so nervous about. He certainly remembered how to kiss a woman, and Winnie sure did kiss him back like she was enjoying herself.

She ran her fingers through his hair and down the sides of his face, and Ty felt so cherished and like he really mattered.

He finally found the willpower to pull away, but he kept his eyes closed and simply listened with his good ear to Winnie breathing in and out. Her breath came a little quicker, and then she sighed as she tucked herself against his chest again.

A moment later, the timer on the oven sounded, and Ty groaned as he rolled away from her and pushed himself up. Getting off a bean bag was no small feat for Ty, but as it was Winnie's preferred place to lounge in her house—and it was quite comfortable while he was in it —Ty didn't dare complain.

Instead, he ignored the protests of his body as he limped into the kitchen, silenced the timer, and pulled the fish fillets out of the oven. He'd set the risotto in a pot of water and turned the heat on, hoping it would boil. It hadn't quite gotten to that yet, but a few bubbles popped on the surface.

Ty turned up the heat and then opened Winnie's fridge. He pulled out her sour cream, some milk, and the bottle of lemon juice, and then moved over to her spice cabinet, where he dug around for several long moments. The lid on the pot clanged and jiggled, and he turned toward it and turned the heat off underneath the risotto.

All he had to do now was empty it into a bowl and it would be ready to eat. The fillets rested while he found the bottle of dill and put together a quick sauce for the fish.

"Are we eating out there, sweetheart?" he called.

"No," Winnie said with a sigh.

He got out plates and silverware before she joined him.

"Let's eat at the table like real human beings."

He smiled at her. "Today's been a weird day for sure, and it'll be nice to do something normal."

Ty handed her the plates, and she moved over to the table and started to set it.

"I need to text my momma real quick." He whisked his phone up from where he'd left it on the counter. "Yeah, she's called twice."

He held his fingerprint to the screen and saw that she'd texted a few times as well, the last one saying, *Oh, I can see you're over on Goose Creek Lane. I don't know whose house that is, but I'm assuming Winnie's?*

Yeah, I'm at Winnie's, he said. *We're both fine and safe. We're about to eat dinner. Do you need me to call?*

No, his mother said. *I just wanted to make sure you were okay. Libby and Paul were here saying you hadn't checked in on your rancher's text string for a couple of hours, and they didn't know where you were. Henry said you'd left the moment you could.*

Yeah, Ty said. *Winnie was at a training at the hospital in Amarillo and had to ride the storm out in her car in the parking lot.*

Oh my goodness, Momma said. *Is she okay?*

Yeah, she's all right, but her car got pushed around a little bit, and we had to leave it there. So we're gonna have to figure that out tomorrow.

There's a lot to figure out tomorrow, Momma said. *I think the dust storm hit hardest on the southern side of town, at least according to Libby. She's saying that JJ and the Glovers and the Rhineharts are reporting a lot of damage. We were at Bowman's Breeds, of course, and we didn't have a whole lot. Some fences compromised, and one of Libby's cowboy cabins lost a window.*

What about Courage Reins? Ty asked. *They have that huge front wall of windows.*

Yeah, they lost several too, Momma said. *But they knew about the dust storm, and they'd moved everything out of the foyer and closed all the doors.*

I'm going to eat, Ty said. *And then I'll check in with everyone. I hope I didn't worry you.*

I could see where you were, Momma said. *Say hi to Winnie for me.*

Ty tapped out of the string and saw that he had over *seventy* messages from his ranching friends now. A slip of guilt moved through him, but he flipped the phone over and left it on the counter.

"How's everyone?" Winnie asked.

"They're okay," he said. "I'll go through my ranching texts after we eat." He pushed the dip across the counter where Winnie picked it up.

"You can just put that halibut on the table too," he said. "And I'll get the risotto out."

He went about doing that while Winnie put salt and pepper on the table and started to brew coffee. They sat down together—Ty with his back to the wall, and Winnie with her back to the kitchen—and he looked across the table to her.

"Can we pray?"

They'd not prayed together previously, but he reached for her hand at the same time she extended hers across the table. "Yes. I'd like that."

Ty had taken his cowboy hat off when they'd arrived, so he simply bowed his head and squeezed Winnie's fingers in his. "Dear Lord," he said. "We're grateful to be safe in Winnie's home tonight. We're grateful for emergency systems that work and rescue operations and communities that can come together in times of crisis. Please bless us that we'll have willing hearts and strong hands for anyone who may need help rebuilding. And bless any who have lost something today in the dust storm, that it will be restored according to Thy will. We're grateful for this good food, and ask Thee that it will bless our bodies and do us good and keep us strong and healthy. We pray for these things in Thy name. Amen."

"Amen," Winnie repeated.

When Ty raised his eyes to hers this time, something shifted between them yet again. He wasn't sure if it was because they'd just been through something scary, or because he'd finally cooked for her, or because he'd kissed her, or because they'd prayed together for the first time, but the connection he felt with Winnie seemed to lengthen and strengthen at the same time, driving deep into his heart and binding him to her.

"What do you think I should do about my car?" she asked.

"I can call Link's momma in the morning," Ty said. "She used to own the mechanic shop only about a half-mile from here, and maybe she'll know some small towing companies that won't be inundated with work."

"So will there be lots of cars like mine?" she said. "There were all those ones on the side of the road. Is it because they stopped running in the storm?"

"Sometimes the debris can do that," he said. "Get all up in the engine and clog it, especially if the cars were running at the time. Yours wasn't, so I can't imagine that that will be a problem for you. We've just got to get it to a body shop and get it fixed."

Winnie nodded. "And you can take me to work in the morning? I have to be there at eight."

"Yeah," he said. "I don't work tomorrow, except for the dog training, and I can show up to that whenever I want. It's usually not until nine anyway."

Ty used his fork and slid a piece of halibut across the tray to Winnie's plate. "This is just Parmesan risotto, sweetheart. It doesn't have mushrooms or peas or anything gross in it." He smiled at her, and she reached for the spoon and served herself some risotto.

"It smells amazing," she said. "And how did you make this sauce?"

"Just a little sour cream and milk, lemon and dill," he said. "It's perfect with fish."

He took the remaining fish fillet and a couple of healthy spoonfuls of risotto, then doused his halibut in the dill sauce before he took his first bite. "So tell me how you grew up in Oklahoma without ever having a dust storm."

Winnie took a bite of her fish too, her eyes glittering as she looked at him. She swallowed and said, "I don't know. We've just never had one. How many have you been in?"

"I think that was my third one," Ty said. "The first was when I was a little boy—eight or nine—and then we had another one, I think when I was a junior in high school? Maybe a sophomore. We were at school when it came through, and they herded us all into the gym, and we had to sit in there for a couple of hours, and our parents had to come check us out. They didn't run the bus."

"Wow," Winnie said.

"We had our own bus out to Three Rivers anyway," he said. "Squire bought it—Libby's father?"

"Yeah?"

He nodded. "Yeah, my daddy drove it sometimes. There were a lot of kids that lived out on the ranch, and since my parents worked out there, that was the easiest place for us to go after school. Heck, we all worked the ranch."

"Did you, Ty?"

He nodded. "Every day. I worked at either Three Rivers, my momma's boarding facility, or Courage Reins."

"No wonder you like horses so much." Winnie smiled at him, and Ty returned it.

"Sometimes I think humans don't deserve horses," he said. "They'll do anything we ask of them, and they never quit, and they're always happy to see us."

"Cats are like that," Winnie said.

Ty chuckled and shook his head, though he suspected she was teasing him. "No, they are not. How *dare* you try to compare cats to horses?" He kicked a full grin at her and flaked off another bite of fish.

Winnie laughed too, and Ty sure loved the sound of it. As they ate dinner and Winnie turned the conversation to lighter topics, he barely recognized his life. It continued to morph around him every few months, and the addition of Winnie as his girlfriend was definitely the best change of all.

A COUPLE OF HOURS LATER, Ty finally arrived home. He'd showered, and he currently only wore boxer shorts as he lay in bed, a single lamp giving light to the room from the nightstand beside him.

He needed to go through his texts, so he'd know where to be in the morning to do the most good.

He had several messages from Angel and Henry at Lone Star, four from Colt—just between him and Colt, not whole orchard texts or whole ranching group texts—but over a hundred from his friends.

He started to read through them, and sure enough, it looked like his help would be needed at Conrad's, JJ's, *Signs for Success*, Shiloh Ridge, and the Rhinehart Ranch.

At one point, Rock had mentioned Golden Hour, which Ty knew as Britt Bellamore's place. One of Rock's uncles had married a Bellamore, and he said he would try to get more details about what they needed, and then he'd never come back on the text.

Send me a list of what you need off this thread, Finn said. *I'll make a list and organize us. Anyone who can come help—great. We understand if you can't. We all have our own family and farm obligations.*

Ty smiled at the way Finn took charge. He loved it, because the man loved him, and he genuinely wanted everyone to be taken care of. Mitch had asked about him first, and Ty's heart expanded with love for the man.

Henry and Angel had both chimed in that he'd been at Lone Star, and safe, and then left right away, and Libby had reported that his mother was trying to get in touch with him too and hadn't been able to. The texts went on as others related their experiences with the dust storm and the aftermath of it.

Link: *All of my netting is down in the guinea fowl pasture. It's a tangled mess, and I think we're gonna have to rip it out and start over.*

Wilder: *I'm headed to my place right now. I'm actually really afraid of what I'm going to find.*

Mitch: *We have broken windows on the third story of the house, and over in the Academy dorms. And look at how close this tree came to the house.*

Ty recognized as the back corner of the huge plantation-style house where Mitch and Lacy lived, and his heart dropped to the soles of his cowboy boots.

Dawson: *I lost the doors on the west side of my barn, and the roof there doesn't have a single shingle anymore.*

Ty's heart hurt for the loss his friends had suffered. Everything felt more real when he knew the actual people who'd been impacted, and had been to those places which now bore damage.

Gun: *We're still missing several turkeys, a couple of sheep, three pigs, and a whole slew of cattle. Maybe more animals. I've got cowboys out trying to round up everything we can.*

Rock: *Several fences buckled, so our groups got mixed up, and of course, they sheltered wherever they could.*

Link: *Yeah, we have no way of getting them all to safety on such short notice.*

Wilder: *I was already behind on my construction due to figuring out the swampiness here, and this blasted dust storm tore off all of the plastic sheeting and has pelted the foundation. Look at it.*

Ty stared at the picture of the crumbling cement, his chest tightening on Wilder's behalf.

Wilder: *It's ruined the foundation. It's going to have to be re-poured.*

Condolences had come in after that, and Link had said that he and Gun would come down and help Wilder assess what else needed to be done, as Wilder had reported "debris everywhere."

Ty could feel the man's frustration in his short, clipped texts, and he didn't blame him. Wilder was set to get married in only a couple of months, and his future wife had two little girls that Wilder desperately wanted to provide for.

Finn: *Based on the pictures and things you all have sent me privately, I think we should meet at Conrad's tomorrow morning.*

I know not everyone will be able to. No pressure.

He only has a section of fencing to be fixed, and one wall in his barn, and then his livestock will be back to normal.

In the afternoon, we can head to Signs for Success and help Mitch get his dog enclosure rebuilt and assess his window needs.

I think we should be able to fix Dawson's roof on Friday and get barn doors back on his building, and then we'll focus on Shiloh Ridge.

Link: *Good plan, Finn. We've got tons of men here, though, so I'll keep you updated, and I don't know if we'll be able to send anyone to help. I'm really sorry.*

Rock: *I bet we can send a few people. We can't all ride around calling for pigs.*

Wilder: *Honestly, I'd love to get off Shiloh Ridge. This place is going to be the death of me. I can come to Conrad's.*

Finn: *Chime in if you can come to Conrad's tomorrow morning or Mitch's in the afternoon. Let's try to be there around eight-thirty if we can.*

Ty quickly navigated over to Mitch's text to see what he'd said about having a crew come to *Signs for Success* tomorrow.

Mitch: *I hope you're all right and accounted for. No one's heard from you on the group text. Text me when you get a minute.*

A little while later, he'd said, *We're gonna cancel dog training in the morning and wait and see what Finn sets up for us in terms of getting things put back together.*

He hadn't said anything else, and maybe hadn't seen that Finn had said they'd have a group coming to help out at *Signs for Success* tomorrow afternoon.

No problem, Ty said. *I'll see you at Conrad's.* Then he realized he hadn't told Mitch that he was all right, and he added, *I'm fine. Winnie was stuck in Amarillo during the storm and had some car trouble, so I went there to help her and then brought her back here.*

I'm glad you two are all right, Mitch said.

Ty navigated back over to the larger group text to add his voice to the conversation. *I can be at Conrad's by eight-thirty. I have to drop Winnie off at work, as she was stranded in Amarillo, and we had to leave her car there after it incurred some damage from the storm.*

Not ten seconds later, he got a private text from Finn: *What help do you need with Winnie's car? Anything?*

It got pushed into a cement pillar and the front passenger side is pretty dented, Ty said. *We left it there but need to get it back here to get it fixed.*

Let me talk to Sam, Finn said. *He's been trying to start that roadside assistance thing, and he might have access to tow trucks or a flatbed.*

That'd be great, Ty said. *Winnie has insurance, and I don't know what she'll be able to pay, but I know she needs her car.*

Yeah, I'll text him, Finn said. *Glad to hear from you, Ty.*

And Ty knew he was too.

He navigated back to the big group text, and others had said they were glad to hear from him as well.

Alex: *I'll get my morning chores done and plan to be at Conrad's too. They've canceled school, so I'll bring my boys.*

Brandon: *I'll come through the forest and ride with you, Alex, if that's okay.*

Alex: *Sure thing, brother.*

Mitch: *I'll be there as well, and I'd appreciate any help at Signs for Success, but I understand that we're low on the list, because my dogs can just live in the house with me until we get things fixed.*

Trap: *What about your windows? My daddy has lots of window contacts.*

Mitch: *I've already texted with him, and we have someone coming tomorrow by six p.m.*

Trap: *Oh, great. That goes for anyone else who might need windows. My daddy's able to get them for some reason when other people can't.*

Link: *It pays to know people.*

That triggered Ty to think about what Winnie had said about only having him to help her. She may have felt like that, but Ty knew it wasn't true. The community of Three Rivers wouldn't let anyone go without, and his texts with his friends proved it.

They'd show up for anyone, and Ty would be right there with them, gloves on, pain meds in his truck, ready to work.

Anyone around town would do the same for Winnie.

"But I do want to be that man for her, Lord," he whispered. He'd caught up with the texts, and he reached over and plugged his phone in and left it on his nightstand, his alarm set to go off at seven-fifteen so that he could get over to Winnie's and get her to work on time.

Pure exhaustion pulled through him, but he still managed to murmur, "Thank you, God," believing that God would know that he was grateful for a great many things in his life and just didn't have the energy to spell them all out right now.

21

Jackie pulled off the road and into a dirt parking lot, with Winnie peering through the windshield for some sign that she'd arrived in the right place. So many people had canceled their PT that day, the clinic had closed at lunchtime and sent everyone home.

She'd immediately texted Ty to find out where he was working, and where she might be able to help.

We just found out that Tate and Clara Jean could use help at their produce farm, he'd told her. *We're done at Conrad's place, and Mitch says he can fix up his dog enclosure himself. So we're heading over there.*

He'd sent the address, and Winnie now searched for an entrance to the one-story building that had come into view. "I'm sure here is fine," she said to Jackie, the friend and co-worker she'd asked for a ride here.

"Are you sure?" she asked.

She caught sight of a cowboy walking along a downed line of something, and Winnie nodded. "Yes, I'm sure this is it."

"I had no idea Wilde and Organic grew a lot of the produce they sell."

"I just learned that myself." Winnie smiled over to the other woman. "Thank you so much. I'll see you tomorrow."

"Watch your texts," she said. "We might close the clinic again."

Winnie nodded, grabbed her bag, and got out of the car. She strode toward the entrance of the building with all the confidence in the world, but when she stepped inside, she paused, her uncertainty coming back.

The building didn't seem very deep, with another set of doors in front of her that led straight back outside. She could go right or left, down different hallways, and she went to the left when she heard voices coming from that direction.

Winnie wasn't sure what she could possibly do, but she wore reliable shoes and had willing hands, and she supposed God had made do with a lot less than that in the past.

As she neared, she heard a man talking, but she didn't recognize the voice. Then a woman said, "No, I think we should send people over here first, and get the orchards cleaned out while we have Colt to help."

She came to a stop in the doorway and found several people in the tiny conference room, including Ty. A woman stood by a whiteboard, and she wore jeans and a sweatshirt with the Wilde & Organic logo on the front and had her dark—almost pitch-black—hair up in a ponytail. Her eyes switched to Winnie, and everyone in the room turned toward her too.

"Hello," the woman said at the same time Ty scrambled to get to his feet.

"Hey, you found it," he said. "Everyone, this is Winnie." He smiled at her, but Winnie could see the pain in the lines around his eyes. He'd probably been working himself too hard that morning, and Winnie immediately wanted to bring him under her wing, park him on the bean bag at her house, and take care of him the way he had her last night.

"Are you all right?" she whispered, her hand automatically seeking his as he drew closer.

"Yeah, I'm okay." He took her hand and turned to face his friends at the same time. "You've met a few people here—JJ and Finn, for sure—at the wedding and the birthday party."

"Sure," Winnie said, smiling at the familiar faces. "Good to see you again." She nodded at them, her smile firmly stitched in place.

"That's Tate and Clara Jean up at the front," he said. "They're married, and they own this farm and Wilde and Organic. We're here to help them."

"Thank you so much for coming," Clara Jean said, and she rushed forward and gave Winnie a hug.

"And you remember Colt and Conrad," Ty said when Clara Jean stepped back.

"Yes," Winnie said. "And Libby's here too. Hi, Libby."

"Hi, Winnie," Libby said, and then everyone's attention thankfully moved back to the whiteboard. A huge map had been affixed to it, and Clara Jean and Tate had clearly been going over the areas that needed to be cleaned up.

"I think we can probably split up," Tate said. "And send a crew with Colt over to the orchards, and then a crew with me over to the netting. We've got to get that back up over our tomatoes and lettuce and onions." He looked at Clara Jean with some sense of urgency, and she nodded.

"Winnie and I will go with Colt," Ty said. "I'm used to running a crew at the orchard, and Winnie is a quick study."

The rest of them quickly divided themselves, and before Winnie knew it, she led everyone out of the room. Thankfully, Ty stayed right at her side and tugged on her hand to take her further down the hall instead of back toward the door she'd come in. They exited the building on the far end, and the good, rich scent of earth and green growing things filled Winnie's nose.

"They lost a lot of topsoil," Ty said.

"Yeah, this ground is terrible." Colt toed at it as he came up beside them. "Look, you can see tree roots and everything."

He wore an unhappy expression, and Winnie let him take the lead. Finn had come with them, and the four of them had to get over to the orchards, which took up the northern part of the farm.

"Tate said we can take this golf cart," Finn said as Colt walked by it.

"Oh, right," Colt said.

Winnie got in the back and slid over to make room for Ty beside her. Finn and Colt piled in the front, and Colt started to drive them down a well-kept path. Winnie realized as she rode that the farm looked like it had gone through complete upheaval, with bushes with bent branches, more exposed roots, plants broken off at angles, and what she could only describe as debris everywhere—equipment turned on its side, now-empty bags of fertilizer, overturned black trays that had probably held seedlings, and more.

Anything and everything that Winnie could imagine someone needed to grow produce and be a gardener looked like it had been put in a giant bucket, shaken up, and then dumped all over the ground.

She looked over to Ty, pure concern radiating from her. He wore his mouth in a tight line and only met her eyes for a moment before he went back to surveying the damage.

"I feel like a fool," Finn said.

"What for?" Colt asked.

"This is way worse than I thought," he said. "Clara Jean said they needed help with 'a few things,' but this looks like a tornado came through."

"That's because one practically did," Ty said.

"Conrad's place wasn't this bad," Finn said, and Winnie caught the frown on his face. "I'm really glad Mitch said that he can handle his own dog enclosures, because I underestimated this farm. I didn't even put it on the list."

"That's not your fault," Colt said. "Clara Jean and Tate know how to ask for help."

"Do they?" Finn asked.

Winnie actually found it a fair question. A lot of people, in fact, didn't know how to ask for help. She once again looked at Ty as he took her hand in his. She gave him a quick smile, and then Colt came to a stop at the edge of what was probably once a beautifully kept apple orchard.

He switched off the golf cart and got out. "All right," he said. "Here are the ATVs Tate mentioned, and the trailers. Let's get those hooked up, and then we'll start clearing away the broken branches."

He and Finn set about doing that, and soon enough, Winnie found herself behind Ty on an ATV while Finn climbed on with Colt. After a few minutes, Winnie realized it would be far easier if she just walked alongside Ty as he drove. And they did that, making their way up and down the long aisles of trees and filling the trailer with the organic debris.

When it got full, Ty would take it to the dump spot, and when he returned, he said, "Tate's gonna go rent a chipper, and he'll turn those trees into bark. He said any of us could have some. Do you need any at your house?"

Winnie thought about her front flower beds and back garden area. She'd moved to Three Rivers in May and missed the most important planting season, but she'd done a little bit of work on her yard throughout the fall. "Yeah, sure," she said. "I'd take a load of bark."

"Great," Ty said. "I'll have him put it in the back of my truck, and we can unload it when I take you home."

"Are you sure you're okay?" she asked. "You've been working hard for a long time. Are you really going to be able to unload bark at my house?"

"We can cover it with a tarp if I can't," he said. "It keeps."

She nodded, and he leaned over a little closer to her. "You don't need to worry about me."

"No, I'm sure I don't," she said, suddenly feeling shy. She ducked her head. "But that's what I do, Ty."

He kicked her a smile. "I mean, I kind of like it, but it's not necessary. I know when to quit."

She wasn't sure he did, but she didn't want to argue with him either. He was a grown adult, and he could decide when he'd had enough and when he could do more.

"They've got a lot of trees," Winnie said when Ty returned from the second unloading, straightening from where she'd been grouping branches together in Ty's absence.

"Yeah, they sure do," he said. "I mean, they grow produce for a whole grocery store, but I thought they bought a lot of apples from Colt."

"They do," Colt said as he pulled up beside them. "My orchards are at least fifteen times this big."

Ty grinned at him. "Yeah, I guess they are."

"Tate texted and said he needs more hands over with the netting," Colt said. "Finn and I are gonna go over there. Are you guys okay here by yourselves?"

"Yeah, we'll be fine," Ty said. "I'll just take Winnie to help me unload, instead of letting her rest in the shade." He grinned at her.

Winnie rolled her eyes. "Yeah, because that's what I'm doing in the ten minutes you're gone."

Finn grinned at them. "Well, you guys have a good system going. Just do what you can. There's days and days of work ahead."

Ty nodded, and Finn and Colt did a wide U-turn and headed back the way they'd come. Winnie bent and picked up another fallen tree limb and muscled it into the trailer. Ty went behind her and picked up the smaller ones, and she noticed him bending less and less at the waist and just grabbing onto branches that poked up high enough for him to grab without having to lean over.

She said nothing, but when the trailer reached maximum capacity again, she hurried in front of him. "I'll drive over to the drop point."

"You sure?" he asked. "You'll have to unload it. Colt was helping me with that."

"I didn't put anything in that I can't take out," she said.

He had done branches and limbs smaller than hers. She turned back to him and put her hand on his chest. "I know you don't want me to worry about you, but that doesn't mean I know how to just turn it off. So I want you to rest while I'm gone."

He hooked his arm around her waist and pulled her close. "All right," he whispered when she'd expected him to argue. "I'm glad they closed the clinic today."

"Me too," Winnie murmured just before he pressed his lips to hers.

She could really get used to this kind of attention. Kissing Ty so openly, where one of his friends might come along and see them, made this kiss a little more thrilling in a different way than her passion-filled, almost desperate first kiss with him yesterday.

He pulled away. "But I don't know where you expect me to rest out here," he said. "It honestly might be nice just to ride on the four-wheeler with you."

"Okay," she said, looking up to meet his eyes.

"You think you can drive that thing?"

"Yes," she said. "Do you think I can't?"

"I think you can do anything you want, Winnie." He didn't smile as he said it, keeping the moment between them serious and meaningful.

"This way I can give Tate my keys too," he said. "And he can move my truck and load it with the bark."

Winnie nodded and tucked herself back into his arms. "Things just feel sort of blue," she said. "Like, I don't feel happy, but I don't feel unhappy. I just feel...blah."

"Yeah," he agreed.

"I've never seen an aftermath this up close and personal," she said. "And I guess it's just hitting different."

"That's allowed," he said. "But I'm a little surprised. You work with patients every day who have to deal with the aftermath of something similar to this. I mean, look at me."

"Yeah, I know," she said. "But usually by the time they get to physical therapy, they're months out from the event. They've had surgeries, their pain has receded quite a bit, and they've had time to accept what's happened. This was only about twenty-four hours ago. And I don't know...it feels raw."

She stepped back and looked around. "The earth still feels like it's suffering a little bit."

She didn't quite know how else to explain it, but she eased back to Ty's side and said, "I'm glad they closed the clinic, because I just want to be here with you, and it feels good to help others get cleaned up."

He nodded toward the four-wheeler. "Well, let's get this load back, then."

Ty climbed onto the four-wheeler first, and then she swung her leg over and sat in front of him. He wrapped his arms around her and scooted right up behind her, his chest pressing against her back. She smiled as he laid his head against her shoulder blade and murmured, "Yes, I can definitely rest right here."

Winnie had never felt so close to another person as she did to Ty in that moment, not even Carver, who she'd been *engaged* to. There was simply something about Ty that, when he opened up, a real connection was made. Winnie loved having him close to her—physically and emotionally—like this, and she found herself praying as she bumped over the well-kept roads to the drop point that she and Ty could continue getting to know each other and build a true, lasting, loving relationship.

22

"It's right up here," Ty said, and he glanced over to Winnie, who rode in the passenger seat of his truck. She'd been ready when he'd pulled into her driveway to pick her up, and they'd made the almost hour-long drive to Lone Star together.

She'd perked up after he'd driven through the Java Hut to get coffee, but then her mother had texted and she'd fallen into her phone.

She looked up now, the cutest little frown between her eyes. "It's not a bad drive," she said. "When there's not a dust storm." She smiled, erasing all the cares from her expression.

Ty wondered if she realized that she'd shown them to him, as Winnie definitely broadcast more sunshine than anything else.

"I don't know what we'll have to do here today. I usually work until about two," he said. "And Finn said Sam would be calling or texting when he got to your car."

"That's right," Winnie said. "I told him just to take it to that little mechanic shop on the south side of town—the one that Link's momma used to own?"

"Yeah," Ty said. "It's only a few minutes from you, and I'm sure they'll take good care of it."

She reached over, and he gladly gave her his hand. "Thanks for helping me so much with that."

"Of course." Ty put on his blinker and eased off the brake. "What's going on in Oklahoma?"

Winnie sighed and sighed and *sighed*. She sighed for so long, Ty was sure she'd run out of air, and he glanced over to her, his adrenaline kicking a nervous beat through him.

"That bad, huh?"

"It's just my daddy," she said.

"That's all I get?" Ty asked when she didn't go on. "Just your daddy?"

She turned toward him then, and Ty knew immediately that he would not be able to hear this whole story before he had to report for work. Winnie was more talkative than him, but the same could be said for almost any human being on the planet.

The truth was, she processed things as she spoke, while Ty internalized everything first. He liked listening to her talk, and he could ask an occasional question or just affirm what she'd said, and she kept going. In the end, Winnie worked things out in her own mind, and Ty was perfectly happy to be her sounding board when she needed it.

"He's diabetic, right?"

"Okay," Ty said, though he hadn't known that.

"But he doesn't take care of himself. He doesn't regulate his insulin the way he should. So then his hands and feet fall asleep. Then my mother texts me and wants to know what we should do about it, because apparently *all* physical therapists know how to diagnose and deal with every problem dealing with diabetes."

Her frustration poured from her in waves, and she even rolled her eyes. Ty simply gave her the kindest smile he could.

"I've told them a thousand times I'm not a doctor, and he needs to go to the *doctor*, and he needs to manage his blood sugar levels.

Anyway." She waved her other hand like all of this was trivial. "The real problem is his back. He's had some disc problems for a while. One was broken. He had some nerve issues because of that, and of course, the diabetes doesn't help that."

"Of course it doesn't," Ty said as the huge boarding stable came into view. The gate was closed today, and a man stood there. "Hey, that's Caldwell. Remember—he was the one who I stayed with during the dust storm?"

"Oh, right," Winnie said, brightening.

Ty pulled up and rolled his window down. Caldwell approached, a clipboard in his hand. "Howdy, Caldwell. Henry said you guys needed some extra help today, and I brought Winnie. He and Angel knew about it."

Caldwell looked down at his clipboard. "Yeah, I've got you and Winnie working inside today, at the southwest stable. Stable C?"

"Sure," Ty said, as he had worked there before.

"Henry and Angel want everything taken out of the tack room. They want it cleaned and reorganized, and then they want all hallways swept clean and all outdoor doors checked on stalls one through ten. We want to make sure all the locks still work, that none of the hinges were blasted with sand, and we want to make sure that the horses have easy outside exits. So if there's debris and other things that need to be cleaned up, that has to be done."

"Yes, sir," Ty said.

"Your team lead over Stable C today is Burt Hallahan. Do you know Burt?"

"Oh, we know Burt," Winnie said, practically singing the words. "He went out with my sister for a little bit."

Caldwell leaned in the window and blinked at Winnie. "Okay. You check in with him when you're done, and he'll let you know what else—if anything—needs to be done today. Henry and Angel are hoping to have everyone out of here by noon. I guess Henry's going to his daddy's place to help clean up some fences."

"Yeah," Ty said. "Three Rivers Ranch." He glanced over to Winnie and briefly met her eye. "We may go out there too."

He hadn't committed on the group text, because he'd really worn himself out with everything that had happened on the day of the dust storm, and then all day yesterday working at Conrad's farm, and then Tate and Clara Jean's produce plantation.

He honestly hadn't been sure he'd be able to make it to work today, but when Winnie had found out before they'd even left the orchards that the physical therapy clinic would be closed today, she'd volunteered to come with him.

"They're asking for you to park near your zone," Caldwell said. "That way, they don't have vehicles in the way. And we've got parking lots set up, so if you'll just turn left here at the first road, you'll find someone down by the Stable C waiting to help you park."

"Thanks."

Caldwell moved to open the gate, and Ty eased through it, not at all surprised with how efficient Angel, Henry, and Trevor ran the clean-up at Lone Star. Everything they did was managed down to the second, and they employed a lot of people and trained them with a customer-service-first attitude.

Ty was actually surprised he'd stayed on as long as he had, though he could put a smile on his face and do what someone told him pretty easily. Therefore, he found a man named Marcus waving people into the parking lot, and he did what he said.

Just as he put the truck in park, his phone rang, and Ty glanced over to the screen in his truck while it connected. Winnie watched it too.

When the name *Jerry Bozeman* popped up on the screen, Ty's heart went into a spin. "It's the real estate agent." He looked over to Winnie as his pulse actually started to throb in his throat.

"I'm going to answer it."

"All right," she said. "Do it."

Ty reached out and touched the screen, gave the call a moment to connect, and then said, "Hey, Jerry, you're on speaker with me and my girlfriend, Winnie."

"All right," Jerry said good-naturedly. "I know we haven't looked at any places yet, Tyson, but you'd given me a short list from the website that I sent you."

"Yeah," Ty said, unsure of what he might say next.

"Well, I followed up with a couple of them late yesterday, after the dust storm, and unfortunately your number-one pick has decided to withdraw their listing from the market for right now."

The breath left Ty's body, and he slumped back into his seat. "Was that the one out there on the western side of town?" he asked. "Kind of in that last neighborhood before you get down near the crop-dusting hangars?"

"That's the one," Jerry said. "Apparently they took a lot of damage, and they don't want to sell it for cheap because of that. So they're going to take some time to get it fixed up first."

"Well, how long is it going to take?" Ty asked.

"They didn't give me a timeline," Jerry said. "Apparently her niece is living there right now, and they're not even in town, so they might not be doing anything with it for a while."

"Sure, okay," Ty said. "What about the other places?"

"Everybody has a lot going on right now," he said. "So nobody wanted to show this weekend, but I got you a couple of showings for next Saturday, if you're interested."

"I am," Ty said, and he swung his attention back to Winnie, lifting his eyebrows at her. She gave him an encouraging nod, and Ty recognized how pleased her approval made him.

"Great," Jerry said. "All I can go on is what we've been talking about, so it'll be nice to go out and do some actual showing. It always gives me a better idea of what you're looking for, so don't be discouraged if the first property we walk onto isn't exactly what you want. It gives me a better idea, and then I can keep looking."

"Okay," Ty said.

"It's a great time to be looking, too, Tyson. It's a buyer's market,"

Jerry said. "Pricing is down, and people who've had enough of their farms and ranches are looking to get off before spring."

"Perfect," Ty said. "Thanks so much."

"Yeah, I'll send you the time and address of the first showing, unless you'd rather meet at my office."

Ty didn't see why he needed to do that. In fact, he'd never been to Jerry's office. After Finn had given him the man's number, Ty had texted the man, and Jerry called him. They'd talked for a good twenty or thirty minutes while Jerry wrote down all of Ty's preferences, and then they'd been texting since.

"You can just text me where to meet you," Ty said. "And we'll be there."

"Sounds great," Jerry said. "I'll talk to you soon."

"Yeah, thanks."

The call ended, and Ty turned off the truck.

"That's very exciting, cowboy," Winnie said. "Some showings next weekend."

"Yeah," Ty said, trying to muster up his enthusiasm for such a thing. "I guess we'll see." He slid out of the truck and met Winnie at the front corner of it.

As they walked toward the south stable, he reflected on everything that had happened in the last month. He was thrilled he didn't have to go through the clean-up around town alone and feeling more and more like himself now that he had Winnie in his life. He'd taken some big steps forward in his love life, in his personal life by looking for a new house of his own, and in his spiritual life by going back to church and letting the Holy Spirit guide him and direct him more than ever.

Ty wasn't sure that life would ever be perfect, and he knew he never would be. But all of that felt more manageable now, with Winnie's arm linked through his, than it ever had before. *And maybe,* he thought. *Life doesn't have to be perfect for me to be perfectly happy.*

They reached the stable's entrance, and Ty reached to open the door. "Dear Lord," he prayed right out loud. "Bless us that today will be easy, and that Winnie's car will get back to Three Rivers without incident, and that we can enjoy spending time together, even if the work is dirty."

"Amen," Winnie said, grinning at him.

He held the door for her and gestured for her to go first. "Now, come on," he said. "Today's your lucky day, because you get to meet some of my favorite horses on the planet."

23

Winnie grinned at the black and white horse Ty had just cooed at. Yes, *cooed*. The cowboy had never spoke as softly as he did when working with horses, and she stepped up to his side and ran her hand down the horse's nose.

"So you're Matilda, huh? Ty talks about you all the time. Did you know?"

"All the time?" Ty scoffed. "I don't talk about her all the time."

Winnie gave him a dry look. "Please. I hear about Matilda every day—even days you don't work here."

"That is not true."

"Should I go through our texts?"

Ty grinned at Matilda and stepped over to the notes at the side of her stable. "We'll get your stall cleaned out in a bit, girl. We have to do the tack room first."

Matilda stood deathly still, her eyes only halfway open and Winnie stroked her neck. No wonder Ty liked her. "I wish you could tell me what he whispers to you," she murmured.

"She can have a candy," Ty said, and Winnie turned toward him.

"She can?"

"This stable is mostly Lone Star horses," he said. "Angel's, Henry's, Trevor's, and any cowboys who work here and have equines, plus a few others."

"So we got the posh job, is what you're saying." Winnie grinned at him. "And I haven't met Trevor, have I?"

"I don't think you have, no." Ty moved down to the next stall. "This is Gypsum. Hey, you. How you doin' today?"

Winnie stood with Matilda and simply watched Ty interact with the next horse. Gypsum, an eggshell white horse, lifted his head over the half-closed gate and snuffled at Ty.

He chuckled at the horse. "Yeah, I know, You'd just gotten here, and then the world turned sideways, didn't it?" He leaned in close to the horse and actually touched the brim of his cowboy hat to the horse's head.

"My life has changed a bunch too in the past couple of days, believe it or not."

Winnie left the safety of Matilda's side then, and she leaned into Ty's side. "So this is Gypsum."

Ty tucked her in close. "He's my favorite."

"Shh," Winnie whispered. "You can't say it so loud. Matilda is *right there*, and you literally just said *she* was your favorite." She beamed at him, because Ty was simply adorable with his horses.

He grinned, first at Winnie and then at Gypsum. "He understands that life is unpredictable and changes constantly." He stroked one hand down the horse's neck. "Don't you, bud?"

"He does? How do you know?" Winnie envied the horse in that moment, being tended to by Ty, without a care in the world. Not only that, but she and Ty would feed this animal, clean out his stall, and make sure he felt like a king before they moved on to repeat the process for the next equine.

"He was born to be a racehorse," Ty said fondly. "He even trained for a few years, but then he got sold. No more running." He sighed like this was terrible news. "Gypsum loves to run, and he got a little fat and lazy at his new home. Then he got some foot rot, and his owner's sold him to a hobby equestrian.

"She got him fixed up, and he started training to be a show jumper. He only did that for a couple of years, and then, the woman's daughter got too old, and Gypsum came to Amarillo."

"Wow," Winnie said. "How do you know all of that?"

"Horses come with history," he said. "Just like people."

"Like, a written file?"

He smiled at her. "Sort of, yeah. His owner now is an ER doctor who works thirteen days on, and then has the rest of the month off. So we get him while he's working."

Gypsum blinked at Winnie, and he put off a more intimidating air than Matilda. "Do you tell him any secrets?" she asked the horse. "Is that how he knows so much about you?"

"This is Winnie," Ty said matter-of-factly. "Remember, I've told you about her?"

Winnie's eyebrows cocked up. "What have you told him?"

"Just that I was a little conflicted about you." He glanced at her and seemed to realize what he'd said.

"Conflicted?" Winnie asked, her voice pitching up like her eyebrows.

"I mean, in the beginning," Ty said. "I'm not conflicted now."

"I should hope not." Winnie's stomach pinched slightly. "What were you conflicted about?"

He took a beat to think about it. "You being my physical thera-pist," he said. "What people would think of that."

"No one's said anything."

"No, I know." He gave her a quick look with slightly narrowed eyes and left Gypsum. "This is Laura Ingalls. She belongs to Trevor, and she's one of his best cutting horses."

"I'm not sure I know what that means."

"They cut cattle out of the herd," Ty said. "Trevor's one of the best horse trainers in these parts, and he sells his cutting horses for tens of thousands of dollars."

"Wow, he does? I thought you said he couldn't walk?"

"He uses arm crutches, yeah," Ty said. "He's actually one of my heroes. He gives me hope."

Winnie wanted to know more about that, but she also thought Ty had more to say about what he'd been conflicted about when it came to her. "Why's that?" she asked, deciding to stick with this thread for now.

"Because," Ty said. "He's struggled physically for years. He's endured surgeries too. And yet, he just got married to the love of his life, and he runs this boarding stable." Ty shrugged. "And he's happy."

"Did you think you couldn't be happy?"

"After my accident? Absolutely. I thought I'd never be happy again."

"Were you happy on the rodeo circuit?"

Ty checked Laura Ingalls's chart, and then looked over to Winnie. "Happy enough, I guess. I wasn't *un*happy." He exhaled and turned to get something from the wall in front of the stable. "She gets oats this morning."

He went about giving Laura the feed bag, and then he took Winnie down to the next stall. "I don't think I knew what happy and unhappy meant."

"And you do now?"

"I one hundred percent do now."

Winnie refrained from telling him that perhaps God had given this experience to help him learn, and grow, and change. No one wanted to hear that half of their body had to be shattered so they could learn the difference between being happy and being unhappy.

"What were your other reservations about us?" Winnie asked quietly as Ty continued to stand there with Laura Ingalls.

"I don't know," he said.

"Don't do that with me."

Ty looked at her, and Winnie let her eyes hook into his. She worked with plenty of men like him—hurting, broken men.

Ty was no longer the man who'd first walked into their initial PT appointment. He'd changed right before her eyes, and oh, Winnie felt herself falling for him right there in Stable C.

"I was worried I'd asked you out just so Trap couldn't." He cleared his throat and shifted his feet. "Winnie, I'm still learning how to listen to myself. How to feel things and understand what they are."

She nodded. "I understand that."

"Yeah?"

"Yeah." She tried to shrug and only pulled it off halfway. "Imagine you were a week away from marrying someone you love with your whole heart. And you think they love you too. They've said it lots of times. You've been together for over *three years*. And then, she shows up and says she actually doesn't love you, and hey, I'm also leaving town. Good luck to you."

Winnie heard the very clear bitterness in her voice as the last word came out of her mouth. She couldn't hold Ty's gaze any longer, and she focused on Laura's shiny, chestnutty coat. "That makes you wonder if you know anything. If you'll ever be happy again. If you're really as stupid as it seems, and you can actually hear the shattered pieces of your heart as the taillights drive away down the street."

"Winnie, honey." Ty brought her close to his chest.

"So yes," she said. "I know what it feels like to be happy, and unhappy, and to second-guess literally everything I've ever thought, felt, or believed."

"I'm sorry. Of course you know what this feels like. I'm so stupid."

"Hey, no you're not." Winnie pulled away and looked at him. "It's okay for you to have this be a new experience for you." She tilted her head and watched his gaze flit around. "Can I tell you something that will feel like a lecture, or would you rather I not?"

Ty took the now-empty bag of oats from Laura Ingalls and re-hung it on the wall. He nodded down to the next horse. "Yeah, I can hear a lecture." He gave her that sexy, lopsided grin she loved so much. "If it's in your voice, it'll sound like sweet music."

Winnie giggled and shook her head, moving down to the next stall. "Now you're just sweet-talkin' to me."

"Is it working?"

She ran her hands down the sides of the next horse's neck and glanced over to the nameplate. Light glinted off it, and she couldn't make out the letters.

The words she wanted to say stormed through her head, and she debated whether she should say them out loud or not. She reminded herself that she wanted a partner she could speak her mind with, and she'd asked first.

He'd said yes.

"This is a new experience for you," she said. "Learning how you feel, and if it's true or whatever. But you're not alone." She lifted her eyes and met his. That tether that had always been there between them reformed, stronger and tighter than ever.

"You're not the first person to experience this, and you won't be the last. God knows you, and He knows what you need to become the man He wants you to be."

"I want to be someone who's good for you," he whispered.

Winnie's heart leapt and sang, causing a smile to come to her face. "You might be," she said. "But you might not be. We'll figure it out, but you shouldn't try to be who you think I want you to be. You should try to be the best person you can be, because I might not be the one for you, and then—"

"Don't say that," he said. "I can't think of a single reason why we shouldn't be together."

Winnie nodded. "I honestly feel the same right now, but Ty, we're only one month in."

"How long does it take?"

"How long did you date Jenn?"

He flinched and blinked like she'd thrown ice water in his face. "Okay," he said. "Point taken."

"We're together," she said, linking her arm through his as he checked the clipboard. "And I'm really enjoying it. I'm just trying to do what I think is right, and I know you are too."

"Yeah," he said.

"Hey, you guys."

Winnie dropped her arm at the introduction of another voice to the conversation. She looked past Ty to see Burt headed their way.

"Morning, Burt," Ty said, all diplomatic and professional. "I was told to check with you when we've finished our list."

"Did Caldwell give it to you?"

"Yep." Ty dug in his pocket for the paper, and he passed it Burt. "We're just checking the horses right now and doing the special feeding. Then I'll get them fed, and we'll work on the tack room."

Burt scanned the list. "I have a couple of guys on the tack room already."

"Oh," Winnie said. "That's not what Caldwell said."

Burt glanced at her, his expression darkening. "Henry and Angel brought in a lot more people than we need." He checked something on the paper and thrust it back toward Ty. "Did your sister change her phone number?"

Winnie blink-blink-blinked at him now. "Not that I'm aware of."

Burt growled something that sounded like, "So she's just ignoring me," and then spun on the heel of his boot.

Desperation clawed through Winnie, her need to apologize for Taylor right there on the tip of her tongue. She held it back, because she didn't think Burt would appreciate knowing that this was just how Taylor was. It didn't truly reflect on him.

"Poor guy," she murmured as he disappeared around the corner.

Ty scoffed. "Poor guy? He'll have another girl by dinnertime."

Winnie rapid-blinked again, in complete disbelief at how some people lived their lives.

"Come on," he said. "Just because we don't have to do the tack room anymore doesn't mean we have time to stand around and chat."

"Can we stand around and kiss?" Winnie teased as she caught up to him at the next stall.

He looked at her out of the sides of his eyes. "Maybe later."

Winnie tipped her head back and laughed, which caused the horse in front of her—a beautiful brown-and-white pinto named Freedom—to whinny too.

"Settle down, you," Ty said, his voice a touch harder than usual. "This is Winnie, and I've told you all about her."

Winnie felt like someone had plugged her in, what with the glowing warmth that flowed through her now. She truly enjoyed spending time with Ty, and seeing his equine side? That had only accelerated her feelings for him, and now all Winnie could do was pray she didn't fall too far too fast.

———

WINNIE KNEW time was the great healer, and she witnessed it around Three Rivers as the days passed. She saw debris piled out on the street in the morning when she drove to the clinic that had been picked up when she went home at night.

Ty kept her up-to-date on his friends and their ranches and farms, and everyone except Shiloh Ridge had been put back together in only a few days.

Valentine's Day was coming up next weekend, and Ty had asked her on an official date, and she'd been shopping for something new and nice to wear.

They'd be going to look at a couple of places for Ty in only two more days, and Winnie had just pulled into the parking lot at the clinic when her alarm went off. She silenced it, her eyes catching on the note she'd left for herself.

She tapped out a text to Ty. *I hope you have an amazing day off! Don't do anything but rest and rest and more rest. And remember, I'm treating you to dinner after our ASL class tonight.*

She sent it, tucked her phone in her purse, and reached for her bag. Her phone rang, and Winnie's heart jumped for a moment.

"That's so loud," she complained to herself, reaching to turn down the volume on her device. *It's your mother calling* sat on her screen, and Winnie inwardly moaned.

Still, she grabbed her stuff and got out of the car before answering the call. "Hey, Mom, I'm walking into work right now."

"I figured," her mother said.

"How's Daddy?" Winnie asked, because she'd spoken to her parents every day since last week's text-fest on the way to Lone Star.

"He's doing pretty good," Momma said. "I'm actually calling to see how you are."

"How I am?" Winnie repeated.

"It's February," Momma said, as if Winnie should be falling apart.

She did trip over her own feet, because of course she knew the calendar had changed. She still thought of Carver every single day, though she no longer blamed herself for what had happened.

"Right," Winnie said. "And I have a date for Valentine's Day next weekend, Momma."

"I just—" Momma sucked in a breath. "What? A date?"

Winnie smiled to herself and found her confidence all over again. "Yes, Momma, so this call better be about Daddy, because I'm not talking about him yet, and I'm not going to spend my time pining over the past either."

Winnie had never really been one to wallow, but the lost wedding had sent her into a tailspin for a while. One large enough to send her to another state, with a new job.

And yes, now a new boyfriend.

Momma exhaled, and Winnie could just see her gearing up to start a stream of talking. It made her smile, and she was definitely prepared when her mother said, "I finally got him to make an appointment with the doctor, and now *all* he talks about is canceling it," followed by a great big sigh.

24

Ty had not been on a Valentine's date in a very long time. Three years. No, four. Four long years, and every step he took down this road with Winnie felt like he was trying to run when he should be crawling.

He'd managed to get himself dressed as if going to church. Fine, a really fancy church sermon. A wedding.

"Yeah, your own." He half-scoffed and half-chuckled as he made the turn onto Winnie's street. His gaze zoomed in on her house, and everything looked peaceful and normal on this golden-bathed-in-sunset-glow evening.

If only he felt peaceful and normal on the inside. He pulled into her driveway and killed the engine. After reaching for the roses he'd bought after breakfast with his parents that morning, Ty dropped to the ground and started up the sidewalk to the front door.

"Howdy, ma'am," he called to Valerie Thompson, and the woman waved to him tonight, a smile appearing on her face.

Ty moved in a slow, steady way up the steps to the porch, and he knocked on the door before falling back. One hand automatically moved to his throat, where he wore a red bow tie for the first time in his life.

Definitely something a man would wear to get married, he thought, though this one had tiny white hearts all over it. He'd bought it at the downtown mall, along with the sleek, almost shiny black jacket he wore tonight.

He dismissed his thoughts about weddings and marriage. This was Valentine's Day, and he was going out with Winnie. That required polished boots, a new hat and jacket, the blood red roses in his hands, and yes, that bow tie sitting neatly at his throat.

He dropped his hand just as the door opened, and Ty's smile started to spread across his face before he even saw his girlfriend. Just the *idea* of her had him grinning like a lovesick schoolboy.

His heartbeat struck against his ribs like a rattler attacking, and every coherent thought Ty had ever possessed flew right out of his head.

Winnie stood there in a jumpsuit that defied every law of physics and good sense. The fabric shone a deep, rich purple, and it clung to her curves in ways that made Ty's mouth go dry.

One shoulder remained completely bare, the fabric draping elegantly across her collarbone and down her other arm in a way that was both modest and devastatingly sexy. Her hair fell in loose waves around her shoulders, and her lips were painted the same shade of red as his bow tie.

"Hey, Ty," she whispered, her eyes traveling down to his boots and back to his eyes.

Ty couldn't speak. He could only stare at the expanse of bare shoulder, the graceful curve of her neck, the way the purple fabric made her hazel eyes look more green than brown.

"Ty?" Winnie's smile faltered and fell off her face. "Are you okay?" She nodded to the roses. "Are those for me?"

He stepped forward, crushing the flowers between them as he cupped her face in his free hand and kissed her. Not the sweet, hopeful, blazing kisses they'd shared before, but something deeper. Something that tasted like need and want and...*mine.*

Winnie was his, and he was hers, and that thought burned through Ty's mind, heart, and soul as strongly as anything else ever had.

Winnie gasped against his mouth but didn't pull away. Instead, her hands fisted in his suit jacket, pulling him closer as she kissed him back with equal fervor.

When Ty finally pulled away, it was because of the ache in his left knee and not because he wanted to stop kissing Winnie. "You're beautiful," he said, his voice rough and yet tender at the same time. "I mean, you're always beautiful, but tonight you're—" He shook his head, unable to find adequate words. He did find the wherewithal to back up a step and get his weight settled in a better way.

Winnie's smile radiated pure sunshine. "You're not so bad yourself, cowboy." She touched the red bow tie. "I like this bow tie. Very festive."

"You said red was your favorite color."

"It is." Her eyes sparkled with this sense of knowing. "And you wore it for me?"

"I'd wear any color under the sun if it made you smile like that."

Giggling, she took the roses from him and lifted them to her nose. "These are gorgeous." She looked up at him again, a pure playful, desirous edge in her eyes. "Let me put them in water, and then we can go."

Ty followed her inside, unable to stop watching the way she moved. When she reached up to get a vase from a high cabinet in the kitchen, that bare shoulder flexed, and Ty found himself moving closer without conscious thought.

"Here," he murmured, reaching past her to collect the vase. But instead of handing it to her, he set it on the counter and turned back to face her. His hand came up to trace the line of her collarbone, and she shivered under his touch.

"I need to know something," he said quietly, pressing her back into the counter beside the refrigerator.

"What's that?" She didn't look away as her gray-and-white cat came meowing into the kitchen.

Ty likewise ignored the feline as he leaned down and pressed his lips to her bare shoulder—just once, soft and reverent. Then he raised his head to look at her, his fingertips tracing down the slender column of her neck until his hand fell away and he tucked it into his pocket.

"Why don't you wear dresses?" he whispered.

Winnie's expression shifted, something vulnerable flashing in her eyes. But she didn't push him back, and she didn't sigh, and she didn't look away either.

She took a breath, swallowed, and then all of her anxiety dissolved into a softness that Ty really liked. "Carver told me once that he preferred me in a dress. So I wore one every time we went out after that. Every single date, every church service, every family dinner. I wore what he wanted me to wear."

Ty's jaw tightened, and he felt something spark down in his ribs.

"After he broke up with me and left town," Winnie said, her voice steady despite the pain flowing through it. "I burned them in my backyard, my wedding dress included." She laughed, but it came out hollow and made Rocky yowl again. "I haven't worn a dress since."

She reached up and wiped the corner of her eye. "I know it's stupid, and I shouldn't let him have that power over me, but it's actually how I've taken back some of the power I gave him."

"Good for you, Win," Ty said fiercely. "Because this?" He indicated her jumpsuit, and brushed his fingertips along the hem of the single sleeve. "This is perfect. You're perfect, and I don't want you to be anyone—or wear anything—but exactly what you want."

Winnie's eyes stayed bright with her unshed tears. "Thank you, Ty."

"I mean it, sweetheart. Dresses, jumpsuits, those bright purple scrubs with trains—I don't care. As long as you're happy, I'm happy."

She rose on her toes and kissed him again, this one softer but no less meaningful. When she pulled back, she whispered, "But you did say tonight was more formal, right?"

Ty's mind had gone a little mushy, but he opened his eyes and came back to reality. "Yeah, I did say that."

"So the scrubs with trains wouldn't have worked."

"But you could've worn them," he said.

Winnie gave him that playful, *I-want-to-kiss-you* look again and gently pressed against his chest. "Let me put the roses in water, and you better behave yourself."

Ty couldn't quite make himself remove his hand from her waist as she fiddled with the blooms. She didn't swat him back, and in fact, her smile stayed etched right there on her face.

Rocky meowed again, and Ty leaned in close. "Does he need to be fed?"

"No, he's just begging, and he knows you'll cave." She gave him a pointed look and stepped back. "How cold is it outside? Do I need a jacket?"

Ty's eyes swept her bare skin all the way from wrist to earlobe. "I absolutely forbid you from wearing a jacket." He took her hand. "I'll blow the heater in the truck."

She grinned at him. "You'll keep me warm is what I'm hearing."

Heat flamed through Ty right now. "That's right, sweetheart. I'll keep you warm." He took her hand and led her out to the truck. Once he got behind the wheel and got the engine growling and the heater going, he met Winnie's eye.

She watched him with obvious curiosity. "So where are we going? You've been very mysterious about tonight."

"I told you to dress nicely." Ty grinned as he backed out onto the street. "Link and Mitch told me about this place. Apparently, it's where all the Glovers go when they want to impress someone."

"The Glovers have a secret romantic restaurant?" Her eyes widened. "Is it on their ranch?

Ty laughed and shook his head. "No, it's not theirs. It's just this place they know." He aimed them north and west, like they'd go to Amarillo.

As he drove toward the setting sun, the landscape opened up into rolling hills dotted with cattle and the occasional farmhouse. After only about ten minutes, Ty turned left down a long, tree-lined drive that opened up to reveal a stunning stone building that looked like it had been transplanted from Tuscany.

Relief painted through him, because he hadn't had time to come scope this place out himself. They were only open on weekends, and Ty hadn't been in town long enough—with the need to take someone on a very romantic, very expensive date—to know about it.

He honestly wasn't sure he was fancy enough to dine at a place like this. How many forks would there be? Ty's mind whirred as he tried to remember his teenage etiquette lessons, which his momma and daddy had insisted he take since he'd have to go to banquets and galas as a rodeo star.

"Wow," Winnie breathed out as she leaned forward and looked up and out the windshield. "What is this place?"

"Bellissima," Ty said, proud that he'd managed to pronounce it correctly after practicing with Link. "It means 'most beautiful' in Italian."

The honey-colored stone stood two stories tall, with arched windows and wrought-iron balconies. Soft golden light spilled from inside, a fountain bubbled in the courtyard, and the whole place had an air of quiet elegance that made Ty glad he'd dressed as well as he had.

He pulled through the circle drive as Winnie stared up at the building with wonder. "Ty, this is incredible."

"I hope the food is as good," he said as someone opened his door.

A valet grinned at him, and Ty nodded at the man. He'd ridden in limousines, with drivers, and the pop of photography in his eyes when he'd won the National Championship in Las Vegas.

He knew how to shutter everything away behind a mask of

nonchalance, but he could scarcely believe a place like this existed in Three Rivers, Texas.

He moved around the truck and helped Winnie down, tucking her arm in the crook of his elbow as he noted the overhead heaters warding off any chill in the covered drop-off zone.

A man opened the doors for them as they approached, and Winnie looked at him while he looked at her. He grinned, nodded to the man, and then entered Bellissima through carved wooden doors. As he stepped into the restaurant, it felt like he'd stepped into another country entirely.

Exposed stone and dark wood beams stretched everywhere, with an enormous fireplace crackling in the center of the room. Fresh flowers overflowed from vases on every surface, and soft Italian music played from hidden speakers. The maitre d'—a man in an actual tuxedo—greeted them with a wide, warm smile.

"Mister Greene, welcome to Bellissima." He nodded to Winnie, his voice filled with radiance. "Ma'am. Your table is ready."

He led them through the main dining room and out onto a covered terrace that overlooked the Texas hills. Even Ty wanted to take a moment to soak it all in—the beauty of the earth, the way it rolled and rose, the evergreen trees, and those that were still bare of leaves but absolutely stunning.

Heaters kept the February chill at bay, and their table sat in a private corner with a view of the sunset painting the sky in shades of pink, violet, and gold.

"This is perfect," Winnie said after she'd sat down, they had their menus, and they'd been told their waitress—a woman named Liv—would be with them in a moment.

"Ty—"

"Welcome," a woman said, and Ty looked up at Liv. It really had only been a moment. She came with a man holding a wine bottle and glasses, both of them exuding Southern charm.

"Happy Valentine's Day," she said, glancing from him to Winnie. "Are you two celebrating anything special?"

Ty looked at Winnie too, his mind once again a blank slate. But Winnie raised her chin, grinned with all she had, and nodded.

"Yes, ma'am," she said, and Ty thought she sounded a little more Texan in that moment. A smile curved his lips as he watched a hint of pinkness come into her cheeks.

Winnie reached across the table, and Ty met her halfway, feeling the tension in her touch as she squeezed his hand. "We're celebrating the fact that I didn't marry the wrong man a year ago."

"Oh, uh." Liv glanced at Ty, who ducked his head and started to chuckle. Winnie was *such* an incredible woman, and he realized in that moment that he'd have to continue to work to be the man she deserved.

And he'd never wanted to work so hard for something in his life than to be the man on Winnie's arm.

"It's okay," Winnie said. "I mean, for a long time, I wasn't sure it would be okay, but it is." She smiled over to Ty. "And now I'm on a date with someone who treats me like a queen, and wears a red bow tie for me when he never wears anything but black, and has found this gem out in the country to make the whole month of February something brand new for me."

Liv smiled too, and the man said, "We're very happy for you."

"Thank you," Winnie said, and she released Ty's hand with a small nod.

He looked up at the waitstaff. "I'm sure you have wines that will pair amazingly well with the food, but neither of us drink. What have you got in terms of mocktails?" He nodded over to Winnie. "That one likes something fruity and fun, and I want something sour."

He looked up at Liv, who beamed down at him, nodded to her second, and said, "Yeah, that about tracks."

Winnie burst out laughing, and even Ty joined in, because tonight was Valentine's Day, he'd worn a red bow tie, and Winnie had said so many things, done so many things, and wore so many things that had him spiraling into a freefall. If he wasn't careful, he was going to be in love with her before he dropped her off tonight... and right now, Ty was okay with that.

25

"This is unbelievable," Travis Walker whispered to himself. He tilted his phone toward his friend, Colt, who sat on his right side. Colt, in turn, dipped his head to read the text that Trap had just received.

Disgust ran through him, and he had no idea what Pastor Glover was even saying anymore.

The words from the text had been ingrained on the back of his eyelids, and he kept his eyes open for as long as he could, simply so he wouldn't have to see them again.

I need you to meet me at the build site in one hour.

Lila Mae Dixon had said more than that—something about how she'd found a last-minute flight on that Sabbath day—and she'd see him in sixty minutes. Not only that, but the text had come in twenty minutes ago during the sacrament service of church where Trap currently sat with his friends, and Pastor Glover had only been speaking for about ten minutes.

"Who's The Heiress?" Colt whispered, and Trap turned toward him with burning, stinging, watering eyes. He finally blinked.

"That woman who wants to build the cat sanctuary at the Hensen place."

Colt's eyes widened, and then a smile bounced across his face. "Good luck with that one, brother."

Trap sighed like he'd just been told he needed to wave a magic wand and get the church building to fly. That would actually be more possible than cleaning up the Hensen place to the specifications of a cat food heiress who felt like she could text him with sixty minutes' notice to meet her somewhere.

He looked over to Ty on his left side, and his friend looked at him, his eyebrows raised. Trap had been sitting with him, Colt, and Jacob at church for months now, and Ty had started bringing Winnie to their pew in the past couple of weeks.

Trap didn't mind it so much, only that she served as a reminder of how female-free his own life still was. Thankfully, he'd gotten past his *insane* crush on his cousin's wife, as he and Ruby had to work together at the construction firm and interior design center that his parents owned and Trap was set to take over.

The screen on his phone went dark, and Trap had half a mind to ignore Lila Mae's text completely. It was the Sabbath Day, for crying out loud. Wasn't anything sacred anymore?

At the same time, Trap would love to work on the Hensen place, as it would be his first solo project, one that he'd gone out and found himself and that his daddy would have no part in.

Sure, Trap could consult with him on anything, anytime, but Daddy wanted to slow down and ease into retirement at Seven Sons Ranch the way some of his brothers already had. Trap was more than ready and willing to take on the construction firm, as he'd been learning at his father's knee for twenty-five years. He was excited to take MSW Building & Design into a new direction while still living up to his parents' high expectations for the firm.

"I've gotta get out," he whispered to Ty, and his friend turned his knees so Trap could slither past him in the pew. "Sorry. Sorry, Winnie."

He left the church at a good clip, sure he would have to answer some texts from other cousins and friends and his parents who had seen him leave. He didn't mind. He could handle them.

The Hensen place sat west of town, and Trap could admit he'd been frustrated at how slow the project had been coming together. He and Ruby had done an initial assessment of the property almost two months ago now, and the dust storm had slowed everything down. Lila Mae had almost backed out, but the Hensen property really was the best fit for what she had in mind.

She wanted to build a cat rescue operation that her cat food dynasty would pay for. This would technically be a nonprofit arm of that, where Lila Mae would take strays, rehabilitate them, and adopt them back out into the community. She also intended to be a safe house for cats who couldn't be readopted, and she'd told Trap and Ruby that she planned to have two full-time veterinarians on staff, as well as groundskeepers, vet techs, and others to help her run the sanctuary.

Trap couldn't imagine dedicating his life to *cats*, but he supposed he'd dedicated his to wood and hammers, and there were probably plenty of people who didn't understand that.

He went out past Aunt Marcy's airplane hangars and Payne's Pest Free, which she still owned but didn't operate, and where Trap had spent plenty of time growing up, as his daddy and Uncle Wyatt were good friends.

All of Wyatt's kids now lived out of state in a small town called Coral Canyon in Wyoming, and they operated their own rodeo animal-training ranch. While his aunt and uncle hadn't made the move up there permanent yet, everyone in the Walker family knew they would eventually.

Trap beat Lila Mae to the Hensen property, where he had to stop at the gate, which was chained closed. He got out because spring had started to thaw the Texas Panhandle, and the sun felt good on his face today.

"Ten bucks says she doesn't have a key to this place," he muttered.

The Hensen ranch had been empty for years, and the previous family had been trying to sell the land and all the outbuildings for the past half-decade. Everyone wanted turnkey these days, and the Hensen property was about as far from that as one could get. That didn't concern Lila Mae at all, because she wanted Trap and Ruby to gut the place and rebuild it—basically from the ground up.

"Really, but not really," Trap muttered, which were words that Lila Mae had said herself when he'd asked her that very question.

"You want me to tear it all down and rebuild it? Why don't you just buy a piece of land that's bare bones?"

She'd given him a healthy pause over the phone and then proceeded to lecture him about renewal and recycling, as if the concepts were brand-new to Trap. To be honest, he'd never hurt for money, and he never would. His grandpa had been a billionaire due to his investments in the tech industry throughout the seventies and eighties, and Trap himself had inherited quite a bit of wealth from his own father. Still, he'd grown up watching his parents work hard for their company, and he wanted to do the same.

The sixty-minute mark came and went, and Trap's irritation with Lila Mae only grew. She finally arrived thirteen and a half minutes late, in the back of a sleek, black, oversized SUV. He expected her to drop from the driver's seat, but as he peered through the windshield, he could see a man with a buzz cut and a pair of shiny sunglasses sitting at the wheel.

So...not Lila Mae Dixon.

Truth be told, Trap had never met the woman face-to-face. They'd only spoken over the phone, and he'd looked her up on the Dixon's Delights website.

She wasn't the CEO. Her momma still ran the company, but Lila Mae had been labeled the Environmental and Social Impact Director. Trap had no idea what that meant, and everyone he'd asked hadn't either.

His gaze switched to the back doors, where he expected Lila Mae to emerge. A man on the passenger side—whom Trap had not even seen—opened his door in the front and dropped to the ground.

"Are you Travis Walker?" he asked.

"Yes, sir," Trap said with a tip of his cowboy hat.

"Praise the heavens," the man muttered, and he moved to the back door and opened it. "This man says he's Travis Walker," he said.

Still, Lila Mae did not get out of the vehicle, and Trap took a couple of hesitant steps toward it. The man, who wore a pale yellow polo and a pair of black slacks along with his own shiny pair of sunglasses, leaned in further. He sighed and turned toward Trap.

"She wants you to produce some identification."

"*I* have to produce identification?" Trap's eyebrows went up. "Why doesn't *she* produce some identification?"

The man rolled his eyes. "Your guess is as good as mine." He held the door open and stepped back, and Trap stood there and gaped for several long moments before he sighed as loudly as well and pulled his wallet from his back pocket. He flipped it open and walked over to him. "See? Travis Walker."

"Dude, I don't even care," he said. Then he looked into the vehicle. "It says Travis Walker."

He hadn't even looked at Trap's ID. That made Trap smile, and he backed up and stuffed his wallet away as—finally—Lila Mae emerged from the vehicle.

The driver got out and opened the other door, removing a classy black bag and placing it near the front corner of the SUV. A very unhappy yowl came from a cat carrier, which the driver had just set on the ground beside Lila Mae's bag.

"One can never be too sure," Lila Mae said. "Thank you for checking." Her voice rolled in a smooth Eastern accent, and Trap could only stare at her.

She wore emerald green from head to toe, including a hat that was tilted and pinned just-so on her head.

"Thank you, Franklin," she said, and she nodded to the man, who seemed relieved to get rid of her as he closed her door.

She pinned her smile on him as the SUV backed away and left, and Trap wasn't sure if this was a joke or not. "It's wonderful to meet you in person, Travis."

"You can call me Trap," he said. "Only my momma calls me Travis, and only when I'm in trouble." He threw a smile at her that Lila Mae didn't seem to know what to do with.

Another protest came from the carrier, but Lila Mae ignored it as she extended her hand toward Trap, but not the way someone would to shake his hand. Oh, no. She extended her hand like royalty, like she expected him to take it and kiss the back of it.

Trap did exactly that, because he knew when he willingly played with fire, he would get burned. Part of him wanted to see what Lila Mae would do if he scoffed at her and simply turned toward the land where she'd insisted he meet her. His lips buzzed against her skin for the tiniest of moments, and then he fell back a step.

"All right, Miss Dixon," he said. "You got me here on short notice. Now, what do you need that was so urgent that you had to call me out of my church meetings?"

His question seemed to stun her, for Lila Mae simply stood there and blinked at him, her long lashes painted dark though she had straw-colored hair and oceanic eyes. Trap could get lost in a woman's eyes like that, and he cleared his throat and looked away.

"I—" She seemed at a loss for words, and that definitely pushed the tension riding the air between them up to a new level.

Had she forgotten why she'd flown here?

Could she not hear him?

Trap did have Deaf friends now, and the longer the silence went on, the less sure he became.

26

Lila Mae Dixon blinked again and reminded herself of who she was, and why she wanted to be there.

She'd handled board meetings far surlier than this cowboy, and she moved over to the cat carrier, as Cleopatra once again voiced her displeasure at being left inside. "Oh, you're fine," she scolded the feline, and she crouched down right there in an almost muddy spot where she'd been dropped off. Her nerves beat through her now, though coming to Three Rivers and opening this cat sanctuary was everything she wanted. More importantly, it was everything her brother *didn't* want, and Lila Mae was determined to prove him wrong.

"There you go," she said in a soothing tone as she pulled the Bengal out of the carrier. She quickly grabbed the leash that rode with Cleo and snapped it to the cat's collar before she could bolt. "Now sit down and introduce yourself properly to Travis." She glanced over to him. "I mean Trap."

She'd never heard of the nickname Trap for a man named Travis, but this was only Lila's second time in Texas at all, and she once again threw a question heavenward as to why God had wanted her to come here. She didn't know why, only that she'd gotten the impression multiple times in the past couple of years about opening a cat sanctuary, and leaving the boardroom and company politics to someone more suited to it. That certainly wasn't her, though she had spent some time in slacks and heels, trying to get men to listen to her.

"You have a cat on a leash," Trap said.

"Yes," Lila said crisply. "This is Cleopatra. You may call her Cleo."

Now that was a nickname that actually made sense. Trap blinked at her, his eyes getting even wider. "I may, huh?" He moved closer and crouched down.

"Sit down, Cleo," Lila Mae commanded, making her voice as crisp as possible. The Bengal hardly listened to anyone, and she wanted to make a good impression on Trap for some reason that had nothing to do with how handsome he was, with that full, dark beard and dressed in slacks and a white shirt and tie for church.

Lila Mae would like to see him scruffy and dirty too, and she scolded herself strongly that she was not making a near cross-country move to find a boyfriend. No, she needed to find herself first, and her purpose, and something beneficial to do with the vast fortune the good Lord had blessed her with. Her parents didn't understand why she couldn't do that in Atlanta, and Lila Mae had given up trying to explain it to them.

Of course, no one knew the whole truth about Lila's desire to branch out on her own while staying close to something familiar, and a flash of regret moved through her.

Thankfully, Cleo sat, and Lila beamed at the cat as Trap reached out hesitantly toward her.

"She's a Bengal," she said.

"She looks like a tiny tiger."

"Yes," Lila said. "They're a beautiful and rare breed, and she came to me injured. I nursed her back to health, but couldn't bear to adopt her out again. She has quite a bit of anxiety, but she made the flight here just fine."

"You flew with her?"

"How else do you think I got here?" Lila Mae shot back at him.

Trap blinked his eyes, leaving Cleo and coming to meet hers. "You didn't tell me you were coming."

"That's not true," she said. "I said I might try if I could get a flight."

"You couldn't have texted me before you took off?" he asked.

"You didn't have to leave your church service."

"Didn't I?" He pulled out his phone. "Did you read your text? It wasn't a question. It wasn't, 'What are you doing today, Trap?' It was, 'Meet me here in sixty minutes. I'm on the ground in Amarillo.'"

Lila Mae swallowed, because yes, that was what she had done. Her brother had told her she was too demanding, but Lila Mae had grown up being demanded of, and she didn't know another way.

"I apologize," she said, because she needed this man's help. He would be her only tie to Three Rivers and the success of this place, and she wanted nothing more than to show her family that she had good ideas and would do honorable things with their name. "This week happens to be the best time for me," she said. "I apologize if that's not the case for you."

"You're going to be here all week?" Trap asked.

Lila Mae nodded. "If it's a terribly awful time for you, I understand." She reached into her handbag and pulled out her phone. "Perhaps we should schedule some appointments right now for this week."

"All right."

Lila Mae tapped on her phone. "I'll work around you." She looked up, hope streaming through her at the reminder that she would be here in Three Rivers for a week by herself. No overbearing older brother bossing her around, telling her what to do and making her feel small. No mother sighing wistfully and saying she wished she had grandbabies by now.

After all, it seemed to only be Lila Mae's job to provide them, as Kent had been engaged last year and unable to tie the knot, but her mother never talked about that. Oh, no. It was always about Lila Mae. She could hear her mother's disapproving tone even from thousands of miles away.

Lila Mae shoved the thoughts out of her head. She didn't have to deal with them this week, and she could finalize the plans for the build and the design with Ruby and Trap, and make the permanent move here come summertime.

"Well, what did you want to go over?" Trap asked, and Lila Mae blinked herself back to the conversation.

"I was hoping to walk through things with you today," she said. "So we can meet and go over some designs later this week." She looked up, hopeful. "I've been making a few sketches based on what you and Ruby sent me previously, but I need to see it for myself."

Trap nodded and then indicated the chained gate connected to a fence that ran north and south for acres and acres. "How are you planning on getting through that?" He looked over to her again, his gaze dripping all the way down to her shiny black heels and then climbing back to her face. Heat filled her, and she wasn't sure what kind of look Trap Walker wore on his face, but Lila had dated plenty of men in the past, and she recognized her own flash of attraction to this tall, dark, grumpy cowboy.

"You don't have a key?" she asked.

"I don't own this property, ma'am." The words came with a hint of frustration embedded in them. "Don't *you* have the key?"

Lila Mae huffed and surveyed the gate once more. It came together in two pieces of metal curved along the corners, each side with three rungs. It stood taller than her, to be sure, but surely she could duck between two of the slats and be on the property in a couple of seconds.

"I suppose I should have called the realtor," she said.

Trap chuckled. "Yeah, probably while you were waiting for your flight to take off."

She gave him a dry look and rolled her eyes. "Your point has been taken, Mister Walker. This morning was a bit of—well, it was a mess, okay?"

She sighed and took a couple of steps toward the gate, bringing Cleo with her on the leash. She put her elbows up on the top rung and gazed out at the land before her. Yes, it was a complete mess, just like the morning had been, and just like the past couple of years had been at Dixon's Delights.

All in all, Lila Mae's whole life had been a mess for the past couple of *years*, and she was ready to rebuild it into something she could be proud of, something that she could put her mark on, something that would bear her name and do good in the world.

"I'm sorry about this morning," Trap said. "And honestly, you probably saved me from a boring sermon anyway." He gave her half a smile and sighed as he too looked over the land. "I mean, it is your property, and we can probably duck under the fence here and walk around."

"No," Lila Mae said. "You're right. I'm not dressed appropriately for a walk-through anyway."

"You're not dressed appropriately to get on a plane," he said. "How do you walk through an airport in shoes like that?"

Lila Mae turned toward him and blinked once, twice, her heart pounding through her whole body. Then, for some inexplicable reason, she tipped her head back and laughed. It took Trap a couple of seconds to join her, but his deeper chuckle sounded among her higher-pitched laughter and reminded her that, though she would move here alone, she would at least know him.

So don't drive him away, she told herself. *Don't act like he owes you something, because he doesn't. And don't act like you're better than him, because you're not.*

"I don't know how you wear those boots, cowboy," she said as she quieted.

He smiled and simply shook his head. "I'm sure I can meet you out here sometime tomorrow," he said. "Probably later in the afternoon, because I know I'm meeting with a family to do a tree house in the morning."

"That should work really well," Lila Mae said, and she turned away from the chained gate and the property she had purchased. "We can go over a timeline and final design this week."

"Sure," Trap said, and they started back toward his truck, Lila Mae gently leading Cleo along. They reached her bag, and she stooped and lifted it.

"Let me get that for you," Trap said quickly, and he reached across her and took her suitcase from her. Then they both faced his truck, and Lila Mae realized that she had not arranged transportation from the property—uninhabitable at the moment—to the rental she had secured for the week—what she'd done at the airport before taking off.

She looked over to Trap and found him blinking blankly at his truck. "Can you give us a ride?"

He whipped his attention toward her, his eyes dropping to the cat and back to her. "Will she go in her carrier?"

Lila Mae grinned and shook her head. "Oh, no. She yowled the whole way here. I couldn't bear to put the poor thing back in the carrier." She bent and picked up Cleo, hugging her tightly to her chest, while Trap's mouth hung open and a look of disgust drew his eyebrows down into a frown.

Lila Mae grinned at him. "She's very clean. We'll just ride in the back." She took the first step toward his truck, and he dodged in front of her.

"I am *not* your chauffeur driver," he said. "You are *not* riding in the back. If I'm going to give you a ride to wherever you're staying here in town, you can ride in the passenger seat like a normal person."

He huffed at her and then stomped past her to the bed of his truck, where he threw her bag over unceremoniously before turning to pin her with a look that said, *Well, are you coming or not?*

Lila Mae liked him, and she liked that he'd stood up to her, and that he didn't seem to know that she was worth billions of dollars.

And why would he? She was just some woman obsessed with cats who had bought a dilapidated ranch and wanted to turn it into a feline sanctuary.

So she kicked him a smile and went to get in the front passenger seat.

27

Lacy Glover rolled over for the umpteenth time, emitting a long, loud sigh as she did. Beside her, her husband, Mitch, continued to snore, though she had woken him with her tossing and turning in the past.

She and Mitch had struggled to get and keep a pregnancy, and Lacy wanted to be grateful for every moment. She pressed her eyes closed against the tears, because she was now forty-*one* weeks pregnant with no sign of her little girl making an appearance anytime soon.

That wasn't entirely true, as Lacy had an appointment with her doctor the following afternoon. She'd spent the first hour of the night before falling asleep worried that Dr. Marsdon would induce her, and Lacy didn't want to have the baby on April Fool's Day.

One hot tear slithered out of the corner of her eye, and she quickly moved to wipe it away. Then, with another sigh that would wake anyone except those who were deaf, Lacy pushed herself up and balanced on the edge of the mattress. She reached for her phone, which she plugged in and left on her nightstand.

The clock read just past four in the morning, which made sense for the amount of darkness pouring through the window. Lacy really couldn't get up this early and expect to make it through the day, but she'd been on maternity leave for two weeks now, having planned to have a temporary administrator at *Signs for Success,* so she could focus on their baby.

She put one hand on her belly and used the other to balance herself against the nightstand as she stood. No matter how she sat or stood or lay, she was uncomfortable, and something hurt, so she didn't think too much of the pain radiating in a quiet, almost aching way through her lower back.

She'd never been pregnant before and had never gone into labor, and she honestly wasn't sure what to expect. She and Mitch had taken two birthing classes, as he'd wanted to be ultra-prepared for what they might experience at the hospital. He had accompanied her to every doctor's appointment in the past nine months, and their doctor—the sweetheart that she was—had started to learn some key signs for Mitch, like *baby, healthy, girl,* and *name.*

Oh, the name.

Lacy sighed as she got up.

She and Mitch had not been able to agree on what they should name their baby yet, and perhaps that was why Lacy had not delivered her yet.

She'd just stepped onto the cold tile of the master bathroom when a pain unlike anything she'd felt before ripped through her abdomen. She automatically threw out one hand, and thankfully, the vanity stood there ready to support her.

Lacy cried out, knowing immediately that she'd just experienced her first contraction. Panic reared through her, but Lacy reminded herself that she had done a great many difficult things in her life, and she would not be alone through this one.

"Mitch," she said, her voice loud among the dark silence of the house.

Of course, her husband could not hear her, and Lacy didn't dare twist to look over her shoulder toward the bedroom.

"Sunshine," she said. "Alert Mitch."

The dog barked, and Lacy wished she'd brought her phone with her into the bathroom so she could call Mitch and a light would flash.

"Champ, alert Mitch," Lacy said, the aching in her lower abdomen radiating around her back now—all signs of her going into labor. She didn't dare move.

She heard Mitch groan behind her. "Wake him up," she said to his hearing dogs. "Wake him up...Mitch."

He'd trained them to alert him when his name was spoken, and Lacy said it one more time. A moment later, Mitch made another noise, but he wasn't verbal and didn't actually speak. Only a few seconds after that, the bedroom light snapped on, and Lacy managed to reach up and turn the light on in the bathroom too. That brought her husband to her side.

"I'm going into labor," she told him, her hands flying through the signs.

He was devastatingly handsome, rumpled and fresh from sleep. He looked confused for a couple of heartbeats, and then he said, *I'll get dressed and get your clothes.*

Lacy nodded while Mitch returned to the bedroom. She survived another contraction before he came back, and she said, *I need my phone to time the contractions.*

He jogged away from her and returned with it, as well as her favorite maternity pants and one of his oversized T-shirts that she had taken to wearing as the weather warmed.

Tell me what to do, he said.

Lacy nodded to the shirt. *Help me get dressed and make sure I don't fall down.*

They'd talked extensively about how to communicate during the labor, as Lacy might not be able to use her hands to sign as much as she normally did. *Just watch my face, baby, remember?*

He nodded, his jaw tight and a fierce frown of protectiveness between his eyes. He helped her get dressed, and then he picked up the baby bag and kept his arm around her as they slowly made their way out of the house and into her SUV. Mitch growled as he moved the seat back, so he could drive them to the hospital.

They had sat down with Jacob and his parents, so everyone knew how to communicate with them when Lacy went into labor. She often acted as a go-between for Mitch and the rest of the world, and as he pulled around their circle drive, she reminded herself that she, Jacob, Mitch, and his parents could all sign.

Lacy didn't want either of Mitch's parents or her brother in the delivery room with her, and she and Mitch had decided they would manage on their own. They had promised to call Jacob, Cactus, and Willa when they were on their way to the hospital, so they could help with the academy, the dogs, and Mitch, if necessary. Mitch had brought Champ and Sunshine with him in the truck, as his two main hearing dogs went everywhere with him, but he had a few others he worked with on a daily basis.

"I'm going to call everyone." She typed the message on her phone and turned it toward Mitch.

He read it while driving down the lane and nodded. Her brother would be up in another hour and a half, as he got to *Signs for Success* early to start on the groundskeeping, so she sent a text to Jacob first.

Mitch and I are on the way to the hospital. We'll let you know what we need beyond help with the dogs. If you could take care of them today, that would be great.

She called Mitch's mother, because when she had first suggested that she would just text, Willa had looked like Lacy had lit the world on fire. Mitch's mother didn't answer, but Lacy simply dialed again—right as another contraction began. She quickly hung up and checked the timer.

"Three and a half minutes," she said out loud, and then she showed it to Mitch.

He nodded again, flexed his fingers on the wheel, and sped up. They lived about twenty-five minutes away from the hospital, but they'd driven it before, and Lacy thanked the Lord that she'd gone into labor early in the morning when there was no traffic.

Mitch pulled up to the emergency entrance of the hospital, and Lacy opened her own door and turned her legs to get out. In that moment, her water broke and she froze, her mind racing.

Mitch jogged around the front of the truck, which he'd left running—a habit he always had, no matter where they were.

"My water just broke," she told him.

Mitch nodded, his eyes tracking down to her knees. *Can you walk?*

Lacy wanted to say yes, but she honestly wasn't sure. *Maybe you could go find me a wheelchair*, she said. *Type it on your phone.*

He quickly pulled out his phone and typed the message, then turned and jogged inside.

Lacy hated that he had to communicate everything through text, but despite there being more accessibility for the hearing-impaired and deaf population, very, very few people in small-town Three Rivers knew sign language. Thankfully, most people they had to interact with could read, and Mitch returned only a few seconds later with a nurse and a wheelchair. He held her arm tightly—possessively —as he helped her into it.

The nurse asked, "Who's your doctor?"

"Doctor Marsdon," Lacy said. "I had an appointment with her later today."

"We'll page her," the nurse said, and she started pushing Lacy into the hospital.

"My husband is deaf," Lacy said. "You have to tell me where we're going, so I can tell him."

"Labor and delivery is on the third floor," the woman said pleasantly.

Lacy raised her hand and waved it so Mitch would look at her. "We'll get you checked in up there," the woman said. "And they'll give you a room number." She stopped by the emergency desk and said, "Call Doctor Marsdon for Lacy Glover."

"Yes, thank you," Lacy said, marveling that Mitch had been able to tell her that.

Up they went to the third floor, and Lacy got put in Delivery Room Three. Mitch helped her change into a gown, and her contractions continued.

I never called your mother, Lacy said.

Mitch nodded, and he lifted his phone to do it. *She's not answering*, he said. *It's still really early.*

I called once, she said. *She's got it on that three-call thing. Call her again, and then again, and then it'll ring.*

He did, and his momma finally did pick up, and Mitch was able to get her on video and tell her that they were at the hospital.

A nurse named Mindy came in and checked Lacy. "Doctor Marsdon is on her way, and you're dilated to a five already." She beamed at Lacy like this was fantastic news, but all her statement did was send a round of nerves through Lacy's whole body.

She leaned her head back against the pillow and nodded, everything rushing by while also moving incredibly slow.

Dr. Marsdon arrived; Lacy got her epidural; they received confirmation from Jacob that he and Ty would take care of the dogs that day.

My mom and daddy are here, Mitch said. *I'm going to head outside and talk to them for a minute.*

Lacy nodded and watched him depart mere moments before the doctor entered for probably the third time.

"How we doing?" she said. "I feel like you've got to be getting close."

"I feel like I've been in labor for hours," Lacy said, the discomfort coursing through every cell in her body rivaling that of being a week overdue. "I've been praying for this baby to come. Now I'm not so sure."

Dr. Marsdon laughed and asked, "Lots of pressure?"

"So much," Lacy said, as another contraction moved through her. She groaned and tried to sit up.

Dr. Marsdon took her position. "I think you're ready to push."

"Can you grab my husband?" Lacy said. "He just went out to see his parents."

The nurse went to do that, and Lacy made it through the first push by herself before Mitch came running in, pure panic on his face.

I'm so sorry, he said as he came to stand behind her and shore her up. He hadn't wanted to miss a moment of this, and he'd been worried sick for months that their baby would be born deaf. He brought it up every single day, while it was not something Lacy had worried about. Once she'd realized how much it concerned Mitch, she'd done her best to assure him and reassure him that they would do the best they could with whatever happened. After all, God never expected more than that.

Mitch seemed to agree most days, but he really didn't want a deaf child, because so many opportunities for him had been limited, and he'd had to work harder than most people to be where he was and do what he did.

Several long, tiring minutes later, the doctor finally said, "And here she is!"

The beautiful, gut-wrenching sound of a newborn baby's wail filled the air, and Lacy burst into tears.

Mitch, she said, waving his name sign with one hand. *Go see her. Go see her.*

He left his position at her shoulder and moved to the end of the bed. The doctor held up the baby, a look of wonder on her face. "I know you guys were expecting a girl, but I hope you have some male names picked out too, because your baby *boy* is here."

Lacy could only stare at the bright, angry red infant as *he* screamed. Then the doctor handed him to a nurse, who wrapped him up in a warm blanket and turned to put him on a table.

Mitch stood there at her side, pressing in close and asking, *He's a boy? We were supposed to have a girl,* to no one in particular. The nurse certainly couldn't understand him, and Lacy smiled. He looked over to her, and she loved him all the more when she saw tears rolling down his face.

Stay with him, she said. *I'm fine. I want you to stay with him.*

Mitch nodded, and Lacy called, "Remember, my husband's deaf, but he wants to stay with the baby. Just show him what you want him to do, and he'll do it."

"We've got it," the nurse said. "We're gonna get his blood to do all of our newborn testing, and I know you want a hearing test."

"Yes," Lacy said. "And Mitch wants to give him a bath and show him to his parents, if he can, before I have to nurse him."

"Well, let's deliver this afterbirth," Dr. Marsdon said. "And then whatever you two want to do is fine with me."

28

Mitch Glover finished gently dripping the warm water onto his son's head. The baby had absolutely no hair whatsoever, and joy coursed through him in a way he'd never felt before. The baby looked up at him with deep eyes mostly made of pupil, and nothing but love lived inside Mitch.

Everything inside his mind felt noisy, and he wanted to tell the baby how much he loved him.

The nurse at his side handed him a diaper, and Mitch put it on the little boy, being careful of his umbilical cord. She handed him the onesie that he'd gotten out of the baby bag Lacy had packed, and it took Mitch a few minutes, but he managed to get the floppy infant's arms and legs into the clothes.

How's Lacy? he asked, using his phone, as he'd been gone from her side for about thirty minutes now, while they'd done tests on his son and then given him a bath.

The nurse took his phone and typed into it. *She's doing great. You can take him to see your parents, if you'd like, or we can take him back in there to see if he'll nurse.*

Mitch wanted to be able to introduce his son to his parents with a name, and he and Lacy had thought they were having a little girl. He typed out a quick *Lacy,* and the nurse led him through a maze of white, fluorescently lit halls to a different room, where Lacy now lay in a hospital bed.

Her face brightened as Mitch walked in, their little bundle of joy held tightly in his arms and close to his chest. She reached for him, and Mitch passed the baby to her, and then crowded in beside her and sort of behind her, so she could lean back into his chest. Her voice vibrated through her shoulder, and though Mitch couldn't hear what she was saying to their son, it comforted him.

She looked up at him and signed with just one hand in slow, stilted ASL. *Did you show him to your parents?*

Mitch shook his head. *He needs a name.*

Lacy's shoulders slumped, and she looked down at the baby again. *Something strong,* she said. *The way your daddy is Cactus and stands sentinel over the family.*

Mitch started tapping on his phone, because he'd learned early in life that there was hardly anything he couldn't figure out on the internet. He hadn't even been thinking about male names, and he wasn't sure if he wanted to go with something cowboy, something biblical, or something normal.

Mitch had been praying with everything he had since the moment he'd found out Lacy was pregnant the first time that their baby could hear and that he or she would be happy and healthy, even though they had to deal with him as their father.

He typed in his search and then started showing names to Lacy. *Caleb—loyalty and courage. Ezra—helper and steadfast.*

I like Brooks, he said. *Feels rugged and strong.*

Lane—quiet strength, he read, and then he saw *Knox,* and that rang a bell in his heart. He typed it onto a list, knowing that the names in the Glover family meant something and could be a little unusual. He saw *Shepherd* and *Bridger,* and liked the symbolism of both of those.

He showed his short list to Lacy, and it included Ezra, Knox, Griffin—a mythic guardian—Shepherd, and Bridger.

She considered the list while their beautiful boy slept in her arms. He didn't seem too terribly concerned with eating, and Lacy looked good, with plenty of color in her face, as she studied his phone. She looked up and then pointed to *Knox*, and then *Shepherd*.

Those are my top two. You choose, she said.

Mitch looked at the phone, but she put her hand over it and he looked up again. She spoke slowly so he could read the words on her mouth—something she rarely made him do.

"I want him to have your name as his middle name."

Mitch marveled at the perfect way in which Lacy loved him. He let his tears fall again as he looked at the list and tried out the names with his name in the middle.

Knox Mitchell Glover.

Shepherd Mitchell Glover.

Then he erased one and showed it to Lacy. She smiled and nodded, and Mitch tucked his phone into his back pocket and said, *I'm going to take him out to meet my Momma and Daddy, but I'll bring him right back.*

Lacy hugged him close and placed a gentle kiss on his forehead. Her mouth moved as she said something to the baby, and then she passed him back to Mitch. He found his way out to the waiting room, where his momma stood only ten feet from the door, watching it.

"Cactus," she said the moment she saw Mitch, and she started to cry too.

Mitch loved his momma so much, as she had sacrificed and sacrificed for the people around her. Daddy stood up too, both of their eyes wide, somewhat anxious, and yet also crinkled with happiness. Mitch passed the baby to his momma and then signed to Daddy, *We named him Shepherd Mitchell Glover.*

Daddy wiped his eyes and relayed the message to Momma, who leaned down and whispered something to the baby, and Daddy put his hand on Mitch's arm, and when their eyes met, he nodded.

Behind him, Mitch turned and found Dr. Marsdon walking toward him with the delivery nurse. She had learned a few words of sign language, but not many—enough to say *good news* with her hands. And of course, her entire persona radiated it as well.

Still, his heartbeat thrashed against his ribs, though good news shouldn't make him nervous. Dr. Marsdon smiled at the nurse next to her and then, with slow, stilted signs that were almost correct, she said, "Baby Shepherd is not deaf."

A sob branched its way out of Mitch's throat. Had he just been spared his worst fear? He would have loved his son no matter what, and Mitch did not think he was any less than a hearing person, but it could not be denied that life was easier for those who could hear, and Mitch did *not* want his son to have to struggle the way he had.

He turned toward his daddy, who received him into his arms and held him tightly while Mitch's gratitude overflowed and his emotions continued to pour out of him.

29

Ty couldn't help grinning at the picture Mitch had just sent. "He's the cutest thing on the planet," he said out loud, though Jacob couldn't hear him. They'd both been on the text, along with Mitch's thankfulness that they'd taken care of his hearing dogs for the past four days since Shepherd had been born.

Ty hadn't met him in person yet, but Shepherd, Mitch, and Lacy had just been discharged from the hospital, and they would be back at the house soon. He and Jacob had been there for the past couple of hours, working with the dogs, then cleaning up the house, and making sure lunch would be ready when the now-expanded family arrived.

Then, later that afternoon, Ty had another showing, at yet another farm. This one sat out near Henry and Angel's place, but Ty almost didn't want to go. He'd looked at seven properties now, and none of them seemed like they'd ever been inhabited.

Or, if they had been, it had been a while. Or they were too big for him to manage on his own. Or they were completely inaccessible for a single man with a limp and limited use of his left arm.

Which isn't really true anyway, Ty told himself sternly. He could use his left shoulder, arm, and hand almost normally. He simply felt weaker on that side, and he sometimes didn't trust himself if he had to carry anything too heavy, bulky, or cumbersome.

He'd learned that very few farms in the Three Rivers area were accessible. They all had big, wide front porches that required eight to ten steps to reach. Most were two levels—hardly any single-family ramblers or farm-style houses—and the outdoor property? Nowhere near accessible. Barns had lips he had to step over, uneven terrain, and disheveled walkways.

After Ty's last showing a couple of days ago, Jerry had actually suggested he buy a piece of land and build what he wanted. Ty wasn't entirely opposed to that, except for the fact that it would take longer. A lot longer.

Another picture came in—this time of Mitch and Lacy and Shepherd together—and both Mitch and Lacy looked happier than Ty had ever seen them. He loved his friends, and he remembered what Mitch had told him: he'd looked for *Signs for Success* for a long time, bought something he could work with, and then turned it into what it needed to be.

With his smile still on his face from the picture, Ty closed his eyes and prayed that God would lead him where he needed to be too. He could fix walkways and level land—or pay someone to do it. While he and Winnie sure had gotten serious fast, Ty could admit he'd started to think more long-term about his life with her. She had not verbalized any objection to him buying his own farm. In fact, she'd encouraged him and gone with him on some of the showings when she was able.

Women saw things differently than men, Ty knew that, and he didn't worry so much about the pantry or the closet or storage or laundry facilities the way Winnie did. He wanted to be able to plant a garden and live comfortably with his horse and maybe a few more dogs. And yes, maybe a miniature donkey or two.

"A pygmy goat," he whispered, because that was what Winnie

had teased him with when he'd told her he might have a few other pets in mind.

He immersed himself in the listings, though he had them all memorized at this point. He'd been looking for a few weeks now, and his favorite pastime was to see if something new had come up, though Jerry had told him he would alert Ty the moment he saw anything that suited him.

He looked at the two-story white house in the listing where he would meet Jerry later that day, until the lights flashed in the kitchen and both William and Maven alerted Jacob.

"They're here," Jacob said, and Ty got to his feet and followed his friend into the living room, where, sure enough, Mitch carefully led Lacy through the front door while she carried their baby in her arms.

They all radiated pure joy—even the infant—and Jacob laughed as he engulfed his sister and brother-in-law in a hug. Then he took Shepherd from Lacy like he ran a day care instead of mowing lawns, weeding flower beds, and working with hearing dogs. Sunshine and Champ sniffed their hearing-dog buddies while Ty stayed out of the way, somehow feeling perfectly at home and definitely out of place at the same time.

When Mitch and Lacy looked his way, he said, *Congratulations, you guys. He's perfect,* in flawless sign language.

They both grinned like fools.

We have lunch for you, Ty said, gesturing toward the kitchen.

"Oh, bless you," Lacy said right out loud, and she stopped at Jacob's side as he settled onto the couch and handed him a burp cloth. *He'll have to eat soon. Are you okay with him?*

Fine, Jacob said, his smile suggesting he was definitely more than fine.

Ty grinned and followed Mitch and Lacy into the kitchen.

I'm sure your family will bring a lot of food, he said. *If I know the Glovers at all.*

I think Link's Momma has already been here. Lacy moved to the fridge and opened it. *Yep, look at all these casserole pans.* She closed the fridge, beamed at Ty, and then took the wrapped sandwich Mitch handed her. "Thank you so much, Tyson. We really appreciate everything you've done the last few days while we've been gone."

"Of course," he said, speaking and signing, the way Lacy did. "I'm happy to do it." He bent and patted William's head. "I really liked having him with me at night."

Did you? Mitch asked. *Maybe I should have you take him more often.*

It took Ty a moment to catch up to Mitch's fast signing, and then he said, *If you think he's ready, I'd love to have him.*

Ty didn't need a full-fledged hearing dog, and he'd learned a lot from Mitch about how to train one. He'd learned so many things since returning to Three Rivers, including being kinder to himself and increasing his patience with everything.

Mitch's hands flew again, and Ty caught *place*, but not much else. He grinned and said, *You sign too fast for me.*

Mitch chuckled, picked up Ty's phone, and pointed. *Looking at this place?*

"Oh, yeah. I'm looking at it this afternoon," Ty said.

Looks nice, Mitch said. *At least the sidewalks aren't all cracked up.*

"I didn't know you were looking for your own place," Lacy said as she sat at the bar. "That's great, Ty."

"It's not going great," he said. "I'd really like something one level, but there's not a lot out there. I want something already on flat ground, with immaculate buildings, no cracked sidewalks, and no trip hazards."

He grinned at Lacy and picked up his own sandwich. "Wishful thinking, I know."

"Mitch built the entire academy," she said. "If there's something you like about it, you can use the bones to flesh out everything else."

Ty nodded. "I have a hard time envisioning the flesh."

"Maybe you should talk to Ruby and Trap," Lacy said. "Isn't that what he does?"

"Yeah," Ty said, thinking it over. "Maybe I should have him come on a few showings with me."

Lacy nodded encouragingly and took a bite of her sandwich. After she swallowed, she asked, "How are things going with Winnie?"

"Good," Ty said, and he didn't even mind the question. "She's really great."

"Yeah, we really like her here," Lacy said. "The students love her."

She's very...positive, Mitch said, and he didn't seem super jazzed about that.

Lacy grinned at him. "He's happy to have Winnie on board," she said. "He just acts like positivity is a negative trait sometimes."

I do not, Mitch said, and Lacy only laughed and shook her head.

Ty grinned at Mitch, because they were definitely cut from more of the same cloth than he was of Lacy's. Lacy finished her sandwich and said, "I'm going to go feed the baby, and then maybe I'll lay down for a nap too."

Same, Mitch said, but he stayed at the counter, though he'd finished his lunch, while Lacy went into the living room. Ty caught her moving through the mouth of the hallway and down toward the master bedroom.

"You want an update on the dogs?" Ty asked Mitch, who nodded. Ty didn't much like speaking to Mitch because he felt so inferior in his language skills compared to his friend, but he did his best, and the message got across. Thankfully, Jacob came in and helped too, and eventually Ty got to his feet and said, *I'm gonna head out. You guys go take your naps.*

Mitch stood, gave him a big hug, and said, *Thank you so much again.*

Ty started northwest, and then suddenly didn't want to go to the showing alone. He pulled into a gas station parking lot and picked up his phone to call his mother.

"Hey," Momma said. "What's up?"

Ty sighed. "Nothing."

"Yeah, sure sounds like it."

Ty let the corners of his mouth lift slightly. "I don't know. I just wanted to hear your voice."

"Where are you right now?" she asked.

"Sitting at the gas station," he said. "What are you and Daddy doing this afternoon?"

"About the same as every other afternoon," she said. "Working with the horses."

"If I send you an address, would you want to come walk through a place with me? I've looked at six or seven, and I just don't know if I can go alone. It's so depressing."

"Yeah, you sound kind of sad."

"I don't really feel sad," Ty said, trying to find what he did feel. "I just don't feel like being alone."

Momma hesitated for a moment. "That doesn't sound like you at all, Ty. Out of all of us, you love being alone."

"Maybe short-term," he said. "Maybe I'm just tired. I just got to see Mitch and Lacy's new baby."

"Oh, how are they doing?" she asked, a new softness in her voice.

"Amazing," he said. "And... I don't know. They seem so happy, and they're together, and I just have to go back to my sad apartment by myself. And it sure would be nice if I could go to my own place and see Juniper."

"Yeah," Momma said softly. "Horses are good friends. Let me talk to Lucas and make sure he'll be okay here this afternoon without us."

"Daddy doesn't have to come if he's too busy," Ty said.

Momma scoffed. "Are you kidding? Out of the two of us, I'm way busier than your daddy."

Ty chuckled, because that was true. "I'll text you the address. I'm meeting Jerry at two-thirty. If you can make it, great. If it's too hard, no big deal."

"Nothing's too hard for you, baby," Momma said. "I'm sure we'll see you there, and you can think about what else is making you sad. Because you know I'm going to ask, and I'll need you to answer."

"I'm not sad, Momma," Ty said, almost regretting the call.

"Okay, well, what are you and Winnie doing tonight?" Momma asked.

"I don't know," Ty said. "I usually go over to her place after work, and we decide if we want to go to dinner or if she wants me to cook."

"Maybe the four of us could go to dinner," Momma said.

Ty hesitated, recognizing his mother's behavior in his own. "You know, I think I would like that," he said. "Because I really like this woman, Momma." He took another moment, the "but" hanging between them.

"But I think I need more than a few hours' notice to be prepared to go to dinner."

"All right," Momma said. "Maybe we should put something on the calendar, then."

"I'll talk to Winnie tonight," Ty said. "I do think it would be fun, but a little stressful."

"Why would it be stressful?" Momma asked. "You don't have to be anyone but who you are."

"No, but *she* might feel like she needs to," he said. "I would be stressed if I was going to dinner with her parents."

"Oh—Lucas is right here," Momma said. "I love you, bud. Text me the address."

"Love you too, Momma," Ty said, and he ended the call.

He looked at his phone, wishing he could call Winnie, but she had a much harder time answering at work. So he typed out a quick message to her and sent it before reminding himself that he'd traveled the continent with only a rodeo manager, his horse, and a couple of bags of personal items for years.

"Yeah, but you don't have that life anymore," he told himself, and he didn't even want it. He wanted to be able to call his mother and have her come to a showing, or text his girlfriend and let her know that he missed her and felt lonely.

He arrived early at the farm, but he knew from Jerry's intel that no one lived there right now. He drove down the dirt road, which was pretty well-kept considering they were coming out of winter and had endured a couple of pretty major storms in recent months. Ty loved all the trees that hid barns and buildings, as it gave a sense of privacy he really liked.

He rounded the corner and the house came into view. His heart leapt and bobbed against the back of his throat when he saw that he could drive right up to it and only had to navigate three steps to the front porch.

"This is not what was in the listing," he said, frowning at the single-story house. The one online had been white with pale-blue shutters—and two levels. This one was pale blue with white shutters, and just the one story.

He quickly pulled out his phone, just in case he'd come to the wrong place. He scrolled to Jerry's text, tapped the link, and flipped through the photos. He recognized every single one. He'd definitely been looking at the right property. Then he realized he'd never noticed there were *two* houses on this parcel.

"What in the world am I going to do with two houses?" he muttered, looking up. He wasn't sure, but something inside him told him to be patient and to have an open mind.

His phone chimed with a text from Winnie, but movement out his side window drew his eye as his parents' truck rolled to a stop beside him. He smiled and waved at his mother and then quickly looked at Winnie's text:

I can't wait to hear all about the house tonight. I'm really craving some cheesy enchiladas. Can we go to Marco's for dinner and you can tell me all about it?

Of course we can, Ty said, and then he got out of the truck and stepped straight into his Momma's arms, where she held him close to her heart the way she had when he was a baby, a little boy, and now a grown man.

Ty was once again reminded that life didn't have to be perfect to be wonderful. He stepped back and grinned at his mother. "Thanks for coming," he said. "This is actually one of two houses, believe it or not."

"Wow," his daddy said, peering at the house like it might hold secrets he really needed to know. "What are you going to do with two houses?"

Ty burst out laughing, because he had literally just asked himself that very same question.

30

"Anyway," Ty said in Winnie's ear. "I just pulled up to your house. I'll get the cats fed, and we can go to dinner when you get here."

"Okay," Winnie said, and she dipped her hand into her purse to find her keys. "Wow, the wind is terrible." A flash of fear moved through her, as if she might have to endure another dust storm in her car. Winnie looked to the western sky, which remained clear and dust-free. The sun stayed up longer and longer these days, but it would be down in probably the next hour.

"Oh, hey, Rocky." Ty's soft coo for her cat came through the line, and Winnie's heart filled with appreciation for Ty. As much as he claimed not to like cats, he sure took good care of Rocky and Salmon.

When she pulled her keys out of her purse and clicked to unlock the door from several feet away, she practically dove into the safety of it, shivering just a little bit.

"It's really cold today," she said.

"Yeah, we've got a little spring cold snap coming through," Ty said. "I can't wait to tell you about this place."

He'd already told her quite a bit, as he'd dialed the moment he'd gotten back in the car after wandering around a smaller hobby farm that he thought might actually work for him. It was the first time she'd heard any true excitement in his voice after a showing, and it did Winnie's heart good to hear him so happy.

She pushed the ignition button and her sedan roared to life. Thankfully, it had not been in the shop for very long—the bumper had just had to be pulled out and the engine cleaned.

"Okay, I'll let you go to drive," he said. "I'll see you soon."

"All right," Winnie said, though she loved making her quick fifteen-minute evening commute with Ty on the line. He went to work earlier than she did and was usually done a few hours before her. They'd fallen into a nice rhythm of dating, where she called him after her final paperwork was done for the day and he kept her company on the drive home, though she usually found him already at her house, feeding the cats or stirring something on the stove. The man loved to cook, and he was very, very good at it.

Tonight, they were going out, and Winnie couldn't wait to have some of her favorite chicken tortilla soup and chips and guac while Ty told her everything about the property.

She arrived home, called, "Let me just change my clothes real quick, and we can go," as she walked inside, and tossed her bag on the dining room table.

He didn't answer, and Winnie looked out the sliding glass door. Ty loved to sit on her back deck, and he was brave enough to let the cats out with him. She found the three of them out there—Salmon prowling around the top of the stairs that led down into the yard and Rocky sitting right on Ty's lap, the cowboy using his big, capable hands to give the cat a rub.

Winnie had never been jealous of one of her cats until that moment, because she knew what luxury it was to have Ty's hands touch her. She slid open the door a foot or two and said, "I'm home. I'm just going to change and then we can go."

Ty turned toward her, and she caught a glimmer of joy in his eyes. "All right," he said. "No rush."

"Oh, there's a rush. I'm starving."

He gifted her with her favorite lopsided smile and turned back to the river. "We'll go when you're ready, then, sweetheart."

Winnie got ready quickly, chastised Salmon for taking so long to come in off the deck, and before she knew it, they had arrived at the Mexican restaurant she'd requested.

They seated themselves on this Thursday evening, and a waitress approached with a basket of chips and a bowl of salsa. "It's open taco-bar night," she said. "Or I can bring menus."

"I don't need a menu," Winnie said. "But I also don't want open taco bar."

"I do," Ty said. "That sounds amazing."

The woman grinned at him and then focused on Winnie. "What can I get you, hon?"

"I want the chicken tortilla soup, the guacamole sampler, and the beef enchiladas."

"You got it." She nodded to Ty. "Taco bar is open. You grab a plate and eat as many tacos as you want in one night, cowboy."

Ty clapped his hands together, his smile wide and glorious. "Someone's speaking my language."

They laughed together, and she left, promising to bring water and a drink menu.

Ty did not immediately jump to his feet and head for the buffet, and Winnie was actually surprised he'd ordered that, as he hated buffets and having to carry a plate while he walked.

"So tell me about this place," she said. "You've been mysteriously quiet about it since you called."

"Yeah." Ty took off his cowboy hat and set it on the seat next to him. He ran his fingers through his hair, and Winnie couldn't help the way her hormones fired at his handsomeness. She liked him in the black cowboy hat, but she liked it when he took it off too. The man had a great head of hair—one she'd had the opportunity to run her fingers through a time or two when he kissed her.

She blinked, trying to focus on the conversation. "I actually feel really good about it," he said. "I've been trying to sit with it instead of just pouring everything out. And it's not much when you first pull up to it, but it's got two houses."

"Yeah, you said that."

"I don't know, I just think it's kind of perfect. The smaller one is more move-in ready, and I could live there while I fix up the bigger one."

"That's the two-story one, right?"

The waitress returned with ice water, and Winnie reached for the glass. "Can I have the virgin tequila sunrise?"

"Yep. Anything for you, cowboy?"

"You know what? I want a really big Diet Coke tonight."

"You got it." She set down the platter of guacamole and added, "You can have as many chips as you want, hon. Just let me know when you need a refill."

"Thank you," Winnie said, and the waitress moved away again.

"What did your parents think of it?" Winnie asked, reaching for a chip. She swiped it through the guacamole that had corn and pico de gallo in it—her favorite variety—and put the whole thing in her mouth.

"I think my daddy was more impressed than he let on," Ty said. He dunked his chip into the salsa. "And Momma kept asking so many questions."

"Oh, boy," Winnie said, smiling. "Did that drive you nuts?"

"At first," he admitted. "But then I realized they were good questions I should be asking. So it turned out all right."

"What was she asking?"

"If the place has a well, what the water rights were, can more than one family live on it—that kind of thing."

"It's your property and it has two houses. Surely the county can't tell you who can live there."

"Jerry said it's zoned for residential use. And I'm not trying to start a business or anything, so that would work for me."

"That's great, baby. Do you want me to go get you a taco?"

He finished his chip and shook his head. "No, I can do it." He slid to the end of the bench and stumbled for a moment as he got to his feet. Instead of heading for the taco bar, he came to her side of the table and leaned down. "It's good to see you, Win." He pressed a kiss to her temple that shouldn't feel so erotic, but did, and then walked away to get his tacos.

Winnie watched him go, wondering when her feelings had started to feel like love.

Her phone chimed as she filled a chip with regular guacamole—her second-favorite variety on this platter—and she knew it was her mother without having to look at the device. Winnie sighed, because it was Thursday, and she wasn't sure she had the patience to deal with her parents tonight. Her mother needed constant advice—though she'd already looked everything up on the internet and wouldn't listen to anything Winnie suggested. She simply wanted to vent, and Winnie supposed everybody needed somebody like that.

She checked the screen and found that her mother's text wasn't the only one she hadn't read. She had a couple from Jerome at work, and one from Colt, who was more Ty's friend than hers, that sent her heartbeat tumbling. She tapped on his, though her mother sent in another message that started with *you need to call me.*

Hey, Winnie, Colt said. *Ty's birthday is coming up next month, and me and Trap and the boys want to do something for him. I'm sure you guys have some romantic plans, so will you let me know what day works for us to kidnap Ty and show him a good time?* He'd added a smiley-face emoji, and his second text read, *Don't worry—it'll be good, clean fun.*

Winnie grinned at the text and then tapped over to her mother's, because she had not known that Ty's birthday was in May and therefore didn't have any romantic plans as of yet.

Winnie, your father has fallen down, and Brad has told us to go to the hospital. I just don't know if it's necessary or not. And you know how your father is—he thinks the doctors might be trying to trick him about everything. Can you please call him and tell him that he needs to go to the hospital?

The next text, which had to come in only a few seconds after the first, said, *You need to call me, please. It's really urgent.*

Her heartbeat sprinted through her chest as pure indecision raged through her. Ty had not finished telling her about the property, and she wanted to ask him about his birthday too. She glanced over to the taco bar and found him standing there with a plate of food in his hand, resting his left hip against the counter as someone she didn't know spoke with him. Ty knew everyone in town, so this encounter wasn't unique or unusual, and Winnie quickly dialed her mother.

Her mother answered after only one ring. "Oh, praise the heavens, Winnie. I called nine-one-one."

Alarm rang through her. "You called nine-one-one?"

"Your father was in so much pain, he threw up," she said. "I didn't know what else to do, and I don't need you yelling at me too."

"I didn't yell at you," Taylor uh, yelled, from somewhere on the other end of the line.

"I'm not yelling at you, Mother," Winnie said in a calm, placating voice, quickly employing the role she'd always played in her family: a peacemaker between her parents and her sister. "How far out are they, Momma?"

"Seven minutes," Momma said. "Can you come?"

"Momma, I live three hours away now, remember?"

"But you could be here soon," her mother said.

"Mom, I have a job. I can't just leave town. You're capable. You'll go to the hospital with Daddy, and you'll figure out what's going on, and you'll text me."

Not only that, but Taylor lived right there, and Brad only lived thirty minutes away. Winnie wasn't sure why *she* needed to rearrange her life when her parents had other people to rely on.

"I'll tell Taylor to be nice," Winnie said. "And I'll text Brad so I get all the updates, okay?"

"Okay," Momma said a second later, the sound of Taylor's voice silencing. "I swear that girl was getting on my last nerve."

"She's been on mine for a while," Winnie said, a flash of sympathy moving through her at the same time. Her parents could kick Taylor out anytime they wanted, and they didn't, so they must not hate having her live there as much as Momma sometimes said she did.

"Oh, they're here," Mom said. "That was so much faster than I thought."

"I'll let you go," Winnie said. "Keep me updated."

She hung up just as Ty sat down across from her. A sigh moved through her whole body, and she instinctively reached for another chip, because guacamole made everything better.

"What's going on?" Ty asked, a hint of weariness in his voice now.

"My dad fell," Winnie said.

Ty pulled in a breath, his eyes wide as panic played across his features. "Is he all right?"

"I don't know," she said. "My mother was freaking out. Taylor was yelling. They called the paramedics."

She swiped her chip through the third sampling of guacamole on the plate, which was a fruity guacamole with pineapple and onion. It wasn't her favorite, but she tried to have a bite of each whenever she came.

She picked up her phone and quickly texted her brother.

"I told Brad to call me later," Winnie said. She raised her head and looked directly at Ty. "I'm not going to let it ruin my night. My parents have plenty of help. My sister lives with them, for crying out loud."

Ty watched her for a moment, and then his gaze turned compassionate. "All right," he said. "But feel free to take calls and answer texts."

Winnie silenced her phone and flipped it over. "Nope. He's not going to die tonight. I know that he fell and probably hurt his back, because he has broken discs there anyway."

"Do you think he'll have to have another surgery?" Ty asked.

"I don't know," Winnie said. "I don't know anything." She gave him a glare. "I don't want to talk about it."

"All right," he said, his voice pitching up.

Her soup arrived, and she gave the waitress the best smile she could, then reached to put all of the sour cream from the little cup into the soup. "Tell me about the property," she said. "I want to hear about the houses. And you said one of the barns was actually in good shape."

"Yeah." Light returned to his eyes.

Ty wasn't one to go on and on, and so when he did talk, Winnie wanted him to keep going. He told her that the land was in decent condition and he could probably pay someone to grade it better and put in real concrete sidewalks instead of gravel walkways that would allow him to be steady on his feet and get out to the barn to his horse and other farm-animal pets he might add.

He made it clear that he was not trying to homestead like his friends Brandon and Lenore. Any animals he brought to his farm would be for fun, the way Conrad had mini donkeys, Mitch owned too many dogs, and Wilder's fiancée, Savannah, had ducks and llamas and chickens.

Winnie loved this wild cowboy side of Ty, and as he spoke, she was able to set aside her worries over her dad and simply enjoy being out with the man who made her feel like a princess and treated her like his queen.

When he'd eaten his fill of tacos, and Winnie had eaten her chicken tortilla soup and the enchiladas she dreamed about, she drained the last of her mocktail and smiled at him.

"Well, there's one more question for you tonight."

"I'm tired of talking," he said, because he'd detailed that the fences needed to be fixed and that the bigger house needed a new roof. But the chicken coop had good bones, and the land seemed like it had been parceled thoughtfully for pastures and fields. Ty didn't want to plant alfalfa or hay, but he wanted to garden—an activity Winnie encouraged. It did require a lot of bending and use of his hips, so he'd detailed how he could put in raised beds and that there was the frame of a greenhouse, though it needed to be cleaned out and rebuilt.

She worried about who would do all this work, as Ty was usually pretty exhausted at the end of his day now, and he only worked at Lone Star for about six hours three times a week and a half-day at the orchards on Tuesdays.

She kept her concerns to herself, because they'd never gone over well with Ty, and she knew he just needed her support over this property. He'd looked at so many and been disappointed over and over. This was the first time he'd actually been excited, and Winnie would not take that from him.

"It's just a fast question," she said. "I heard it was your birthday next month."

Ty's gaze went back to hers. "You heard it from who?"

"Colt texted me," she said. "He and the boys want to take you out, but he doesn't want to interrupt any of our—" She lifted her brows, feeling flirty and fun despite everything going on that night. "—And I quote, 'fun romantic plans.' I didn't know it was your birthday next month."

"I'm sure I've brought it up," he said.

Winnie gave him a look. "Ty."

"I don't want it made a big deal of," he said. "My Momma makes this huge deal of it—which, by the way, she wants us to go to dinner with her and my dad."

A flash of anxiety moved through Winnie, but she kept it off her face and out of her voice. "Okay. We can set that up."

"My birthday is on May eleventh," he said. "And I'd much rather spend it with you than my friends."

"I'm sure we can do both," Winnie said matter-of-factly. "Let me look at my calendar."

She flipped over the phone—which was a huge mistake—as she now had missed calls from her mother, Taylor, and Brad. Her mouth turned dry and her stomach swooped. She had eaten far too much Mexican food for that to be comfortable, but she tapped on her calendar and slid it from April to May.

"The eleventh is a Thursday," she said. "That's perfect—your day off." She grinned at him. "I'll take that day off too, and we can spend the whole day together, and you can go out on the weekend with your friends." She looked at him, her eyebrows raised. "What do you think?"

"Yeah, that sounds fine," he said.

"And your parents...." Winnie let the words hang there, waiting for Ty to tell her they didn't need to set anything up with them. When he didn't, she added, "What about just next Thursday? You're always so tired on Mondays and Wednesdays, and I teach on Tuesdays and Thursdays, so it would give us an out. We'd have to be done by six-forty-five."

Ty looked at his phone. "Yeah, we've got to be done here in about fifteen minutes."

Winnie was suddenly so glad that he'd driven so she could check texts and find out what was going on with her father as he drove them to *Signs for Success* for her evening sign-language class.

"I'll tell them about next Thursday," he said. "And see if that works. It probably will. They don't do much."

Winnie nodded, the texts about her father already consuming her while Ty asked for the check. She read that her father was getting an MRI and would be attached to an IV for stronger pain meds to deal with his back.

Taylor's text was a lecture that Winnie had not answered her phone. She ignored it and texted her brother: *I'm getting all the messages. I'm just busy tonight. It's Thursday, remember? I'm teaching.*

Oh, sure, got it, Brad said. *Don't worry, Win. We've got everything handled.*

Do you? Winnie asked. *Because Taylor seems like she's about to lose her mind.*

Brad sent a few laughing emojis and then: *When does Taylor not act like she's about to lose her mind? Daddy's fine. He's in the hospital, and they're administering pain medications. I'm taking Momma something to eat, and I'll be able to talk to the doctor.*

Thank you so much, Brad, Winnie said.

Of course. I live right here. Don't let Momma guilt you into coming up here. They're fine. They have doctors who know what they're doing.

He was right, of course, but Winnie couldn't help the guilt that streamed through her.

Love you, sis. We'll keep you updated.

Love you too, Brad, she said, and Winnie thanked the Lord above for her brother, because it seemed like the two of them were the only ones who didn't completely freak out when something went wrong.

She looked up and reached for Ty's hand, grateful for him too.

"Everything all right?" he asked, and she tucked her hand safely and securely inside his.

"It is now," she said, as if holding his hand made all the difference, because to her, it did.

31

Ty sat on Winnie's back deck listening to the river roll over the rocks, late-afternoon spring sunshine soaking straight into his soul. This was the kind of life he wanted, but he frowned, keeping a tight grip on the knife in one hand and the wood he was whittling in the other.

It was an exercise Winnie had asked him to do to build strength in his fingers. And the reason he couldn't seem to find even a vein of happiness was because his next physical therapy appointment would be with someone else.

"It's fine," he muttered to himself.

Salmon lifted his head at the sound of Ty's voice. He loved being outside more than Rocky and alerted on every bird and movement in the backyard. Winnie had told Ty a dozen times she enjoyed coming home to find him in her house, but he still felt a little strange about it.

So, on evenings when he hadn't planned to cook, he sat on the deck with the cats, read his scriptures, texted family and friends, did his physical therapy, or, like today, he whittled.

Winnie had told him he could stay at the house to take care of the cats—another reason for his grumpiness: She was leaving that evening to drive the three hours home to her parents' house.

"Home is not the right word," Ty grumbled as he reached down and stroked Rocky's back.

The cat rubbed against his ankles and then settled at his feet, leaving Salmon to do all the reconnaissance work of keeping the backyard safe for the three of them.

The sliding glass door opened, and Winnie said, "Hey, there you are."

"Hey, sweetheart," he said, immediately putting a smile on his face. He didn't want her to go, but her father had fallen and needed a fairly major surgery, and her brother and sister had been dealing with things for a week now. Being surly about it wouldn't help either of them.

"You got Rocky out here," she said, coming closer.

"He likes the outdoors. It just takes him a little longer to realize it."

Winnie grinned, sighed, and walked past him to the edge of the steps.

"Hey, it's gonna be fine," Ty said. "It'll be good to see your momma and daddy again."

"Yeah, I know." She turned back, a fierce look on her face. "I've only packed enough clothes to stay through the weekend. I'm going to get there tonight, get all my questions answered, assess a few things, and tomorrow, I'll make sure he has appointments with the right people."

Ty nodded and gestured for her to come closer. When she did, he took her hand, gently tugging her between his legs. "Sit with me, sweetheart."

Ty could sometimes barely hold up his own weight, but Winnie didn't protest or complain. She simply settled onto his right leg and curled into his chest. He'd never felt more like a man than he did in that moment, and he pressed a kiss to her temple.

"You'll be back on Monday night," he said. "And I'll have dinner ready."

She nodded. "I have to work Tuesday."

"Maybe I should move my appointment, because I don't really want to see Jerome."

"Oh, please. He'll be good for you," Winnie said. "I think I've been babying you."

"Give me a break." Ty rolled his eyes. "You haven't been *babying* me."

Winnie giggled and pressed further into him. Ty wanted her to be happy above anything else, and he wondered if that was what love felt like. He'd thought he'd been in love before, but it hadn't been this warm, wonderful feeling—this keen sense of missing, even though Winnie hadn't left yet.

"Are you going to stay in the house?" she asked.

"I haven't decided yet," Ty said.

"You can. It'd be a lot easier with the cats."

"I know." He couldn't quite articulate why it felt strange to stay at his girlfriend's house while she was out of town, only that it did.

"It smells like something's cooking," Winnie murmured.

"Yeah. I put one of my curry chicken bags in when I got here. It should be ready in the next few minutes."

"I suppose I should finish packing."

"You're not ready?" He grinned at her as she straightened. "I'm shocked by that."

She grinned back and nudged his chest. "I'm mostly packed. I just need to get my toiletries from this morning."

"I miss you already," he said.

A softness entered Winnie's face that told him she missed him too.

"So we'll eat," she said. "And then you're going to kiss me goodbye and tell me everything will be fine."

"I like that."

"Then what are you going to do?"

"I'll probably go by my parents'," he said. "I want to talk to them one more time about that farm."

Winnie's expression crumpled. "I thought you felt good about the farm."

"I do. Jerry should have the papers ready for me to sign tomorrow. I just want to ask my daddy's opinion on a couple things."

She nodded.

"And then, to be honest, I'll probably go home, pack a bag, and come stay here with the cats."

"I know they'd like it," Winnie said.

Ty realized then that *she* wanted him to stay with her cats. He nodded and brushed his fingers along the back of her neck and into her hair.

"Do you miss me already?" he asked, needing to hear it.

"I do," she whispered.

Ty pressed his lips to hers. Her mouth trembled under his, and he wished he could erase her anxiety and fears. But he couldn't change her sister or her parents, and he told himself he didn't need to try. Winnie was a grown woman; she knew how to handle her family.

"Maybe I'll come on Saturday," he said.

"It's a long drive," she said. "I'm going to be making sure my daddy has everything set up at home, so it's really accessible."

"Okay. I just want you to know that I'd come."

"Of course I know that," she said. "And you'll tell your parents how sorry I am that I had to cancel dinner."

"They understand."

"It's still frustrating," Winnie said, frowning out at the river.

"Someone told me once that how we deal with the frustration is what matters."

Winnie whipped her attention back to him. "Are you seriously quoting me...to me?"

He laughed and pulled her tighter. "Sometimes you say really smart things, sweetheart."

"Sometimes?" she screeched, laughing.

Ty laughed too, glad Winnie relaxed in his arms and leaned her head against his chest.

"All right, we better get going," she said a minute later. "Or I'm going to be pulling into Oklahoma really late."

"You'll text me when you get there?"

"Yes, cowboy." Winnie slid off his lap and turned back to offer her hand. Ty didn't need help getting up, but he slid his hand into hers and let her pull him to his feet.

"Don't let your sister make you feel small," he whispered. "Because you are mighty." He swept a kiss across her cheek and tucked one against her ear. "I think you're the most incredible woman I've ever met. Don't let her make you think otherwise."

Winnie sniffled and nodded, then stepped out of his arms, took his hand, and led him into the house for their goodbye dinner together.

———

AN HOUR LATER, Ty pulled into his parents' driveway, Winnie's final goodbye kiss still burning against his lips. She might not have said everything in plain words, but the way she gripped his collar and clung to him told him everything he needed to know, at least for now.

He parked on the street in front of his parents' house and looked at it. He'd lived here until very recently. His parents had been very, very good to him and always there for him no matter what. Now that he knew more about Winnie's family, he realized how good he'd had it.

He sat with pure gratitude streaming through him. Momma stepped onto the front porch, clearly worried, and he grinned, waved, and got out of his truck.

"Winnie feels really bad about canceling dinner," he said as he started up the steps.

Momma and Daddy had installed new railings when he'd first come home after being injured, and he still used them to this day.

Momma waved a hand and pulled him into her arms. "Oh, it's fine," she said. "It's dinner. We eat it every night."

"That's what I told her, but she still feels bad."

"She get going okay?" Momma asked.

Ty hugged her tighter, his emotions storming through him. "Yeah," he said, his voice breaking.

She held him and waited him out; no questions, just Momma's strong, steady heart.

"Is Daddy here?" Ty asked when he'd found his center.

"He's on his way," Momma said as Ty stepped out of her arms. "We ran into some trouble with Molly."

"That can't be true." Ty kicked her a grin. "That horse is a saint."

"Yeah, well, she was," Momma said dryly, her gaze sharpening the longer she looked at him.

He'd come to ask Daddy about a few projects on the property he'd be buying tomorrow, but he realized he had a few questions for his Momma too. "Momma, you know I don't like it when you look at me like that."

"Like what?"

"With all those questions in your eyes."

"I'm not doing it on purpose," she said.

"I know." He breathed in the comforting scent of home and faced her. "I'm going to be staying at Winnie's while she's out of town," he said. "It's just easier with the cats."

"Of course."

He blinked, then raised his chin. "Momma, how do you know when you're in love?"

Her eyes widened, and her chest rose sharply.

"Wasn't expecting that, were you?" he asked, a smile tugging at his lips.

"You think you're in love with Winnie?"

"I don't know," Ty said. "But it hurt letting her go, and I don't like that I won't see her tomorrow, even though I know she'll call me tonight and tell me everything. It just feels...like too much distance."

Momma nodded. "Well, she might be a keeper then, Ty."

Before she could say more, the back door opened and Carolina's voice came inside. "Is Ty here, Momma? His truck is out front."

Momma's eyes flew toward the kitchen. "Yeah, he's right here," she called.

Ty gave Momma a nod that said he was fine. Then he turned as his sister came in. "I'm right here, Carolina."

"I thought we'd watch a movie tonight." Her brows went up, asking him if he'd stay and do that. Ty never wanted to watch movies, but his sister always did when she was sad and needed to be surrounded by people who loved her.

"Yeah, sure," he said. "I'm always up for a movie."

She moved in and hugged him. "What are you sad about, brother?"

"I'm just feeling anxious about a few things right now is all."

"And Winnie left today," Momma said.

Carolina gasped and pulled back. "Oh, of course. I'm sorry I'm here, Ty. I can go—"

"Why would you need to go?" he asked. "So I can have Momma all to myself? I don't think I'm ready for that."

It was Momma's turn to scoff. She brushed past him into the kitchen. "Daddy's gonna be here in ten minutes with pizza, so I suggest you treat me nicely."

"Oh, come on, Momma," Ty said, following her. "I was just joking."

He hugged her again, both of them laughing. Ty had just settled at the counter with a Diet Coke when Bryan and Ellie walked in.

"Wow, Ty's here," Bryan said, and then he stopped. "What's going on?"

Ty rolled his eyes. "For the love of eight seconds, I come home all the time."

"Do you, though?" Carolina teased.

"Where's Winnie?" Bryan asked, and Ellie nudged him, her eyes wide. "Oh—I mean, maybe you two aren't—"

"It's fine," Ty said. "She had to go to Oklahoma. Her daddy fell, remember?"

"Oh, right," Bryan said. "So you decided to join us for our midweek dinner?"

Daddy stepped in, calling, "All right, the food's here!" before Ty could answer. Thankfully.

He didn't want to be reminded he didn't come around as often as his siblings, or that he was obviously still the black sheep among them. But in that moment, with them rallying around him and Daddy pulling him into a big hug, he certainly felt like he belonged.

32

Winnie glared at the console in her car as her phone started to ring yet again. "Taylor, I swear I'm going to kill you," she muttered.

She had just crossed the border from Texas to Oklahoma and stabbed the button to take the call. "Hello," she said as politely as she could. Her sister had been badgering her for a solid week, as if Winnie didn't have anything going on in her life and could simply uproot everything and come home to take care of Daddy.

Taylor's crying came through the line. "You have to come home, Winnie."

"I know," Winnie said. "I'm on the way right now."

"I just can't bear them anymore. Momma thinks I should stay home all the time, and I can't be trapped in this house with them twenty-four seven."

Winnie gripped the steering wheel and worked not to roll her eyes. "Taylor, I just crossed the border," she said. "I'm probably an hour away."

"You should see the way they order me around. It's like Mom

hurt her back too, but she didn't, and she's perfectly capable of making dinner."

Winnie sighed, the fight leaving her body. She didn't want to argue with her sister. She'd listened to plenty of her mother's complaints about their father, and while Winnie agreed with a lot of them—and had no idea what it would be like to live with a chronically ill person—she knew her mother didn't handle stress very well.

Just like Taylor.

"Taylor," she said, this time louder. "I'm on the way, and I already told Momma—and you—that I was going to bring dinner. Remember?"

Taylor sniffled. "Yes. You're right."

Winnie nodded encouragingly, the way she would to a small child. "All right, so it's going to be fine. I'm going to be there in a few minutes. Remember, I shared my map location with you so you can see how far away I am."

"What are you going to get for dinner?" Taylor asked, all traces of distress now gone. Of course.

"I told Momma I was going through the drive-through at Roadkill Barbecue, and she texted me your orders, so I already have everything I need." Winnie made her voice very firm. "I'm not making extra stops, Taylor. I worked all day, and I've been driving for hours."

Once she got to her parents' house, she'd have to haul her bags in, figure out where she would sleep in the cramped house, and listen to at least three different versions of the same story—one from her mother, one from Daddy, and one from Taylor.

"It's just that we're out of Doctor Pepper," Taylor said.

"Then use that app and order some. I'm not making an extra stop." She glanced down at her phone where her map was up, though she'd made this drive before and it was a straight shot north. "It says I'm fifty-seven minutes out, which means I'm not going to get there until a quarter past nine. I'm tired, and I'm not stopping."

"Fine," Taylor said. "But just so you know, I'm going to be gone all day tomorrow. I have had enough of dealing with them. It's your turn."

"I'm aware—" Winnie started, then cut off as a loud beep filled the car, indicating Taylor had hung up on her.

Winnie stared at the dashboard. Incredulity ran through her in hot, rampant waves. Taylor had *not* been alone in taking care of their dad. Brad had been there until Monday morning, when he'd gotten up early and made the long drive back to work. Not only that, he had a wife and a family to take care of, and Taylor had no one but herself.

I don't know why you're surprised, Winnie thought, glancing out her side window. *Taylor is a narcissist, and everything is about her.*

The radio came back on, and Winnie let the country station Ty had introduced her to whisk her cares and worries out the window.

She drove through the barbecue restaurant as planned and arrived at her parents' house exactly when her map app said she would. She left her bag in the car, hoping to use it as an excuse to escape for a moment later, gathered the plastic sacks of food, and headed inside.

"I'm here," she called. "And I brought dinner."

"Praise the heavens," her momma said from the couch near the front door. She jumped to her feet and approached Winnie, tears streaming down her face. "Oh, it's so good to see you, my girl."

Winnie believed her. She knew without a doubt that her momma and daddy loved her, and she let her own powerful feelings of love flow through her as well. "I got the smoked turkey," she said, her voice a little thick. "And plenty of mashed potatoes. I think you'll have extras for a week."

She managed a giggle and then pulled back from her mother. "Where's Daddy?"

"I already have him set up in bed," Momma said.

Her father bellowed something from down the hall, but Winnie couldn't make out the words.

"I'll fix him up a plate," Momma said. "You go say hello." She took the bags and bustled into the kitchen while Winnie took a moment to get her bearings and find her sister.

"Where's Taylor?" she asked when she didn't find her in the living room, dining room, or kitchen.

"She ran out to get a soda pop," Momma said.

Winnie wondered what time she had left, chose not to say anything, and went down the hall to see her father.

Her parents had a bed where the head and foot could both be lifted or lowered, and Daddy sat up on his side closest to the door. A fond smile coursed through her. "Daddy." She rushed to his side and leaned over gently to hug him. "Tell me if I hurt you."

"Oh, you're not going to hurt me," Daddy said, and he gripped her fiercely, the tight hug telling Winnie she was loved. She thought of Ty and the way he held her on his lap and in his arms and close to his heart.

"Momma's bringing in dinner," Winnie said as she stepped back. "What can I get you? When's the last time you took pills?"

She surveyed the nightstand beside him. It had been cleared of his usual Bible and books; his reading glasses sat on top of an e-reader, and he had a half-drunk bottle of Gatorade, a tall hospital water bottle with a straw, and an array of creams and pill bottles.

"Momma writes everything down," Daddy said. "She can't seem to remember what she gave me and when, so we started doing that."

Alarm tugged through Winnie, but she didn't let it ring too loudly. She reached for the small notebook on the far corner of the nightstand. Her mother's familiar handwriting shone back at her, and she found Daddy had taken his pain pills at five-thirty.

"It's been a little over three hours," she said. "Are you feeling all right?"

"We time it that way on purpose," Momma said from the doorway. "So he can take his strong narcotics right before bed. Then he sleeps the best."

"Okay." Winnie actually thought that was a smart move.

"I could use some more water," Daddy said. "And I'm not going to drink that Gatorade."

Winnie reached for the offending items and cleared them from the nightstand as Momma approached with Daddy's Styrofoam container of barbecue on a plate.

"She remembered the bacon on the mac and cheese."

"That's a good girl," Daddy said, and he took the plate from Momma.

Winnie noted the color in his face and how well he seemed to be doing. Of course, he lay in bed wearing a back brace, probably in the most comfortable position he'd been in all day. She turned to fill his water bottle and toss the Gatorade and went to do that in the kitchen.

"I'll take it," Momma said, and Winnie handed her the refreshed cup of ice water.

Instead of following her down the hall, Winnie moved to the French doors and stepped outside, taking a deep breath as she hugged her arms around herself.

Her parents had a half-acre property here in Redwood. Nowhere near what Ty was going to buy for his horses and the small farm animals he'd count as pets, but she found their faithful border collie, Lucky, near the back fence. Winnie walked across the deck and down the steps to greet him. He was thirteen now and clearly excited to see her. She smiled, opened his run, and crouched to scrub his neck and face.

"How you doing, Lucky?" Lucky whined and licked her, turned in a circle, his rump wagging in joy to see her.

"Winnie," her momma called.

Winnie rose and faced the house again, the motion light blazing as she made the trek back, Lucky bounding ahead of her.

"Oh, don't let him in," Momma said. "He's a pain."

"Momma, how long's he been in the run?" Winnie asked.

"Um, Taylor put him outside...when your Daddy fell." Momma glared at the dog as he dodged past her into the house. He went straight to the water bowl in the corner and started lapping vigorously.

More alarms rang through Winnie, far louder now than the fact that her aging mother needed to write down her father's medication schedule. "Momma, when's the last time you fed him?"

"Taylor takes care of him," Momma said.

Watching Lucky sniff his empty bowl and then turn to look at her, Winnie very seriously doubted that. "Momma, I don't think he's been fed today."

"I'm sure that's not true," Momma said.

"Have you met Taylor?" The words slipped out before Winnie could stop them. She shook her head. "Never mind."

She walked to the pantry and opened the doors, expecting to see Momma's neat rows of baking supplies, canned goods in holders, bags of flour and sugar and rice, and the bucket of oatmeal on the floor. Instead, pure chaos stared back.

More packaged food than Winnie had ever seen in her parents' home stared back at her. Mac and cheese, bagged noodles, rice dishes, lentil cups, the list went on and on.

"Where's Lucky's food?"

"We had to move it into the garage," Momma said.

Winnie turned a long look on her mother. When Momma didn't meet her eyes, Winnie's heart started to pound an irregular rhythm.

"Come on, Lucks," she said, trying to sound casual. "Let's go get your food." She scooped up his bowl, opened the door by the dining table, and stepped down the three steps into the garage, flipping on the light as she went.

She'd parked on the street, because her parents' minivan was in the driveway, and she'd wanted to leave room for Taylor's SUV. She hadn't realized the minivan was there, because they couldn't pull it into the garage.

She blinked at the disarray and magnitude of items swallowing the two-car garage. Momma had always kept a standing fridge and freezer beside the door, as well as a chest freezer. Daddy had hunted in Winnie's childhood and filled the freezer with venison every year. For a few years, they'd invested in a cow co-op and gotten half a beef with a neighbor down the street, and Momma was a good cook, especially with soups and stews.

Now, moving boxes and a couch and loveseat set filled the second parking spot in the garage, and a queen mattress and box springs leaned against the wall covering Daddy's tools. Trash bag upon trash bag, most of them clearly tossed from the entrance and left where they landed, littered the other half of the garage. One had liquid oozing onto the concrete.

With the sight of all that garbage, the smell hit Winnie, along with the realization that things here in Redwood were far worse than she'd known.

Lucky whined and circled her legs, and Winnie jolted back to the task at hand. She'd never been to the landfill, but she could figure it out. She cringed inwardly at loading up her parents' and Taylor's trash and driving it somewhere, but she would do whatever she had to do to be able to drive away in good conscience on Monday night.

After all, she had a job, a little house by the river, two cats, and Ty waiting in Three Rivers. She couldn't stay here, even if Taylor forgot to feed Lucky and everyone in this house had forgotten how to walk the trash an extra twenty feet to the big black barrel outside.

She looked to the shelves above the chest freezer and found a bag of Lucky's food there. "Thank you, Lord," she whispered, because she did not want to get back in her car and drive to the grocery store. She would have, though, because Lucky needed—*deserved*—to be taken care of.

She filled his bowl and set it on the floor right there in the garage, needing another moment before she went inside and confronted her mother about what had really been going on.

Unfortunately, Momma opened the door a few seconds later. "Oh, you found it."

"Momma," Winnie said, sweeping an arm across the garage. "What is all this?" She turned to watch her mother's reaction. Anxiety, and then resignation, filled Momma's gaze. "Why didn't you tell me things had gotten this bad?"

Winnie took a step toward her, then another. From the bottom of the steps, she asked, "Mom, why doesn't Taylor take any of this trash out?" As far as Winnie knew, her sister didn't even have a job.

"She's just so busy," Momma said.

"Doing what?" Winnie bit out. "Momma, she is *not* busy."

"Taking care of your dad takes a toll," Momma said next, excuses lining her voice.

"Momma, how long has Daddy been bad enough that you can't walk the trash to the barrel and put the barrel out on Thursday mornings?"

Her mother swallowed, hands fretting around one another. "He's been in a lot of pain for months," she whispered.

"Why didn't you tell me?" Winnie asked. "Does Brad know?"

"He does now," Momma said.

"What is the point of hiding this from us?"

Tears ran down Momma's face and Winnie's heart broke, though she found it very hard to have sympathy for her mother. Empathy, yes, but sympathy came much harder.

"You and Brad are off living good lives," Momma said, voice choked and full of emotion. "And Daddy and I don't want to burden either one of you." She wiped quickly at her face. "We're fine here. Come on, Lucky. Come inside."

Winnie didn't know how to argue with *we're fine* and *I didn't want to burden you*. She turned her back, collected Lucky's half-eaten dish, topped it off, and urged the canine inside. She refreshed his water with fresh, cold water, set it next to his food, and moved to the kitchen with her mother.

She opened her own Styrofoam container. "Did you eat, Momma?" she asked quietly.

"Not yet," her mother whispered back.

Winnie nodded, picked up Momma's order, put the container on a plate, and faced her. "Where do you want it? Couch or table?"

"On the couch, please," Momma said, and turned that way.

Winnie followed, waited while her mother put up the footrest, helped her tuck a blanket around her legs, then handed her the plate. Their eyes met, and pure understanding moved between the two women. Winnie knew her mother was doing the best she could. She had never worked and didn't have many skills that would bring money in.

Daddy had retired a couple of years ago, and as far as Winnie knew, they had what they needed—the house paid off, no car payment, and health insurance from the state. Momma had always claimed that having Taylor here was not a burden, as she paid for her own Dr. Pepper—though now Winnie wondered how exactly she did that if she didn't have a job.

No matter what, it was a conversation for another time. Winnie turned back into the kitchen to get her own food. She'd eaten with Ty before making the drive, so she'd only ordered cheese fries. She sat at the dining room table to eat them, Lucky still chowing down and reminding her that he had been very hungry.

She had shared her location with Tyson during the dust storm and had never rescinded it. She smiled at the word he'd once used with her, then pulled out her phone to text him, her heart heavy even as her fingers flew.

33

Things are so much worse here than I thought. Winnie's message glowed on Ty's screen. He read it again, waiting for the next one.

The garage is full of trash, and our family dog wasn't even fed. Momma's pantry looked like a bomb had gone off, and Daddy was in good spirits but already in bed. I have no idea what tomorrow will bring. I'll keep you updated.

Ty's jaw tightened. He could read between the lines. *I'll keep you updated* meant she would likely be in Oklahoma longer than just through the weekend.

He glanced at Rocky as the cat jumped onto the bed beside him. He'd gone back to Winnie's house instead of his apartment. Her guest room was immaculately clean and smelled like fresh linen—probably a room spray. He reached for the cat and stroked him once before focusing on his phone again.

I'm sorry things are a mess there, sweetheart. Do you want to call?

Taylor's not here, Winnie said. *And I honestly don't know when she'll be back, and I think I may be too tired to talk.*

"Okay," he said aloud as he typed. *I'm back at your place, and the cats are fine.*

Thank you so much, she sent, followed by a couple of cat emojis, a couple of smiley faces in cowboy hats, and three pink hearts.

Ty grinned despite himself and sent three black cats, three red hearts, and then three potatoes. *Did you get your cheese fries at least?*

Yes, and they are delicious.

I can't believe you eat at a barbecue place called Roadkill. He smiled, though a cold feeling slid through him, like Winnie might be slipping through his fingers the way smoke lifted from dry ice. He reminded himself she had a job, a house, and her cats here. Surely her father's health in the present wouldn't define their entire future.

Of course, his own life had changed because of his injuries, so he knew better than most that everything could blow apart and be gone. He didn't like thinking so fatalistically. He'd been working to see the glass half full—through a Winnie-lens instead of his own.

"Redwood is only three hours away," he told himself. "And you know how to drive."

Momma might throw a royal fit about a trip that long by himself, and he couldn't imagine showing up on Winnie's parents' front step, having never met them.

Besides, when he'd first come home after being injured—and after every surgery—Momma had stayed by his side for at least a week, bringing medication and food and making sure he got to appointments. If Winnie had to take on that role, she wouldn't have time to see him.

He racked his brain for something he could do. *What do you need? Breakfast in the morning? A maid service? Tell me, and if I can make a few calls, I'll get it done.*

She sent three 🚫 emojis. *No—don't do anything yet. I'm going to take a full assessment of everyone and everything tomorrow, and we'll see where we stand.*

Ty sent praying hands and flopped back on the bed, curling onto his side as Rocky settled against his chest. "Salmon," he called softly.

He had no idea if the black cat would sleep with him. Winnie had said sometimes Salmon came into the bedroom and sometimes he slept under the bed, and sometimes he chose his cat palace in the third bedroom.

Even without Salmon, Ty liked the coziness of the guest room. It had close walls that didn't press in, and gave him somewhere solid to be.

Winnie didn't text again, and his hand drifted along Rocky's back until he finally fell asleep.

———

HE WOKE EACH MORNING, and by Sunday, Salmon had decided he could tolerate sleeping in the same room as Ty. He fed the cats morning and night, went to work and to church, and on Monday night he sat on Winnie's deck again, this time with his computer open on the table, working through an online sign language lesson Lacy had given him.

He'd spoken to Winnie every day since Thursday, and her assessments were not good. She hadn't said she wasn't returning yet, but at Ty's PT appointment that afternoon, Jerome had mentioned he wasn't sure when she'd be back. As the supervisor over the PT unit, the man would know.

The quiet stillness of the suburb threatened to smother him. His ribs felt heavy against his lungs, but he felt so loud and chaotic inside. He moved through the lesson without a sound from his mouth, only his hands whispering through the air.

He finished, his impatience peaking. He snapped the laptop closed and tapped to call Winnie instead of texting.

The line rang twice. "It's Ty, and I'm going to talk to him for a few minutes. You're fine without me," she said to someone, her voice full of frustration. A door slammed, then a sigh. "Hey, cowboy."

"I can call back if it's a bad time," he said.

"It's always a bad time," Winnie griped. "It's fine."

"Things aren't goin' well there?" he asked. She didn't have to answer for him to know. He'd expected her on the road by now, but her pin still showed her in Redwood.

"Honestly, everything is a dumpster fire," Winnie said, and he could see her wiping her hands down her face. "It's like everyone in this house has turned into a child. I think my mother is doing the best she can, but Daddy's ornery and in pain all the time, so he's short and mean, and Taylor's—well, you've heard me talk about Taylor, and this has only made her worse."

"I'm really sorry," Ty said. "You never let me send anyone or do anything. What can I do?"

"Just calling is perfect," she said, her voice softening.

"You want me to drive up some more clothes?" he asked, keeping his voice even and without judgment. "I'm sure I can find something in your closet or dresser."

"The last thing I want is you rifling through my clothes," she said, then giggled. "I'm fine."

"How long are you going to stay, sweetheart?" Ty asked.

"I don't know," she said, her voice turning into pure frustration. "I'm really sorry, Ty, but I don't know. I called Jerome, and he said it's fine. I can stay as long as I need to, and you're taking care of the cats, so...."

The word hung there, and Ty hated it. "Okay," he said, thinking of this weekend and Wilder's wedding. He and Winnie had planned to go together. He wasn't going to mention it and make her feel worse. "You'll tell me if you need something, right? I can't read your mind, Winnie, and I want to help."

"You're the sweetest man alive," she said. "And you know what I would really love tomorrow?"

"What?" he asked.

"There's this place in Redwood called Waffle-All, and they have a Belgian waffle with fruit."

"I'll order it for you," he said. "When's a good time?"

"Taylor's been leaving around ten, and we get a little peace and quiet then. Daddy has a physical therapy appointment at one."

"Anytime between ten and one," Ty said. "What do your parents want?"

"My daddy will love you forever if you get the sweet-and-hot bacon, and they both love French toast."

"Okay," Ty said, his heartbeat finally steadying. "Winnie, you're my favorite person. You know that, right?"

"Yes," she whispered. "And you're my favorite person too."

Warmth flowed through him, properly assured. "All right, then," he said. "I'll let you go, and I want pictures of your fruity Belgian waffle in the morning."

She giggled, and he smiled as the call ended.

They hadn't broken up. They simply weren't in the same physical space. "So how can I get us in the same physical space?" He leaned back as darkness painted over the yard.

"I could text Henry and Colt and get out of the rest of the week," he mused.

Rocky startled him with a loud "Mrow," and jumped into his lap.

"Then there's the cats," he said, already making a short list of people he could con into taking care of them so he could make the three-hour trip to Redwood, Oklahoma—and his beautiful girlfriend.

34

"I call." Colt set down his hand at the same time his phone made the beeping sound that indicated Finn Ackerman had texted. He loved his ties to the other cowboys and ranch owners in Three Rivers, and all of that stemmed from Finn.

Personal news thread, Finn had said. *We have a massive agenda at tomorrow's meeting, so try to be on time, get some food, and get ready for a spring planting seminar from the agriculture professor at Baylor.*

Therefore, personal news thread.

Colt frowned at his phone, because he wasn't sure he had personal news. His mother had finally—*finally*—backed off on the orchard, and Colt ran it full-time now. His way.

But his personal life had been in a stagnant holding pattern for a long time. He'd finally figured out how to be there for Jonas while doing all he needed to do with the apples, and his relationship with his ex-wife was just fine.

He certainly couldn't put *I'm lonely* on the personal news thread. Nor could he text his friends and ask them for advice about asking out one particular woman.

Tate: *We got the last of the orchards and fields cleaned up and fixed!*

Brandon: *Lenore is having a baby girl, and her due date was updated to July 21.*

Congratulations started flying in from other cowboys and cowgirls, and Colt let his thumbs add his own *Amazing, Tate!* and *Congrats to you and Lenore!* to the mix.

Alex: *Nikki and I are thinking about fostering. Prayers appreciated, and not that it'll happen, but that we'll know if it's the right thing for us and the kids.*

Libby: *Rusty and I are going to name our little boy Gavin. Just so I don't have to answer the same question another 5000 times.*

Mitch: *I hope you actually have a boy. You might want to have at least one baby girl name as a back-up.* 😂

Wilder: *Savvy and I are still getting married in three days.*

Conrad: *My brother Easton is going to ask his girlfriend to marry him. They're thinking a Christmas wedding.*

Colt's heartbeat bumped strangely in his chest, and he wasn't sure why. Fine. He knew why, one hundred percent. If the Walkers were having a holiday wedding, he'd get to see Elaine in a gorgeous, sequined dress. *Probably red*, he thought, and his blood ran red-hot through his veins.

He had no idea how to deal with this insane crush on his buddy's little sister, but Elaine wasn't much older than Fawn, and he had no idea how to ask out one of his friend's sisters. If only Wilder or JJ would suggest it, then Colt could seize onto it and casually shrug one shoulder to judge Conrad's reaction.

Dawson: *No news. Just trying to survive three kids with constant spring rain.*

Link: *Ditto. I'm really looking forward to having the llamas, I'll admit that. My boys are super excited about them.*

Wilder: *I'm glad. Savannah is so grateful.*

Clara Jean: *Leave it to my husband to give our good news about* the FARM. 🌚 *I told him to tell everyone that we're expecting our first baby right after Halloween.* 🎃

More congratulations poured in, and Colt glanced at Trap, then Jake. They were glued to their phones too, but their thumbs didn't move.

"No news, boy?" Colt asked.

Trap looked up at him, his dark eyebrows drawn down. "No," he clipped out. "What am I supposed to say?"

Elaine was Trap's cousin, and perhaps Colt should try to bring her up with him. At the same time, Trap had been struggling to find a girlfriend too, and Colt didn't want to rub salt in any wounds.

"How about that you now have three projects on the books?" Jake suggested.

Trap looked at him, his expression lighting up. "Okay, I can do that."

Rock: *Smiles is graduating in another couple of months and will be back at Shiloh Ridge. We're making preparations for that.*

Finn: *Edith has agreed to another dog instead of another baby. I'm relieved!* 🐕😅

Ty: *Winnie's still out of town, and I'll be at the wedding this weekend alone. Prayers for her father would be appreciated.*

Conrad: *Dogs are good, Finn. Prayers coming, Ty. I'm excited to have Smiles back in town.*

Rock: *Oh, and by the way, Clover and I are having a baby in October too.*

Henry: *Leave it to Rock to casually lay down the fact that he's going to be a first-time dad in only a few months.* 😄

Finn: *Yeah, "by the way," guys, Rock's gonna have a baby.*

Link: 🤣 🤣 🤣 *Congrats, Rock! Tell Clover we love her too.*

Paul: *Congrats on all the amazing good news, guys! Nothing much going on at Courage Reins, other than the fact that Brielle and I have decided we're getting a puppy for Christmas.*

Finn: *Christmas is in eight months, brother.*

Henry: *Paul's the type that commits early.* 🐕🎄

Gun: *Camila is not pregnant, but the end of the school year is hard, and while you're praying, add her to the list, if you would.*

JJ: *We're doing great at Seven Sons too. Jason has himself a new girl.*

"Aha!" Trap yelled, and Colt jumped in his seat. He looked at the triumphant expression on Trap's face. "I *knew* he was dating someone, and he wouldn't tell me."

Colt grinned at Trap's indignation. "Who do you think it is?"

"It's one of my aunt's new pilots," Trap said, his attention already back on his phone. "Melissa, or Marissa, or Maggie, or something."

Trap: *I've got three or four projects I'm working on that I got myself, so that's exciting.*

Jake: *Things are going well at Three Rivers. I finally feel like I'm settled in.*

Colt started typing, his pulse pounding in the back of his throat. With the orchards humming along, *I think I'm ready to try dating again. Any suggestions?*

He couldn't send the text quite yet, as more congratulations and comments came in about the most recent news that had been shared.

Then Angel sent a picture.

Angel: *Trevor and Janie want to let you know that they're going to*

a cutting horse show next month, and Trev's pretty optimistic that he can win it.

Finn: *Way to go, Trev!*

Henry: *He's totally going to win, and any of you who haven't seen him work with his cutting horses are MISSING. OUT.*

Colt erased his text and typed a different one. *When can we come watch, Trevor?*

Angel: *I'll ask him.*

Henry: *He trains with Little Sister every morning, right after roll call.*

Ty: *It's about nine by the time he's saddled and LS is warmed up.*

Mornings were rough for Colt, as he had to get his son off to his mother's, and then get over to his orchard crews and get assignments out. Making the drive to Lone Star by nine would be hard. No, impossible.

Or, you can just take Jonas with you one morning and go. Colt owned the orchard, and he could definitely do that. He loved taking his son on little trips around the Texas Panhandle, and he couldn't wait to take him to Lubbock for Texas Tech football games, or up to the Oklahoma state line to sit on the tailgate and drink root beer floats, the way Colt had done with his father.

He loved being a dad, and he wanted more kids. To do that, he needed a wife, and his thumbs flew across his phone as he re-typed his message.

This time, he sent it.

35

Savannah Calloway woke on her wedding day to the sound of the wedding march blasting through her house.

Today was the last day she would wake up in this bed alone. Today was the last day she would live in this house with her mother and her twins. For today, she was becoming Mrs. Wilder Glover.

She smiled as the door creaked and the twins came in.

"Momma," Gal whispered in a not-so-whisper. "You awake, Momma?"

"It's time to get up," Sequoia said. "Gramma says."

"I'm awake," she said. "Come here, my beauties."

Little feet pattered across the floor, and Sequoia and Gal climbed into bed with Savannah.

"It's wedding day," she told them.

"It sure is," Sequoia said.

"Gram said we gotta give you breakfast and a kiss," Gal said. "And then we get to go get our nails done."

"Mm, that's exciting." Savannah tucked her girls close, one on each side. "Then you're going to go with Daddy for a week or two."

She and the girls would be moving into their new home once she and Wilder returned from their honeymoon. Wilder had first suggested taking the girls with them, which had made Savannah fall in love with him all over again. But they still had the end of their kindergarten year to finish, and selfishly, she wanted her new husband all to herself.

So, with that idea vetoed, Wilder had booked them a twelve-day river cruise in Europe. Savannah had protested because she had two dozen chickens, twelve llamas, and a whole flock of ducks to care for, but Wilder had simply cocked an eyebrow and asked, "Really? You don't think there are enough Glover cousins to handle a few ducks and chickens?" He'd laughed and wrapped her in his strong arms, and Savannah had agreed to the cruise.

Link, Gun, and Rock, along with Fawn, Pearl Jo, and Chaz—had all agreed to make sure her animals not only survived while she was gone, but thrived. The twins would go with Jack; he would keep getting them to school on time, and her mother would help if he was driving the cement truck and couldn't.

Once she and Wilder returned, the twins would have a month of school left, and Savannah would have to make the long drive from the outskirts of Three Rivers to their current elementary school. She and Jack had met at a coffee shop a couple of months ago to work out a new custody schedule for after the wedding. She wanted to enroll the girls in the Three Rivers elementary school, which meant they'd be with her on weekdays. Jack had agreed, and they'd both signed a paper stating she would drive the twins to his house for his custody times, and he would bring them back.

He'd talked about getting a job in Three Rivers to be closer to them, but so far he hadn't. Honestly, Savannah wasn't sure she wanted him to; she simply wanted him to be happy. The girls loved their father, and he was very good to them.

"You got in bed with her?"

Savannah giggled at the sound of her mother's incredulous voice.

"Oh, you girls are in trouble," Momma said. "You were supposed to wake her up, not steal snuggle time."

Savannah grinned over to her. "Can't we just have a few more minutes? It's so nice and warm in here."

"It's a nice day outside, Momma," Sequoia said. "We feeded the chickens already."

"You did, huh?" Savannah smiled as her mom perched on the edge of the bed. "My alarm hasn't even gone off yet, so you guys are early."

"Well, the girls and I have manicure appointments," her mother said. "You just need to get to Shiloh Ridge."

"True." Savannah kissed Sequoia's head and then Gal's. "All right, you two go with Grandma. Get your nails all pretty and I'll see you up at the ranch."

"Okay, Momma," Gal said, as she loved all things girly, from sequins to sparkles to dresses. They'd gone shopping for the wedding with Oakley's mother, who had bought Gal an actual tiara, something that had endeared the woman to Gal immediately. Of course, Gal loved everyone, and everyone loved her too.

Sequoia, the more serious and quieter twin, sat up, leaned over, and hugged Savannah properly. "We'll see you at the wedding, Momma. Love you."

"I love you too, sweetheart."

She watched Sequoia slip from the bed and skip to her grandmother. "I'll see you up there, Mom. Thanks for taking them this morning."

"Yep, no problem."

Savannah listened to her mother herd the girls down the hall, the front door click, and then the house—once her complete solitude—settle into silence. The quiet rang through her soul, and she needed it badly in that moment.

I love Wilder, and he loves me. All she had to do was think of those few weeks when he'd left town last summer to know she didn't want to go that long without him again. That thought alone got her out of bed and on her way to getting ready for her own wedding.

She showered, and an hour later she pulled up to the house Wilder had designed and built on a corner five-acre parcel of Shiloh Ridge Ranch. He'd consulted with her every step of the way—closet space, barns and sheds, stables and pastures for the llamas, ducks, and chickens she relied on at Llama Mamas.

They'd talked about having more kids. Savannah wasn't sure she wanted to run big weekend events *and* have a newborn. Wilder had told her she could do whatever she wanted, and he would facilitate the coming true of her dreams.

She was getting ready here at their new house, which Wilder himself hadn't even moved into yet. Electricity and plumbing were on, but there were still a few finishing pieces to complete. Trap Walker, one of Wilder's best friends, had assured him it would all be done before they returned from their cruise, so the date they'd set months ago had held.

Before Savannah could get out of the minivan, the front door opened and Wilder's sister Fawn spilled out of the house. She jogged over as Savannah got out and said, "You are not to do anything today. My brother's orders."

Savannah blinked as Fawn opened the back door and lifted out the dress bag.

More Glovers came out fast and furious. Gun's wife, Camila, smiled and picked up her makeup bag.

"Is this hat box coming?" Pearl Jo asked.

Savannah nodded, because she'd loaded the van with everything she needed for today and the next twelve days.

"Hey, how're you doing?" Glory Rose asked. Savannah had been out with her and Conrad several times over the past months.

She reached for the baby boy in Glory Rose's arms. "If I can't lift anything, does he count?" She kissed the four-month-old's chubby cheek and grinned. "He is the cutest thing ever." Chance's dark hair and eyes glowed in the April sunlight.

"You can have him," Glory Rose said with a smile. "But I'm pretty sure my momma will take him from you in a few minutes. He's teething, and we don't want drool on your wedding gown."

"Today is definitely a drool-free day," Oakley Glover said as she approached. She wore a wide, warm smile and opened her arms to Savannah. "Hello, my dear. Are you ready for this?"

"I think so," Savannah said, giving her a quick side-hug with Chance between them. "I'm more worried about Wilder than anything."

"Oh, we always worry about Wilder," Oakley said, smiling as she stepped back. "But he's proved to be more than capable in a great many things, and I've stopped underestimating him."

Savannah blinked and mentally backpedaled. "I didn't mean I was underestimating him."

"I know you're not." Oakley tilted her head, taking in Savannah's shoes and luggage for twelve days—one large suitcase to check, a carry-on, and a backpack. Savannah trusted Fawn would make sure it all got inside.

"What are you worried about?" Oakley asked. "We sat with Wilder for a long time last night, and he's not worried about anything."

"I'm not really worried," Savannah said. "But I'm used to having two little girls around, with their many moods and swings and attitude shifts. Wilder has seen a lot of that, yes, but it's different when you live with them."

"I imagine there will be some difficult days. Every marriage has them," Oakley said. "And yes, you're bringing two darling girls to the mix. But my son knows this, and whatever he's not ready for can be learned—because he has you, and he has God."

Tears pricked Savannah's eyes at such a beautiful testament. She pressed her lips together and nodded. Oakley slipped an arm around her and guided her into the house.

"I haven't been inside for weeks," Oakley said. "The cabinets are amazing, aren't they?"

Savannah's mood brightened. "I was a little skeptical of the robin's-egg blue, but Gal was insistent. Trap showed me pictures of it in other houses and said it could be changed, so we ran with it."

"It's amazing," Oakley said.

Savannah had no trouble knowing where to go; Fawn stood next to a barstool, waving her in like an air-traffic controller. Savannah sat, and from there she let Wilder's sister, cousins, mother, and aunts fix her hair and makeup, feed her breakfast, chat, and keep her company.

With only an hour to go, the front door opened and little-girl voices burst into the room.

"Momma! Momma, we're here!" Gal called.

Fawn went to meet them. After quick hugs and a flash of their pretty new nails—Gal's a bright pink and Sequoia's a pale violet—Fawn herded them down the hall to get into their dresses.

The three of them would walk down the aisle together. Savannah's dad had died a few years ago, and she could give herself away as long as her girls were at her side.

Things moved quickly from there. Her mother and Oakley helped her into her dress, doing up every pearled button and placing the veil just-so.

Camila rose from the couch. "Gun says the llamas are ready."

A nervous flutter moved through Savannah's stomach. She pressed both hands over it. "Well, if the llamas are ready, sounds like it's time to get married."

Oakley laughed with her, and everyone joined the exodus out of the farmhouse and up to the main part of Shiloh Ridge Ranch.

They parked in front of the main homestead, where Wilder still lived with his parents in the West Wing—at least until after the honeymoon. She found Mocha, Nacho, and Sheepskin in the front yard.

"Momma, where's Carl?" Gal asked. "You said Carl was going to be in the wedding."

"Carl is going to be with Wilder, baby." Savannah checked the rearview, unbuckled, and turned. "It's how we're going to get the llamas down the aisle without causing a scene. Remember?"

She smiled at her mother and let everyone get out first. Many of the Glovers had gotten married at True Blue down the road, but today the ceremony sat in the large family gathering area by the fire pit, outdoor barbecues, and ring of seats. Cars lined the road in front of the ranch house where Wilder's aunt and uncle lived, and all the way to the end where another aunt and uncle always hosted a Christmas light show.

Nerves ran rampant through Savannah now. She gathered Gal and Sequoia to her side like a hen protecting her chicks. "Stay right by me, babies," she said. "Remember, Grandma and Granny Oakley will have to go sit down as part of the wedding party."

"When is it going to be our turn?" Gal whispered, though they were outside and alone.

"Very soon," Savannah said as her mother and Oakley crossed the street in their diamonds and heels. Savannah's best friend, Cissy, had been tasked with telling her when everything was ready. In the rehearsal yesterday, Cissy had met her at an opening between two buildings; that sidewalk became the aisle, leading to an altar at the back of the graveled area where Wilder would be waiting with Carl.

"Let's get our llamas," Savannah said. "Remember, Gal, you're taking Mocha, and Sequoia, you've got Sheepskin."

She expected Gal to argue—they'd fought about who got to lead which llama—but either Savannah had been forceful enough earlier, or God had comforted her child, because Gal simply skipped to Mocha and picked up the lead. "Come on, girl," she chirped. "Momma's getting married today."

Once everyone had a lead secured, they started across the street at a slow crawl. Savannah didn't have her phone and would have to rely on others for cues. Back in the more private area behind the buildings, trees ringed the space and a slight breeze ruffled across Shiloh Ridge.

"Let's wait here, girls," she said, her nerves growing wings. Yesterday, Cissy had showed up almost immediately. Today, seconds ticked by, and still her best friend didn't appear.

Savannah was about to send Sequoia ahead when Cissy stepped out from between the buildings in a gorgeous, apricot dress with wide shoulder straps and her hair piled on top of her head. She smiled widely, her peach-tinted lips gleaming, and beckoned. "They're ready," she whispered as Savannah got close. "Now remember, you girls go down side-by-side and then wait for your Momma."

"Yes, ma'am," Sequoia said, drawing a deep breath like she was about to make the hardest walk of her life. Savannah loved her with her whole heart and watched Sequoia reach for Gal's hand. The two latched on to one another and took the first step. Tears pricked Savannah's eyes at the way her girls loved one another.

Cissy hooked an arm through Savannah's. "This is a gorgeous dress."

Savannah glanced down at the lace bodice and the frilly tulle that started just below her bust and flared in every direction. She had no train; the dress stopped at her heels, her cowgirl boots peeking out—perfect for marrying a cowboy billionaire like Wilder, and sure to make him smile, laugh, pull her close, and say how much he liked them.

She floated down the sidewalk, and the entirety of her future opened before her. Then she stepped into place, and everything snapped into reality.

Across the gravel stood Wilder in a deep black suit with matching boots and a cowboy hat. One hand rested lazily in his pocket; the other held a rope loosely, Carl at his side. The llama stood nearly as tall as Wilder.

Their eyes met, and electricity flowed freely between them. Chairs curved around the space, Wilder at the epicenter and Savannah at the other end. "Go on, girls," she said.

Sequoia walked to the left, along the back row to a secondary aisle at the same time Gal went right. They would meet in the widened middle, where three girls and three llamas could walk together. Potted plants spilled bluebonnets, red poppies, crimson roses, and bright yellow sunflowers along that aisle—a nod to the flower cowboy her girls had fallen in love with long ago.

Savannah took careful, measured steps, noting Sequoia's eyes locked on hers while Gal waved at everyone she knew, drawing giggles and twitters from the crowd.

Savannah stopped in the middle, grinning at Wilder while the girls brought their llamas back over to her. She threaded Nacho's lead over her elbow, then took Gal's hand in her right and Sequoia's in her left. The three walked side by side, flanked by Mocha and Sheepskin, with Nacho hurrying them all along to Wilder.

At the altar, Wilder crouched and opened his arms. The twins rushed into his embrace. He said something in his calm, quiet cowboy way; they both nodded. He kissed their cheeks, then stood. "Go put the llamas where they belong."

The girls obeyed. Savannah handed off Nacho's lead, her eyes never leaving the cowboy she loved.

"Sorry we're running a little late, sweetheart," he said. "Were you worried?"

Savannah shook her head, though she had been a touch concerned. "A story you'll have to tell me later."

"Definitely."

The girls returned to her side, and they all stepped forward together. Wilder slid a hand to her waist, pressed his cheek to hers, drew a deep breath, and murmured, "I love you so much, Savvy."

"I love you too, Wild." She felt shiny, full of glowing energy.

"Time to get married," Gal announced.

Savannah and Wilder laughed with the rest of the crowd—because yes, it was definitely time to get married.

36

Smiles Glover kept his eyes on his best friend. Wilder shone like the brightest rainbow in a sky that still harbored gray clouds but promised a glorious day of sunshine to follow, and he knew his mother had been right.

He often joked with her that she was right only eight times out of ten, and he really wanted to prove this was one of the two times *he* was correct.

He looked over to her and found tears trickling down her cheeks, both hands pressed against her heart. He knew she wanted him to get married too, and she *was* excited about his new girlfriend.

One look to Wilder and Savannah—Aunt Willa and Uncle Judge both joining them at the altar—told Smiles had he brought Canessa, he would have outshone Wilder, and that would have been catastrophic.

Smiles didn't mean to outshine anyone, and his momma had warned him that his charisma and big, bright personality would have to be contained at some times in his life.

At other times, she'd told him. *You'll be able to let it loose.*

He'd first heard her tell him that when he was only ten years old

—and again last week when he'd called to ask if he could bring his girlfriend to Wilder's wedding. His momma hadn't said no instantly, to her credit. But after only a single moment's hesitation, she'd said, "I don't think it's a good idea, Stetson."

His heart had settled somewhere in his stomach and stayed there, because he didn't know how to explain to Canessa the many, varied, and complicated family dynamics of the Glovers. He wasn't even sure such a thing *could* be explained.

Secondly, his momma had used his real name, and that told him all he needed to know.

What he saw now was that today belonged to Wilder and Wilder alone, and yes, him bringing a girlfriend would have shifted all the focus to him. Number one, it would be a road trip—and that indicated something very serious for the Glover family, even if Smiles himself didn't think it was that big of a deal.

Smiles hadn't handled the situation that well, and Canessa's feelings had gotten hurt. But she'd stayed in Amarillo while he'd made the trip home for the weekend and the wedding.

The truth was, Smiles would have his pomp and ceremony soon enough, as he would be graduating with a DVM in only another six weeks. He wasn't sure what would happen with him and Canessa at that time anyway, as he planned to move back to Shiloh Ridge and finally step into the role that had been reserved for him for the past eight years.

Canessa was a first-year veterinary student and had three more to go after this. Smiles knew by experience that she couldn't finish her degree here in Three Rivers. And there was no way someone could commute that far for that long, so they'd probably break up anyway.

While Momma hadn't said that, she had told Smiles their relationship was fairly new and not super established, and therefore he probably shouldn't bring her to the wedding.

Smiles did like her, and he felt time ticking away toward some unknown zero where a bomb might go off and everything in his life would shatter. He wasn't sure why he felt like that, only that he did.

Part of him, he supposed, had assumed he would be married before he graduated from veterinary school and subsequently returned to his homey, rural ranch

After all, who was he going to meet here? Everyone in Three Rivers knew him and he knew them, despite being gone, and he'd never had much luck finding someone he wanted to spend more than a few months with here in Three Rivers. So while he was graduating with a medical degree, with certifications in ranch animal care and small-farm animal expertise, the fact was, Smiles dealt with feelings of massive failure on a daily basis.

"They are so cute together," Clover said at his side, and Smiles threw a smile in Rock's wife's direction.

For a while there, Smiles had entertained daily phone calls from Rock as he worried over whether Momma and Daddy would ever accept Clover into their family, or if she'd ever fit in on the ranch. He'd once told Smiles, *She's not exactly ranch-wife material, but blast it, I love her.*

Smiles had told him to follow his heart and that if he loved Clover, they would make things work, whether that meant he didn't live on the ranch and just came up to work every day, or something else. They'd moved into Uncle Cactus's house out on the Edge, and that suited them perfectly, because Clover loved the outdoors and hiking, and she was able to do those things a little farther from the epicenter of the ranch without too many scrutinizing eyes.

Of course, she did it while wearing pink, her hair in full curls, and plenty of makeup—something Smiles and Rock definitely weren't used to with their own momma and aunts—but that didn't make Clover a bad person, or a bad wife.

She loved fiercely and deeply and loyally, but her presence only reminded Smiles how isolated he'd become from his own family, and how Rock had achieved so many things that Smiles had not. So again, while he had a degree, his brother had a wife and a baby on the way, and Smiles honestly wasn't sure which was the greater accomplishment.

"Smiles," Rock said under his breath.

He looked over to his dark brother, who wore a fierce look that said, *get going.* In that moment, Smiles looked around and realized all the other cousins were moving to the end of the aisles the way they'd rehearsed—but only with Savannah. Wilder's eyes met Smiles's, plenty of surprise in the dark depths.

"What's going on here?" he asked, and Smiles noted that he looked to him for the answer. Not Rock, not Gun, not his own sister or his parents, but Smiles. His daddy had told him he was a natural-born leader, and he'd better figure out how to lead people to the right and good things.

A hint of bitterness cut through Smiles, because he'd never *asked* to be a leader in the Glover family, and he'd never asked to shine the brightest. Truth be told, his time away from the ranch for the past eight years had been very freeing, because he didn't have anyone looking at him to see what he would say or do. He didn't have to lead, and he got to be himself without considering what his last name meant and who might be watching.

"Just a little musical number, brother," Smiles said, his trademark grin sitting widely on his face.

He stepped next to Wilder and turned to face the crowd, while all the other male cousins—up to Ollie at age forty and down to Mister and Libby's youngest, Brantley, at age twelve—joined Wilder and Savannah at the altar.

Jewel—Rory and Oliver's oldest daughter—stood down at the end of the wide aisle Savannah had walked down with her daughters and three llamas.

In moments like these, Smiles loved being from a small town, and he loved his family, and he loved watching a wedding with llamas in it. He wondered if anyone anywhere else in the world did things like this, and he sure hoped so, because they were good, and they fed a man's soul.

"A musical number?" Wilder asked right out loud. "Savvy, what is going on?"

"Just relax and enjoy it," she said.

Jewel raised both hands like a classical conductor about to lead the world's greatest choir. Music piped through the space. Smiles, a natural tenor, took a deep breath to sing his part.

Wilder loved Garth Brooks, and the man had plenty of love songs. This one Savannah had chosen wasn't exactly a love song, because it spoke of a couple that didn't end up together, but he hung on to the memory of her through a single dance they'd shared. Wilder loved it, and Savannah knew that, and she'd arranged for all of his male cousins to sing it.

Our lives
Are better left to chance
I could have missed the pain
But I'd have had to miss
The dance.

Halfway through the song, Gal and Sequoia played their part perfectly, with Gal grabbing onto Wilder's hand and Sequoia towing Savannah out in front of them.

"Dance, Momma," Gal said, and since she'd choreographed this and knew what was coming, she took Wilder by both hands.

"Will you dance with me, cowboy?"

No man in his right mind would say no to a woman wearing a dress like that at his own wedding. And Wilder wasn't going to be the first. He easily opened his arms and took Savannah into them.

Everyone, including Smiles, could see how blissfully in love the two of them were. His heart ached, because he wanted something like that with someone as special as Savannah, and he had yet to find it.

On the last stanza, the Glover women came out of the crowd to dance with their husbands, or brothers, or cousins.

Smiles had asked Hailey to dance with him. When he had been praying about it, God had let him know that it would mean a great deal to her. When he'd texted her, she had called crying and said absolutely she would, and thanked him profusely for thinking of her and not forgetting that she was part of the family too. Smiles hated that she felt like that at all, and she'd been going through a very rough time in the last year.

So he received her into his arms easily and held her close for just a few bars. When the song ended, he said, "Thank you for dancing with me, so I didn't have to be alone."

She nodded and swiped at her eyes quickly, and when Smiles looked up, he found more than one person watching them. He'd gotten used to all the eyes, but he knew others didn't carry it as well as he did.

The audience started to clap, and Smiles joined in with them, hurrying back to his seat beside his parents. Among other tall, broad-shouldered men, Smiles didn't stand out so much, and relief coursed through him when everyone sat down once more.

He had other single cowboys here at the wedding who he could hang out with after the ceremony, including Trap and Colt and Tyson, and he let his heartstrings sing as Judge pronounced Wilder and Savannah man and wife. He whooped and threw his cowboy hat in the air with everyone else as Wilder bent her back and kissed her.

He could be happy for his cousin, even though Wilder had everything Smiles wanted, because he'd kept the spotlight where it belonged—and that was on Wilder.

As Wilder and Savannah lifted their hands in wedded bliss, and the Glovers shattered the sky with applause, Smiles stood still and thanked God for personal revelation and a very, very good mother.

37

Winnie did her best to hold back her own emotions. Her calendar notification had just gone off for Wilder's wedding, and she had a right to be upset that she wasn't there with Ty. Not only that, but she enjoyed Wilder and Savannah and all the cowboys who Ty spent his time with. It was exactly the kind of community Winnie wanted in her life, and she hated that she was still in Oklahoma.

Her father had come home from the hospital fairly quickly, but he needed surgery. Winnie had already endured a dozen conversations about how he could possibly recover on his own here in Redwood without her. Of course it could be done, while Winnie would literally have to quit her job and leave Three Rivers to do what her parents wanted her to do.

Her great sense of duty and loyalty warred with her heart, and Winnie had been searching for a solution to her problem for days now. She was happy in Three Rivers, something she thought she'd never accomplish again, and she was steadily falling in love with Ty and didn't want to give up her relationship with him either.

But didn't she need to honor her mother and father? Her heart told her she should, and she'd started making phone calls to back surgeons in Three Rivers. She actually had an appointment in another week or so with one of them. She just hadn't told her parents that yet.

She first had to figure out how to get them to agree to move to Three Rivers and live with her. Taylor could maintain the house here, doing whatever it was that Taylor did, and Winnie would be able to continue her life in Three Rivers, getting to know Ty and solidifying her friendships with everyone there.

It felt like a good solution, but she knew it would be a fight. Not only with her momma and daddy, but with Taylor too. She wanted all the benefits of being the baby in the family without having any responsibility whatsoever.

Winnie had spent the beginning of the week being angry, but she didn't have it inside her anymore. She couldn't change Taylor, and all she could do was pray that her parents would see reason. She had a single-level, three-bedroom house that they could easily move into.

They didn't have to give up everything here in Redwood, and Winnie saw this as a short-term solution that might be the next six to twelve months of her life, and she'd done much harder things for much longer than that. She could do this too.

She'd need to get supper started soon, but she sent a text to Ty, hoping he might have a moment during the changeover from ceremony to wedding dinner to respond. She'd texted him that morning too, telling him she wished she could be there at the wedding and asking him who he was going to sit by.

He'd replied with *Colt and Trap* and nothing else. She'd asked who they had invited to the wedding, as she knew none of the cowboys liked to go by themselves. After all, that was how she'd gotten her start with Ty, and she fully expected Travis and Colt, Jacob and Jake, and any other single cowboy to have a date.

But Ty hadn't answered.

Winnie had, once upon a time, thought about getting cameras in her house for her cats, but she'd never done it. Ty was a saint, and he'd been taking care of them and staying at her place since the moment she left town, and she hoped they weren't the reason he hadn't answered her.

She didn't truly think they would be, because Salmon and Rocky loved Ty.

As much as you do....

She paused there, her thoughts scattering for a moment. Did she love Ty? In a lot of ways, Winnie absolutely did, but in others, she knew she needed more time with him to truly get to know him and be all the way in love with him.

Winnie let her fond feelings flow through her, choosing them over being anxious and worried about his silence.

I'm sure the wedding is amazing. Send me some pictures when you get a minute.

With that, Winnie put her phone away, because she couldn't bear the thought of sending another text and not getting an answer yet again. She knew he was busy, and he would reply when he could. At least that was what she told herself as she pushed herself off the couch and went to start dinner.

———

Winnie woke the next morning, her eyes feeling crusty and puffy and a certain vein of misery streaming through her that she hadn't felt in a very long time. Since the morning after Carver had stood on her parents' front doorstep and told her that he couldn't marry her, in fact.

She'd been staying here in her childhood home then too, and she could remember the awful, sick feeling in her stomach and the absolute unhappiness that came with it.

This time, it wasn't because her fiancé had ended their relationship one week before they were set to be married, but because her current boyfriend had not texted her back yesterday.

Yes, Wilder and Savannah had had an afternoon wedding with a full dinner afterward, but certainly Ty would have been home by nine o'clock and could have texted.

Winnie had made herself sick with scenarios, thinking maybe he was too tired, that he'd overdone it, that he was dancing with someone else. She'd just as quickly dismissed those thoughts, because Ty was not a cheater, and she didn't believe for one moment that he would do that to her.

She didn't want that negativity brewing in her head, and she told herself that Ty had had a very busy and stressful week—exactly the way she had—and he was entitled to some rest and relaxation of his own.

But the thought of him needing rest and relaxation away from her made her throat tight. Was he having second thoughts about them? He'd asked her one more time since her initial assessment of her daddy how long she thought she'd be in Oklahoma, and of course, Winnie still didn't know.

She wanted to reassure him that she would be home soon, but the truth was, she didn't know that. She'd had a very serious conversation with Jerome on Friday, wherein she told him she fully expected to be back in just another week. She couldn't stand the thought of staying longer than that, and she'd already been in Oklahoma for ten days now.

And though she'd skipped talking to her parents about moving in with her yesterday, she knew she needed to do it today. She picked up her phone just to see if Ty had texted, and then she'd make her way down the hall and into the main part of the house to talk to her parents.

Winnie stared at the text string between her and Ty, trying to come up with something that didn't sound accusatory. She wanted to be flirty and fun, but she wasn't sure how to pull that off either.

In the end, Winnie sent a generic, tentative text that said, *I hope you have a great Sabbath day.*

She didn't want to pressure him to text her back, and perhaps her message popping up on his phone would remind him that he'd meant to send her pictures from yesterday's wedding and had just been too tired to do so.

She sighed as she got up and went into the bathroom before going down to the kitchen. After all, she didn't want her parents to see her tear-stained face and know she'd cried herself to sleep. Or maybe she did. Then they would know how serious things were with Ty and how badly Winnie needed to get back to Three Rivers.

She brushed her teeth, washed her face, and pulled her hair back on the sides. She liked getting ready in the morning, as it made her feel more human. Not only that, but she wanted to be at her best when she started the difficult conversation with her parents.

"I can't stay here," she practiced in the mirror. "You guys need to come back to Three Rivers with me." She sighed, saw the defeat in her own eyes, and dropped her head.

"This isn't going to work," she muttered as she dodged back across the hall to her bedroom. Still, she pulled on her cutest pair of skinny jeans and a flowery top that made her feel feminine, fierce, and powerful.

She *had* to have this conversation. Lord knew there had been plenty of other...lively discussions around the house this week. Winnie had taken not just one trip to the landfill, but three, and she now had everything where it should be. Mostly.

"Lord, I need Thy help." She tilted her head heavenward, but the writhing, snaky feeling in her stomach wouldn't abate. Thankfully, the scent of coffee filled the air, and Winnie could busy herself with sweetening a cup before she started talking.

Her mother had a certain way she liked her morning caffeine, and she didn't let anyone else touch the coffee pot. Winnie simply counted it as one chore she didn't have to do—and she got to benefit from some pretty good coffee too.

The doorbell rang, and Winnie whipped her attention toward her closed bedroom door. Her heartbeat rebounded from somewhere in her stomach, sticking in the back of her throat and hanging there. She quickly moved to open her door and step out into the hall.

"I got it," Momma called, as if Winnie were the butler and Momma was doing her a favor by getting the door at her own house. A flash of her bright blue blouse moved past the mouth of the hallway as she left the kitchen, and Winnie started down the hallway.

Hopefully, whoever it was would drop off the loaf of bread or casserole dish and be on their way. Of course, if someone from the neighborhood or her parents' church had stopped by with food, Momma would invite them in. Winnie might never be able to have the critical conversation about moving her parents to Three Rivers, and pure desperation clawed at her vocal cords.

A male voice met her ears the closer she got to the living room, and Winnie's footsteps slowed. She didn't want to see the pastor—or anyone else from church. She hadn't packed a dress, of course, nor had she planned to attend church while in town. The last thing she needed were all of those people's eyes and whispered judgments about what she was doing back in town—or what she *should* be doing.

She'd had enough of that after Carver's disappearance from her life fourteen months ago.

Winnie honestly felt near tears as the conversation at the door continued. Then Momma called, "Winnie! It's for you, hon."

She got herself moving, and she entered the living room. "Me? Who is it?" She couldn't quite see past her momma, but she stepped back and opened the door wide.

The whole world narrowed to the man standing on the front porch of her parents' house.

Drawn by the force of gravity, which was fueled by joy...or maybe love...Winnie flew toward Ty. Giggling and grinning, she asked, "What in the world are you doing here?"

38

Ty could not have hoped for a better reaction. He did worry for a moment that Winnie would barrel straight into him and the two of them would tumble head over heels down the *eight* steep, concrete steps he had already climbed. He prayed he had the strength to hold her—and himself—upright after a restless, sleepless night and a three-hour drive at dawn with only a cold breakfast burrito and subpar coffee to sustain him.

She grabbed onto him, and he hugged her tightly too, and thankfully, they both stayed on their feet.

Winnie's laughter subsided and she stepped back, her eyes wide and searching. She ran her fingers down the sides of his face. "You're here," she said, as if she couldn't believe it. "You're really here."

His cowboy hat was gone, but Ty didn't need it, because he was ready to expose everything between them. "I couldn't do it," he said.

Winnie's excitement faltered and her expression filled with anxiety. "Couldn't do what?"

"Make it through another weekend without you." He threw one arm out in a gesture, as if to indicate the whole world was awful without her, which it was. "I mean, the wedding was wonderful, but I hated every minute of it, because I was there by myself."

He felt wild and out of control, the way he did after he'd finished an eight-second ride and was waiting for his score to come up on the board. He forced himself to look at Winnie and take another breath.

His eyes met hers, and Ty could see his future in her face.

She spoke of home and goodness, and while he hadn't been sure if he was in love with Winnie Landry or not, as he stood there on her parents' front stoop—movement behind her threatening to steal his attention—Ty allowed the very real feeling of love to fill his heart.

"I love you," Ty said, as if it were a terrible thing. He threw his hands up and let them fall back to his sides. "Yep, there it is. I'm in love with you. And Momma says love shouldn't make a man miserable, but I've been *so* unhappy since you left. And then she said that if I am miserable without you, that maybe I'm in love, which doesn't make any sense, but there you have it."

He forced himself to slow down and take a breath. "And I know I just bought that ranch, and I think it's awesome, but I'd sell it and move here, if that's what I needed to do to be with you." He flicked his eyes behind her, where her mother stood beside a man who had to be her father.

"Or maybe your parents can move to Three Rivers. I've got two houses on my place, and I can take care of them and the cats. I just *have* to be with you."

He looked at her again. "And maybe it's too fast, and maybe it's too soon, and maybe I'm a complete fool, but Rock said he knew he was going to end up with Clover after their first date. And Carolina says that I should never be afraid to speak what's in my heart. And Finn told me to just get everything out between us and then let you decide."

Ty's mind finally slowed and the words in his mouth dried up. When Winnie didn't immediately jump in and repeat *I love you* back to him, he said, "That's it. That's all I've got."

A slow smile spread her lips. "That's it? That's all you've got?"

"Yes," he clipped out.

She cocked one hip and put her hand there. "I don't think I've heard you say so many words strung so closely together."

"All right," he said. "I drove three hours to be here and you're going to ridicule me?"

"No." She reached out and straightened his perfectly flat collar. She watched her own fingers, and then she finally lifted her eyes to his. "Are you serious right now?"

"When am I ever not serious with you?" he asked. "Do I just say stuff off the cuff?"

"No," she whispered, and her chin shook, and Ty wanted nothing more than to erase every hard thing from her life.

"Or maybe you need me to speak a little slower," he said. "Or climb up on the roof and yell it."

She looked up at him again, pure vulnerability riding in her eyes now.

"I'll do whatever it takes," he said. "I called Jerome at home about fifteen times yesterday until he told me that you would not be at work this week. So then I immediately called in sick everywhere." He hooked his thumb toward his truck. "And I have nowhere to stay tonight, but I'm sure there are hotels here and I've got enough clothes for the next week. And maybe we can just spend some time together and talk."

They hadn't really broken up, but Ty felt too far from Winnie to be sane.

When he looked at her again, he found her watching his truck. "Did you bring my cats?" she asked.

"No," he said. "I pawned 'em off on Conrad."

She pulled in a breath. "Ty, that man has a four-month-old baby."

"Yeah, and a six-year-old daughter who loves felines," he said. "Don't worry, I'm paying her."

"You're paying someone to watch my cats?" Winnie shook her head. "No, that is not okay."

"Well, I couldn't bring them with me," he said. "I did manage to look up a few places to stay, and none of them accepted cats."

Winnie grinned at him, and Ty loved this back-and-forth between them.

"I'd offer for you to stay *here*," Winnie whispered, leaning closer. "But one, I don't want you to. And two, there's no extra bedrooms."

"Oh, well, can you properly introduce me to your parents anyway?" he whispered back. "Or give me some indication that you've heard all the things I've said and that I'm not an idiot?"

She glanced over her shoulder and then put one hand on Ty's chest and pushed him back on the porch so she could exit the house too. She pulled the door closed behind her and stayed up on the step so that she stood almost level with his height.

"I'm not sure, because you were talking real fast, and in a way I've never heard you talk before, but I *think* you said you love me."

"I do," Ty said. "And maybe it's crazy, but—"

"It's not crazy," Winnie said. She dropped her chin in that shy way she had that made Ty love her even more. "I was just about to talk to my parents about coming to live with me in Three Rivers." She looked up and met his eye. "Because I'm miserable here without you."

"Yeah?" His lips curved up in a smile. "That's great news."

"Me being miserable is great news?"

Ty tipped his head back and laughed. "Yes, sweetheart, because it means you're in love with me too."

"Hm, I didn't say that," Winnie said.

Ty pressed in close to her, resting one palm at her hip against the door. "You don't have to *say* it, Win. You kissed me like it when you left, and when I kiss you right now, I'm going to feel the exact same thing."

"You think so, huh?" She swallowed, and Ty dropped his head and moved at a snail's pace, giving her every opportunity to push him away or shoot some other barb in his direction.

She didn't, and when his lips grazed hers, Winnie reacted the same way she always had. She pulled in a breath, grabbed onto his shirt, and pulled him closer. She kissed him hard for a moment, and then she let Ty take control again.

He savored his time kissing her, finally moving his left hand up her arm and across her shoulder and into her hair.

"Mm, yeah, I love you," he said. "And you kiss me like you love me."

"Fine," Winnie whispered. "Maybe I do."

He chuckled and touched his lips to her earlobe. "Yeah, maybe you do."

He pulled back; their eyes met, his smile falling away at the tenderness between them.

Winnie breathed out and then pulled in another breath, and Ty recognized her trying to control her emotions. He took her face in his hands again and kissed her for several long moments until he became aware of voices on the other side of the door.

He pulled away just as Winnie said, "My parents."

"Yeah. You want to introduce me to them?" he asked.

Winnie grinned, and though her face bore a bit more pinkness, she nodded. She reached behind her and twisted the doorknob and almost fell backward into the house. She tugged him inside with her, and Ty tried to stand as tall and as strong as possible at her side as she said, "Momma, Daddy, this is my boyfriend, Ty, and he drove here from Three Rivers, because he loves me, and I'm not staying here in Redwood, because of him. So we need to talk about the two of you coming to live with me in Three Rivers, where Daddy can have his surgery and I can then help take care of him in the recovery."

With every word she spoke, her parents' faces morphed through a range of emotions—first from gentle acceptance, then to happiness, and then to disbelief, and then to pure shock.

"We can't go to Three Rivers," her father said.

"Oh, yes, you can," Winnie said.

"I don't have a doctor there," he said.

"I've called several," Winnie said. "And we actually have an appointment in Three Rivers, not this Tuesday, but the next one."

She glanced at Ty, and he nodded at her, hoping to give her the strength she needed to see this through.

"So we have a week to get this house packed up with everything you need, and then Ty and I are taking you back to Three Rivers with us on..."

She turned toward him, and Ty cocked his eyebrows at her. "Saturday?" he guessed.

Winnie nodded and turned back to her parents. "Saturday."

"What about the house?" her mother asked.

"Taylor lives here," Winnie said without missing a beat. "She can handle anything with the house. You guys can come to Three Rivers, where there are renowned back surgeons, Daddy, and you can have your surgery there, and I can keep my job, and my boyfriend."

Ty put his arm around her and watched, once again, as her parents went through a roller coaster of emotions. Neither of them spoke for several long seconds, and then they looked at one another as if they had rehearsed it.

"It might be a good solution, Cecil."

"I don't like it," her daddy said.

Her mother let out an exasperated sigh. "You wouldn't like *anything* we proposed." She shook her head and then stepped forward. "It's wonderful to meet you, Ty. Winnie has told us a lot about you."

"It's great to meet you too, ma'am." He stepped forward and shook her daddy's hand. "Sir."

He grinned around at all of them, though he didn't see Winnie's sister. "Now, it smells like coffee in here, and it has to be better than the glop I drank from the gas station at the Oklahoma border."

Winnie's mother sucked in a breath. "Was it Harrod's?"

He nodded, and she tisked her tongue. "This is terrible news. Come get something good."

Winnie beamed at him like he'd just done something amazing, and Ty honestly felt like he had. For the first time since Winnie had left town, he felt like he was walking on clouds as he followed her mother into a small kitchen where she poured him a fine-smelling cup of coffee.

39

Winnie hummed to herself to calm her nerves as she made the turn, deftly following Ty onto the highway that ran east and west. They'd been in a three-car caravan from her parents' house for the last couple of hours. She was still twenty-five minutes from her house, but to get to the hobby farm Ty had purchased, they had to turn here and go down the highway toward Amarillo for about three miles. Then he made another right turn onto the property, and Winnie's sedan bumped over the dirt road just fine.

It had been a whirlwind of a week, with plenty of crying from both Daddy and Taylor, but Winnie noted that her mother had never once protested again. She didn't have to pull Winnie aside and tell her that she was secretly thrilled about the developments happening for Winnie to know it was true.

"And now," Winnie said to herself, because Ty had his truck and she had her car, and her parents had insisted on bringing their mini-van. "We just need to figure out where they're going to live."

She almost hoped it would be here on Ty's property. He'd said the smaller, single-level house was move-in ready, and she had lain in his arms on a blanket in her parents' backyard and worried that they would displace him off of his own property.

He said he didn't mind at all if it would get them to move here and make her happy. She'd talked with her parents about them getting their own little apartment closer to the hospital and doctor's appointments, where Daddy could just walk and Momma could buy groceries from a shop a half-block away. No car needed.

She'd talked about her parents living in the spare bedroom at Winnie's house, where Ty had been all this time. Any of those solutions would work, and Winnie's parents were planning on staying with her for at least a couple of nights, until her father's first appointment. She honestly wasn't sure if she could handle much more than that, though she wanted to be able to.

Ty came to a stop outside the cute little farmhouse, and Winnie pulled in beside him. Pure goodness flowed through her, along with a sense of calmness and peace. She got out of the car and joined Ty at the front corner of his truck.

"This place is amazing, Ty," she said, because she had never seen it in person.

"This is just one of the houses." He slung his arm around her. "I've had a couple of service people in," he said. "The plumber, and the heating and air-conditioning guy, and they say it's ready. I had the septic tank pumped, and since it's only a half-mile off the road and we're moving into summer, I don't think I need to do any asphalt or concrete yet."

Winnie looked at him. "I can't believe you're willing to let my parents stay here."

"I'm okay with it," Ty said, and he pressed a kiss to her forehead. "What about us?"

"What do you mean—what about us?"

"I mean, I know you said you didn't want to get engaged before six months—that it felt too fast and all that—and I'm fine with that, but there's a lot of things we haven't talked about, and one of those is a family. Do you want kids, Winnie?"

"Yes," she whispered. "I think I'm good with kids."

"I think you'd be a phenomenal mother."

Winnie turned into Ty and fiddled with his collar, something she did when nerves ran rampant through her, and she didn't know how to contain them. Ty seemed to know it, and he simply let her do so until she was brave enough to look up at him and vocalize her thoughts.

"We won't know much about my daddy's surgery until Tuesday, but a full recovery could be six months or more."

"Winnie...." Ty drew a breath and blew it all out.

"I'm worried about them living here and keeping you off your own property."

"There's another house," he said.

"Yeah, but it's not move-in ready."

"I had the same plumber and heating guy check it out," he said. "They've made a few repairs, and I'm on Trap's schedule to make sure that everything is up to code, and he's going to replace the front and back decks. And then, honestly, Winnie, everything's just cosmetic."

"But you've told me you don't want to live in a construction zone," she said.

"I can get painters out pretty quick," he said. "And I bet I can replace the flooring next week with a few phone calls. I'm not going to do any of the work myself."

Winnie turned toward the house and nodded. Ty put his hand on her face, sending a zing of attraction through her as he guided her eyes back to his.

"Win, I'm not going to do any of the work, and that's something you've worried about too. So maybe I just make a few more phone calls and accelerate the remodel. I could still be on the property in a month."

"In the other house," she said.

"In the other house," he confirmed. "And your parents really can stay here right now—tonight."

Winnie's nerves shook at her, and the sound of tires over gravel told her that her parents had arrived behind them.

"Let's see what they want to do," she said.

They pulled in and parked, and both Momma and Daddy got out, with Daddy hemming and hawing and grunting and groaning with every move he made. Winnie had snapped at him in the past couple of weeks, asking if he made those noises if he was by himself, and that she bet he didn't. "So stop being dramatic," she'd told him. But Daddy was Daddy, and he wasn't going to change now.

"This is it?" Momma asked, her voice touched with awe. "Ty, this is a nice house."

"It's three bedrooms and two baths," he said. "Just like what you've got in Oklahoma. It's a single level. But I'm afraid this is what the land looks like. There's no yard or anything."

They'd left Lucky in Redwood with Taylor, though she'd refused to come out of her bedroom and bid them farewell. She was not happy with the changes, and Winnie had left her a notebook page filled with names and numbers of people who could come mow the lawn and walk the dog, so she could continue to pursue her sugar-daddy lifestyle. It angered Winnie that she had to enable her sister in such ways, but if she didn't, she feared her parents would return to Redwood to a dilapidated house full of dog feces and wild vines.

"The whole property is twelve acres," Ty said, gesturing right and then left. "If you go left, down the road here and around a couple of corners, that's where the other house is. It's actually off another road, and it's where the main barns and stables will be. This house over here, I envision as either a mother-in-law apartment, a guest house, or, if we ever get to the point where we need cowboys to live here and work, they could live in this cabin."

"Are you going to plant?" Daddy asked.

"Just a garden over at the main place," Ty said. "And probably not this year. This year I'm going to focus on getting the house where it needs to be so that I can live there comfortably, and all of the farm buildings accessible."

Momma and Daddy both looked at him and then back to the house.

"After that, I'll probably plant a garden next year," Ty said.

"Ty is a very good cook," Winnie said, and she linked her arm through his simply to be closer to him.

They still had a lot to talk about, as Winnie did not want to get married in the winter. As far from February as she could get would be best, and that was August or September. And with May on the horizon, she wasn't sure she could put a wedding together that fast.

Of course you can, she told herself. *What do you need?*

With Momma and Daddy here, she'd only need her brother and his wife to come and Taylor to make an appearance. She was sure she could book one of the little chapels in town, and maybe Willa Glover to officiate, and then Winnie would simply need something to wear. She knew where to buy jumpsuits that complimented the shortness in her torso and the extra curve in her hips, and she'd seen them in white. Or maybe she'd be married in purple.

Or scrubs, she thought, and she giggled to herself.

Ty looked at her, his eyebrows raised. "What are you laughing about?"

"Nothing," she said. "Come see the house, Momma. I haven't even seen it myself."

"We run on a well here," Ty said as Winnie moved with her mother toward the house. "But everything's plumbed, and you've got hot water in the house. I just had it all checked."

He led the way up the wide staircase with only three steps to the front door, and the moment he opened it, Winnie realized why he had fallen in love with this place and purchased it.

It simply felt like home, something invisible but tangible welcoming them onto the property and into the house.

"This is a laminate hardwood," Ty said, scuffing his boot across the floor. "It's more gray than I like, but my momma put down a rug, and this is a new couch."

He indicated the full-sized couch against the window at the front of the house. He didn't have a love seat, but a recliner faced a TV mounted to the wall in front of them. The kitchen—clean, with white appliances—held a six-person dining room table, and a single back door that was almost entirely made of glass.

"Bedrooms and baths down there," he said. "And there's no laundry room, but there is a laundry closet." He took a few steps and opened an accordion door to reveal a stackable washer and dryer.

"It's everything you'd need, and two of the bedrooms are empty. So if there's stuff that you want to bring and store, I'm sure we can make another trip up to Redwood."

Momma disappeared into other rooms, though when Winnie wandered after her, she found them empty, save for the last one in the corner that connected to the second bathroom and made an ensuite. Ty had put a king-size bed there with fresh linens and two nightstands with lamps.

He'd spent a lot of time on his phone this week as he'd made arrangements to have this house cleaned, inspected, and furnished for her parents or for himself. He'd wowed her parents with his good cooking, and he'd even gotten Taylor to laugh a few times.

No matter what, Winnie had fallen more and more in love with him, with everything he said and every move he made, and every preparation he put together on her behalf. He'd had Conrad send pictures of Rocky and Salmon, and he'd assured Henry and Angel that he'd be back at Lone Star next week.

Winnie realized in that moment that his brother was also engaged, and she might not be able to have her non-winter, non-February wedding this year. Worry worked through her gut and then Winnie told herself that she and Ty weren't even engaged. In fact, she'd told him that he was absolutely not allowed to propose to her before they'd been dating for six months, which put them right around the Fourth of July.

Winnie wasn't sure why that mattered, only that it felt fast otherwise. She wanted to be very sure this time.

As opposed to last time? she thought. She and Carver had dated for almost two years before he'd asked her to marry her, and they'd been engaged for fourteen months.

She realized this as she followed her mother out of a corner door in the master suite and onto a private, master-only deck.

The date on which things happened had mattered to Carver. *He'd* proposed to her on New Year's Eve in an extremely romantic grand gesture, and they'd been set to be married only a few days after Valentine's Day.

"This is a really nice place," her mother said.

Winnie leaned her head against her mom's shoulder. "Yeah," she said. "It's really quiet and peaceful here."

"What would you rather have us do, Winnie?"

Winnie didn't think her mom had ever asked her opinion before, at least not about something like this. "I think you should do whatever you think will make you happy, Mom," she said. "And whatever you think will be easiest for Daddy, because he's going to do whatever you say."

"Yeah, probably," Momma said. "I think this would be really nice for before the surgery, but we'll need somewhere with level ground where he'll be able to walk after it."

Winnie nodded. "So maybe you'll stay with me until our appointment on Tuesday," she said. "And then once you know when the surgery will be, you and Daddy can make a decision. You might even be able to go back to Oklahoma for a couple of months."

Momma shook her head and sniffled. "No, I think you're right. We need to be here, and we need to be away from Taylor. That girl needs to figure out her life."

Winnie had listened to her mom complain about a great many things, but her words never turned into actions and things never changed much, so she simply agreed.

"We told her when we come home she has to move out," Momma said.

"What?" Winnie's eyes widened, and she gaped at her mother.

"So we won't go home before the surgery," Momma said. "We

told her she probably has six months, and she needs a job and her own place before then."

"Wow, Momma. Do you think she'll actually do it?"

Her mother sighed and leaned against the railing, gazing out over the fallow land. "I don't know, Winnie. But you know, I think we've enabled her long enough, and she and your father don't get along. I think she's poisoned me a little bit against him, and I want to be a good caretaker for him and a good support." She smiled over to Winnie. "The way you are for Ty and he is for you."

"Do you like Ty, Mama?"

"Yes, Winnie," she said. "He's wonderful."

"Yeah, but we thought that about Carver too," she said.

"Ty and Carver are nothing alike," Momma said.

"How do you think they're different?" Winnie asked, because she had her own reasons, but she wanted to know what her mother thought.

"For one, every single thing Ty thinks or feels is right there on his face. He doesn't have a disingenuous bone in his body."

"He's actually pretty good at hiding things," Winnie said. "At least he thinks he is. He said he had to do it all the time in the rodeo—that he'd just swallow the fear and get on the bull." She sighed and looked out at the untamed Texas wilderness too. "I don't want to be a bull to him. I want him to *want* to be with me."

"I think he does, dear," Momma said. "And like you said, you guys are going to give yourselves a few more months to get to know one another, celebrate some holidays together, experience some birthdays, and see how things go with your father's surgery."

"Yeah," Winnie said.

"For what it's worth, I don't think you need to worry about Ty," Momma said. "I mean, the man babysat your cats—both of them—for ten days, and that Salmon can be a real piece of work."

Winnie pealed out a laugh, and she hugged her momma tightly. "Thanks, Momma. Now let's go see where Ty and Daddy are."

Winnie stepped back into the bedroom and allowed her mother

to go past her and out into the hall first. She really wanted to be one hundred percent sure about Ty in all things, and maybe she didn't have to wait six months for him to propose to her. Maybe they both just needed to be on the same page—ready to write a book about the future of them together—and everything else would work itself out after that.

Winnie paused in the bedroom alone. "Bless me with clarity of mind," she murmured, and she believed with her whole heart that God could and would answer her prayers. She felt brave and indestructible as she stepped out into the hall and joined Ty and her parents out in the main part of the house.

Ty glanced at her. "Your momma says she's just going to stay with you until they meet with the doctor on Tuesday."

Winnie nodded and moved to his side. "That's right. If the surgery is right away, then maybe they'll just stay with me through it. Momma wants to have level ground for Daddy to walk on after his recovery, as we already know that a lot of walking after his surgery will be one of the most important parts of his recovery."

"Makes sense," Ty said. "I'm fine with whatever. I just want you guys to know that this is available."

"We really appreciate it, Ty," Momma said, and she lunged at him. Ty managed to wrap Momma in his arms, and he smiled over her shoulder at Winnie as they embraced.

Winnie stepped back and grinned at all of them. "I'm starving. Let's go find somewhere awesome for lunch."

"I know what that means." Ty kicked that delicious grin at her.

"What does it mean?" Daddy asked, a look of confusion knitting his brows.

Ty considered Winnie for a moment, and she simply watched him back. "Well, Winnie has a way of saying what she wants without really saying it," Ty said.

Both Momma and Daddy looked at him blankly and then switched their attention to Winnie.

"Right now I'm thinking she either wants Chinese food or tacos, and I'm just trying to figure out which." He tilted his head, his eyes narrowing slightly. "Seems to me that I remember her saying there were no good Chinese places in Redwood, so I'm going to go with that."

Winnie clapped a couple of times for him and said, "Chinese food, cowboy. It's only the best cuisine on the planet."

He laughed and took her into his arms and then led the way out of the house, leaving her parents to follow behind them, whether they wanted Chinese food or not.

40

Ty paced in front of the living room windows of his new house. He'd moved in a couple of weeks ago, after Winnie had found out that her father would be doing back surgery the day after his birthday. That day had arrived, and Ty felt no different as a thirty-two-year-old than he had as a thirty-one-year-old. Nevertheless, Winnie had insisted that he should be celebrated, and he knew he had to be ready for guy's night out tomorrow by six-thirty as well.

Winnie had insisted on coming to pick him up at his house, claiming she'd need the thirty-minute drive from her place to his to get in the right frame of celebratory mode. Her parents wore her to the bone, and she already worked an emotionally demanding job.

Ty still spent most evenings with her and the cats, and now her parents, and the number of conversations they'd had about only having to wait three weeks to do a lower disc fusion surgery was such a blessing had worn him right on out too. He knew Winnie just wanted it done, so the healing and recovery process could begin.

Winnie's parents would likely stay in Three Rivers through Christmas, and Ty and Winnie were meeting her brother at their home in Redwood this weekend to get more of their belongings—clothing and a few pieces of light furniture—as they'd found an upstairs rental in a house only a few blocks away from Winnie.

Brad, his wife, and daughter would make the drive back to Three Rivers in a caravan with Ty and Winnie, and they would get everything moved by Monday as her father wasn't expected to come home after his surgery until then anyway. Winnie would be able to run over there and check on them easily, but they wouldn't be living in her house anymore, something that Ty knew would bring her great relief.

They would also be bringing Lucky home with them, as Winnie worried about him day and night. Ty had perked up at that news, asking if he could have the border collie. "Just until your momma and daddy get back on their feet," he'd said.

"You can have him," her momma had said immediately.

"Momma," Winnie had chastised. "He's your family dog."

"Honey, we do not have time to take care of a dog," her mother had said. "Which is why I'd asked Taylor to take care of him. We love him, but he's a lot."

"I can run him at the ranch," Ty had said. "And take him to work with me at Lone Star and the orchards. He'd love it."

He'd trained his gaze on Winnie at that point, and she'd sighed. "Don't look at me with those big, sad cowboy eyes," she'd said.

"You can't take care of a border collie, and I can." He'd seen the moment she'd agreed with him, and Ty couldn't wait to have Lucky on the farm with him.

Yes, this weekend definitely marked a lot of changes. Ty looked out the window, didn't see Winnie's sedan, and marched himself into the kitchen. He pulled open his junk drawer and retrieved the navy-blue velvet box sitting there. The lid creaked as he opened it, and he smiled down at the diamond peeking up at him from all that plush fabric.

"There's already enough changes for one weekend," he said quietly to himself.

Winnie still had not told him in exact words, *I love you,* but they'd talked quite a bit more about marriage. His sister was getting married in only three more weeks, and Bryan and Ellie had set a date for late September, giving Momma four months between the two events.

If Ty and Winnie gave her four more months, that would be... February.

Ty knew without a doubt that Winnie did *not* want to set a date for that month—or anywhere near it. She didn't want to be married in the winter at all.

The only way Ty could imagine they could be married this year instead of next would be if he squeezed in a wedding sometime between Carolina's and Bryan's, and that would be impossible. He hadn't brought it up with anyone yet, because his mother was so busy with Carolina's wedding and running the horse stable during very busy spring and summer months.

Ty snapped the lid on the ring closed and had just shut it back in the drawer when he heard Winnie pull up outside the farmhouse. He headed that way and stepped outside just as she emerged from her car.

"Howdy," he said, giving him his first birthday present—her arrival in a black-and-white striped pair of slacks and a billowy, loose top that looked like someone had splashed black watercolor flowers on a white background. "You are the prettiest woman in Texas."

He wanted to bounce down the steps and take his girlfriend into his arms, but he held onto the railing and took careful steps instead.

She greeted him by reaching up and tapping the brim of his cowboy hat. "This is new."

"It's my birthday present to myself," he said with a grin.

She giggled. "Is that what we do? Buy presents for ourselves?"

"I do," he said.

She put one hand against his chest and leaned into him. "I like that idea."

Ty placed one hand on her back, holding her close as he leaned down to kiss her. "Mm, you taste like mint," he said. "And maybe chocolate." He cocked one eyebrow at her, and Winnie grinned that soft *I'm in love with you* smile at him.

"I may have eaten part of your present on the way here," she said.

"You *ate* my birthday present?" Ty laughed, filling the sky with more happiness than he thought he could ever feel or express. "What was it?"

"There's still some in the car," she said. "Come see." She took his hand and led him over to the passenger door, which she opened for him.

Ty found the package of mint Oreos sitting on the passenger seat. Yes, they had been opened and resealed. After he sat down and she closed his door for him, he pulled back the packaging and saw she'd only eaten a few.

"You were starving, huh?" he asked when she got behind the wheel. "And I just want the record to show that this feels weird." He gestured between them. "That you came and picked me up, and that you're driving me around in your car."

She grinned at him. "It's okay to do new things, Ty."

"Oh, brother." He rolled his eyes. "Thanks, *Doctor* Landry."

Winnie laughed and pulled around in a wide arc to set her car back on the road leading off the ranch. Ty wasn't sure where she was taking him, but she'd promised he would be happy with the food and the atmosphere.

She turned left out of his place and headed back toward Three Rivers while Ty tried to swallow his nerves.

"You're being awfully quiet tonight," she said. "I expected a report on the second level of your house."

"Yeah. It's going good."

"Going good? That's all I get?"

"I wanted to talk to you about something, actually," Ty said.

Winnie glanced over at him, her mood shifting from flirty and fun to a bit more serious. "All right."

He reached over and took her hand in his. "I don't see how we're going to be able to get married until next April," he said. "And that feels like a really long time from now, don't you think?"

Winnie sighed and looked out her side window, though her fingers in his stayed tight and secure. "It does feel like a long time."

"Maybe I'm greedy and selfish," Ty said. "I want you in the farmhouse sooner than that, but with your daddy's surgery and both of my siblings getting married, I don't see how it can be done before Christmas. Unless...."

Winnie gave him a few moments to go on, but Ty's bravery totally failed him.

"Unless what?" she finally prompted.

"Well, I've got a couple ideas," Ty said. "I'm not sure you're going to like either one of them, which is why...."

"We're talking about it," Winnie said, shooting him a look. "Talking doesn't hurt, right?"

He swallowed and nodded. "Right. I've been thinking about asking Bryan and Ellie if we could do a double wedding with them."

"A double wedding?" Her voice pitched high enough to call dogs.

"Or," Ty said quickly. "We could just elope. And I've got to be really honest—the more I think about it, the more an elopement sounds like exactly what we should do." He watched the gorgeous Texas landscape roll by his window.

"We should just take a couple of friends, and the cats, and someone with the authority to marry us, and go to our favorite place and get it done."

Winnie gaped at him, her eyes wide and the road in front of her forgotten. Then she started to laugh.

"What?" he asked.

"Those are both good ideas." She grinned. "I think you're insane if you think you can handle an elopement."

"Why wouldn't *I* be able to handle an elopement?"

"Because you have more friends than any cowboy on the earth."

"That is not true. Have you met Finn Ackerman? He's the most popular cowboy on the planet."

Winnie smiled at him and squeezed his hand. "I kind of like the idea of us just running away and getting married, but Ty. Come on. Your family has lived here for forty years, and I don't think that's how things are done in small-town Three Rivers. Your momma will think I'm pregnant."

Ty rolled his neck, because Winnie wasn't wrong. "Yeah, okay. So maybe I should talk to Bryan?"

"If you want to," Winnie said. "But I was thinking, Ty, that we don't need a big thing like what the Glovers do."

He watched her, looking for any pressing of her lips or that little jump her jaw did when she got a little anxious. "You don't want a big wedding? What had you planned for you and Carver?"

"Too much," she said simply, though he did notice the way her fingers tightened around the steering wheel. "And I don't really need it. It would be great if my family could be there. And yours. And any of your friends." She threw him a quick look and focused on the road again. "But you know I'm not going to wear a dress, right?"

Ty grinned at her. "I'd actually be disappointed if you wore a dress, sweetheart."

She let the breath huff out of her mouth, and Ty simply waited for her to tell him more.

"I guess I'm just feeling like it can be something simple," she said.

"Which is why I think an elopement would be great. We could have your parents meet us at the Oklahoma border and set up a tent and have lemonade and all the Chinese food you want."

Winnie smiled softly. "That does sound amazing."

They settled into silence, no answers decided upon, while she drove back into town. But instead of turning south toward Main Street or the new downtown, she turned north, as if driving him out to Three Rivers Ranch. That was another forty-five minutes, and though Ty hadn't eaten since lunch, he said nothing.

"What would you wear to our wedding?" he asked.

"A jumpsuit," she said. "And maybe we don't have to give Bryan and Ellie four months. I mean, didn't you say a bunch of the Glovers got married last June, one week after the other?"

"Yeah," Ty said. "I just need to talk to my mom and Bryan about it, to make sure we're not stepping on any toes. I can't even imagine what they're going to say if we get married before we've even known each other a year."

"Oh, we've known each other that long," Winnie said. "Don't you remember? You came to your first physical therapy appointment in May."

Oh, Ty remembered, because a man didn't meet a woman like Winnie and forget about it.

When it became obvious that she was taking him to Three Rivers, she glanced over to him. "I just want credit to go where it's due," she said. "Henry, Paul, and Libby have helped a lot with this dinner tonight."

"Where are we eating it?" he asked.

"In one of your favorite spots," she said. "Don't worry."

"Oh, I'm worried," Ty said, but it wasn't really about him. It was about her, because as the weather had heated up, Winnie didn't enjoy dining out on patios or in gardens. So dinner at the ranch didn't really seem like her cup of tea.

They arrived, and Winnie parked in front of Courage Reins. Ty met her near the hood, and she took his hand and led him around the building toward the stables. They walked past them, the shade definitely cooler on his bare arms, and then the ranch opened up in front of him. Ty sighed, because he did love the sight before him as it was as familiar to him as his own face.

"Oh, look, the miniature donkeys are out."

"Yep," Winnie said. "And Henry put out a few other horses as well." She smiled and nodded to a round table that had been set up in the shade of a beautiful live oak. "There's one I think you know."

Ty heard the familiar call of his horse, Juniper, and he turned to face the pasture, stunned that someone had come onto his farm and taken his horse without him noticing.

"How did you get her?" he asked.

"Henry picked her up," Winnie said, with a clap and a bounce in her feet. "Are you excited?"

"Yeah, of course." He grinned at her. "This is great. Thank you."

"Wait until you see what we're having for dinner." She led him over to the table where Juniper met them at the fence. Ty took a moment to stroke his horse and laugh when she tried to take off the offending cowboy hat.

"It's just a new hat, girl," he said. Horses got spooked by the dumbest things.

He moved over to Winnie, because he'd rather spend his time with her than a horse any day, and that said something, because a cowboy had a very special relationship with his horse.

Two places had been set at the table, the plates covered by cloches, and Winnie said, "Sit down and let me serve you."

Ty wanted to argue that none of this was necessary, but instead he did what his wonderful Winnie wanted and let her stand beside him with her hand poised on the cloche for dramatic effect.

"I give you...." She pulled the cloche back and practically yelled, "A Texas cattleman's dinner!"

A gorgeously seared steak sat there with a fully loaded baked potato—steam actually rose off of it. A little bowl of mac and cheese had been paired with collard greens, and Ty's stomach practically roared at him to get a utensil and start eating right now.

"Wow," he said. "This looks incredible." He watched Winnie as she took her seat across from him. "Who made this?"

"I had the chef at Iron Maiden make them," she said. "Paul picked them up on his way home from the IFA, and I'm hoping it's all still warm enough to eat."

Ty picked up his knife and fork and cut into the meat. "Mine looks great," he said at the perfectly pink center. "When did he get these?"

"I think he texted as we were turning onto Three Rivers Ranch,"

Winnie said. "So they've probably only been sitting here for five minutes."

Ty put the single bite of steak in his mouth, everything buttery and fatty and delicious about it singing through him. "This is incredible, Win," he said. "Thank you so much."

"Happy birthday, cowboy." She scooped a cheesy bite of pulp from her potato and paired it with a bite of steak, all of it poised perfectly on the end of her fork. She looked at him. "Now tell me what's going on in the main homestead, and I'll tell you what I know about guy's night out tomorrow."

Ty's eyebrows went up. "Don't I know what's going on for guy's night out?"

Winnie grinned, popped her food into her mouth, and shook her head.

"Great," Ty said, and then he took another bite of steak, and it suddenly didn't matter that the homestead renovation was going to cost more than he'd anticipated, or that he didn't know what his friends were really planning for tomorrow night. He had steak and the woman he loved, and life didn't get much better than that.

41

Trap waited at the bakery, checking his messages to see where everyone else was. Colt had spearheaded this birthday celebration for Ty, and since he spent a lot of time with Trap and Tate, they'd eventually landed on the idea of hosting it at Wilde & Organic. Tate had volunteered the upstairs conference-room space, which had plenty of seating, tables, and a wall where they could hang a dartboard.

Trap loved the idea of being able to come downstairs and get anything he wanted from the grocery store, which was open until ten p.m. on weeknights. He'd ordered the cake, JJ was bringing a few board games, and Conrad was already upstairs, hanging the dartboard.

Colt had put together some decorations that had barely met Clara Jean's requirements for a party. Her comments on what he'd brought for their friend had only served to remind Trap that men and women were not the same. It had also spurred Colt to order a bouquet of balloons to add to the banner he'd purchased online.

They'd invited everyone in their small ranch owners' meeting group, as well as a few of Ty's friends from *Signs for Success* and Lone Star—but men only, as it was guy's night out, whether married or single.

Trap looked up and back into the bakery, but the girl he'd given his name to still had not appeared with the cake he'd ordered. He glanced at his phone again, not even sure if he wanted to check Two Cents or the Panhandle Singles app.

Colt had put it out to the group a few weeks ago that he was ready to start dating again, and he'd been on a few dates. As far as Trap knew, they hadn't gone anywhere. Moving into the summer building season, Trap wasn't sure he was ready to take on a girlfriend. It didn't help that his last few attempts at dating had failed spectacularly.

"Here you go, Trap," the girl said, and he shoved his phone away, his indecision saving him once more.

"Thanks, Miley." He reached for the wide, two-foot-long cake, surprised at how heavy it landed in his hands. As he made his way toward the front of the store—all he had to do was walk through an employees-only door at the customer service desk and go up a flight of stairs—Trap wondered if anyone had thought about plates and utensils.

You probably should have, he thought. *You're in charge of the cake.*

His boots made thunking noises on the gray-painted concrete steps as he went up, and he entered a hallway that only had doors leading off the right-hand side of it. A wide wall of windows expanded to his left, and a few desks sat out in the open space where the security team here at Wilde & Organic worked day and night.

He entered the last door on the right to the biggest conference room, where the long eight-foot tables had been pushed together to make one big rectangle with about twenty-five chairs around it and more pushed up against the wall.

Conrad fiddled with the dartboard near the back corner, and Colt looked his way as he entered. "Oh, you got the cake." He indicated the corner of the table. "It goes right there on the end."

"Do we need paper plates and forks?" Trap asked.

Colt had decided to order pizza, because what man in his right mind didn't like pizza? It was one of Trap's favorite foods, that was for sure. He found a stack of plates on the corner as he slid the cake onto the table, his question answered.

"I got plates," Colt said. "But no forks."

"We need forks?" Tate asked. He had just entered the room after Trap. "We've got some in the cupboards back here."

He continued to where some tall cabinets stood against the back wall. He opened one of them and pulled out a box of plastic forks. "It's just forks. No spoons."

"I didn't get ice cream," Trap said. "I figure if anyone wants some, they can go down and get themselves a pint size, and then they can have the flavor they want."

Besides that, Trap rarely wanted to eat dessert after dinner. He didn't understand big meals like Thanksgiving, where so much energy was poured into the pies that couldn't even be enjoyed because of how much food he'd stuffed himself with. Trap almost always would prefer real food over dessert anyway, and he hadn't wanted to let the ice cream sit out and melt and have no one eat it. It would take all of five minutes for the cowboys to go downstairs, pick out their favorite flavor, buy it, and bring it back up.

JJ and Finn stood down at the end of the table, pulling out board games from a bin JJ had brought in.

"Hey-ho, hey!"

Trap turned toward the door at the sound of Henry's voice.

"The party is here!"

He moved out of the way as his brother-in-law, Trevor, entered. They both wore big black cowboy hats and smiles as wide as the Texas sky, and Trap felt a sense of brotherhood with them that could not be explained.

"Howdy," Trap said, and he moved to shake Henry's hand and then Trevor's. "Do you guys leave in the morning for that cutting competition?"

"It's next weekend," Trevor said. "And we'll leave on Thursday."

"It's only a three-hour drive," Henry said. "But Trev doesn't like to have the horses in the trailer for that long." He grinned at his brother-in-law and moved further into the room.

Trap sometimes felt on the outside of these men, because he didn't technically own a farm or a ranch. He lived in a cowboy cabin at Seven Sons, and he helped JJ whenever he needed it. If Conrad needed help on his farm, he'd go there too.

But Trap had taken over his father's construction business full time now, and he didn't have to deal with spring planting, livestock issues, water rights, or anything else the bulk of his friends did.

Voices came down the hall, and it sounded very much like the Glover clan. Sure enough, Link, Rock, and Gun walked in only a moment later, with Wilder laughing about something with Mitch and Jacob a few steps behind them. Trap shook hands and put his smile on his face as the room started to bubble and vibrate with chatter and friendship.

Ty had not arrived yet, and Colt had been in charge of making sure Winnie knew where to have him and when, though it wasn't exactly a surprise party. Jake walked in with Jason Walker—JJ's younger brother—and then the birthday boy himself made an appearance.

"Okay," Colt yelled. "Ty's here, everyone!"

The man had turned thirty-two years old yesterday, and now the former bull-riding champion in him came out as he raised both hands above his head and waved, the way Trap's uncle often had when he'd won national titles.

"There's no food on this table," Ty said, his smile fading as his arms dropped back to his sides.

Colt stepped past Trap and drew Ty right into a tight hug. "Howdy, brother. Pizza will be here in ten minutes."

He turned toward everyone, his arm still around Ty's shoulder. "Hey, guys, can I get your attention for a second?"

Trap stepped out of the way, taking his place next to his cousin Jason and Jake Ahlstrom, who he'd grown up with. After all, Trap had never needed to be in the spotlight, though he enjoyed praise as much as the next cowboy.

"We're so glad everyone could come for Ty's birthday, and we know it's a busy time of year, and lots of y'all have wives and kids, so feel free to leave anytime you need to. Pizza will be here in about ten minutes, and I got ten of them. I don't want to hear any complaining about fruit on pizza or too many olives. If there's something you don't like, you just pick it off. All right?"

He wore a stern look, but chuckles moved throughout the crowd, as they'd talked about food preferences in their ranch owners' meetings in the past.

"JJ has a bunch of games down on the end, and Conrad brought darts, and I thought it would be fun just to hang out." He indicated the tables. "Some of us play cards every couple of weeks, and I brought those too, but don't feel like you have to have something to do."

He clapped his big hands together. "Let's sing *Happy Birthday* to Ty right now. And if you brought a gift, you can give him that, because when the pizza gets here, I think it's going to be a free-for-all."

He laughed, and then he led them in a rousing version of *Happy Birthday*. Ty stood there, his face turning a deeper shade of red with every moment. After the last purposefully off-key note ended, he said, "Thank you guys so much," and then he stepped out of the doorway and further into the room.

Trap recognized another person wanting to blend in when he saw one, and he welcomed Ty to his little huddle with Jake and Jason.

"Who got the cake?" Ty asked.

"I did," Trap said. It had a couple horses on it and the words *Happy Birthday, Ty,* and Trap didn't think it looked too bad.

"Thanks, brother," Ty said, and he grabbed onto Trap's forearm for a moment, gripped it tightly, and then pulled his hand back. "How are things going with you?"

Trap blew out his breath, letting his lips flap a little bit the way horses did. "Good enough, I guess. I've got your big project and four or five others on the docket, so I can't complain."

"He complains plenty, though," Jason said. "You should hear him talk about the Hensen place."

Trap's gaze shot to his cousin, who had asked to help him on several projects in the last few weeks. "That place needs to be condemned," he said. "And she wants to move here in a month."

"Is there a house she can live in?" Ty asked.

"No," Trap said. "And she seems to think I can build her one just by snapping my fingers." He wasn't salty about the Hensen place, he was salty about the owner's expectations of him regarding the Hensen place.

"We *are* going to build her one," Jason said.

Trap rolled his eyes. "I just don't see how someone like her is going to survive in a tiny house."

"She requested it," Jason said. "And you've wanted to build a tiny house for at least the last five years."

"Yeah," Trap said. "I have."

"We're starting on it on Monday."

He'd actually poured the foundation already, and he'd gotten final approval from Lila Mae on the blueprints just yesterday.

"It's fifteen-by-fifteen-feet," he said. "Kitchen, bathroom, and living on one floor and a loft bedroom. It *is* going to be twenty feet tall, so she should be able to stand up upstairs." He shot a look over to Jason. "I just don't think people understand that simply because a house is tiny doesn't mean there aren't the fifteen thousand checks that need to be gone through—plumbing, electricity, inspections, all of it. It's the same as building a regular house. It's just smaller."

"We'll get it done," Jason said, his perpetual positivity something Trap actually liked about him most of the time.

"Ty, come cut your cake," JJ called. "Some of us are starving, and the pizza isn't here yet."

Ty went to do that, and Trap moved over to the table with him, Colt, and JJ.

"How's dating going?" Ty asked, and Colt slid him a look out of the corner of his eye.

"It could be better," he said. "I went out with that Lisa woman a few times."

"Oh, that tells me everything I need to know," Ty chuckled. "*That Lisa woman.*"

Colt smiled too. "You know who I mean. Lisa Frampton."

"Yeah, I know who she is," Ty said. "I'm the one who suggested her."

"She was nice enough," Colt said, and he took the piece of cake Ty handed him. "I don't know. There just wasn't any spark."

"You know who you should go out with?" JJ asked, and he took the next piece of cake that Ty put on a plate.

"Who?" Colt said. "You've been holding out on me?"

"Yeah, the man asked for suggestions," Trap said. "And maybe I need some too."

JJ grinned at him. "You can't go out with her, brother."

"I can't? Why not?"

JJ looked over his shoulder to where Conrad still stood by the dartboard, now with Finn and Henry surrounding him. "Because it's Elaine. She's looking for a boyfriend."

"Oh, yeah, *I* can't go out with her," Trap grinned and looked at Colt. "But you should."

Colt cleared his throat, and a ruddy redness entered his face. "You want me to go out with your cousin?"

"Yeah, sure," JJ said. "Why not?"

"How old is she?" Colt asked, his eyes on his cake and refusing to be anywhere else.

JJ looked at Trap, who racked his brain quickly. "Uh...."

"I know the triplets are younger than you," JJ said. "By like a year —so, like, twenty-six, twenty-seven."

"That's not too young," Trap said.

"Not too young?" Colt asked. "Dude, I'm thirty-six years old. It's almost a decade of difference."

"She's really mature," JJ said. "She just started that foundation and everything." He put half his piece of cake in his mouth at once, and all eyes focused on Colt.

"I don't know," he mumbled. "Do you think it would be weird with Conrad?"

"Why would it be weird with Conrad?" JJ asked.

"I don't know," Colt said again. "I'll think about it."

Trap had played cards with Colt plenty of times in the past year or so, and the only time the man ever acted evasively like this was if he'd already spent time thinking about whatever they were talking about—which meant he'd thought of Elaine as a potential date all on his own.

He watched as Colt turned away from the group, his face still a healthy, blushing pink. Yes, that man liked Elaine—or at least had thought about asking her out. He simply hadn't done it yet.

"I've got a lot of pizza here for Colt Franklin," a man appeared in the doorway, and he had someone with him, both of them carrying a healthy stack of pizza boxes.

"Yeah, yeah," Tate said. "Pizza's here, boys."

Trap got out of the way as several others came forward to relieve the delivery men of their boxes.

"The darts are ready," Conrad said as he joined the line.

"And I've got Texas trivia," JJ said. "I think we should start with that."

"Oh, boy," Trap laughed. "No one should play trivia with JJ. He's too good at it."

"Hey, that's not true," JJ said.

But it so was, and Finn started in on a story where he'd played trivia with JJ at one of their family nights and lost spectacularly.

The group had a good laugh. The sense of camaraderie and brotherhood permeated the party. And while Trap might live alone in a small, six-hundred-foot cabin, with his fears and worries over growing and maintaining his daddy's business and honoring the Walker family name, he sure did love his friends, and he knew they loved him.

42

Winnie bustled around the kitchen, the brownie batter coming together nicely without much thought. Libby had had her baby a few days ago, and they'd named the darling boy Gavin Rusty Jackson.

Misty—Link's wife—had sent out a call for food and help in the next couple of days, as Libby and Rusty also had a two-and-a-half-year-old little girl, and Libby ran the entirety of Three Rivers Ranch. Winnie had signed up for dessert tonight, and Ty had taken the dinner slot.

She'd actually left work early and beaten him back to her house, where—once she had the brownies in—she'd set a timer and run over to her parents' house to make sure everything was going well with her momma and daddy.

His surgery was about thirty days old now, and it had been a tremendous success. He'd been pain-free almost from the moment he'd awakened, and Winnie worked with him in physical therapy to continue to strengthen the muscles in his lower back, his core, and his legs. He'd started complaining about the pain in his knee, because now that his back wasn't sending complete agony through his body, he could feel the pain there.

Momma went walking with him every morning, and they'd started with a mile loop that had expanded to two miles. Winnie smiled to herself at the progress her father had exhibited, and she thought they might even be able to go home before Christmas. They were very happy in their upstairs rental, as the young couple who had purchased the house lived in the basement and needed the extra help to pay their mortgage. They had three bedrooms and one bath on the main level, with a boxy living room and a tiny kitchen with just enough space for a table for two—perfect for Momma and Daddy.

Lucky was now living his best life with Ty on his farm, and Trap had finished the remodeling and renovations in the main homestead and moved on to other projects. Everything seemed to be going Winnie's way, except for the absolutely oppressive June heat that had settled over the Texas Panhandle. She wouldn't complain about it, because Winnie was exactly where she wanted to be, with exactly who she wanted to be with.

She spread the brownie batter in the pan, then dropped spoonfuls of chocolate-chip cookie dough at random intervals, gently pushing it down into the batter. She slid that into the oven, set a timer for thirty-five minutes, and swiped her keys from the credenza in the living room on her way out the front door.

"All right, guys," she called to the cats. "I have to go check on Momma and Daddy. Ty should be here soon."

She left, thinking of his good Southern cooking and how he'd promised to make extra so they could have dinner also. But they had a long drive out to Three Rivers to deliver dinner and dessert to Libby and Rusty, and they'd probably stay and visit for at least a few minutes.

Ty had Juniper on his little farm now, and he'd bought four goats and a few sheep too. Finn ran a little hobby farm as well, and Ty's next addition would be chickens. He'd been going to Finn's and Brandon and Lenore's homestead more and more to get an idea of how to take care of the animals and the types of enclosures he needed as he continued to improve his land and start his farm.

Winnie pulled up to her parents' place and parked behind their minivan. She jogged inside and called, "Hey, I'm just here to check on you," as she walked into the house without knocking.

"We're on the back deck," Momma called, and Winnie walked through the whole house and right out the back sliding door to a tiny deck that had just enough room for the two chairs Momma and Daddy needed. Winnie called a place like this a postage-stamp house, as it sat on a rectangular property, with the house right up against the road, and a decent-sized yard out the back. It was fenced, and every house on the street looked exactly like it.

"See any good birds out here?" Winnie asked, looking toward her mother's bird feeders.

"Just hummingbirds," her momma said. "They're most active in the morning."

"Sure," Winnie said, because that did make sense.

Daddy slowly and lazily lifted a glass of sweet tea to his lips.

"How you doing today, Daddy?"

"Pretty good," he said.

"He bent for his shoe when he should have waited for me," Momma said.

Winnie could always count on her to rat out Daddy. "Dad, you really can't be bending and twisting like that," she said. "Three months, and you're only in one."

"I was okay," Daddy said.

"His back hurts him a little bit tonight," Momma said.

Winnie cocked her hip and folded her arms. "Daddy."

"I took a few extra pain pills, and I won't do it again," he said.

"You're going to have on days and off days," Winnie said. "Some where you feel really great, and some where you don't. You've got plenty of help. You don't need to be getting your own shoes."

"I'm okay," her dad said, his voice forceful enough that Winnie dropped it.

"What are you guys doing for dinner?" She moved over to a slim built-in bench and sat down—her place in the backyard when they sat out here.

"I think I'm going to make one of my easy shepherd's pies," Momma said. "We've got some of those ready-made mashed potatoes, and I've got some frozen filling."

"That should be easy, then," Winnie said, and they settled into a companionable silence.

Her parents were completely different people here in Three Rivers than they'd been in Redwood, and she wasn't sure why. Were they outside their comfort zone? Were they better away from Taylor?

They went to church with her and Tyson, and they'd settled into their community just fine. Because they didn't live with her, she got along great with them, and Winnie actually enjoyed coming over and checking on her parents as often as they needed her to. She'd come every day in the beginning—morning and night—and now she usually only came by for a few minutes in the evening on her way home from work.

"Ty said he brought you lunch yesterday," she said.

"Yeah, he did." Fondness filled her father's voice. "It was really good, too. He made chicken fajitas, and the peppers were nice and tender."

A brilliant smile filled Momma's face. "He is such a fine young man, Winnie." She sighed and looked over their backyard, which had a single apple tree in the back and tall privacy spruces along the left fence that protected the yard from the neighbors.

"Yeah, he's great," Winnie said.

"When do you think he'll propose?" Momma asked.

"I don't know, Momma."

"Well, he can't propose," Daddy said. "She hasn't even told him she loves him."

She whipped her gaze back to his. "What? How do you know that?"

Daddy gazed at her in a steady, even way that almost felt like a challenge. "Because he told us yesterday."

"I can't believe you haven't told that wonderful man that you love him," Momma scolded. "He *needs* to hear it, Winnie."

"Men like to hear things like that just as much as women," Daddy added.

Guilt streamed through Winnie, the hotness of it testifying to her that her parents were right. "I didn't know I was going to get a lecture when I came over today," she said.

"Now you know how *I* feel," Daddy said. "I get a lecture every time one of you opens your mouth."

"Oh, you do not," Momma said.

Daddy chuckled. "I know. Besides, sometimes I need the lectures."

"We all do," Momma said.

Winnie faced her parents again. "Did Ty say anything else?"

"He said—"

"We are not going to tell his secrets." Momma's louder voice drowned out Daddy's, and Winnie pinned her gaze to him, hoping to implore him with just her eyes to tell her what else Ty had said. But Daddy said nothing.

Momma finally looked over to her. "I think he's waiting on you, dear."

"Waiting on me," Winnie murmured, and then the alarm went off on her phone. "Well, I have to get back to the brownies."

She sighed as she stood up. She leaned over and hugged her momma, and then carefully squeezed her daddy's shoulders.

"You guys call me if you need anything, okay?"

"We'll be fine," Daddy said. "Enjoy your evening."

Winnie drove back to her house—a feat that took all of sixty seconds—and as she walked inside, the deep, rich aroma of chocolate greeted her, as did the meowing of a cat and the sizzle of something sautéing on the stove.

"Oh, you're here." She'd been so preoccupied with her own thoughts, she hadn't even seen Ty's truck parked on the street.

He flashed her a quick smile and went back to stirring with the wooden spoon. "Yep. I'm just getting these bread crumbs toasted up, and I've got the pasta boiling. Your brownies have six minutes left."

Winnie stood on the cusp of her own kitchen and watched Ty work. Her feelings stormed through her, marching left and right and all around. She did love Ty, though she had never told him in those exact words.

He looked over to her, and when he found her standing there, he paused. "What's wrong?"

She had no idea what he saw on her face, but pure vulnerability and anxiety ran through her as she thought about all the times she'd told Carver she loved him and he'd said it back. He hadn't meant it, and Winnie realized in that moment that she hadn't wanted to tell Ty she loved him until she knew *absolutely* for *certain* that she meant it.

She swallowed. "I love you, Tyson."

Air burst out of his mouth, almost sounding like a scoff, and he settled his weight on his right foot, away from her. "What?"

"I love you," she said again. "And I've never said it out loud, and I'm really sorry, because I know you need to hear it."

The jitters in her stomach danced their way right out of her body, and she put a smile on her face. "It feels really good to say it. I love you."

She liked the way the words fit in her mouth, and she absolutely loved the gorgeous man in front of her receiving them.

He still looked like she'd hit him with a two-by-four, and she took a step toward him, ignoring Rocky as he meowed at her. "I'm in love with you, Ty," she said. "And I want to marry you and sell this house and move into the homestead with you on that little hobby farm."

She arrived right in front of him. "I love you."

Ty blinked, and she saw how badly he'd needed to hear those words. "I love you too, Win."

He leaned down and touched his lips to hers, cradling her face in his big hand, the way he did that made her feel so cherished and so loved.

She kissed him the way she had been for the past couple of months—like she loved him—but it sure was nice to match actions with words.

Ty pulled away, his breath a tiny bit ragged. He placed a kiss against her jaw and then right below her ear. "I talked to Bryan and Ellie," he said with a huff of a laugh. "They said they don't care how close we get married to them, but they don't want to have a dual wedding on the same day."

"Okay," Winnie whispered, her eyes still closed and her body feeling a bit disconnected from the earth. She floated, her only anchor Ty's hand on her hip, burning through the thin cotton of her shirt.

"And I know you don't want to get married in the winter," he said. "And I'm absolutely too impatient to wait until next spring."

He stepped back, and Winnie opened her eyes and watched with complete shock marching through her as he gripped the handle on the fridge and got down on both knees.

"So I think I better just ask you, and we can start planning a date for this fall."

He dug into his pocket and pulled out a diamond ring that Winnie didn't even know he had purchased.

"I love you, Win," he said. "You're the first and only person I want to talk to about everything—good, bad, and everything in between—in my life. I was lost before I met you, and I would be a useless man without you. Will you marry me?"

Tears pricked Winnie's eyes, and she nodded, trying to get the lump in her throat to go down, so she could speak. She swallowed once and then twice, and then managed to say, "Yes. Yes, I'll marry you, because I'm desperately in love with you as well."

Ty gave her that beautiful, lopsided grin, and she held out her hand so he could slide the ring onto her finger. He took her hands in his, and Winnie used his strength to balance herself as she got down on her knees and kissed her new fiancé.

"Tell me how long I have to wait until you can be at the farmhouse," he whispered, promptly stealing her ability to answer by kissing her again.

Winnie kissed him back and then pulled away. "Would November be too close to Bryan and Ellie? It was still pretty warm in November last year."

"The *beginning* of November," Ty said, a note of finality in his voice. "Sounds like an amazing time to get married."

Winnie grinned at him and cupped his face in her hands. "I think so too, Ty."

"I love you, sweetheart," he said.

"I love you too, cowboy."

———

I think Ty and Winnie are my new favorite couple in Three Rivers! What did you think? **Let me know in a review now! Just scan the QR code with your phone to do so.**

Keep reading for a sneak peek at the next book in the Cowboys of Three Rivers Romance series, **WHERE PROMISES STAY.**

Sneak Peek! Where Promises Stay, Chapter One:

Travis Walker stood with the rest of the congregation as the choir started to sing the closing hymn. He'd made it through a couple of scorching months already, and not a single cell in his body wanted to leave the air-conditioned church—not even to attend the linger-longer potluck in the shaded field behind it. But he would, because Trap never passed up free food if it was available.

There were some really good small-town Texas cooks in Three Rivers besides, and Trap had been dreaming about Marie Holster's fried-chicken salad for the past year. She only brought it to the linger-longer in July, and Trap would suffer through any heat to pile the crispy chicken bites with chipotle mayo and a pop of crunch from cool celery and sweet corn on a croissant.

As he glanced around, he thought he definitely saw more people at church that day. While it wasn't a requirement to attend the sermon in order to attend the linger-longer, most people had some sort of conscience.

He stayed standing through the benediction, and then the tension in the air broke as the meeting ended.

"She didn't go on too long today," Colt said. "That's something I'm grateful for." He grinned at Trap and led the way out of the pew.

Trap followed him, with Jake Ahlstrom behind him, and Ty and Winnie bringing up the rear. Trap nearly got swallowed by a whole herd of Glovers as they exited their rows in front of and across from where he'd been sitting. He grinned at them and shook hands or knocked knuckles. The Glovers swarmed their aunt, giving her hugs and telling her what an amazing job she did, which provided cover for Trap to simply follow the crowd down the hallway and past the Sunday School rooms to the back door of the building.

To his great relief, fans blew across the space, and several big white tents had been set up to cover any breaks in the sunshine coming through the trees.

A mic crackled to life and then sent a high-pitched wail of reverberation through the air. Cactus Glover pulled it away from his mouth until it stopped. Then he said, "Give us about fifteen minutes, folks, and we'll have all the food set up. If you brought anything, please bring it out now. And of course, everyone can start with a drink from our beverage bar near the back fence. No stampeding now, you young men."

Trap caught a smile on his face.

"Yes, Mrs. Langley brought her famous peach-almond punch, and we know that turns some of you into animals." He pulled the mic away from his mouth even as he started to chuckle.

"Oh, I love that peach punch," Colt said. He lengthened his stride, though the beverage tables had to be fifty yards away from where the food was being set up.

Trap went with him, though he didn't care for the peach punch all that much. He filled a plastic cup half with lemonade and half with sweet tea and stood by Colt in the shade as Colt hummed and moaned over the deliciousness of the almond-peach punch.

Trap liked Colt, though he was a few years older than him, because he didn't beat around the bush. He asked direct questions and said what was on his mind. If he wasn't talking, he didn't think it necessary to, and Trap had grown up in a family with a lot of cousins and a lot of aunts, all of whom seemingly loved to hear the sound of their own voice.

Trap took a sip of his Arnold Palmer, his eye catching on the skirt of a woman's dress as the wind caught it.

"Oh, boy," he muttered behind his cup, then lowered it slowly. "Jessa at ten o'clock," he whispered out of the corner of his mouth.

"You've got to be kidding me." Colt sighed.

Trap watched as Jessa Arnold continued her quest toward them. Not him, really, but Colt, as he'd been out with her a few times before ending it. She'd literally told him they didn't have to be exclusive if that was what it would take for them to stay together, and that had only turned Colt off more.

He'd just turned thirty-seven and had a four-year-old son, so casual dating wasn't exactly at the top of his to-do list. In fact, Colt was a lot like Trap in that he hated nothing more than having his time wasted.

Sometimes, Trap cursed his impatience, and he had incorporated a few things into his life that deliberately forced him to slow down and enjoy where he lived, what he did for a living, and the people around him. If he didn't do that, he would flit from one thing to the next for twelve or fourteen hours a day, only stopping when his body finally told him it was starving and about to collapse.

"Howdy, fellas," Jessa said.

Colt actually turned in the other direction, as if he hadn't heard her. Trap had never seen him be quite so dismissive before, but it was blatantly obvious to anyone with even one good eye that he did not want to talk to Jessa. In fact, he practically pulled Tate into their circle while simultaneously cutting Trap out of it.

It was his turn to sigh. "Howdy, Jessa," he said, his voice feeling and sounding a bit tired.

She looked at Colt, a slight frown between her brows reaching her eyes. Then she focused on Trap and brightened. "Did y'all hear they might be building a water park?"

That rumor had been going around Three Rivers for a couple of months now. And yes, Trap had heard it so often, in fact, that he was sick of talking about it. Everyone seemed to have an opinion on whether or not it would happen, but since Trap knew a lot about the real-estate market and what properties were up for sale and what properties needed what construction done, he happened to know no one had purchased the land rumored to become a water park on the southeast side of town.

"Yeah, I heard," he said. "It's not going to happen."

"You don't think so?" She seemed genuinely shocked. "Why do you say that?"

"Because there's no way the Starlight Ranch owners are going to allow a water park up by them. Can you imagine?"

He shook his head, because the one and only gated community in Three Rivers was on the southeast side of town. His uncle Wyatt and aunt Marcy had a house there, and everyone who lived there had money— and a lot of it. They wouldn't want their quiet, hilly road turned into Water Park Central, Trap knew that.

"Well, I heard it's going to be on the city-council agenda in August," Jessa said, lifting her chin.

"Well, you would know," Trap said airily. "What with your daddy being on the library board and all."

"Exactly."

Trap scanned the crowd beyond Jessa, sure there was someone more interesting to talk to. She was a nice enough woman, but Colt had said it best when he described her as shallow.

"And I don't mean that rudely," he'd said. And Trap didn't either — just that Jessa wasn't that smart. Not everyone was. Heck, Trap had never been to college, and he fought imposter syndrome as much as the next person.

"It looks like they're getting ready to say the prayer," he said. "Should we make our way back that way?"

Jessa threw one last look at Colt, and Trap was so going to cash in on a major favor from the man one day in the very near future.

"Sure," Jessa said, and she turned and started back across the lawn.

Trap prayed with everything he had that someone would call his name and need to talk to him about something extremely important, so he could ditch Jessa and be closer to the food at the same time.

That didn't happen, and he found himself standing with her, as well as Finn and Edith Ackerman and Alex and Nikki Baxter, while the prayer was said. It always amazed Trap that a fairly sizable crowd could calm and quiet enough to say a prayer, and the very moment the "Amen" got spoken, the noise and chatter swelled and resumed once more.

He didn't immediately surge forward like the teenagers and tweens, but he found his feet moving along with the crowd. He picked up a heavy-duty paper plate and deviated to the other side of the table as his friends filed across from him. He got behind a couple of people moving much slower than the other side, but Trap actually found himself smiling down to the elderly woman only a few people in front of him.

He knew Olive Braithwaite, and he wondered where her grandson was. He glanced around, looking for the seventeen-year-old, and didn't see him. His heart pounded in his chest, because he didn't want to overstep. His stomach growled at him and told him he should just keep his place, get his food, and mind his own business.

But a louder, more demanding voice said, *Go help her.*

Trap had only had this voice bellow at him as loudly as it currently did a couple of other times in his life. Usually, God spoke to him in a calm, quiet voice that Trap had to work really hard to hear. But apparently not today.

He took a step back and moved around the couple of people between them. "Howdy, Olive," he said. "Can I help you with that?"

Her plate shook in her weathered, wrinkled, veined hand, and Trap put his palm underneath it right as she dropped it.

"Oh, yes, please," she said.

Trap gave her a smile. "Where's Joel today, ma'am?"

"He's at a summer government camp," Olive said, her voice shaking.

"You hold right onto my arm, ma'am," he said. "Let me get rid of my plate."

He looked up and found Finn watching him. He reached for the plate, and Trap passed it across the table to him. "Just give it to one of your kids," he said. "I'll go through the line again."

Finn nodded, and Trap looked at Olive. "All right, Mrs. Braithwaite, you gotta tell me what you want, because I can't read your mind." He grinned at her, and she linked her arm through his.

"I got in line quickly," she said, her voice also a little bit shaky. "Because it's the July linger-longer, and that fried-chicken salad is here."

"Oh, if they run out of that stuff, I think they know they'll have a coup on their hands." Trap laughed, his heartier voice joining the wheezy one of Mrs. Braithwaite. "And they put it way down on the end, hoping you'll fill your plate before you get to it."

"No, they've got bowls by it," someone said, and that made Trap's heart happy. He could carry a plate for Mrs. Braithwaite *and* a bowl of the fried-chicken salad for himself, and he wouldn't need to go through the line again.

"Oh, is the pimento all gone?" Mrs. Braithwaite asked when they reached a bowl that looked pretty scraped clean.

"They'll bring out more," another woman said from somewhere. Trap's wide-brimmed cowboy hat kept him from looking around and seeing who'd spoken.

"Coming through," a voice said, and Trap once again stepped back from the table, moving a little bit right and in to Mrs. Braithwaite as he thought he'd heard the voice on his left. He bumped into another soft body, his back also registering a hard rim. He flinched away from it, still trying to balance the plate and keep his arm tight against his side for Mrs. Braithwaite to hold.

He automatically moved left and glanced over his shoulder, only to find none other than Lila Mae Dixon standing there, a bowl of fresh pimento cheese in one hand and a platter of pita-bread triangles in the other.

She sucked in a breath, and Trap realized the tray of pita was slipping. He couldn't just whip Mrs. Braithwaite around and use his right hand.

Brains worked fast, but not fast enough, because Trap's first reaction was to use his left hand and help balance the tray. Unfortunately, he carried Mrs. Braithwaite's plate of food in that hand, and as he arced it up, he actually let go of it.

Huge mistake, screamed through his head, even as his fingers clamped around the platter of pita bread and saved it.

Because all he could do now was watch in complete horror as Mrs. Braithwaite's baked beans, mac and cheese, and poppy-seed ham sandwich came down on Lila Mae's head.

Sneak Peek! Where Promises Stay, Chapter Two:

Lila Mae Dixon had had no idea that volunteering at a church potluck could be such a messy job.

She also couldn't believe how quickly various items on the buffet could be emptied. She'd never heard of pimento cheese before moving to Texas, but apparently Texans needed to hook themselves up to it intravenously, or they might not survive.

"Let me take that for you," someone said, and they took both the full bowl of pimento and the platter of pita triangles that Travis Walker had steadied for her.

"Napkins," someone said, and they passed them to Trap.

Lila Mae stood there, not quite sure if the baked beans were hot enough to burn, and wondering how she would ever get the saucy mac and cheese out of the ends of her blonde curls.

"Sorry about that," Trap muttered, and he pawed at her shoulder with the napkins.

"I've got Olive," another man said.

"Thanks, Jason," Trap said, and then he handed the napkins to Lila Mae so she could clean up herself.

"I'm real sorry," he said. "It was just instinct, and I just...sort of threw that plate."

"It's fine," Lila Mae said airily, though she still had plenty of unwanted attention on her. She met Trap's eyes, the dark depths of them completely undoing her in less time than it took for him to blink.

She'd been in town for exactly four weeks now, and she had only been moved onto her new property— that would become Feline Friends— for a couple of weeks. The tiny home she'd commissioned Trap to build for her had not been completed when she'd arrived, and he'd put her up in a cabin right next to his on his family farm.

It's his uncle's place, she told herself, as if these were the thoughts she should be having at this moment in time. But Trap had been very careful to tell her on more than one occasion that his family did not own and run the farm. His momma and daddy owned a construction and interior design firm, and he and his sister-in-law now ran it. They lived on the farm, but another of his cousins actually owned it and managed all the affairs there.

"I'll go get cleaned up," she said. "You can take my place while I'm gone."

"Take your place?" Shock flowed across Trap's face, but Lila Mae grabbed onto his elbow.

"Yes. They need help bringing out food, and I can't just disappear for ten minutes while I get cleaned up."

"It's gonna take you ten minutes to wash off some baked beans?"

Lila Mae rolled her eyes and huffed at the impossible cowboy and turned to head inside. "Just come on."

"I don't see why I have to do it," he said. "It's a few minutes."

"Oh, thank goodness, Lila Mae," Sally said the moment she stepped back inside. "There's a whole tray of bacon-wrapped sausages that need to go out."

"I got beaned," Lila Mae said, holding out her hands, where a baked bean actually dripped from one finger. "I'm going to run to the bathroom really quick, but I recruited Trap Walker to help."

She beamed at Trap, and then Sally said, "Welcome, Trap. The bacon-wrapped sausages need to go out."

Trap blinked like he'd never heard such words put together in that order before.

Sally picked up the tray and handed it to him. "They're down on the end with the meats. You can just slide this tray on top of the one that's already there."

"All right," Trap drawled, and Lila Mae wished she didn't find the sound of his voice quite so alluring.

She scurried down the hall to the restroom, taking a peek just as the dark-haired, broad-shouldered cowboy went back outside. She got cleaned up and then looked at herself in the mirror.

You have a lot of work to do while you're here. You can fantasize about cowboys as you're building cat rooms and equipping them with toys.

She also needed to hire another veterinarian and at least three more people to help take care of the cats before she could open. Right now, she only had thirteen cats, and it was such an unlucky number for her that she really needed to either adopt one out or take on another stray.

She stood there thinking through that week's appointments for who knows how long before she realized this was not the time for it. Lila Mae was getting better at time management and organization, but she still found herself getting overwhelmed pretty easily, as opening a cat sanctuary and feline rescue sounded really easy on paper. After all, it was only a few words.

But in reality, Lila Mae had needed permits and proper enclosures. She needed documentation, and she had to register as a business or a nonprofit. She had to have proper paperwork for adoptions and surrenders. She had to have salaries for employees.

And apparently she'd moved to Three Rivers at one of the worst times a person could: summertime.

There had been three or four cases of heatstroke documented in town already, and she got daily notices on her phone about staying hydrated, wearing sunscreen, getting outdoor chores done early in the morning, and calling for help sooner than she thought she might need it. Water stations had been set up around town, and she'd seen them simply sitting on the corners in neighborhoods and all around the parks.

About the only thing Lila Mae had going for her was the unlimited supply of cat food she had at the sanctuary. Her family owned Dixon's Delights, a world-renowned cat food brand that did over five hundred million dollars annually in the pet business. Her oldest brother had just taken over as CEO, and Lila Mae had left her position at the company to come halfway across the country and start a cat sanctuary.

She knew her brothers didn't understand, and her parents didn't either, but Lila Mae had used all the words she knew to try to explain it to them, finally coming to the conclusion that they didn't have to understand. She had dreams and aspirations of her own, and had been blessed with the good health and fortune to do it.

They dedicated their lives to putting food in cans and plastic containers or bags. Why was dedicating hers to saving abandoned animals any worse?

Lila Mae shook the thoughts out of her head and turned to leave the bathroom. She returned to the kitchen area of the church and took a deep breath as she observed the chaos there.

"What else do you need?" she asked.

"We need more potato chips," someone called, and Lila Mae stepped over to the table.

"I've got them," she said, and she picked up three bags and headed outside.

The heat hit her like a wall, as Lila Mae was also not quite used to the humidity found here in the Panhandle. By the time she arrived at the buffet table only twenty feet away, her bangs had become plastered to her forehead. She managed to put the potato chips out without causing a scene, and then turned to go back inside.

Trap came out as she approached, and he carried a casserole dish with perfectly browned biscuits on the top.

"Wow, those are pretty," she said. "What is that?"

"Chicken pot pie casserole," he said. "Have you ever had it?"

"No, sir."

"It's really good," he said. "And this is from the Eagles. She made three or four pans of it, and I already snagged myself a piece."

"Oh, can we do that?" she asked. "Just get what we want from the kitchen?"

Trap gave her a side-eye. "We can when we've been volunteered against our will." With that, he moved by her, and Lila Mae turned and watched him go. She focused herself much quicker this time and went inside, taking the next direction.

After only a few more trips, Sally, the activities director at the church, told her, "You're all done, Lila Mae. Go get some food."

"Thank you so much. Can I get you anything?" she asked.

Sally picked up a plate of cherry pie. "I've been eating the whole time, honey."

Lila Mae giggled with her, realizing that Trap had been right. Everyone in the kitchen seemed to have what they wanted, and Lila Mae hurried outside to the table, where the crowd had thankfully died down.

She picked up a plate and started through the line, wishing she could take a little bit of everything and get a history lesson on it, as well as an ingredients list. The pimento cheese was gone, and she'd have to have some another day.

She'd actually found a cute little bistro next to the courthouse on Main Street, and they served an English high tea every day, South-ern-style. She'd had her first pimento finger sandwich there and a dandelion tea that had left her mouth wanting more.

She managed to get a little bowl of the fried-chicken salad and a half of a biscuit from the chicken pot pie casserole, as well as some cheesy, bacony tater tots and a healthy slice of Texas sheet cake. She picked up a fork and a napkin and turned to face the vast array of tables and tents.

She'd been in town for a month, but she didn't know very many people, as Lila Mae wasn't exactly outgoing, and she'd rather work with pets over people. She knew a few of her employees, but she didn't see any of them, and she knew a couple of the Walkers, as she'd lived on their ranch for those couple of weeks.

Unfortunately—*or fortunately?*—for her, her eyes landed solidly on Trap himself. He sat at a table only two back, and he had a spot on the end next to him.

Lila Mae's heart pounded in her chest, sprinting through her veins and making her head feel lighter than ever. Combined with the heat, she knew she needed to get off her feet, and fast. So she started toward him.

The man next to him saw her coming first, and he nudged Trap with his elbow. Trap glared at him and then swung his attention toward her. His eyes narrowed slightly, and she wasn't sure why the man didn't like her. She'd paid him a lot of money to assess the property she'd bought, and he still had months of construction to go.

"Can I sit here?" she asked.

"Yeah, sure," Trap said, and he even grabbed onto the back of the chair and pulled it out for her.

Lila Mae set down her plate. "Thanks. I'm going to run and grab a drink."

"I'm going to get a drink right now," a man a couple down and across the table from her said. "What do you want?"

"Oh, um, just some lemonade," she said, and the sandy-haired man got up and left.

"That's Alex," Trap said. "His wife, Nikki, and their boys."

Lila Mae nodded to the kids directly across from her. They couldn't be more than eight or nine years old, and they only seemed to have sandwiches and potato chips on their plates.

"You got some of the chicken pot pie casserole," Trap said, and he gave her a rare smile.

"Yeah," she said. "It looked pretty rich, and it was almost gone, so I only took half."

He nodded and put another spoonful of mac and cheese in his mouth.

"Oh, shoot. There's not a chair here anymore?"

Lila Mae looked up at the cool female tone, the tension doubling as a brunette came to a standstill only a few feet from him.

"Oh, sorry," the man next to Trap said, but he didn't sound sorry at all.

"Yeah, sorry." Trap looked up. "Jessa, Lila Mae's new in town, and she needed somewhere to sit."

Lila Mae looked up at the dark-haired woman, who wore daggers in her expression. The last thing Lila Mae needed in town was enemies, and she swallowed quickly. "I can find—"

"No, it's fine," Trap practically yelled over her.

She swung her attention back to his and found his eyes a little bit wider and filled with more urgency, clearly trying to convey something to her nonverbally.

"I see Jessa's brother right over there," Trap said. "Jessa, he's got a seat for you. Sorry." He actually did sound a little bit sorry, but Lila Mae didn't think he truly was.

"You'll call me about game night, right?" Jessa asked. When no one answered, she added, "Colt?"

"Yeah," Colt said, but he didn't even look at her.

She huffed and walked away, taking all the horrible tension with her.

"I didn't mean to take someone's seat," Lila Mae said.

"You didn't," Trap said.

"She seemed to think it was for her."

"Yeah, well, it wasn't."

Lila Mae frowned. "You don't like her."

"I like her just fine," Trap said. "But she's Colt's ex who doesn't seem to think they've broken up yet."

She leaned forward and looked past Trap to the cowboy on his other side. He nodded at her. "I don't think we've met. I'm Colt Franklin. I own the apple orchards in town."

A smile sprang to Lila Mae's face. "I *love* those apple orchards. I come every Monday and get your fresh cider. The cats love it."

Colt grinned at her, and even Trap snickered. "You feed cider to cats?"

"Apple cider has a lot of health qualities," she said. "And not just for humans."

She looked at Travis, and she thought his smile looked a little bit wicked.

"Are you making fun of me?" she asked. "Maybe I don't want to sit by you."

"You can't leave," he said, his smile drying right up with the words.

"Why not?" Lila Mae suddenly wanted nothing more than to do exactly that.

Colt leaned forward and said, "Because *that* is Trap's ex-girl-friend, and he doesn't want to sit by her." He pointed his plastic fork out into the crowd. "And if you thought I didn't want to sit by Jessa, he doesn't want to sit by Chelle times ten."

"She's not my ex," Trap said at the same time Lila Mae turned to see a beautiful, honey-haired woman looking for a place to sit. "We went out one time," he muttered. "And it was torture."

"Yeah, but she wants to go out with him again," Colt said.

Lila Mae scoffed. "You cowboys seem to have a lot of women who want to go out with you that you don't want to give the time of day to." She gave them both a cocked-eyebrow glare. "Seems to me like you'd be happy for someone to go out with."

Colt's mouth hung open for a moment, and then he started to laugh. Trap simply blinked at her, his frown deepening by the moment. Lila Mae had half a mind to pick up her plate, claim she was finished, and offer her seat to Chelle.

She had the words formulated in her head too, and the whole scenario played out in her mind. Then she remembered she needed this man on her side, and that he had dozens of construction projects still to do at Feline Friends.

So she shut her mouth and picked up her fork to try her first bite of chicken pot pie casserole. As the creamy, salty sauce exploded across her tongue, Lila Mae moaned.

Trap laughed. "It's good, right?"

"We do not have food like this in Maryland," she said.

"I thought you were from Atlanta."

"Our corporate headquarters are in Atlanta," she said. "But I grew up in Maryland and worked out of the social media office there."

"I don't even know what a social media office is," Trap said.

"Oh, yes, you do," she fired back. "You post on social media for your business. I've seen your videos. It's how I found you."

He turned toward her. "Is it? Tell me more."

Lila Mae wasn't sure if Trap was quiet and shy or cocky and arrogant, but she wanted to find out. She put a bite of chocolate cake in her mouth and picked up her phone.

"Let me find the first video I saw," she said. "I saved it. It's what made me come back and look you up online." It only took her a few seconds, as Lila Mae had been doing social media marketing for a very long time and knew her way around a mobile device.

"Here it is," she said. "You're even in it."

He practically yanked her phone out of her hand, and she peered over his forearm at the video, where none other than Trap Walker himself said, "Hi, I'm Trap Walker, and welcome to Three Rivers and MS Designs, a family construction and interior design firm that can meet any needs, big or small. Come with me as I show you everything from a new barndominium build, to an old farmhouse kitchen remodel."

"I've got to say," Lila Mae said as the video continued. "You're a lot more personable online than you are in person."

That caused Alex, Nikki, and Colt to all start laughing. Lila Mae took her lemonade from Alex. "Thank you."

"Well, she's got you pegged, Trap," Alex said.

"I hate this video." Trap handed her phone back. "I shot that thing like a thousand times."

"Well, you're very good," she said. "It made me want to work with you."

"My daddy will be thrilled," Trap deadpanned. "But let's not tell him, okay?"

Lila Mae grinned at him. "I think I'll drive straight to Seven Sons and hunt him down." She'd met his father, and she could do it too. Trap looked mortified, as if he'd never been teased before, and Lila Mae sighed and shook her head.

"You Texans don't have as good a sense of humor as I thought you would."

"That's just Trap," Colt said. "He takes a while to warm up."

"Does he?" Lila Mae said. "I feel like I've been talking to him for about a year now."

"It's been six months," Trap said. "And trust me, it feels like six years."

A sting of hurt moved through Lila Mae. She lifted her chin slightly. "Well, I'm sorry if my project has put you out."

"He loves your project," Colt said. "Don't listen to him at all."

She looked at Trap. "Is he right? Do you love my project?"

"It's fine," Trap said.

"You're going to be out later this week, right?" she said. "I believe Thursday."

"Yeah, Thursday morning."

"Great," Lila Mae said, something new and slightly sinister entering her mind. "I'll give you until then to figure out why you dislike me so much and what I've done to offend you."

She picked up her napkin and her plate and stood. "I won't torture you with my presence any longer."

"Come on, Lila Mae," he said.

Lila Mae gazed at him. "If we can't get along, Mister Walker, I'll simply hire someone else."

"Don't go," he said, but Lila Mae walked away, thinking maybe these Texas cowboys had a different sense of humor than she had, but if that were true, she didn't like it.

She didn't want to be ridiculed or have to wonder if every word out of Trap's mouth was a joke or meant to genuinely hurt her.

She'd give him one more chance to explain on Thursday, and if he couldn't, Lila Mae knew Three Rivers offered plenty of other construction firms to choose from.

———

Oh, boy. What will happen this Thursday with Trap and Lila Mae? **Find out in WHERE PROMISES STAY!**

When Love Returns: A Three Rivers Cowboys Romance (Book 1): He's been serving in the military for a decade. She's been quietly grieving a devastating loss. When Finn and Edith reunite in small-town Three Rivers where they grew up together, can their second chance romance provide hope, healing, and the happily-ever-after they both crave?

Scan this QR code with your phone to see this series in eBook, audiobook, large print paperback, or regular paperback:

1. When Love Returns
2. Back to Her
3. Deep in the Heart
4. Undone at Midnight
5. Calling Her Home
6. More Than Words
7. What She Says
8. A Place for Hope
9. Everything He Wants

10. Miles to Go
11. Where Promises Stay
12. Roping Her In

Be sure to check out the other three series set in the beloved town of Three Rivers too!

Meet the cowboys who started it all at Three Rivers Ranch! Scan the QR code below with your phone to check out this complete series.

Scan this QR code with your phone to see and order this series in eBook, audiobook, large print paperback, or regular paperback:

1. Second Chance Ranch
2. Third Time's the Charm
3. Fourth and Long
4. Fifth Generation Cowboy
5. Sixth Street Love Affair
6. The Seventh Sergeant
7. Eight Second Ride
8. The Ninth Inning
9. Ten Days in Town
10. Eleven Year Reunion
11. The Twelfth Town
12. Lucky Number Thirteen
13. The Curse of February Fourteenth
14. Fifteen Minutes of Fame
15. Sixteen Steps to Fall in Love
16. The Sleigh on Seventeenth Street
17. The First Lady of Three Rivers Ranch
18. Eighteen Bowties and Counting

Seven Sons Ranch in Three Rivers Romance™ Series

Meet the cowboy billionaire brothers at Seven Sons Ranch! Scan the QR code below with your phone to check out this complete series.

1. Rhett
2. Tripp
3. Liam
4. Jeremiah
5. Wyatt
6. Skyler
7. Micah
8. Gideon

Shiloh Ridge Ranch in Three Rivers Romance™ Series

Become a Glover Lover by reading all the Glover Family romance & family saga at Shiloh Ridge Ranch! Scan the QR code below with your phone to check out this complete series.

1. The Mechanics of Mistletoe
2. The Horsepower of the Holiday
3. The Construction of Cheer
4. The Secret of Santa
5. The Gift of Gingerbread
6. The Harmony of Holly
7. The Chemistry of Christmas
8. The Delivery of Decor
9. The Blessing of Babies
10. The Networking of the Nativity
11. The Yes at Yuletide
12. The Wrangling of the Wreath
13. The Hope of Her Heart

About Liz

Liz Isaacson writes inspirational romance, usually set in Texas, or Wyoming, or anywhere else horses and cowboys exist. She lives in Utah, where she writes full-time, takes her two dogs to the park everyday, and eats a lot of veggies while writing. Find her on her website at www.feelgoodfictionbooks.com.